OTHER MATT BANNISTER NOVELS

Willow Falls
Sweethome
Bella's Dance Hall
The Wolves of Windsor Ridge

THE ECKMAN EXCEPTION

(MATT BANNISTER WESTERN 5)

KEN PRATT

The Eckman Exception

Paperback Edition
Copyright © 2019 by Ken Pratt

CKN Christian Publishing
An Imprint of Wolfpack Publishing
6032 Wheat Penny Avenue
Las Vegas, NV 89122

christiankindlenews.com

Paperback ISBN 978-1-64119-830-1
eBook ISBN 978-1-64119-829-5

THE ECKMAN EXCEPTION

PROLOGUE

Pick Lawson was aware that Morton Sperry was not known to be a nice man. He was part of the Sperry family from the little town of Natoma, twenty-five miles west of the Jessup county seat, Branson. The Sperry name belonged to a large family known for trouble. No matter what Sperry it was or where they went, trouble was never too far behind. The Natoma Sperrys were a bad bunch, but Morton was perhaps the worst of them all.

Morton had the coldest green eyes Pick had ever seen. They weren't just cold, but they also had no hint of compassion, humor, or any of the other human qualities a normal man would have. His eyes were hard and life-less, devoid of anything remotely resembling joy, love, or even fear. Pick wasn't new to the outlaw world, but he found it hard to relax when Morton was nearby. Pick didn't scare easily, but Morton made him afraid. Pick wasn't alone, though. Everyone in the Sperry-Helms Gang had a heavy dose of respect for Morton. Even

Morton's equally dangerous cousin, Jesse Helms, submitted to Morton's authority within the gang they led.

Karl Digsby was Pick's friend and the newest member of the gang. Karl wasn't a criminal. He worked for a flour mill and barely made enough money to pay for his rented home. It didn't help that his wife spent the money about as fast as he was made it. It was his friends, Deuce McKenna and Pick, who encouraged him to join the Sperry-Helms Gang for some extra income. It sounded like easy money and a bit of excitement, so he agreed to meet the Sperry and Helms brothers who made up the gang. The cousins were all hard men, but there were others in the gang that he'd never dare to betray or want to square off against, men such as Cass Travers or Charlie Walker, both of whom were as dangerous as any of the Sperry or Helms brothers. It was a wonder to Karl at the time how his two friends Pick and Deuce had teamed up with such a hard bunch as the Sperry-Helms Gang.

Karl knew he didn't fit in and had told Pick so from the beginning. Then, one Sunday, Morton, Jesse, and Cass showed up at Karl's home with a saddled horse for him to ride, and he was not given a choice. Karl followed them up into the Blue Mountains that rainy morning.

It was a rare event to have storms in the summer months that lasted for more than a few hours, but two days of continuous rain had left the road muddy. It was a cool morning, with heavy gray clouds hanging low over the trees and a slight drizzle. Karl followed silently, having no idea where they were going, but he had heard of a member of the gang called "Possum" by the others who lived in the Blue Mountains somewhere. Karl remembered Deuce and Pick talking about a man named Possum bragging about buying a prospector's cabin in the mountains for barely any money.

Possum apparently was from Tennessee or somewhere down South, and had somehow wound up in Oregon and served some time in the Oregon State Penitentiary with Alan Sperry, the founder of the Sperry-Helms Gang. When Possum was paroled, he went to Natoma with a letter from Alan to look for Morton and joined the gang. He wasn't well liked by Deuce or Pick, but they hadn't known him for very long, either. Like Pick, Possum was new to the gang and the area. Deuce often joked that Possum's wife must've been either so beautiful he had to keep her secluded in the woods for her own protection, or so hideous it was just safer for mankind to keep her hidden away like Medusa somewhere. Karl reasoned that was where they must be going as they rode farther into the mountains.

They left the main road and followed a trail through a series of bends in the forest for a mile, then came out into a small meadow of grass and got their first look at Possum's cabin. It was nothing more than a small shack thrown together, with scrap hewn boards of various lengths nailed together to make the walls. The shack had neither windows nor a solid roof; an oil-soaked tarpaulin was draped over the hole-filled expanse, and a thin plume of blue smoke rose from the stovepipe that poked through it.

The frame of a small barn in the process of being built stood a short distance from the shack. It was also covered with a tarp to keep the single horse dry. There was no hay storage to be seen, nothing for the horse except the grass of the meadow and the small stream that ran past the shack. It was an uninviting homestead, to say the least.

A frail, homely woman in her late forties to mid-fifties, dressed in a dark-gray dress that was nearly black from filth, stood beside the cabin. Her graying black hair was disheveled and loose, falling to her shoulders like a frayed shawl. She appeared to have never smiled in her life, from the concrete frown on her embittered lips.

"Ma'am," Jesse said with a sly smile and a tip of his hat. "Is Possum around?"

"Who?" she asked nervously.

"Your husband, ma'am. Can you tell him Morton and Jesse are here, huh?" Jesse asked, pleasantly enough.

She nodded slowly. "I git him," she said slowly, with noticeable anxiety in her expression. She stepped closer to the door, but Jesse stopped her.

"Say, ma'am, what is your name?"

"Ingrid."

"I'm Jesse, Ingrid. So, are you Russian?"

"German," she answered with her heavy accent. "I will git him."

"Now, hold on," Jessie said and continued, "I haven't gotten to talk to a pretty German girl before. So, how long have you been hooked up with Ole Possum? He seems way too old for you. Think I could steal you away from him for a while?" he asked with a wry smile.

Cass Travers snickered under his breath.

Ingrid looked at the men skeptically. "I git him," she said and went into the shack.

Jesse laughed as he spoke to Morton and Cass. "Well, now we know why he keeps her hidden away! I've seen finer-looking hogs down at the meat market."

Cass chuckled. "No wonder Possum stays drunk, huh?"

Jesse snorted. "I wonder how many shots it takes for her to start looking good? Well, I guess it's no wonder he's always broke."

A moment later, the door opened, and the man known as Possum stepped outside, pulling his suspenders up over his stained long johns. He was a thin man in his fifties, with thinning gray hair of medium length and an unshaven face with a week's worth of a beard. His dark pants were wool and had been mended multiple times, and they were in need of another mending on one knee. "Are we riding out today? Give me a few, and I will get dressed. I wasn't expecting anyone," he said, looking like he was hungover from the night before. He yawned. "Are we heading to Loveland?"

Morton Sperry shook his head. "No, Loveland's been postponed for a while."

"Really? That's too bad; there's a fortune up there to be had. How long until we go? I'm getting a little low on money, you know. Which reminds me, boss, can I borrow a few dollars until our next job? You know, a draw on my share?"

Jesse Helms answered, "You're not going to have a share left if you keep borrowing money. You borrowed five from me and two from Deuce, and who knows how much from everyone else. We're gonna have to rob that bank in Loveland and two others just to get our money back from your shares."

Possum was taken aback by Jessie's words. "Well...as you can see, we're not bringing home a fortune. But I promise, from what I heard, once we hit the Loveland bank, my share will be big enough to not only pay back my debts but also to be able to build a real barn. All that gold and money in Loveland, boys... Well, that's a big job. And one we can't go wrong on! The way I hear it, the sheriff up there can't find his way home from the outhouse, let alone be able to track us." He smiled a nearly toothless smile.

"So I've heard," Morton said seriously.

"I'd hope so. It was your idea, after all!" Possum laughed, then grew serious when he saw Morton stare at him coldly. "What?" he asked with anxiety in his voice.

Morton spoke seriously. "I heard you've been telling people about our plans. Do you really think we could go rob the Loveland bank now that you've told everyone we were planning it?" he spat angrily.

"No... No, I haven't told anyone! What do you think I am, stupid? I didn't breathe a word of it to anyone. I swear I didn't, Morton! Maybe someone else did, but it wasn't me!"

Jessie smirked. "Oh, come on, Possum. I heard it straight from Ugly John himself. The only reason he gives you any credit is that you ride with us, but that's stopping today. We gave you a chance because of Alan's letter, but Alan isn't here, and we can't have people talking."

Possum shook his head defensively, his concern growing. "I didn't say nothing about anything! John's lying, or he heard it from someone else, but I didn't say anything! Come on, Boss!" He addressed Morton. "I was locked up with your brother for a long time, and he knows I don't say nothing! Hell, he wouldn't have sent me to join you boys if he thought I did. You know Alan."

Morton looked at him sternly. "You talk when you drink, and you drink a lot."

"I won't drink anymore!" Possum exclaimed quickly. "I promise."

"So, you did talk a little too much, huh?" Morton asked.

"No, I've already told you I didn't."

Morton took a deep breath and smiled slightly as he looked into Possum's eyes. Possum averted them quickly. "We can't trust a liar, and I won't have anyone I can't trust riding with me. Our lives are all on the line," he said pointedly, and then continued, "So I am going to give you one last chance to come clean with me. When you were drunk, did you tell Ugly John about the Loveland bank?"

Possum sighed heavily. He spoke like a child being disciplined by his father, even though he was a good fifteen to twenty years older than Morton. "Yeah, I guess I did. I just got too drunk, and my credit line was up. I was just telling him I could pay my tab after I got my share. That's all. It won't happen again, I swear it!" he said with great sincerity. "My drinking days are done."

Morton nodded slowly. "Where'd your wife go?" he asked, changing the subject.

"Huh? Oh, she's in the house, checking on her bread. It should be about done. It's about all we got to eat, but if you want some, I'll go grab it for ya."

"Maybe you better introduce us first. Call her out here."

"Sure, but honestly, I am done drinking. I won't be doing that anymore. Okay? I promise you, I won't."

Morton held up a hand to stop him. "Just get your wife."

"Sure. She's a little shy, but she is a good cook. I will go get her." He walked to his door and opened it. "Ingrid. Come on out here and meet the boss and the boys." A moment later, Ingrid appeared in the doorway, and Possum put his arm around her shoulder and walked her toward the horses. "Ingrid, this is the boss man, Morton Sperry, and over here is the other boss man, Jessie Helms…"

"Hey, beautiful," Jessie said with a nod.

Possum ignored the comment, as did Ingrid. "And that's Cass, and back there is the new kid, who I haven't met yet, actually. What is your name?"

"Karl."

"Nice to meet you, Karl. I'm…"

A sudden glimpse of movement in his peripheral vision pulled Possum's attention from Karl to Morton, who drew his revolver quickly and fired the .45. It was pointed at Ingrid. She fell to the wet ground with a bullet hole in her chest. For a moment, as if in a horrible dream, Possum stood motionless, and then quickly dropped to his knees at Ingrid's side. "No! Ingrid, come on, baby. Ingrid!" he yelled painfully. He picked up her head and held it close while she opened her eyes in shock. She focused on him and tried to touch his face with her fingertips. A tear slipped from her eyes and ran down her face. Her gasps were deep but empty of air. Blood flowed out of her mouth as she tried to exhale.

"Baby, I'm sorry. Lord, I am sorry," he said desperately, not knowing what else to say. "I love you, Ingrid. Baby, please hold on. Please..." He began to sob as he held her, then glared at Morton with pure hatred. "You shot my wife for no reason, you son of a..."

Another .45 shot echoed through the forest, ending Possum's yelling abruptly. He lay beside Ingrid while she labored to breathe. Possum was dead, with a bullet through his head. Ingrid tried to moan, but could only gurgle with every breath she attempted to take.

Morton holstered his revolver casually and sighed. He turned in his saddle to look at Karl. "Here's your first lesson of earning our trust: there's no room for error when you ride with us. If you talk, say anything about anything at all, or about any one of us, that will be you and your wife! Do you understand me?" he asked harshly.

Karl stared with wide-eyed fear at Morton. He felt his head nodding and heard himself say, "Yes."

"Good. Now drag them into the shack. That's your job for today." Morton said and looked over at Jessie. "You kind of liked her, did ya?"

Jessie nodded. "Like I do the plague, yeah. I heard she was a good cook, though. I think I will go get some warm bread," he said, then climbed off his horse and held the reins to look around. "He hasn't got any place to tether the ponies!" he said in disgust.

Cass shrugged. "Tie it to the barn."

Morton looked back at Karl and raised his voice. "I

told you to drag them into the cabin. Unless you want to join them, you better start listening right now! I won't tell you again."

Karl slid out of the saddle and looked at Morton cautiously. "Drag them?"

Morton grimaced impatiently. "Carry them if you want to, I don't care! Just get them in the cabin! For crying out loud, are you sure you understand English?" he yelled irately.

"Yeah," Karl replied meekly and turned quickly toward the bodies. Possum was dead, and his wife, Ingrid, lay still with her eyes staring up into the gray drizzling sky. She was still alive and trying to breathe shallowly as blood flowed slowly from the sides of her mouth. Karl hesitated and spoke to Morton cautiously. "She's still alive."

Morton looked at Karl with great hostility, but it was Jessie Helms who shouted at him, "So? You were told twice to put them in the cabin. Now do it, or we'll leave you in there, too! For crying out loud, why is it all the new guys you let into this gang are soft?" he asked Morton with disgust. "This guy is a soft link in our chain, and soft links break when the pressure's on! And I'm telling you right now, I don't like those other two guys either, Deuce or Pick."

Cass Travers spoke up for his old friend. "Pick's all right. I don't know about Deuce."

Morton took a deep breath. "We'll be cleaning house in this gang real soon. Let's go see what's inside." He dismounted and walked past Karl into the small cabin, followed by Jessie and Cass. Karl grabbed Possum's wrists and dragged him over the wet ground into the cabin, which was crowded with the others inside. He was cursed by Morton for bumping into him and being in the way, but he quietly did as he was told and left Possum in the middle of the floor. He then went back outside and grabbed Ingrid's wrists. As he lifted her arms and upper torso, blood poured a little faster from her mouth. It sent a wave of nausea through Karl as he dragged the suffering woman across the wet ground. He laid her on top of her husband's body. Once again, he was pushed out of the way and cursed by the others for being underfoot when they were searching the house for anything of value and eating the bread Ingrid had made.

Morton ate a piece he tore from the loaf and looked at Ingrid as she laid there struggling to breathe. A tear fell from her eye, or maybe it was a drop of rain; it was hard to tell. "She'll be dead in a bit. No reason to waste another bullet on her," he stated casually. He then added to Karl, "Start bringing in their woodpile and stacking it around their bodies. We're going to burn the place down. It's my understanding no one knows where they live except you, right?" he asked Cass Travers.

"That's what he told me," Cass answered as he searched through the papers in a small wooden box. Finding nothing of value, he tossed it to the floor.

Morton nodded. "If he was found dead and recognized, it would come back on us, so let's just burn the place down, and he won't be recognized. I want no trace of him left, so bring his saddle in here. And Cass, you take his horse out into the woods a few miles from here and skin it. Take the hide to the tannery and sell it. Old

Possum is just going to disappear, but if anyone asks, we can honestly say he went north."

"Or south," Cass offered.

"Or south," Morton repeated with a half-smile. "Yeah, let's say he left Jessup County to go back to California and get settled somewhere before winter sets in. The winter months just ain't warm enough for his wife. Does that sound believable?"

Morton raised his eyebrows inquiringly and spoke to Karl in a threatening tone. "Not one word about this to anyone. Not even your wife, or we will come to meet her, and you two will disappear as well. Do you really understand me? You seem to have a problem with understanding English, so *do you understand me*?"

Karl nodded. "Clearly," he replied nervously.

"Good. Now go bring in the wood."

Karl felt the air leave his lungs as the wickedness of his new career path struck him. It was far eviler than he had ever imagined it would be. He had known the Sperry-Helms Gang was a tough bunch who did their share of stealing and robbing. He had even heard rumors of them killing people, but despite his worst expectations, he had never dreamed of them murdering another gang member—a so-called friend of theirs— and his innocent wife. Worse, they were about to burn a woman alive. The whole idea sickened him to no end. However, he had been warned by Morton and heard Jesse's complaint about him and his two friends, so he dared not question Morton's instructions again. Karl walked outside and began carrying in the split wood, which was covered by a tattered tarp to keep it dry. He stacked the wood all around and on top of the two bodies.

Twenty minutes later, Cass used an axe to break the chimney free from the woodstove, leaving the small cabin full of smoke from the fire. Morton poured out the oil lamps and, finding a can of oil, spread that around the cabin to ensure a nice fire. Finally, he opened the door of the small woodstove and kicked it over, spreading the coals out on the oil-soaked wood floor. Flames began, and moments later, the small home was consumed in a large fire.

The four riders sat on their horses, watching it. Morton, Jessie, and Cass spoke proudly of their finds in the house, including the weapons and knives they had claimed. "Well, let's get going. Let's take the stream bed for a while so we aren't seen or tracked." Morton said.

Cass asked before leaving the group with Possum's horse in tow, "What about Marshal Bannister? He's not like the other lawmen around here. The marshal is the real deal."

"He's gone. He went over to Idaho somewhere to track down some woman killer yesterday, I hear, so we are good," Morton told him.

Jessie smirked while he watched the flames consuming the cabin. "That fire is hot as hell! Too bad Possum left us; he was a good man. Being a family man with a sick wife to feed, a man needs a more reliable job in a warmer climate. I hear he got hired on as a mule-skinner by an old friend down in California somewhere. Isn't that what you heard?" he asked Karl pointedly.

Karl nodded nervously. "That's what he told me."

"Good answer," Morton said, looking at him closely. "Keep it up, and maybe you'll fit in just fine. Maybe."

PICK LAWSON REMEMBERED Karl telling him in detail what had happened up in the Blue Mountains at the little cabin belonging to Possum and his wife. Pick and his friends, Deuce and Karl, feared for their own lives after Possum was murdered. With the new marshal's office in town, Morton and Jesse were on edge and weren't taking any chances with members of their gang they could not trust. Who was to say when they might decide they couldn't trust Deuce, Karl, or him?

They decided it was best to take action to preserve their lives by framing Morton and Jesse and a couple of others by robbing the Loveland Bank. Deuce's nephew, Brent Boyle, joined up with them to do it. They covered their faces before they entered the bank, but they identified themselves as Morton and Jessie as they left.

Deuce decided it would be best to cut across the Wallowa Mountains back to Jessup County, but it turned into a bloodbath of unimaginable proportions. Unknown to them, the man they had beaten and robbed of his gold in the bank was the Venetta Creek Killer, who had been terrorizing miners along the creeks and rivers. That man was forced to lead a posse after the bank robbers, and for unknown reasons, murdered everyone in the posse, according to the newspaper.

That man, Octavius Clark, a killer through and through, was traced back to the ferocious and violent Champ Ferguson guerrilla force during the Civil War.

Bloody Bill Anderson was more famous, but the men who rode with Champ Ferguson were more brutal. They murdered Union and Confederate soldiers and civilians. They murdered just to murder. Octavius, it turned out, was one of the worst of the bunch. Champ was hung for his war crimes, but Octavius and the others he rode with were all pardoned for their sins. Octavius had never stopped killing and shot Karl Digsby in the back without warning when he caught up with the bank robbers. Karl, Deuce, and young Brent all died in a valley on the other side of Windsor Ridge. Pick survived, but it wasn't without injury and some cunning, and maybe a little bit of luck and treachery.

Pick escaped the mountains on foot, stole a horse from the first homestead he came to, and rode straight to Natoma to tell his tale to Morton Sperry. He changed the truth to a lie and blamed Deuce for deceiving him into thinking the bank robbery was at Morton's orders. As evidence of his loyalty to Morton, he told him about killing Deuce's nephew, Brent.

Pick had been worried about getting caught from the beginning, and his name was carved on the underside of his saddle, so he carried it for a mile before hiding it inside a thick brush-covered ravine deep in the Wallowa Mountains, in a crevice between two fallen trees. He had hidden it well and doubted anyone would ever find it.

Upon hearing Pick had lost his horse and had stolen another, Morton took the stolen horse to the Heather Creek Tannery in Natoma to be immediately butchered and the hide tanned. For a receipt, the description was written in detail to match his missing black and white

paint mare, which everyone knew he rode and was probably dead in the mountains. Morton gave him another
horse and saddle, along with the receipt, to prove he had
been nowhere near Natoma when the bank robbery was
committed.

Pick tried to tell his employer he had influenza and
that was why he had missed four days' work, but he was
fired from the lumber mill. Having inside information
that there were three openings at the Premro and Sons
Milling Works where his three dead friends had been
employed, he applied and was hired. It was strange to
listen to his new co-workers talk about their old friends
who had inexplicably decided to rob the Loveland Bank
and been killed in the Wallowa Mountains. All the
mysteries of why and what had happened were common
conversation for a while, but the shock was wearing off
now. The question of what had ever happened to the
fourth bank robber was perhaps the greatest blessing.
The paper had written that the fourth bank robber had
committed suicide by hanging himself, but the exact
location where he had done it was unknown, so somewhere, a corpse was rotting on a limb. Pick had literally
gotten away with murder, but he not only got away with
it, he had also gotten Brent Boyle's job.

It had been over a month since then, and he sat at his
dining table, drinking a cup of coffee, amazed at what he
was reading in the local paper. The US Marshal Matt
Bannister had discovered that the burnt bodies six miles
up in the Blue Mountains were those of the missing
daughter of multi-millionaire Louis and Divinity Eckman
and her husband, Nathan Webster. The burned bodies of

Nathan and Catherine Eckman appeared to be a murder-suicide since she was shot in the chest, and he had obviously taken his own life with a close-range shot to his head.

The bodies were burned beyond recognition. However, Matt had found evidence that confirmed it was them. A metal box found under debris contained some letters, which, though burnt, still had her name legible, and an enclosed picture of her parents. He also discovered an ivory Roman soldier chess set.

According to the article, the evidence proved their identities beyond any doubt, and Catherine's remains, which had been buried in the Branson Cemetery under "Jane Doe," were transferred to Sacramento, California, where her parents could inter her in their family plot. The Eckmans had been looking for their daughter for three years and had offered a ten-thousand-dollar reward for her return. The article explained Louis Eckman declined to pay the reward, quoting him as saying, "The reward was for her safe return, not her body. Although I appreciate the marshal identifying her remains, I will not reward him for failure! If he had done his job, she'd still be alive. I won't reward him for her death."

Pick was dumbfounded and laughed in disbelief. The bodies were not those of Nathan Webster and Catherine Eckman, they were the bodies of Possum Overguard and his wife, Ingrid. He didn't know Possum's given name, but Possum had always talked about his wife, so Pick knew her name. He read the article again, and couldn't believe it. The marshal was pulling a scam. Pick knew a good scam when he saw one, and the marshal was pulling the wool over the Eckmans' eyes, and the whole community's.

He would have believed it too if he didn't know the men who had killed Possum and his wife. But where did the marshal get the real Catherine Eckman's personal belongings?

"That bastard," Pick said with a chuckle. "He knows where they are!"

CHRISTINE KNAPP LOOKED as beautiful as ever in a lavender dress. She had her long, dark hair woven delicately up underneath a wide-brimmed white hat with decorative flowers on it. Her large brown eyes shone brightly as they looked at Matt Bannister. He was sitting behind his desk in his private office with the door closed, as it usually was when he was talking to someone. He wore a plain brown flannel shirt with his US Marshal badge pinned to his left breast pocket. His long, dark hair was in a ponytail, and the beard on his strong, handsome face was trimmed neatly.

"Matthew, I wanted to express my appreciation for what you've done for me, so I sat down at the piano and wrote a song about you. It's not much, but it's from my heart, and I think it's ready to share. It's just my way of saying thank you for saving me from the sheriff and his friends. I'm singing the song I wrote for you tomorrow at the dance hall at nine o'clock sharp. I would really like for you to be there," she told him.

Matt's smile broadened. "Will I cry?"

Christine laughed lightly. "Maybe. But I think you're tough enough to take it."

"What's it called?"

"You mean, 'titled?'"

"Oh, forgive me. Yes, what's it titled?" He laughed.

Her eyes looked up to the left slightly as she paused before answering. She returned her gaze to him and answered, "*Heroes.*"

Matt smiled kindly. "I'll be there, and I can't wait to hear it."

"And you have to dance with me afterward."

"I'd be honored to."

"Now that that's out of the way, how are you, Matthew Bannister, really?" she asked with the utmost sincerity.

Matt tilted his head. "Tired. I'm afraid being gone for a few weeks and then leaving again for one trial and then a second has worn me down. My life's been non-stop since coming back from Sweethome, and if it's not one thing, it's another."

"I read the article about the Eckman family's daughter. That is so sad. At least you gave them an ending to their frantic searching. It's too bad she got hooked up with that man, though."

Matt frowned and nodded. He spoke softly. "It was."

"Were you offended by what her father said about you?"

Matt shook his head slightly. "No. He's been looking for his daughter for a long time, and he had just buried her. It would be a hard blow. He was just blowing off steam. Besides, in my position, or any lawman position, you can't take anything too personal. I shook it off like a wet dog and left it there."

"That's one of the character traits I admire about you, Matthew—your ability to see through other people's eyes. That's a rare trait nowadays. Do you know how many men would've been furious about it?"

"A few. But it doesn't matter. He wasn't my friend beforehand, and he sure isn't now, so it means nothing. Maybe since his daughter ran away to begin with, the fault lies with him and his relationship with his daughter, not me."

Christine nodded. "That may very well be true. So, are you planning on getting some rest this weekend?"

From out in the main office, Matt's deputy, Nate Robertson, said loudly, "Matt? You better come see this."

Matt glanced at Christine and laughed lightly as he stood up. "I wouldn't count on it. We better go see what's going on, huh?" he asked as he reached for his gun belt and wrapped it around his waist.

"You don't go anywhere without that, do you?" she asked with a hint of sadness to her voice.

He answered with a chuckle, "Not when Nate sounds like that."

"We better go see what it is, then," she said, standing up.

"And then if you'd like, we could go get some lunch?"

"I'd love to."

Matt stepped out of his private office into the main area.

"What's up, Nate?" he asked.

Nate Robertson was a young man in his mid-twenties

who had little law enforcement experience, but he was learning fast and had shown his grit a few times now. He was a big guy, with broad shoulders and neatly trimmed blond hair on a strong, clean-shaven face. Nate pointed toward the large bay window at the front of the office.

Out front were three horses tethered to one another, led by one rider. The man had two dead bodies tied over the saddles of the two horses, and he was in the process of cutting the ropes and pushing the bodies off the horses and onto the street.

Matt wordlessly walked outside. "Excuse me, what do you think you're doing?" he asked.

The man was older, perhaps in his early to mid-sixties, and had a grizzled and tough appearance. He had unkempt shoulder-length heavily graying brown hair and a long gray goatee that grew past his chin about three inches or so. His face was long and narrow, with a slender nose that had been broken in the past. His eyebrows were thick, and still had a touch of their original dark brown color to them. He was an average-sized man and was dressed in dirty buckskins with bloodstains on them. Over them, he wore a black bearskin coat. He had a shotgun close at hand on his saddle and a longer-range Henry rifle on the other side. He wore a gun belt with his revolver held in place with a hammer thong, like Matt himself carried. The man ignored Matt, cut the ropes to the second body, and let it fall to the dirt street with a deep thud.

"Oh, my word!" Christine said, covering her mouth.

"What do you think you're doing?" Matt asked with more authority.

The grizzled old man looked at Matt for the first time. His light blue eyes were hard and cold like steel. He spat out a mouthful of tobacco juice and stepped to his saddlebag to pull out a roll of papers tied with a rawhide strap, then grabbed the top two papers off his collection and moved toward Matt.

"Are you the marshal?" he asked in a deep, rusty voice. He held the two sheets out for Matt to take.

"I am," Matt said, already annoyed with the man.

"I'm delivering the bodies of Pat and Truman Flanders. You will see for yourself if you take the damn papers that they're worth two hundred and fifty dollars apiece since they're dead."

Matt frowned and took the papers. Each one was a wanted poster for one of the two brothers. Each had a drawn likeness of the wanted man. The Flanders brothers had taken to robbing stagecoaches in southern Oregon. If the man had brought them in alive, it would have been a five-hundred-dollar bounty apiece, but their dead bodies brought half the price.

People begin to gather on the street and boardwalks to stare at the two dead men. Matt spoke plainly. "I can identify the bodies for you and write up a bond note, but you're going to have to load those bodies back up and take them to the undertaker because you're not leaving them here."

The man narrowed his eyebrows and responded quickly, "Like hell I will! It says to deliver them to a law enforcement office. I have done my part." He glared at Matt with his steely gaze.

"Yup, and I am telling you to load them back up on

your horses and take them to the undertaker. I'll give you directions."

"Do it yourself! I've done my part. They're your problem now." The man spat again.

Matt looked at the man with annoyance. "No, they're not. Take them to the Branson Sheriff down the road a few blocks. I have no interest."

The man glared at Matt irritably. "Do you think just because you've got a pretty lady beside you and a crowd here watching that you can act like a big shot and fail to do your damn job?" he asked loudly.

Matt smirked lightly. "Take your papers and bodies to the sheriff. His name's Tim Wright. I'm sure he'll be happy to help you."

"I've earned my money. Now, are you going to help me or not?"

"No, I'm not."

The man grimaced. "You're Matt Bannister?"

"I am."

"I thought you'd have more backbone."

Matt spoke uncaringly. "Take your papers."

The man snatched the papers out of Matt's hand with unexpected speed. "You better not break the law, because if I ever see a bounty with your name on it, I'm coming for you!"

Matt chuckled. "I'll try to stay on the straight and narrow path, but just in case I cross over, what name should I be listening for?"

"Jim Hexum."

Matt nodded in recognition. "Your reputation proceeds you."

Jim nodded curtly. "It should!" he said with a hard glare at Matt. He looked at Christine. "Ma'am." He nodded goodbye and went to load up the bodies again.

"Have a good day," Matt said in a friendly tone.

"Go to hell!"

After he rode off, Christine asked, "Do you ever just meet someone, and you don't like them? I just had that bad feeling. Not just because he was rude, but also, something about him doesn't feel right. Who is he?"

Matt took a deep breath as he watched Jim Hexum ride down the street. "They call him Bloody Jim Hexum. He's a bounty hunter of the worst kind. He probably could've brought those two boys in alive if he wanted to, but he is known for killing everyone he brings in. It's legal enough, but it shouldn't be. He's what I'd call a legal killer. A predator is what he is."

"He doesn't seem to like you."

Matt laughed slightly. "That makes us even, I suppose. So, where do you want to have lunch?"

"I don't know if I can eat after seeing those bodies, Matt. I think it ruined my appetite. But how about Regory's Italian Restaurant if you're hungry?"

"That sounds good."

PICK LAWSON WATCHED Matt Bannister step into Bella's Dance hall and paused inside the door to quickly scan the crowd of men. The marshal's eyes stopped on an older man with long gray hair and a three-inch-long gray goatee standing at the bar. The hard exterior of the stranger left no doubt that he was not to be trifled with, even at his age. The man had seen Matt step into the dance hall and nodded slightly, and Matt had returned it. It hadn't been friendly on either one's part, but rather a nod of acknowledgment, with perhaps of a bit of respect.

Pick watched Christine Knapp nearly run across the floor to Matt, and his smile widened as she took his arm and lead him across the large dance floor to a small table with a white tablecloth set in front of the stage. The stage curtain was open, and a silver candle-holder with three tall lit candles burned on top of the piano. Pick had been there enough times to know it meant Christine was going to sing a song tonight. He watched Christine sit down at the table with Matt and couldn't help noticing the excitement revealed in her expression and body language as they began to talk.

Christine was the most beautiful of all the dancers, and maybe in the whole world, at least of the women Pick had seen. Everyone seemed to dream of winning Christine's heart; she was often the talk of the town. Certainly, young Brent Boyle had sworn he was in love with Christine. Pick smiled as he thought of how desperate Brent had been to win her heart. He'd had a dream of building a cabin out in the solitude of the Wallowas where they could be alone.

It had been a farfetched fantasy for a nineteen-year-old boy, but Pick had to agree it would be nice. It was unfortunate that Brent was dead by Pick's hand, but Christine had never known knew Brent existed anyway. He wished he could speak to Brent one last time, just to tell him he was nothing more than a dance ticket to put in her pocket.

Pick would've liked to get to know Christine, but she was like a summer's gentle breeze: she was soft, kind, and warm, but always passing him by. She had a way of making a man feel good about himself for a moment, but then she was gone to dance with someone else. The expression on her face when she was with Matt was even more appreciative and tender than the expression she had worn over the summer when his old company manager Travis McNight would walk in. Travis never set foot in Bella's Dance hall anymore. Pick was curious as to why.

Pick had never spoken to Matt, because quite honestly, Matt made his chest tighten anxiously. He knew that if Matt figured out he was the mysterious fourth bank robber of the Loveland heist, he'd wind up on the end of a rope. There were only two people outside the Sperry-Helms Gang who could identify him as the fourth robber, and both of those men were related to Matt.

However, on the other side of that coin, Pick was one of the only people aside from the Sperry-Helms Gang who knew Matt was lying about the Eckmans' daughter and his attempt to scam them out of ten thousand dollars. The real mystery was, where had Matt found the evidence that proved it was Catherine Eckman's and her husband's bodies?

He couldn't fake the belongings; they had to be real. According to the paper, it had been a very rare chess set and a box containing partially burned photos and papers that verified it was them. It was a scam, because Pick knew Possum, and Possum's wife wasn't a twenty-something millionaire heiress. Where would a young lady hide where Matt could find her? Pick began to smile as he looked around the dance hall. Sometimes a person had to step back and look at the full picture before he could see the puzzle pieces fall into place.

Before he went to Loveland, Christine was rumored to have been courting Travis McNight. He'd come in late at night for the last dance, and outbid everyone else to dance with her. Soon after Pick returned from Loveland, the gossip had changed from the bloody massacre of a posse and the suicide of the fourth bank robber to Christine being accused of murdering some fella from Willow Falls.

Pick didn't know what was happening within the law offices, but when Matt came home from Idaho, suddenly those murder charges were dropped. Just so happened the sheriff, Travis McNight, and Josh Slater all three looked like they'd been in a lethal train wreck. The rumor spread that Matt had beaten them behind closed doors at the Monarch Hotel for some reason that never came to light, and it was about then that Travis quit coming to the Dance hall.

Not long after that, Matt had begun his own investigation into the two bodies found in the burnt cabin. Pick knew the Sperry-Helms Gang was edgy at the time, but they were dumbfounded when Matt provided the evidence that proved the bodies belonged to Catherine Eckman and her husband.

Pick watched Christine leave Matt's table and walk up

the four steps to the piano. Pick leaned against the bar and ordered another drink.

Christine played the instrument with such a master-fulness that everyone stopped talking to pay attention to the beautiful notes in their sweet-talking harmony. She began to sing with her soft angelic voice:

"When I was a little girl and had a bad dream, I'd cry out for my grandfather. A man of strength to battle the fear away. A man of comfort to wipe the tears away. A hero...meant to forever be.

Heroes step in and play the cards of fate. Heroes always do what's right. Heroes, my hero...meant to forever be.

Men of might, men of valor, men of courage, men who stand before a stampeding herd to save an unwanted lady of the night. Men who just know it's right. Grace and love, yet able to fight.

Heroes step in and play the cards of fate. Heroes always do what's right. Heroes, my hero...meant to forever be.

And you never ask for a thing in return. You just chase the nightmare and fears away and say, 'It'll be all right.' So much strength behind the kindest eyes. A man among men, a hero...my hero. You're my hero, and you're forever meant to be my hero."

The crowd was momentarily silent, then erupted into loud applause, shouts, and whistles. Christine stood up and wiped her damp eyes before smiling brightly and curtseying. Then she walked off the stage.

She headed to where Matt stood clapping with a smile. She put out her hand and said, "Come dance with me."

"It would be my honor," he replied and took her hand in his as he followed her out to the middle of the dance floor. She turned into him, and he put his arms around her before the band began playing.

"Honestly, what did you think?" she asked softly.

Matt smiled sincerely. "I have never heard anything more beautiful. I'm...stunned. It was a beautiful song, and you sounded wonderful."

She looked up at him, pleased by his answer. She spoke softly. "I wrote it for you, and I meant every word of it."

Matt looked into her eyes seriously. "It means a lot to me. I am more honored than you know."

"Matt?" She paused.

"Yes?"

She smiled sadly, changing her mind. "Let's dance."

The music started, and the song the instrumental band played was a slow waltz. She drew closer to him than she did anyone else when a slower song was played.

Matt asked, "How did you know it was going to be a slow song?" He realized they had been holding each other before the band began to play.

She looked up at him with a soft, sad smile. "I asked them to play one."

He shrugged. "Nice."

"Do you want to stay late tonight?" she asked. "I know

I should have asked you first, but I took the rest of the night off so we could go sit up on the roof and look at the stars and talk. If you want to?" she added nervously.

Matt hesitated. "Um…"

Christine spoke quickly. "I know you're courting Felisha, and I don't want to interfere. I just thought we could have some time to talk as friends. I promise I won't tell you that I'm falling in love with you or anything like that. I just thought we could enjoy the stars and talk for a while."

"It's a little cold out, isn't it?"

"Not if we sit up against the chimney and wrap ourselves in a quilt. Trust me, if it's too cold, we'll come down to the reading room. But we'd have time to talk. Some deep conversation would do us both good, I'm sure."

He smiled as they danced slowly. "I'm sure it would."

"Then let's finish this dance and go," she said with a pleased smile as she rested her cheek against his chest.

PICK WATCHED Matt and Christine leave the dance floor hand in hand, walk out of the ballroom, and disappear up the stairs. He frowned since no men were allowed upstairs at the dance hall. They hired a man just to stand by the stairs to make sure none tried to go there, but he had let Matt walk upstairs with Christine without a care.

Pick looked around to see if any other men noticed Matt going upstairs. Christine was the most sought-after lady of them all, so most of the men had noticed, and it was being discussed. Many, like Pick himself, felt a twinge of jealousy to see Christine leading Matt upstairs by the hand while the music still played.

It felt like the wall of a mine shaft caving in on him when the final puzzle pieces fell into place. The whole picture became clear, and it was more obvious than the scar on his face. Christine Knapp was Catherine Eckman! He was dumbfounded, and filled with an excitement he had not felt since his youth. He had solved the puzzle of one of the world's greatest rewards for a missing person. Catherine Eckman was hiding in plain view of the public, and no one had figured it out yet.

She was beautiful, she was educated, and she was a lady through and through. Everything about her manners and etiquette hinted of a wealthy upbringing. She had been married, but her husband was deceased, and now she lived in the dance hall. The final puzzle piece was the song she had written for Matt about being a hero. The timing was very suspicious since Ingrid Overguard's burnt body had been accepted as Catherine's and moved to the Eckman family plot in Sacramento, California.

The missing pieces all fit like a Natoma-made glove. She and Matt had partnered up to swindle her parents out of ten thousand dollars and fake her death. If she was dead, the two of them could live their lives in the open, and no one would ever be looking for her or suspect a thing. Pick had to admit it was a good plan. They just hadn't expected someone like him to catch on to them.

When the dance was over and the music stopped, Pick looked around to see if anyone else had twigged to the opportunity. The men went back to their drinks or bid to win a dance with an attractive lady before someone else beat them to it. It was then that Pick noticed the only other person still staring toward the stairs was the older man with the long gray hair and goatee.

The stranger had a look of bitter indignation in his eyes. It was obvious the man didn't like Matt. Pick recalled Matt nodding an unspoken personal acknowledgment to the stranger when he entered, which made Pick curious to know who the man was. It was possible the old man had caught onto Christine being Catherine as well. Now that he could see the full picture, he couldn't believe no one else had seen the obvious deception taking place right in front of them.

He moved down the bar a few steps and said to the older gray-haired man, "Pretty, ain't she?"

The man looked at Pick irritably. "Who?"

Pick nodded toward the stairs. "The lady Matt went upstairs with. I couldn't help but notice you watching them."

"What's it to you?" he asked shortly.

"Nothing. Whether you agree or not is up to you. I thought you might be staring at her like I was, but maybe not, huh?" Pick asked, taking a drink.

"She's pretty."

"Do you know Matt?"

The man shook his head once. "I met him."

"You don't sound like you were too impressed with him."

The man gave Pick a cold glance and didn't respond.

He put his attention back on the dance floor. It was obvious he didn't want to talk.

"Is this your first time? I haven't seen you in here before."

The man nodded.

"Are you from around here?"

The man shook his head wordlessly.

"You don't talk much do you? My name's Pick. Pick Lawson." He put his hand out to shake.

The older man looked at him uncaringly, then half-heartedly raised his own hand. "Jim Hexum."

"Nice to meet you, Jim. Wait...Jim Hexum. Bloody Jim Hexum? The bounty hunter? Really?" he asked, amazed as an idea came to him.

Jim nodded. "I suppose so," he said and began to step away.

"Wait, who are you looking for? I might be able to help."

"I doubt it."

"Are you here looking for that girl? The one the marshal found?" Pick asked with interest.

Jim shook his head. "Not anymore."

"Why not?" Pick asked with a slight smirk.

Jim looked at him with a no-nonsense expression of irritation. His voice was sharp as he answered, "She was already found," he said bitterly and began to walk out of the dance hall.

Pick followed. "Jim, wait. Let me buy you a drink down the street where it's quieter. I have a business proposition you might want to hear about. Trust me, you'll be glad you took a few minutes to listen to me."

. . .

"So, what do you want?" Jim asked bluntly as he sat at a corner table in the Thirsty Toad Saloon. The one-time failing business had a new owner who had livened the place up with pictures of nude women, a piano player, and a few women to work the room. The drinks were cheaper than the dance hall's, and the atmosphere was more exciting than it had been in years.

Pick looked around the saloon to make sure he wouldn't be overheard, then spoke quietly. "You're the most famous bounty hunter around, so you probably knew about the Eckmans' daughter, right?"

Jim nodded, unimpressed.

"What if I was to tell you that the couple burned in that cabin wasn't the Eckmans' daughter and her husband?"

Jim frowned skeptically. "Your marshal proved it was. You're walking up a dead trail and wasting my time. It's been a long day, and I need some sleep before I hit the trail north. Goodnight." He began to stand.

"Wait! I know for a fact it wasn't them because I know who was killed and who killed them. It was not the Eckmans' daughter unless she was married to a dirt-poor old man," Pick said urgently to get Jim to sit down. "Have a seat and hear me out. Please..."

Jim looked at Pick and narrowed his eyes in thought, then sat down. "Go on."

Pick leaned forward to get to the point quietly. "She's still alive and around here, and I know who and where she is. Her husband was killed in Colorado a few years ago, so he's not around. But she is! Now, I believe we can get the Eckmans to pay top dollar for the resurrection, let's say, of their daughter. Their bounty was ten thousand, so I think we should get twenty thousand for such a miracle, huh? I'm the only person who knows what really happened up there at the cabin and where their daughter is hiding. I think they'll pay top dollar for that knowledge."

Jim shook his head doubtfully. "The marshal found their belongings in the cabin. It was them."

Pick laughed. "Our good marshal is pulling a scam! He tried to get the money, but the Eckmans wouldn't pay for a dead body. We can return her back to them alive. Look, I'm no angel, but I've never done anything like this before. I'm asking you to be my partner in this because you have tracked men down and held them captive while you took them back to town. The job's too big for a one man. I need a partner, and I'm asking you to do this with me."

Jim looked at Pick coldly. "Where is she?"

Pick chuckled and shook his head. "Oh, no. I'm not saying a word until you and I have an agreement on paper. I could do it alone if I had to, or I could let my friends in on it, but your name would get their attention, trust, and a reply faster than mine would. You're a godsend. You can write the letter, and we can blackmail them up to twenty thousand dollars. Ten thousand each for a few days' work. What do you say, Jim?"

"You think you can blackmail the Eckmans? Once you notify them, they'll send a battalion of Pinkertons here to snoop around, and if she's here, they will find her."

Pick shook his head. "They haven't found her yet because she doesn't want them too. She's not missing against her will; she's hiding from her parents. I wouldn't trust Louis Eckman as far as I could throw him from what I've heard about him, so I'm not going to tell him where she is because I'd never get my money. I'm talking about taking her and keeping her hidden out of town until Louis gets here with the money. Once I have the money in my paws, we'll hand over Catherine Eckman. What happens to them after that is their concern. Just imagine, twenty thousand dollars for a few days' work."

"You're going to kidnap her?" Jim asked skeptically.

"I am with your help. Do we have a deal?"

Jim thought it over. "How do you know it's her? I've been looking for her for a long time and found no trace of her. What makes you think your girl is her?"

"Common sense and observation. She wasn't killed in that cabin. I know *that* for a fact. Matt Bannister planted that evidence there. I know *that* for a fact, which means she is around here somewhere, and Matt knows where. But he's apparently not expecting anyone else to know that. I know who she is and where. All we have to do is take her and wait for the money."

Jim yawned tiredly and looked at Pick. "If you kidnap a woman, the marshal's going to be on your trail, especially if he's in on it too. A rabid dog's dangerous, and if you corner it, you're going to get bit. Aside from Matt, even if you successfully got the money, Louis Eckman will have the Pinkertons hunt you down even after he has his daughter back. That is his preferred way to deal with his enemies. I talked to one of his Pinkerton hunters in

Nevada one time, and I'll tell you, Louis Eckman didn't get rich being a nice man. Trust me on that. He'll put a twenty-thousand-dollar bounty on your head."

Pick frowned in thought. "Don't you think he'd be a bit angrier with Matt for trying to scam him out of ten thousand dollars for a stranger's body? Or do you think he'd be grateful enough to have his daughter back alive to part with a bit of money? I think his rage will be at Matt, myself, and Matt will be shamed out of office, and probably arrested for something once Louis gets done with him."

Jim smiled slowly. "You know who she is?"

"I do. This is an opportunity, Jim, that we will never have again. Trust me, I know who she is! Partner up with me. Let's write up an agreement between us to split the money, and then I'll tell you who she is. With your name and reputation, no one is going to doubt us. The Eckmans are going to thank us."

He nodded. "Get some paper and ink. But you better be right about this."

Pick smiled. "I'm right." He raised his voice and waved a hand in the air. "Hey, barkeep, do you by chance have two pieces of paper and some ink?"

The barkeep nodded and disappeared into a side office. He came out carrying two sheets of paper and an ink bottle and pen. He set them down on the table. "Anything else? Another drink?"

Jim nodded. "This round's on me."

After the barkeep went back to the bar, Pick began writing the same words on both hand-written agreements. When he had finished, he slid both pages across the table for Jim to sign. He read both identical pages and signed. It was a simple agreement to split the reward money earned from Louis Eckman evenly. The two men shook hands and put their contracts to the side for the ink to dry.

The barkeep set two drinks on the table and said, "My name's John Briggs. I'm the new owner of this establishment."

"I'm Pick Lawson, and this is Jim Hexum, the bounty hunter."

"Bloody Jim Hexum? Well, welcome to the Thirsty Toad Saloon! I hope it becomes your favorite place in town. It's a tough competition between Ugly John's, Bella's Dance Hall, and the other saloons in town, but I'm up for the fight. Let me ask you, Jim..." he said as he pulled up a chair to join them uninvited. "Were you on the hunt for the Venetta Creek Killer or the Sperry-Helms Gang members who robbed the Loveland Bank? If so, you're too late. They're all dead now. Rumor has it one's still hanging up there somewhere, but he hasn't been found yet."

"We've heard," Jim said, clearly having no interest in talking to him.

"I was there," John offered. "I had a saloon up in Loveland when the bank was robbed. I was part of the posse that went after them, and we probably would have caught them if I had stayed with the guys. My horse hurt its leg when we jumped down into a riverbed. I couldn't continue with my friends. Which is too bad, because they'd still be alive if I had gone with them. I knew right away that Octavius Clark was bad news. I never trusted him, and man..." He paused with a hint of sadness on his expression. "I wish I was there to save my friends. Try to, at least."

Pick asked anxiously, "Did you see the bank robbers?"

John shook his head. "No, I was sleeping when they hit the bank. It's strange, though; the paper listed everyone's name in the posse except Nathan's. His brother Cal was killed along with everyone else, but not a word about Nathan. I don't know if he survived or ever came back or not. Shame, though. He had a very pretty wife named Sarah. I wonder if she's still single?" He laughed lightly.

Jim spoke soberly. "Nice to meet you, but I have business to talk about."

John raised his hands as if surrendering. "Well, don't let me stop you. You gents have a great time, and I hope you'll be coming back to the new Thirsty Toad."

Pick frowned at John. "If you were part of the posse, how come you don't know if that man ever came back or not? I thought you said you lived in Loveland?"

John looked at Pick with a blank stare for a moment, hesitating. "I was moving here that day," he said unconvincingly.

"With an injured horse?"

John nodded. "Yeah. It wasn't fit for mountain climbing, but fine for road travel," he said and walked away quickly.

"He's lying," Pick said simply.

Jim couldn't care less about that. "I signed the agreement with you, so tell me—who is she, and where can we find her?"

Pick smiled. "Didn't you listen to Christine's song

tonight? It's Christine! You saw them together. It's so blatantly obvious, and nobody knows it except me. Jim, nobody is allowed upstairs, but where did they go? He's keeping her for himself!"

"No, that isn't her. The Eckmans' daughter don't look like her. I have her likeness on a poster in my room, and she don't look like that. I believe you're wasting my time," Jim said and began to stand.

"And that's exactly why no one has found her yet! The artist who drew the picture may not have been all that talented, so of course, they walk right by her night after night. No one knows what she looks like for sure."

"Her hair is supposed to be blonde or light brown," Jim said, sitting back down.

"She dyes it. We have the tannery in Natoma, and they dye skins various colors every day. All she has to do is buy dark dye and dye her hair. It goes clear back to the Roman days, so it's nothing new. That chess set was bought in Greece or somewhere over there, the paper said. She is very well educated, so you think she won't know that? She has to know if she's running from the law, or her parents, that dyeing her hair is not a bad idea."

"Hmm," Jim said thoughtfully. "Her hair's in a bun in the likeness. She is a pretty girl, it looks like."

"A likeness is right, not a photograph. It has room for error, and that explains why no one has found her. Until now," Pick added pointedly.

"So, what kind of plan do you have?"

"First, you write a letter to the Eckmans and make arrangements for them to wire you a date they'll be here with twenty thousand dollars."

"Why me?"

"Because your name brings credibility. If they agree to our deal, we'll find a way to kidnap her. If we must, we'll set the dance hall on fire and sweep her up in the chaos, but we have a week or so to plan before we take any risks. We need to think about it."

"Who was killed in the cabin if it wasn't Catherine Eckman?"

"Possum Overguard and his wife. They were closer to your age than mine. Possum was paroled from prison eight months ago or so, and joined up with the Sperry-Helms Gang. That was an order given by Alan Sperry from prison. They were both killed by Morton Sperry for talking too much and burned. Catherine Eckman is alive and well. Trust me, when her parents read your letter, they will respond. It'll probably take the letter about a week to get there, and them a week to get here, so we have about two weeks to come up with a plan to take her and get her holding cell prepared. I'll get it all figured out. It's what I do—figure things out."

Jim squinted his cold eyes and gave Pick a quick smirk. "You're not exactly a law-abiding citizen, are you?"

Pick looked at Jim in the eyes, his own coldness revealing itself. "Not exactly."

"Sperry-Helms Gang?"

Pick nodded.

"How come you didn't call upon them to help?" Jim asked.

"Their name can't be trusted, but yours demands respect. Besides, I don't want her hurt, I just want the money. Once I get the money, I am leaving this area and getting far away from the Sperrys and the Helms boys. I don't trust them for a minute, and this is my ticket out. Tomorrow, I'll show you the old mine shaft we'll keep her in. It's isolated, and long since forgotten. I think you'll approve of the plan I have so far. Trust me when I say this is the easiest money you'll ever make."

Jim looked at Pick carefully and then smiled slightly. "I like it. But what I really want to see is the marshal stripped of his badge. That's what I want out of this, and I know your Sheriff Wright would love that too. He isn't too fond of the marshal, I discovered."

Pick shook his head. "I bet not. Matt broke the sheriff's nose, and I don't even know why. No one does, apparently, but they don't like each other very much."

"Obviously. Well, once the sheriff gets hold of this, he won't let go until Matt's done for. I look forward to that."

"So is the Sperry-Helms Gang. I'm doing them a favor, and they don't even know it."

Jim laughed. "I think you may be doing a lot of folks around here a favor, but that's what keeps me busy. So, let's get it done. Let's go back to my hotel look at her likeness to verify it's her, and write the Eckmans a letter if there's any resemblance."

IT WAS a clear and cold October night, with a crescent moon and a sky filled with bright stars. It was indeed a beautiful night to sit on cushions from the chairs in the reading room against the warm chimney on top of Bella's Dance Hall. Christine Knapp had brought up a large and heavy quilt her grandmother had made her to cover Matt and her as they sat together to watch the stars.

Christine pointed at the moon. "Do you see that star nearest the moon? When I was little, I used to think it was my mother in heaven watching over me. Even when I got older, it still held a special place in my heart. It's my favorite star in the whole universe. I guess you could say it's special to me...like it's my own personal star."

"From now on, every time I'm out at night and see that star, I'll know that's Christine's star," Matt told her with a smirk.

She smiled and nudged his shoulder with her own at his sarcasm. "I hope so. Do you have a special star, or a favorite, anyway?"

Matt pointed to the Big Dipper. "I don't know why... yes, I do know why. The Big Dipper is the constellation I always look at. It reminds me of home and my mother. When I was little, my mom and I would go outside and look at the stars, and she always pointed at the Big Dipper. During all the years I was out tracking people down, I'd find myself staring at it often and missing home. I suppose it's my favorite constellation."

Christine smiled as she watched his face in the dim light. "So, the Big Dipper is your favorite series of stars. I must correct you, though—it's not a constellation. It's actually part of the Great Bear constellation. It's interesting...the Little Dipper over there," she pointed, "is part of the constellation of the Little Bear. I don't know their technical names, but they are both bears, and both only part of a constellation."

Matt looked at her. "So, you *don't* know everything?"

She laughed. It was a pleasing sound that made Matt smile.

"No, I don't know everything, just the things you don't know."

He laughed. "Then that's quite an education you have!"

She shrugged and said seriously, "My grandparents didn't want to leave an uneducated girl to face the world after they passed on, so they taught me what they could. It was enough to know the big dipper is *not* a constellation." She smiled.

"They did a good job," he said simply, watching her angelic face shine in the starlight.

"Thank you. I loved them very much. You know, I never heard them fight. They would have disagreements once in a blue moon, but I never heard them argue or say anything hurtful to one another. It made for a very happy and love-filled home. They had a good marriage. I don't think I understand people who just want a wife or a husband and are willing to jump headfirst into marriage without first taking the time to get to know the person.

"My ex-husband was my best friend for years before we got married. Working here at the dance hall, so many of the girls are just anxious to marry whoever asks them before they get too old to dance. It's a real fear for some of the older ladies here. My friend Helen is probably the worst about that, but I think she found the real deal with her beloved Sam. I told her to make a list of the qualities she wants from her husband and compare those to Sam before marrying him, but I don't think she did. Let me ask you, Matt...if you were to make a list of qualities you wanted in a wife, what would they be?" Christine turned on her cushion to face him.

Matt exhaled and thought for a moment. "The qualities I would want in my wife, huh? Well, first and foremost, she'd have to be a Christian. We wouldn't be equally yoked together if she wasn't. I want someone I can talk to and share my dreams and frustrations with without the fear of being ridiculed, made fun of, or gossiped about. I want a marriage that is built upon friendship and intimate conversations, where we can talk for hours and not tire of each other. We should be able to keep the fire burning as we each bring our own pieces of oak to add to it from our lives every day.

"I'm not a romantic, so I really can't write a love poem here, but what I want from my wife is someone I can trust to help me to be a better man and not tear me down. I want someone to laugh with, and whose sense of character and humor I absolutely honor and adore. I want someone who I can trust with my deepest secrets and tell everything to without any doubt of it not being shared. I want someone who can see me at my worst and still love me. I want someone with integrity, a gentle heart, compassion for others, and a whole lot of love for me. And I will not marry anyone who is bitter-hearted or easily angered." He looked at Christine. "How's that?"

Christine smiled. "I'm glad you're not going to marry a bitter and angry woman. That's not anyone's dream, is it?"

Matt smiled. "I'd hope not."

"They wouldn't say it if *I* asked, probably, but if you asked most of the men who come in here what qualities they were looking for in a wife, I'd bet cooking, cleaning, and bedding would be the first three things they answered."

"Those guys downstairs spend a whole lot of their lives looking for something to satisfy their emptiness. Food, clean dishes, and sex won't do it. I'll bet most of them who do jump into a quick marriage for those qualities soon wish they never married at all. I want more out of my life, and out of my relationship with my wife. I want a best friend, and someone to raise a family with and love for the rest of my life. What about you? What qualities are you looking for in a husband?"

She smiled slightly. "A man who loves the Lord. A man who will be my best friend and love me for who I really am. A man of the utmost integrity and character. Gentle, kind, and affectionate, and not afraid to share his dreams with me. And like you, I think it's very important to have someone who supports and encourages me. I want someone I can be real with, and who will hold me when I need to be held and comfort me when I cry and allow me to do the same for him. I'm waiting for a partner in life, fifty-fifty, and a hundred years to go."

"I don't think you'll have a problem finding a good husband, Christine. You're a diamond in a gold mine. When the right prospector finds you, he's going to hit the greatest mother lode of a lifetime," Matt said sincerely.

Christine smiled slightly but had a sad expression in her eyes. "Thank you. But that prospector hasn't noticed me yet. As your friend, I have to ask: does Felisha have the qualities you mentioned?"

Matt nodded slowly. "Yeah, she does. At least so far."

"When do you get to see her again?"

"Saul and Abby's wedding is in two weeks, and she is coming over for that."

Christine was silent for a moment, and a slight mist covered her eyes as her heart plummeted into her stomach. The man who had the desired qualities on her list was sitting beside her. She wondered how long it would take the prospector in the gold mine to notice the diamond right beside him. She fulfilled every need and want he had listed, and he acted like he was blind, deaf, and dumb to the obvious. She frowned. "Are you going to ask her to marry you while she's here?"

Matt shook his head. "No, it's a little too soon, I think. I'll wait a while if that's okay with you?"

She smiled to mask her sadness. "Marriage is a lifelong commitment. You might want to take your time and make sure she's the one you want to marry. There might not be too many diamonds in a coal mine."

"Gold mine. You can't twist my own analogy on me. A coal mine is just dust and coal, but a gold mine has value. It's a precious metal all on its own, but a diamond is the rarest of rare finds. A true treasure."

Christine looked at him gently. "I hope you find the diamond, Matt."

"You too, Christine."

1

Matt Bannister walked down Main Street with a smile on his lips. It couldn't be helped, really. In two hours, the stagecoach carrying Felisha Conway and her son Dillon would pull into town. He hadn't seen her in over a month, and he was excited to see her again. Even more, he was excited to show her around Branson and the surrounding county where he grew up. He was excited to introduce her to his family and friends. He was excited to see her pretty smile and to hold her in his arms again and kiss her. He was excited to see little Dillon's reaction when he showed them the Premro Island waterfall. There was so much to show them, and his excitement at seeing Felisha especially was hard to contain.

As he walked down Main Street's boardwalk past businesses of various kinds, he heard some laughing and loud encouragements of a vile kind as he neared a four-foot alley between buildings. A lady walking toward him holding her coat tight against her dress to fight off the cold glanced down the alley and then stepped quickly away to distance herself from whatever was happening with a disturbed expression on her face.

Matt peered into the alley and stopped. It took a lot to make Matt mad, but he was suddenly angered. Four teenage boys surrounded an old Indian man who was lying on the hard ground, vaguely trying to protect himself from the boys. They were spitting, and one boy was urinating on him while his friends laughed.

"Hey!" Matt shouted. "Get your filthy asses away from him!" He walked quickly into the alley, and three of the boys ran toward the other end as fast as they could. The boy who was urinating tried to get his pants buttoned and run at the same time. He was quickly caught by Matt, who grabbed the boy and forced him back to the old Indian man roughly by the hair. "What's your name?" Matt asked the boy harshly.

The boy grimaced at the grip on his hair. "Tad. Tad Sperry."

"Sperry?" Matt asked. "Are you related to the Sperry-Helms Gang?"

"Yes, sir. My uncles, and they'll get you if you don't let go of my hair! Now, let me go!" Tad Sperry was a slight fifteen-year-old with ear-length blond hair, and he was dressed poorly.

Matt turned Tad's head by his hair to look into his eyes as he said, "You can tell your uncles I'll be at my office if they want to come 'get' me. I highly doubt they will. You, your family, your uncles, your cousins, and anyone else you can muster can find me easily enough. Your family does not scare me. But since they didn't teach you any manners, I am going to teach you some right now!" He turned Tad around to face the old man and forced him to his knees in a puddle of his own urine that had run off the old man.

"That's pee! You can't do that to me! It's cold out, and I have to ride back to Natoma with wet knees now because of you! Let me up, you son of a ... Ouch!" he cried as Matt twisted his fistful of hair.

"Shut up! Apologize to this man."

"No... Okay!" he agreed after Matt twisted his hair forcefully again. "I am sorry! Okay?"

"No, tell him you're really sorry."

"I'm really sorry!" Tad cried out, with the encouragement of Matt tightening the hand in his hair.

"Good. Now tell him, only girls like you pick on drunk men. And say it so loud the folks out on the street can hear you."

"No! *Okay!*" he screamed as Matt yanked his blond hair. "Only girls like me pick on old drunk men! Okay? Now will you let go of me?" Tad yelled. He was turning red from embarrassment because the crowd that was forming at both ends of the alley was laughing at him.

"No," Matt said. "You have to say it louder so your cowardly friends can hear you too. Go on, yell it out proudly."

Tad looked up at Matt with angry blue eyes. He grimaced painfully, and using his hands, tried to break free of Matt's grip. "Only girls pick on old drunk men!" he finally yelled.

"Girls like *me*," Matt emphasized.

"Girls like me!" he yelled after enduring the pain from his scalp as long as he could.

"Very good. Now stand up." Matt allowed the boy to stand and let go of his hair. He held the boy's ragged coat so he couldn't run away. "I don't mean to humiliate you, young man, but you had no problem humiliating this old man. You plainly see he is not able to defend himself. If I ever catch you doing something like this again, I will throw you in jail and hold you there until this man, or whoever you are harassing, *can* defend themselves, and I'll let them do so in your jail cell. Are we clear?"

"Yes," Tad agreed in a quiet yet restrained voice. His sneering lip and angry expression signaled just one thing, and that was trouble with the law in the boy's future.

Matt nodded. "Get out of here."

The kid walked a safe distance and turned back toward Matt. "I'm telling my uncles!"

"Be sure to tell them what I said." Matt knelt beside the old Indian, who was dressed in red wool pants and an orange shirt that was buttoned up to the top. He had no coat on and shivered in the cold. The man's shoulder-length black hair was heavy with gray and matted into a tangled, filthy mess. He smelled of whiskey and vomit. He had more than likely spent the night drinking and sleeping in the alley where he'd passed out. Matt shook his shoulder.

The man stirred. "Dogs of the moon don't bark when the lightning strikes," he said in a muffled, slurring voice.

Matt nodded. "Whatever you say, Chusi. Come on, let's get you up and out of the street. You can use one of my beds for the night." He grabbed his arm and helped him stand, and the crowds began dispersing from the ends of the alleys. Some folks commented on the boy, but Matt ignored the talking.

Chusi Yellowbear claimed to have been a fierce Shoshone warrior but was now just one of the town drunks. He lived somewhere outside of town in the woods along the river, but no one seemed to know exactly where, or really cared. He had no family and spent a large part of his days begging. One thing he could do well was catch fish with his nets, and he made a little money selling fish when he wasn't begging or drinking.

"Where's your coat, Chusi?" Matt asked after he got the man standing.

"Don't know."

"We'll keep you warm tonight anyway, and get you a coat if need be tomorrow." Matt wrapped his right arm around Chusi and helped him walk out of the alley and toward the marshal's office.

Chusi mumbled something unintelligible, and Matt ignored him.

Two businessmen striding toward them stepped out of the way. One encouraged Matt to lock Chusi away for good, the other to put him out of his misery. Matt looked at them harshly and kept walking Chusi toward his office, which was still two blocks away. A moment later, a well-dressed lady walking toward them pressed her back against the wall of a building with a disgusted expression on her face.

"You're going to get lice, scabies, or smallpox from that savage. You shouldn't be touching him!" she said as they passed her.

Matt paused and turned to look back at her. "He's a human being, not a savage!"

"Well!" she said with a huff. "Not to me."

Matt nodded. "That says everything I need to know about you, then." He started walking down the board-walk again.

Chusi, who had been watching as the lady degraded him, began to mumble, then spoke irately in his native tongue, and finally said in English, "Sleep!" He turned toward Matt and swung his right arm to hit him unexpectedly. Matt blocked it easily with his left arm, but Chusi's forceful spin caused Matt to lose his grip on him and the Indian fell, hitting his lower back on the edge of the boardwalk, while his head and shoulders hit the dirt street. He groaned, arching his back in pain.

Matt shook his head with frustration and stepped into the street to pick Chusi up. He didn't look around, but he could hear people laughing, including the lady he'd just spoken with.

"Wait, Matt. I'll help you," Christine Knapp said from across the street. She was with Bella and a few other ladies shopping. Christine handed her bags to one of the ladies and crossed the street. She looked as beautiful as always in an olive-green dress with a light green pinstripe. She wore a long gray wool coat over her dress, and her long dark hair was woven into an attractive chignon with an elegant hairclip holding it all in place. "Oh, my goodness, is he okay?" she asked as she came near.

"He's drunk. I'll pick him up," Matt explained, irritated. He lifted the man to his feet again and guided him back onto the boardwalk.

"Well, let me help you anyway." Christine slung Chusi's right arm over her shoulder and put her left arm around his lower back, touching Matt's arm. "Where are we taking him?" she asked.

"My office. I'm going to put him in one of my jail cells for the night, or until he sobers up, anyway. He was passed out in the alley back there." Matt continued, "You might not want to touch him, Christine, He isn't sick, but he was being spit on and urinated on by some boys."

"Ugh! Is that why he's wet? Well, my hands and coat will wash clean. Do you know him?" she asked.

Matt nodded. "Yes, this is Chusi Yellowbear. And you drank too much, didn't you, Chusi?" Chusi mumbled something neither of them could understand. "I think that means yes," Matt said with a smile.

Chusi glanced at Christine, then stared at her.

Christine smiled. "Hello, Chusi. My name's Christine."

The man slurred, "Christine...beauty like an angel."

Once back at the marshal's office, Matt and his deputy Nate Robertson took Chusi into the cell, laid him on a bed, and covered him with blankets. When they had finished, Matt asked Nate to go to the store down the road and charge a change of clothes and a coat for Chusi to Matt's account. Once Nate left on that errand, Matt looked at Christine, who was leaning against the three-foot partition that separated the entry from the main office. She was gazing at him fondly.

"What?" he asked with a slight smirk.

"You are a wonderful man, Matt. Not many would do that for him."

Matt frowned. "It was the only right thing to do. I'll probably keep him locked up until tomorrow, and have Nate walk him to the Chinese bathhouse to get him clean, then throw his old clothes in a fire someplace. A man shouldn't smell that bad, especially an elder. Seeing that kid urinate on him and the others spitting on him infuriated me, though. Anyway, what are you out doing today?"

"Shopping for dinner. It's my turn to help cook for the ladies."

"Anything good?"

She gave a laugh. "Always. I am a very good cook, mind you. Remember I told you my grandparents taught me a lot? Well, cooking is one of the things I do best. Tonight, I'm making a chicken casserole, pie, and sour-dough bread. Edith's making another dessert, but I make an excellent..." She stopped and looked at Matt oddly. "No, I'll just make you dinner one of these nights. But I do have to get back to the dance hall. Are you up to walking me back?"

Matt nodded. "Sure. I have time. Felisha's stage is due in around four."

"Are you excited to see her?"

"I am."

"How long will she be in town?"

"Four days. She is going back on Tuesday."

"Do you have plans?" she asked as Matt opened the gate to the partition for her to walk through.

56

"Saul and Abby's wedding is tomorrow. Beyond that, just showing her around and visiting."

"You're not asking her to marry you, are you?" she inquired.

He shook his head. "You already asked me that up on the roof. No, I'm not planning on it. I want to be sure she's the one for me before I ask for her hand in marriage. Are you okay with that idea?" he asked sarcastically as he held the office door open for her step outside.

"I am. Should I get your approval when a guy asks for my hand in marriage?"

He laughed as he locked the office door behind him. "Yes, you should. Because I'll tell him right up front, 'If you're a smart man, you'll run for your life! She's horrible!'"

She laughed and gave him a sharp shove into his door. "No, you wouldn't! You'd probably wish he was you! Anyway, before I forget to ask, what is your favorite kind of pie? When I make you dinner, I want to make your favorite pie, too."

"Yeah, what *is* your favorite pie, Matthew?" Felisha Conway asked, sounding a bit bitter. She was standing with her son Dillon and their friends Richard and Rebecca Grace about ten feet away on the boardwalk. She was carrying her traveling case, as were Richard Grace and Rebecca, who had their children with them.

"Felisha!" Matt said, surprised to see her. "I thought your stage was supposed to be here at four?"

"Hi, Matt!" Dillon said. He broke free from Felisha's hand and ran to hug Matt's waist.

"Hi, buddy. How are you?" he asked Dillon with a smile.

Felisha eyed Christine sourly and suspiciously and said, "Well, answer the lady, Matthew. What is your favorite pie?"

Matt laughed as he hugged Dillon and looked at Christine. "Apple. I like apple pie the best. Christine, this is Felisha, Felisha, this is Christine."

Christine held out a hand to shake. "I've heard a lot about you, Felisha. It's nice to meet you."

Felisha shook her hand half-heartedly. "I wish I could say the same, but Matthew hasn't mentioned you to me. So, Matthew, respond to the lady. Will you wish you were the one marrying her when someone finally asks for her hand in marriage?"

Her jealousy was noted by Christine, and the awkwardness became quite pronounced when she saw that Rebecca Grace and her husband were staring at her questionably too.

"What?" Matt asked, surprised by her tone. "Oh!" He laughed, remembering what Christine had said. "She was joking."

"I was," Christine said, trying to ease the tension in Felisha's eyes. It was filling the sidewalk.

Richard Grace spoke in a friendly manner despite the awkwardness of the moment. "I'm Richard Grace, and this is my wife, Rebecca. We came over with Felisha for the wedding tomorrow. Will you be there?" he asked.

Christine shook her head. "No, I won't. But you all have a wonderful time, and enjoy your stay."

Rebecca reached her hand out to Christine. "I'm

Rebecca. You're a very beautiful young lady, Christine. You must have dozens of successful young men trying to court you."

Christine looked at Rebecca with a puzzled expression. "A few. Well, I must go. I hope you all have a wonderful weekend, and it was nice to meet you all. Especially you, Felisha. Matt, have a great weekend."

"You too, Christine," Matt said and broke free from Dillon to step closer to Felisha and put his arms around her.

After she left, Felisha raised her eyebrows inquiringly. "Pie? Dinner? Who is Christine?"

"Just a friend," he said and put his arms around her. "I've missed you."

She smiled for the first time, although it was a troubled one. "I've missed you too."

"Well, welcome to Branson. I think you're going to love it here."

"I don't so far," Felisha said with a hint of jealousy in her tone despite her smile.

2

Friday night was spent in the living room of Matt's house with Felisha Conway, her friends Richard and Rebecca Grace, Saul Wolf, and his roommate and deputy marshal, Truet Davis. It was a wonderful time of relaxing and catching up on each other's lives since they were all last together. For Saul, it was the last night he would be a bachelor since he was marrying Abby Lesko the next day. For the Graces and Felisha, it was their first time reconnecting with Truet since his wife had died and he'd left Sweethome. For Matt, it was a time to visit with new friends and spend time with his beloved Felisha.

Matt's house was a two-bedroom brick single-level structure that had ornate dark wood floors and wainscoting and light-cream-colored wallpaper with a light-pink ornamental design. The colors and design of the house had been done by Lee and Regina Bannister since it had been their first home. Now that they lived in their new three-story Victorian on a city block near Kings

Court on Liberty Street, they rented this house to Matt. Since he had two bedrooms, he allowed his friend Truet Davis to live with him. Felisha and Dillon and the Grace family were staying in the Monarch Hotel as Lee Bannister's personal guests.

"Truet," the Reverend Richard Grace said, "if you're ready to move on—and maybe I shouldn't even say this because you probably aren't—we met Matt's friend Christine today. She's very attractive. I don't know if she's a Christian or not, but she seems very nice."

Rebecca slapped her husband's arm harder than anyone expected her to. "That's rude, and no, you shouldn't have said that!"

Richard laughed despite himself. "I'm sorry. If I offended you, Truet, I really am sorry."

Truet smiled sadly. "It's all right, Richard. No, I'm not over Jenny Mae, but life does go on, no matter how hard I try to hold onto her. But I haven't met anyone who I'm interested in yet," he said, then glanced at Matt quickly and back at Richard. "Christine is very pretty, but I don't think she's what I would be looking for if I was looking."

Felisha said, sounding slightly jealous, "Well, she seems interested in Matt to me."

Matt chuckled uncomfortably. "She's only a friend. You'd like her if you got to know her."

"Hmm," Felisha said with a sarcastic and doubtful gaze.

Truet offered, "She is a nice lady, and she is a Christian. Matt helped her out of a tough situation, and she appreciates him. He has no interest in her, Felisha. She really is just a friend. Whether she wants to be more, I don't know, but she's not the only one who does if she does. Matt's a single man with a future, and most of the ladies around here..."

"He's not single," Felisha said defensively. "We are courting, and they had ought to know that."

"They do," Truet said quickly. "Matt told Christine right up front that he was courting you, and he's told every other woman who has approached him the same thing. They know about you, but you're not here, so they think of him as single. Some, like the Slaters' daughter, are rather aggressive, but Christine is very respectful of your relationship. At least, from what I've seen and heard."

"She did say she had heard a lot about you," Richard offered to Felisha.

Rebecca Grace couldn't hold back any longer and asked Matt, "Why would she want to make you dinner? Isn't that crossing a line? Maybe it's just me, but why tempt yourself with a young and beautiful lady when Felisha is being loyal to you?"

Felisha added, "That's what I was wondering. Why even risk temptation when you could avoid it? Would you have dinner with her if I was here?"

Matt's face turned red from being put on the spot in front of his friends. "No, I wouldn't."

"Then why would you agree to it when I'm not? I wasn't going to mention this in front of everyone, but since it was brought up, I must. I came all the way from Sweethome on a very uncomfortable stagecoach ride to see you. Sure, I came for Saul and Abby, but I wanted to see you, and when I got here, you were making dinner plans with a beautiful young lady. How am I supposed to feel?" Felisha's eyes misted over with emotional tears.

Matt could see the hurt in her eyes and felt the rush of awkwardness from being questioned in front of a room of people. "Felisha, she is nothing more than a friend, just like Truet and Saul are friends of yours. It's very...innocent. We talk, and that's all we do. But what you said makes sense. I never thought about being tempted, because that temptation just isn't there. I am loyal to whoever I am committed to, and I am committed to you. I won't have dinner with her and will make sure she knows I am committed to you. She already knows that, though, because I talk about you all the time," he said uncomfortably.

Felisha grabbed his hand and nodded. She leaned over to hug him on the davenport and whispered in his ear, "I just love you."

He smiled. "I know."

Saul said in his deep voice, "This is supposed to be like my bachelor party or something, and it's turning into a bigger fight than any of mine. Well, my money's on Felisha."

Felisha laughed with the others. "Good choice," she said. "We're not fighting. I was just hurt and...I'm tired. Tomorrow will be a better day."

"It better be. It's my wedding day!" Saul exclaimed with laughter in his voice.

❧

An hour later, Matt walked the Grace family and Felisha and Dillon to the Monarch Hotel and said good-night to the Graces. Felisha's room was two doors down the hall, and like all the rooms, had a bedroom separate from the living room. They put Dillon to bed, where he slept soundly. Felisha and Matt sat on a small davenport, cuddling under a blanket to keep the slight chill of the room at bay. Their fingers twined as they talked.

"You know, I've been thinking that maybe I could move over here and get an accounting job or something in an office somewhere. This courting over the miles is very hard for me, and getting harder all the time. It's not a light decision, because my life is in Sweethome, and I don't want to throw away what I have if this doesn't work out. I never thought it wouldn't until today."

"Are you talking about Christine?" Matt asked, slightly agitated.

"Yes. Well, understand my point of view. I had just come to town, and caught you making dinner plans with another woman who thinks you'll wish you're marrying her when she does get married."

"No. You didn't hear the conversation. I had just told her I would tell her husband not to marry her. It was all in fun anyway. It didn't mean anything. You just over-heard the tail end of something and assumed it was more than it was."

"Well, I didn't know who she was or how you felt about her or me anymore because the distance between us is only filled by letters. Writing is great, but often the feeling doesn't come through the words, and it can be taken the wrong way. It made me think tonight that something must change. I have been considering moving over here so we can see if this relationship is going to grow or...not. I've been married, Matt, and I don't want to make the same mistake twice. My husband was faithful, but we weren't altogether close. There was space between us, and I'm afraid if our relationship is based upon letters over the distance, that's the way it will always be. Distant. So, if you want me to, I will make plans to move over here."

Matt smiled. "I'd love for you to be here. I can get you set up in one of Lee's places, so housing is no problem. A job? Well, between Lee, Albert, and me, we'll find something."

"So, you guys will help me get situated and the details taken care of for me?"

"Of course."

"Um, Matt, don't take this wrong way, but I'm not selling my house in Sweethome until we are married...if we do get married. I hope you understand that I won't throw away what I have to start a new life that isn't written in stone yet. I just want to be careful. I have Dillon to raise." She said softly, "I love you, Matt, but until we are married, it's what I have to do to make sure I have a life just in case."

Matt smiled. "I understand, and I think we are on the same page. I would like for you to be here with me. I'm excited about it, actually."

"Are you?"

"Of course."

She smiled slowly. "Does that mean you want me to move over here?"

"It does."

She leaned over to wrap her arms around Matt. "Kiss me, you handsome man, you! I've been looking forward to kissing you since I left Sweethome."

3

Six miles outside of Branson, there was a narrow series of deep gorges that splintered off one another known as the Spider Creek Ravine. One short and narrow finger of the ravine held a forgotten mineshaft that went into the cliff about a hundred and fifty feet. The origin of the mineshaft was a mystery since it had long since been forgotten about, and only a few people knew it existed. It had become a hideout for the Sperry-Helms Gang to hole up in when necessary, and that was how Pick knew about it.

The letter Jim Hexum sent to Louis Eckman was received about a week after they sent it. Louis wired back as instructed in the letter with a simple yes or no answer to the letter's demand for twenty thousand dollars. He was also to keep it quiet until he had his daughter to show the world what a liar Matt Bannister was. The wire came in with a "Yes. Noon, Tuesday the 23rd." The meeting place would be the local newspaper office, where it could be immediately printed in the Branson Gazette. The 23rd was now three days away.

When the wire came in, Jim and Pick began working on the mineshaft to make it more comfortable, bringing in two old civil war medical cots with heavy blood stains on the canvas and blankets for Christine and whoever stayed to watch her. A firepit was built, and a supply of wood to burn was stacked along the wall. Cooking utensils and canned food were stored, and board scraps and weathered sticks they found on the gorge floor were either wired or nailed together as a door to close the entry.

Picked looked around the mineshaft and nodded in satisfaction. "I think we have everything here. All we need now is Catherine Eckman."

Jim nodded his agreement. "Yep. It's all coming together well. Tonight, after you start the fire, get out to the wagon. When she comes outside, I'll get her away from the crowd somehow and bring her near the back of the wagon. When I say go, you take off. As long as you get a good fire going, no one's going to notice a thing."

He pulled a flask out of his coat pocket and showed it to Jim. "I'll get a good fire going, don't you worry about that!" He laughed. "In three days, we are going to be twenty thousand dollars richer, Jim. What are you going to do with your share?" Pick asked.

Jim grunted. "You better hand that over here so I can make sure whatever whiskey you put in there isn't watered down."

"Oh, no. You won't like this since it's kerosene. Did you notice the water bucket behind the bar? It'll be the first thing they throw on it, and that will spread the fire quicker than I ever could. The place is burning down tonight, and the beauty of it is, everyone will be there fighting it and not paying any attention to us leading her out of town," Pick said with a chuckle. "So, what are you going to do with your share, Jim?"

Hexum looked at Pick with a growing smirk of approval. "I'm surprised you're not a wanted man, Pick. I don't know if I should be honored or ashamed to be doing business with you," he said. "Maybe I'll fill a newly evacuated marshal's office. With Matt gone, this place will need a county sheriff, at least. I could fill that role."

Pick laughed. "You picked a hell of a way to become a lawman, Jim. Appointed by arson and kidnapping!"

Jim raised his eyebrows pointedly. "That's better than lying about her dying just to get some easy money and keeping her for himself. We're the lesser of two evils, I think. I lost all respect for Matt Bannister when he refused to touch my two bounties. Anyway, what about you? What do you have planned?"

"I'm leaving if you're going to become a lawman! No one's going to be safe if that's the case. No, I'm going to San Francisco. See what kind of trouble I can get into there."

Jim smiled and looked at his pocket watch. "Well, it's getting close to lunchtime. Let's get moving toward town and find something to eat. I want to see if the marshal's around so I can wish him well before I ruin his life."

"Agreed. You know, the hardest part is going to be getting her into the wagon without causing a scene, so if you pray, pray it works," Pick requested pointedly.

Jim sighed. "I outgrew that when I was a kid. Brains are what we need, not prayers. I'll get her in there whether I have to carry her or drag her. You just start a good fire and be ready."

They rode their horses out of Spider Creek Ravine and through two miles of forest to the main road leading to Branson. They passed the Slater Silver Mine, and a mile later, the mine's company housing, which was known as Slater's Mile, or more commonly, the Slater Slums of shacks and rats. It was there they saw a small one-horse carriage coming toward them. Matt Bannister was driving it, with a woman sitting beside him. They were covered with a blanket and snuggling closely.

Jim stopped his horse unexpectedly. "That's the good marshal driving that buggy, and if he's with our goods, we won't need a fire. We could take her out here with less witnesses," he said, squinting to try to see the woman's face more clearly.

Pick said simply, "It's not her."

Jim asked, "Do you know who this woman is? His wife, perhaps?" He spat out a mouthful of brown tobacco juice.

"Matt's not married. No, I have never seen her before."

"Hmm. Looks like they have something romantic going on, though. I'll bet you I can start a fight between them. Wanna bet? Watch this..." Jim said with a small smirk and waited for Matt to drive closer. He held up a hand to stop them. "Hello there, Matt."

Matt slowed the buggy down to a stop. "Jim," he said, with a nod to Pick. His eyes scanned both men quickly for any signs of aggression.

Jim spoke before Matt could say anything more. "You must have a harem of pretty women lined up. I found it a bit disappointing to learn you're the only man allowed to take the girls in the dance hall upstairs. Isn't that where their rooms are?"

The expression on the face of the woman sitting beside him brought Jim a great sense of joy. Her eyes widened, and her friendly smile faded to a downturned expression of jealousy and anger as she glared at Matt, surprised by what she had heard.

"You're not learning much then, because no one is allowed up there," Matt responded irritably.

Jim's eyes hardened as he leaned over his saddle horn to glare at Matt. "Are you calling me a liar, Matt? Did you not go upstairs with that girl a couple of weeks ago? The one who sang you that love song? You should remember. You went upstairs with her for the night, right?" He turned to Pick. "Didn't he go upstairs with her? If I remember right, it was right after a romantic dance, and then she led you upstairs by your hand. I remember it because everyone was talking about it. Why do you get such special privileges with...what's her name, Catherine?" he asked Pick.

"Christine," Pick answered, looking uneasy.

"Yeah, Christine. You two looked pretty close. Too close. Closer than you two, and that's pretty damn close if you ask me." He pointed his finger at Matt and Felisha.

Matt's anger rose to the surface. Jim was talking nonsense, and Matt knew he was doing it intentionally to create friction between Felisha and him. It was easy to see the entertainment Jim was getting from watching Felisha grow angrier at Matt by the minute. She let go of his arm and moved an inch away from him. "That's enough," Matt warned.

"What? Am I lying?" Jim asked with a hard glare. There was now more aggression in his voice.

Matt looked at him evenly. "No. I went upstairs..."

Jim chuckled. "I know you did, and you never came back down! And now you got yourself another lady, I see."

Matt smirked, shook his head, and said, "Good day, gentlemen." He looked at Jim coldly. "You're not worth my time."

Jim laughed. "Of course not! So, who will I see you with tomorrow, Christine, this woman, or some other woman? Maybe some Molly from the flesh market on Rose Street?"

"I know what you're trying to do, Hexum, and I don't appreciate it," Matt stated firmly.

Jim smiled. "I don't care what you appreciate. I believe in being loyal to one woman. Some men don't," he added with a shrug of his shoulders. "Oh, by the way, I just went up to that cabin where you found the Eckman girl. I'm surprised you could find anything made of paper that survived. If a human body can't outlast a fire, I'm surprised paper did."

Matt nodded. "Me too. We'll talk later, you and me," he said, his irritated clear from the hard look in his eyes. He gave the horse some reins and the signal to go.

"Nice to meet you, ma'am!" Jim yelled and then laughed as they drove off.

Pick grinned at Jim. "You are about half-crazy, do you know that?"

"I must be to join up with you and attempt what we're going to do."

"Do you think it was wise to mention the cabin, though? Now he might suspect us when she disappears."

Jim shook his head, still pleased by the friction he had caused between Matt and his lady friend in the buggy. "No. He'll be too preoccupied with the argument he's about to have." He chuckled.

4

Matt drove the buggy in silence for a few minutes, knowing Felisha was angry. He could feel her hostility, and the distance grew between them as she tried to move farther away from him, with her arms tight to her sides and her hands tucked in her underarms. He was afraid to speak, not knowing how she would respond. "That was Bloody Jim Hexum, the one bounty hunter I was afraid would get to Truet before me."

"Hmm." She grunted.

"He showed up a couple of weeks ago with a pair of bodies and wanted me to take care of them for him. I refused, and we haven't been too friendly since."

Felisha turned toward him on the short bench seat and said heatedly, "Is it true? Were you led upstairs by some girl holding your hand? Is this the same Christine who wants to make you dinner and an apple pie?"

Matt stopped the buggy and said slowly, "Yes, it's true. I went upstairs so we could go watch the stars..."

"*Stars*, Matt? You and Christine went upstairs to her

room to look at the stars? How stupid do you think I am? Maybe you better just take me back to the hotel so I can be alone for a while. I'm suddenly not feeling like going for a buggy ride!"

"We weren't in her room; we were on the roof. The only way to the roof is upstairs. I told you last night that you could trust me, Felisha."

"Yes, you did! But you didn't tell me that you were dancing with her! You didn't tell me that she, what...sang a song for you? You didn't tell me she works at a dance hall! You didn't tell me a lot of things, so how am I supposed to trust you? Because you say so? I'm afraid I can't. Just how close are you two, Matt?" she asked with a wide-eyed glare.

"We are friends. I've already told you that. And that's all we are."

"It sounds like a little bit more than just a friend. Are you attracted to her?"

"She's very attractive, but I'm not in love with her. I am with you. Look, Jim Hexum was trying to cause a fight between us. That was his whole intent, and we have nothing to fight about. We don't," he repeated with a shrug.

Felisha looked at Matt sternly. "I am debating about moving over here to be with you, and last night I was committed to it. But...I don't want to come over and compete with Christine for your attention. Maybe you have no interest in her, or maybe you do, and if you do, even in the slightest, tell me, so I don't uproot Dillon's and my life for nothing!"

He said, his frustration evident in his voice, "Felisha, I

have already told you multiple times that she is a friend. I want you to move over here, but you have to trust me enough to believe me over a fool who wants to cause trouble. I will deal with him later, but I refuse to sit here on a beautiful day and argue and bicker over absolute nonsense. I have never been tempted to be unfaithful, no matter how beautiful she or anyone else is. I'm committed to you!

"If you can't believe that, then you probably never will. I help people; I enjoy helping people. I helped Christine out of a horrible situation, and she is grateful. If she wants to make me an apple pie, fine. It's no big deal. It's her way of saying thank you." He paused for a moment before saying in a softer voice, "We're not getting off to a very good start this weekend, are we? And I really wanted it to be great. I don't want to talk about Christine, I want to talk about you and Dillon. I want to talk about you moving here, I want to talk about us."

Felisha smirked as she looked at him. "Okay. How long did you watch the stars with her?"

Matt sighed. "A couple of hours."

"Why do you spend so much time with her and not everyone else you help?"

Matt laughed despite his aggravation. "Felisha, can we change the subject, please? I swear I don't know why you're so insecure. I have never done anything to make you so."

"I never said you did!" she responded with a venom he wasn't expecting. "Take me to the hotel. I think our conversation is over for today."

Matt stared at her for a moment. She pulled the

blanket up tighter around her neck and glared at him. "Now!"

Matt took a deep breath. "Fine. I've said all I can say anyway."

"Really?" Felisha snapped. "Then how come you didn't answer my question?"

"Which one? Your questions are coming one after the other like a Gatling gun, with no time to answer. Which one is not answered by 'we're just friends' and 'you're the one I love?'"

Felisha spoke slowly to be clearly understood, although she loaded her words with a heavy dose of angry sarcasm. "Why. Do. You. Spend. So. Much. Time. With. Her?"

"Because. You're. Not. Here!" Matt responded in the same fashion. "For crying out loud, Felisha, she's a friend. People spend time with their friends. Why in the world are you so upset about something as simple as that? I have no interest in courting her. I am in love with you, so why are you so... I don't know. What, threatened by her? Do you even know why you're acting like this?"

Felisha's eyes softened a little and got moist. "Because she is so beautiful. I am ugly compared to her, and I don't want to lose you," she said as a tear fell from her eye. "She's falling in love with you. She must be, because how could she not? Why would you want to be with me when you could be with her?"

Matt's face softened. "She is beautiful, but so are you. I didn't fall in love because you're beautiful, I fell in love because of who you are. You're my lady, and you don't need to worry about losing me. I'm hooked on you. I love you, Felisha."

"So, you're not falling in love with her?"

Matt laughed. "No. You're the only one I love. And I would really like to enjoy our time together while you're here without talking about her."

She smiled and wiped her eyes. "So would I," she said and kissed him.

"Do you still want to go back to the hotel?" he asked.

She shook her head with a slight smile. "No, it's too nice of a day to stay inside. Let's finish the buggy ride, and no more talk about her."

Matt nodded. "Agreed."

5

Louis Eckman was no one to be trifled with. He was a powerful man who had no mercy for anyone who wronged him or, if the stakes were important enough, opposed him. Blackmail, extortion, intimidation, and when called for, murder, were all a part of his business dealings.

He didn't commit the crimes himself. He hired paid toughs who worked for a former Pinkerton detective named Carnell Tallon, who still carried the Pinkerton badge and identified himself and his men as Pinkertons. He was just as corrupt as Eckman gave him and his men money to be. They were paid to take care of Louis Eckman's problems and strong-arm anyone who got in his way, but not everyone knew that, of course. He kept his dirty work as quiet as he could so it wouldn't tarnish his reputation as an upright Christian man.

The Pinkerton Detective Agency had an issue with Carnell using their name for his personal business, but there was nothing that money couldn't buy, including the

Pinkerton Agency's turning a blind eye to Louis Eckman's personal team of Pinkerton detectives.

Louis and his wife Divinity were held in high esteem by Sacramento's upper society. They had a reputation for having high standards, charitable giving, and solid integrity they were expected to uphold. They were local royalty, and their daughter Catherine had been a princess. Like the days of old-time royalty, she was an asset to show off and use to further their wealth and power.

Louis had made a vast fortune investing in multiple railroads, but there was an even greater future in shipping cargo by sea. He could ensure a close working relationship with the Bertrand Ship Builders Company if Catherine married Gaius Bertrand, the son of the founder of the company and a mechanical engineer himself, who would take over the company by the time he was forty. A marriage between Catherine and Gaius meant a fruitful future for Catherine and a doorway into the shipping industry for Louis. A little backdoor politics and Pinkerton persuasion would help him to control a large portion of the cargo leaving San Francisco with his own shipping company. The advantage he wanted over the competition was having inside access to the newest ships available that promised to be faster and safer than anything the competition had. It was important for his future that Catherine marry Gaius since then he could buy the ships he needed at a lower cost from *family*. Over time, Louis could soften the ground to plant the seeds for a monopolizing partnership between the two companies with his son-in-law and control the ports of the West Coast.

A lot of preparation had gone into introducing the young couple at the Governor's Ball. Louis had coached his daughter on how she should act and what to say and to show interest in the young man. However, the night he had introduced them, Catherine had shown no interest in Gaius, and for some god-forsaken reason, demonstrated more interest in one of the entry door's security guards.

The young man was a mere private in the Cavalry named Nathan Webster, who Louis had despised at first sight. Somehow, he had known immediately that Nathan would become a thorn in his side. Louis hadn't become a wealthy man by being a fool, so he recognized a threat when he saw one. Not long after that, Catherine invited Nathan over to meet her parents. Louis was most displeased and wasn't shy about ordering her to end the relationship immediately.

He expected far more from his daughter than associating with a military private without a future. The boy could never provide for his daughter, and simply had no business courting the most coveted princess of Sacramento's upper society. She was a treasure to be protected and an asset to use to fulfill his plans. Nathan was no more than a cockroach looking for a feast, and Catherine was his meal ticket. Louis forbade Catherine to associate with the low-class peasant again.

Then one morning, they had found a note stating she had eloped to marry Nathan. Louis was enraged and immediately sent his dog pack of Pinkertons after them. Three days later, Carnell caught them in San Francisco before they boarded a steamship bound for Astoria, Oregon. They were already married, but Carnell and his men took Catherine and Nathan to the basement of a building, where they were forced to sign annulment papers to end their two-day marriage.

Catherine had refused to do so at first but had changed her mind after seeing Nathan being beaten up and hearing Carnell threaten to cut off his fingers one at a time. Once she had signed them, she was whisked away to face her parents back at home. Nathan was left on the pier unconscious and bleeding heavily as a warning to never come back around her again.

Louis and Divinity did all they could to keep her from associating with anyone until she was ready to get to know Gaius. Everything seemed to be going fine, until one morning they unexpectedly found a note saying she had eloped with Nathan again.

Louis had been furious, and sent his dog pack of Pinkerton Detectives after her again with one demand: to kill Nathan. As a bonus, he offered twenty-five thousand dollars to the hired man who killed him and brought his daughter home. With a thirst for blood, the detectives used every asset they had to track them, but she was not found.

It had been three years, and there had never been a single report of Nathan or Catherine being seen until the day Louis received a letter and a package in the mail from US Marshal Matt Bannister, notifying him that he had identified two bodies found in a fire as those of Nathan Webster and his daughter Catherine Eckman. The evidence was in the wooden box the letter accompanied

—the ivory chess set he had bought her in Greece and a photo of them that was scorched by fire.

The letter stated the bodies had been found in a cabin deep in the Blue Mountains. Each had been killed by a single bullet wound, and their bodies burned. It appeared from the evidence to be a murder-suicide. Matt Bannister stated he would have her body exhumed and sent to Sacramento if they wanted to have it reinterred in California. He then offered his deepest sympathies.

The day the letter from Matt arrived with the evidence was a day the whole Eckman estate mourned and wailed. It was proof Catherine was dead. They had her body exhumed and shipped to Sacramento. The funeral for their daughter was expensive, and nothing was spared to give her the finest of everything to say their final goodbye. Hundreds of Sacramento citizens showed up to share in their grief and offer their sympathy as the casket was placed in the ground. It was the worst day of Louis' and Divinity's lives.

They had just been getting to where they could move forward when a letter came from a bounty hunter named Jim Hexum. Louis had never heard of him, but his most trusted associate Carnell Tallon most certainly had and didn't doubt the integrity of Hexum's letter at all. The letter gave some details Matt Bannister had left out, like Nathan Webster had been killed in Denver years before, and Catherine was alive and well. She was in a relationship with the marshal, and everything the marshal had said was a cover up for them to marry without having anyone looking for her again.

Reading the letter and going back to the evidence

Matt sent them, it made sense. Louis conferred with Carnell, then agreed to Jim Hexum's conditions and made plans to go to Branson.

The fastest route would've been by railroad up to Portland and then up the Columbia Gorge, which went about halfway to Branson. However, Divinity was terrified of trains. She had been traveling by train to a social event in San Francisco with her lady friends when a train unexpectedly derailed around a bend and the rail cars flipped. One of her friends was killed, and several others were seriously injured. She had been lucky to come out of it with nothing more than bruises and scratches, but she had refused to ever ride on a train again. To make long trips together, they'd had a coach specially designed for extended road travel so they could relax in comfort.

With the railway not being an option, it was decided to take their coach to Branson, cutting across Northern California into southeastern Oregon and on up to Branson. It would be a long and uncomfortable trip across some tough terrain, but Carnell had had the idea of hiring experienced local drivers and horses all along the way to keep the stock fresh.

He wanted to keep the coach moving as continuously possible, and stole the idea of trading drivers and horses at certain points from the Pony Express. Local drivers who knew their own territory could get them through it faster than anyone else could. The object was to get the Eckmans to Branson as quickly as possible to see their daughter. Coming home, they could take their time on a sternwheeler down the Columbia River and back to San Francisco.

It had been a long and rugged trip, but they were less than fifty miles from Branson now and ahead of schedule. The road through the Blue Mountains was rough, and the coach bounced as the wheel went into another rut in the road. Divinity Eckman was jarred awake and looked out the window at a wall of giant Douglas Fir trees and the dark forest behind them. It was nearly noon and the sun was bright, but the darkness within the forest wall was unsettling. A man could be standing ten feet off the road, and they'd never see him in the shadows. She looked at her husband, who was reading a book, and asked, "Where are we?"

Louis Eckman lifted his eyes from his book and glanced at her. "Somewhere in the mountains. These are apparently the Blue Mountains, where we were told Catherine was killed. I can't wait to get my hands on that lying marshal. I swear he won't have anything left to live for when I'm done with him!" Louis was a stocky man with short, dark hair and a short mustache. He was wrapped in a thick wool coat and wore a derby hat. His face was square, and he had an intensity in his eyes which left no doubt that he was a serious man with no time for nonsense.

Divinity had light-brown hair that was pinned up under a wool blanket she had wrapped around her to keep warm while she napped. She had an attractive oval face with green eyes, but the lines around her eyes had doubled and become deeper since her only daughter had eloped.

Catherine hadn't disappeared, and she wasn't missing; she was intentionally hiding from them. It had been three years, and Divinity still didn't understand why Catherine would rather live in poverty and hardship than to return home and be in luxury. The letter from Jim Hexum had been a blessing, and had brought on a wide range of emotions when she learned Catherine was alive and well. However, Divinity began to wonder if she was an unwanted mother to her only daughter. She wondered if she had failed, but then pushed the thought away. She had given Catherine everything money could buy, a lavish home, and the best of everything in life. It didn't make sense why she would choose to stay away.

"Louis," she asked quietly, "why wouldn't she come home when Nathan was killed?"

He frowned. "What's that mean?" he snarled, irritated to hear the name "Nathan" spoken.

Divinity shrugged. "It means if Jim Hexum told us the truth in his letter and Nathan was killed in Denver, then why didn't she come home instead of living in poverty? Do you think she's afraid to face us because of her shame? I mean, she could have come home any time, and she didn't. Maybe she was too ashamed to."

"I don't know. What I do know is she's coming home now, and the marshal is going to pay for what he did to me! Isn't he, Carnell?"

Carnell looked up from his book and nodded. "I'm already working on it."

Divinity spoke to her husband. "Us, not just you, Louis. He deceived both of us. Does that not tell you something?"

"What's it supposed to tell me?" he asked sharply, setting his book down with a hint of frustration.

She looked at him sadly. "She still has the worst taste in men. I don't understand why she'd want to live out here in the woods instead of in Sacramento. How does anyone even make a living out here? I'll bet she's wearing rags."

Louis spoke angrily. "And her choices are a damn embarrassment! She's my daughter, and a representation of me! She is rebelling against everything we taught her and raised her to be. I will not allow her to treat us like this! I don't care if she lost her damn husband. Good! He was a louse, if not a flea on my ass! We are taking Catherine home with us and breaking this spell he put on her. I don't know how he turned her against us, but he did. I'm glad he's dead!

Now she's shaming our name by getting mixed up with a backwoods marshal. We raised her better than that. I'll put her in an institution if I must to get her thinking straight. She's an Eckman, and it's about damn time she starts appreciating that and acting like it." He paused. "She's supposed to take over our kingdom someday, and I can't even get her to write home!" he shouted. "She's been brainwashed by mere pawns in the game of life, and it's time to get her thinking like a queen again."

"I'll agree to whatever it takes to get my daughter back," Divinity told him.

"What do you think, Carnell? You have daughters?" Louis asked the third man in the coach. He was a slight man with short light-brown hair and a fragile disposition. He was clean shaven, had a narrow facial structure, and wore thin metal-frame round spectacles over his eyes.

Carnell Tallon appeared to be the least of threatening men, but his appearance was quite deceiving.

Carnell answered in a soft voice, "I think if you want your daughter back, then we'll need to dispatch every anchor she holds dear, including the marshal. When you're all she has left to go back to, she will. If not, then an institution will get her thinking straight again right away."

"See?" Louis asked Divinity. "They brainwashed her against us."

Divinity shrugged tiredly. "I just want my daughter back like she used to be. I would like for her to go to Europe with us this summer and be my little girl again." She rested her head on her pillow and closed her eyes. "Do whatever it takes to get that done."

Louis smirked at Carnell. "Only you would risk dispatching a US Marshal."

Carnell shrugged. "Matt Bannister is only a man. Accidents happen."

Louis laughed. "Yeah, so I've learned."

The wagon slowed to a stop unexpectedly. It caused a moment of concern on the face of Carnell, and he quickly opened the door and swung halfway out to ask the driver, "Why are we stopping?"

The driver climbed down out of the driver's seat and looked anxiously at him. "I have to relieve myself. Sorry!" he said and ran into the woods.

Carnell pulled himself back into the coach and closed the door. "I explicitly demanded no unscheduled stops! This driver just broke his contract," he said. "You won't be paying him for his driving time today."

Louis nodded. "A dollar saved is a dollar earned."

"What's going on?" Divinity asked quietly, her eyes still closed. She was glad to be free of the bumps and rough ride for a few minutes, anyway. She hoped to fall back to sleep before the coach began moving again.

There was an unexpected rifle shot, and the Pinkerton riding beside the driver and holding a shotgun fell from his seat to the ground with a heavy thud.

Carnell's eyes widened, and he looked out the window to see his employee and friend lying dead from a well-placed gunshot to his heart. He glanced at Louis and Divinity sternly. "Stay calm! No sudden moves, and don't offer them any reason to become violent. Give them whatever they want and stay quiet! We've been betrayed by the driver, no doubt. Be calm," he repeated as several horses neared the coach.

Divinity asked with great uneasiness, "What's going on?"

"We're being robbed," Carnell answered simply. "Stay calm."

"Think it's the marshal's doing?" Louis asked with a sneer on his lips.

"The driver..."

"Get out of there, or we'll start shooting!" a man on a horse shouted to the three occupants. He wore a gray cloth bag over his face, with holes cut out of it for his eyes. He held a revolver in his hand, and it was pointing it at the coach. "Hurry up!" he shouted in a deep voice.

Three more riders surrounded the coach, all of them wearing the same sort of bag over their faces and holding guns. "Give us your money and goods, and you can move on!" the man demanded.

Carnell stepped out of the coach first and turned to help Divinity to the ground. He kept his eyes downward and whispered for Divinity to do the same. He didn't need to, though; she was too afraid to look the masked men in the eyes. Louis stepped out of the coach and glared at the man who had demanded their money. "The money's for my daughter, and you're not taking it!"

The man pointed his revolver at Louis. "Stop me." He looked at one of his riders. "See what they got."

The man slid off his horse and walked to the coach. He began to step into the coach, and Louis turned around, grabbed him by the back of his coat, and pulled him out of the coach before forcing him to the ground. He kicked the man in the face when he landed, and shouted at the leader of the four-man gang, "You're not taking it!"

"Louis, knock it off and let them have it!" Carnell suggested anxiously.

"No! I'm not losing my daughter again because of some cockroach highwaymen don't want to work for their money!"

"Cockroach?" the man holding the revolver asked.

Louis glared at him. "Yeah, you are a cockroach! A damn worthless cockroach that needs to be stomped upon before your nit-headed children grow up to be the same kind of pestilence on humankind. Do you know who I am? I'm Louis Eckman! If you rob me, every law enforcement officer from the Mexican border to Canada will be looking for you! Including Matt Bannister, who happens to be my friend, so take your cockroach friends and get out of here!" he shouted.

"Louis, shut up!" Carnell hissed under his breath.

"Louis Eckman...of the railroad?" the man asked.

Louis sighed, relieved his importance was being recognized. "Yes, I am. Now please leave us to our travels. I'm nothing but trouble for you."

The masked man pointed his revolver at him. "My father was killed digging a tunnel through a mountain for your railroad. They blew some dynamite in the tunnel, and a rock from the blast hit him in the head. He died working for you, and you got rich off his labor. Let me ask you: do you have a list of the men who died so you could get rich?"

Carnell interjected quickly, "Sir, the railroad does. I'm the company bookkeeper, and I could send you that list. I am confident your father's name would be on it. The railroad kept careful records of the lives lost tragically while building the greatest accomplishment in humankind. You should be quite proud of your father for his labors. What he helped build will last forever."

"Shut up!" the man warned. "The railroad couldn't care less now, nor did it then! Do they, Mister Eckman?"

Louis smirked. "Your father should've ducked. I weep every day for the men who never went home to teach their nits how to work," he said pointedly.

Carnell yelled, "Damn it, Louis, shut the hell up and give him the money!"

"You weep every day, you say?" the masked man asked. "Well, I did too for a long time. But what the hell, I got over it. Your daughter will too," he said and pulled the trigger, shooting Louis in the stomach. He backed up against the coach with an expression of shock while Divinity screamed. He stared at the masked man as he fired his weapon again, hitting Louis in the forehead. He crumpled onto the ground, dead.

Divinity dropped at her husband's side, screaming in horror over his dead body. Carnell cursed and looked at the gunman. "Please, just take whatever you want and go! You didn't have to kill him."

The man shrugged. "He should've ducked," he said simply, then to his men, "Take what they have and let's go. Check the late Louis Eckman's pockets, and their bags, too. He's a rich man, so he must have money. Don't hesitate to take it all. And take her wedding ring and jewelry. That might shut her up!"

Carnell was thrown against the coach to be patted down by one of the men. "Here!" he yelled. He pulled his leather billfold out of his jacket pocket, opened it, pulled out over two hundred dollars of cash, and handed to the man about to search him. Carnell feared they would discover his Pinkerton Detective Agency badge pinned inside his wallet. "Take all I have, just please don't hurt us." The man took it the cash and began counting it. Carnell covered the badge with his palm and opened his billfold to show it was empty. "Mister Eckman's billfold is in the coach. There's more money in it. Please, take whatever you want, but don't hurt Missus Eckman or me. Please!" He bent down near Divinity like a coward and put his billfold back in his coat. It was the only day since the beginning of their journey that he hadn't put on his shoulder holster with his silver-plated .38 revolver. If he had worn it, he could have killed three of the four men right now.

The robber counted the money in his hand with excitement while another man climbed into the coach to find Louis Eckman's billfold. He laughed in excitement when he found it. "Oh, my! Dang! There's like two thousand dollars in his billfold!"

The leader ordered the masked man hovering over Divinity to take her rings and jewelry. He did so without any mercy while Divinity screamed. Carnell remained on the ground with his face hidden, acting afraid for his life.

The driver walked out of the woods, horrified to see Divinity helpless on the ground beside Louis' body. She screamed while her wedding ring was ripped off her finger by one of the hooded men. "Why'd you shoot him? You were just supposed to rob them!" he questioned loudly.

The leader turned his horse toward the driver, and without saying a word, shot him in the chest and watched the man fall. He turned his horse back toward the coach while yelling, "Let's go!"

Carnell Tallon watched the four men carefully as they prepared to leave. He noticed what they wore, any accent to their voices, the color of their horses, the style of their saddles, and looked for any marks or other helpful information that might help identify the robbers, especially the one who had killed Louis. When the men rode off in a hurry, Carnell went quickly to the driver, hoping he was still alive so he could get a name or two. He got one before the driver died. "Dall..."

He went back to Divinity and put a comforting hand on her shoulder.

"I want you to kill them, Carnell!" she sobbed. "I want them dead!"

"I plan to," Carnell said, watching the robbers ride away. There was no hint of cowardice in his tone.

6

Felisha was Abby's bridesmaid and was in a side room getting prepared with Abby for the wedding. Saul Wolf had asked his friend Truet Davis to be his best man, and they were in another room waiting for the wedding to begin. Matt walked into the Baptist church, waved at a few people he knew, and went to go sit by his brother Lee and sister-in-law Regina. He was surprised to see his sister Annie sitting with them.

He sat down and looked at her oddly. "Annie, what the heck are you doing here? Do you even know Saul or Abby?"

Annie shrugged. "No. But if you're here, and Lee's here, I figured I might as well be here too. They'll like me. I'm pretty sure of it, anyway." She was wearing a very elegant green dress and looked prettier than she usually did at home on the Big Z Ranch.

Matt nodded slowly. "Good thinking. You look very pretty."

Annie smiled. "Thank you. So, I understand your Felish-a is here? Is she the hound I saw peeing on the grass out front?"

Matt chuckled. "No, probably not."

Regina asked, "Did you two have a nice day together? Lee said you were taking her on a buggy ride."

"It started off a little rough, but it finished well."

"Where'd you go?" Lee asked.

"Around town, and then up past the silver mine."

Annie laughed. "Only you would try to impress a lady by taking her to a filthy and annoyingly loud stamp mill. Very romantic, Matt. Let me guess, is that where the roughness began?" she asked with a laugh.

Matt smiled. "Actually, we were at Slater's Mile when things got rough."

Lee looked concerned. "You didn't tell her I owned it, did you?"

"No."

Lee turned to Annie. "Felisha's thinking about moving here, and I told Matt to take her by my cottages."

Annie laughed. "If you don't want her moving here, all you have to do is say no. You didn't have to take her out to that sewer pit and say, 'Welcome to your new home.'"

"Funny. No, we ran into Bloody Jim Hexum along the way, and he said some stuff that upset Felisha. I would've liked to have knocked his teeth out, but didn't want to escalate the situation in front of her. I'll chat with him soon enough."

"I heard he was in town. What was he saying, anything insulting? Because you probably should have if he was insulting her," Lee said.

"Not insulting, but he was alluding that I was unfaithful. It's a long story, but he was just being an ass. I knew what he was doing, and he wasn't lying, but it was out of context by a mile. Anyway, it caused a bit of an issue. It's all good now, but for a little bit, Felisha was pretty upset. I had to reassure her that she is the only one I am interested in."

Lee frowned. "Don't tell me it has something to do with that dancer girl? She seems to be trouble through and through. First, it was with Kyle." He looked at Annie fondly, then at Matt and continued, "And then it was my friends, Josh, Travis, and Tim, who you beat the hell out of. And now she's causing problems with you and Felisha. Take my advice and leave her alone. It sounds like Felisha is moving over here, and you don't want to ruin that."

"Your friends deserved it. Felisha and I had a long talk about Christine today. It was kind of forced by Jim, but we got it straightened out. All is well. And trust me, I have no romantic interest in Christine,"

Annie leaned forward and looked seriously at Matt. "I don't ever want to meet her. I understand she had nothing to do with Kyle, but it isn't something I want to be reminded of, either." She took a breath, then added more thoughtfully, "I am looking forward to meeting Felisha and seeing what she looks like, though. I'm hoping she's cuter than Boris my boar, but she likes you, so I don't know. If she's not cuter than Boris, then I suggest you buy a dog and name it Felisha, so at least people will say she's cute."

Matt smiled. "Annie, I cannot wait for you to finally meet someone and start courting, because I'm going to scare him so bad you can watch him empty the urine out of his boots."

Annie smirked. "You might try, but I'll smack you around like a spoiled child and show him what a frightened sheep looks like when it runs away."

Matt laughed. "Well, it was an idea."

Piano music began to play, and soon Truet walked Felisha down the center aisle toward the altar. Felisha was wearing a red dress made and fitted by Abby's mother and looked beautiful.

"That's Felisha," Matt said to Annie.

Annie looked at her with a smirk on her face. "Well, I approve."

"Me too," Regina said, smiling at Matt.

"And that's my deputy Truet Davis with her," Matt said. "He's also my roommate."

Annie smiled. "I approve."

Regina laughed. "Me too,"

Lee just chuckled.

7

It was Saturday night, and Bella's Dance Hall was full of men wanting to drink and dance with a pretty lady. Pick Lawson watched Christine Knapp dance with a middle-aged logger, by the looks of his clothing. He was smiling gleefully. She was wearing an elegant two-tone ballgown that was simply stunning. It was a very faint shade of gold silk that shimmered in the light as she danced. It had ruffles that flowed over her bustle, and the gold silk ended just above her knees, then a faint shade of light blue fell in pleated layers to just above the floor. Christine looked amazing as always, and her smile was bright and joyful. Her long auburn hair was artistically styled, and her large brown eyes shone with the smile that could light up the darkest night. There was something about Christine dancing that always brought a sense of joy to Pick. He didn't understand why exactly, but she had that effect on him. Her smile was infectious, and joy was the disease she spread around her.

He looked at Jim Hexum and spoke just loud enough

to be heard over the band playing and the men clapping their hands along with the song. "It's going to be a shame to burn this place down."

"There's another one in San Francisco that you'll like better. I'm going outside to wait. You move toward the kitchen and set the fire and get out to the wagon. Let's earn our money."

Pick nodded and made his way down the bar and farther down the wall to a door that had a sign saying Stay Out. He leaned against the wall next to the door to watch the dance floor, then reached his hand down behind him and turned the knob. The door was unlocked, and when he was sure no one was watching him, he slipped inside and closed it behind him. It was the kitchen where the meals for the ladies were prepared. He pulled a flask out his coat pocket and poured kerosene across the floor to the door, then laid a cut candle about a quarter-inch tall with a short wick in the puddle of kerosene and lit it. He then peeked out the door to make sure no one was too close, and seeing that it was mostly clear, he stepped out of the kitchen and closed the door behind him. To look less suspicious, he turned toward the door and acted like he was locking it behind him before walking to the bar. He didn't have time to order a drink, but paused there to lose any interest of anyone who'd been watching him. He made a casual departure, and just as he was stepping out of the dance hall, he heard a man yell, "Fire!"

Pick ran across the street to where a covered wagon with the rear canvas flap closed sat waiting a half-block away. It had been decided to place the wagon on the opposite side of the dance hall because with everyone's attention on the fire, no one would be paying attention to what was happening behind them. Pick couldn't see Jim anywhere, but he knew he was around.

Within moments, panic occurred in the dance hall, and like cockroaches being exposed to light, a flood of men and the dancers came running out the front door. Many of the men ran to a nearby water trough with a pump and dunked their coats into the water to run back inside to fight the flames. Others began to emerge from other buildings with buckets, gunny sacks, blankets, and coats to soak in the water. One man began pumping more water into the trough, while another grabbed a shovel and ran to the kitchen window, broke out the glass, and began shoveling dirt in.

"No more water! It's spreading the fire! No water! Get shovels and fill the buckets with dirt. Hurry! Go now!" Dave, Bella's husband, screamed from the front door. "No water! Dirt! We need dirt and shovels! Someone started this fire with kerosene or something on the floor, and it's spreading! Dirt! Fill the buckets with dirt!"

Branson had a volunteer fire brigade, but it was doubtful they had been notified of the fire yet, even though men were running in all directions screaming, "Fire" to alert the need for more men and more buckets to come help douse the flames before the city went up in smoke. Men ran from all directions to help create a line of overflowing buckets but paused when they heard water was spreading the flames. Men began running back to their homes or wherever they could find a shovel. The band members carried their instruments outside and went back in to help Bella and the other ladies carry out armloads of papers and other things they did not want to lose in the fire. They coughed from the smoke that was filling the dance hall. The ladies were crying, and some wanted to go back in to get some things out of their rooms, but Bella refused to let them. Christine got to her knees and began praying, and she was joined by a few others who shared her faith in Jesus and some who normally didn't but now did. Every face in the crowd was either expressing fear or great concern to get the fire out since the fire could destroy not only the dance hall but the entire town if they didn't stop it from spreading. Some men who weren't fighting the fire were carrying furniture and items out of the dance hall to save what they could.

The man with the shovel dug into the hardened ground as fast as he could to fill the buckets with dirt to throw on the floor of the kitchen. Kerosene didn't burn very hot or fast, which unfortunately meant it burned longer and spread farther. Pick watched the men anxiously waiting to get a bucket of dirt, and others ripping their coats off to go throw them on the fire to help smother it. Everyone's greatest fear was allowing the fire to get into the walls and climb to the second story, spreading throughout the building. "Urgent" couldn't describe the importance of getting the walls put out before the flames worked their way into them. Not using water to do so made the fight much harder. There were many men using their hands to fill buckets with whatever topsoil they could gather to help extinguish the fire. One man began digging in the street with a grub hoe, another a pick to help provide the dirt needed. Three men came running with large bags of flour. The commotion was the perfect situation Pick had wanted to create, but Jim Hexum was nowhere in sight.

Smoke billowed out of the broken kitchen window and the front door, but as of yet, Pick hadn't seen much flame come out of the building. He stood by the wagon waiting, not caring if the building stood or fell. A man ran up to him frantically. "Do you have flour in there?" he asked, pointing at Pick's wagon.

"No."

"Don't just stand there, come help!" the man demanded.

"I can't walk. Gout," Pick said lifting one leg and feigning a painful grimace.

The man turned and ran back toward the dance hall. The crowd was quickly growing; every building on Rose Street and those around it emptied as the men came to help or watch. Soon there were so many people crowded around the building that Pick had lost sight of Christine completely. Yelling, crying, prayers, and cursing were all heard as the firefight continued. For Pick, it was a wonder what a flask of kerosene could do when spread by water. He had been counting on that to create the chaos he had wanted. Now if Jim could only get Christine. No one was looking toward the wagon; everyone was focused on the fire and the smoking building. With so many people helping, he guessed the fire would be out soon enough, and if they were lucky, it hadn't gotten into the walls. What he most feared was Jim not accomplishing his task of getting Christine into the wagon.

"Water! We need water now!" Pick heard Dave yell. "Grab an axe and bust the walls open!"

A ringing bell and the hoofbeats of fast-approaching horses signaled the arrival of the fire brigade, driving the only steam-engine pump wagon Branson had. The crowd began to make room for them as they approached.

Pick double-checked the harnesses of the three-horse team that pulled the wagon and inspected the wheels, and did about everything else he could to look busy and the least suspicious. He grew anxious as more time went by, and angrier with every minute. "Where the hell are you?" he asked while looking for his partner.

Jim Hexum had stood back in the shadows watching with approval as the fire had done all it was supposed to do and maybe more than he expected. Certainly, the damage would be significant if they got the fire out, and if not, the building would be no more. He didn't have time to wait and see which it would be, though. The crowd was large enough now to get lost within it and out of sight of Christine's friends within seconds. He worked his way out of the shadows and into the crowd toward her. When he was close enough, he tapped her shoulder as she prayed and bent down close to her ear. He spoke with urgency. "Matt needs you now. He's been hurt. Come quick!"

She looked up at him with concern. "What?"

"Matt needs you. Come on!"

"Okay!" She stood up to go but was grabbed by one of

the young dancers named Angela, who was crying. "Where are you going?"

"To see Matt. I'll be back." She began walking with Jim. "What happened to Matt? Is he okay?"

"No, ma'am, he's been hurt. He sent me to get you. I don't know why."

"What happened? Was he burned?"

"No, ma'am, stabbed."

Christine stopped where she was, and tears quickly filled her eyes. "Stabbed?" she stammered. The sense of horror that filled her when she heard her husband had been stabbed to death in a saloon in Denver echoed loudly in her mind now. People always feared guns, but she knew all too well how deadly a knife could be. 'Oh, Lord, no. Please let Matt be okay. Not him too, Lord.' She prayed silently as she stood in place, trying to regain some control over the fear of someone else, she cared deeply for, being stabbed.

Jim stopped and looked back at her. "Yes, ma'am. He's asking for you."

Christine stepped forward as the wave of déjà-vu filled her soul like a sinking ship. She began to cry as she walked with Jim through the crowd. They neared the wagon, and Pick walked around to get onto the bench seat.

"Get in, and we'll take you to him," Jim said as he lifted himself into the back of the wagon and held the flap open for her.

"Where is he?" she asked as she climbed into the wagon without a second thought.

"Um...across town," Jim said, then, "Get going, Pick."

Pick released the brake and urged the horses forward, leaving the fire behind them.

Christine kneeled on the buckboard and rested her hand on the saddle horn of one of three saddles lying beside each other to keep her balance as the wagon jerked ahead. She looked at Jim. "Is Matt going to live?" she asked, a tear floating down from her eye.

Jim closed the flap and looked at her. "Yeah. He'll live, but he won't be much anymore."

Her eyes closed, and she contorted her face to keep from sobbing. With a gasp of breath, she asked in a broken voice, "How bad is he?"

Jim peeked out of the back of the wagon to make sure no one took notice of them leaving. He groaned before answering, "Oh, let's just say he's going to be unemployed very soon."

Christine began to get a bad feeling in the pit of her stomach. She watched his face harden like stone while he peeked out from under the tarp like a criminal. "I don't understand. How bad is he hurt?"

"No, you wouldn't understand, would you?" He looked at her with a knowing expression of raised eyebrows and a pleased smirk. "Catherine, your parents are on their way here to get you."

"What?" Christine asked, confused. "Where is Matt?"

Jim chuckled as he moved to block the back of the wagon. "Probably with his other woman."

"You said Matt was stabbed?" Her breath quickened with alarm as she realized she had been deceived and was being taken against her will to only heaven knew where. Her heart beat faster, and her stomach dropped as her adrenaline spiked.

"I lied. And now you're going back with your parents, and my friend and I are a lot richer."

"Let me out of here!" Christine shouted, and a surge of alarm ran through her faster than a lightning strike. She knew she couldn't get around Jim since he was blocking the rear exit of the wagon. She was afraid, but she had to act. She looked at the canvas flap to the front of the wagon and leaped over the saddles toward it, intending to crawl over the bench and fall to the road where she could run for her life. However, as she leaped to do so, Jim Hexum dove on top of her and pulled her back to the center of the wagon.

"I'm afraid not, young lady!" Jim exclaimed bitterly.

"Let me go! Help!" she screamed. "Someone help me!" Without any warning, Jim's right fist landed full-force against the side of her head. It stunned her enough to keep her from fighting to get away from him. He flipped her onto her back and sat on her stomach. Her eyes focused on him and she began to scream as loud as she could, horrified as she was to be helpless and to see him on top of her. Jim drew his fist back and hit her with a solid blow to her face, and followed it another blow to her head. He drew back and hit her again. The combined four blows knocked her unconscious.

The wagon stopped suddenly, and Pick stepped force-fully through the flap and pushed Jim off her. His eyes were enraged and burned into Jim, and he had his revolver in his hand. "Don't you hit her again! Touch her again, and see what happens! I'll end our partnership right now and blow your damn head off if you touch her again! I swear it!"

Jim leaned against the buckboard as he looked up at Pick. He was surprised by the explosiveness with which Pick had come through the flap. "We don't need her screaming through town, do we? She's out now for a bit, so drive."

Pick kneeled beside Christine's head while she laid in the bed of the buckboard unconscious and bleeding from her nose. Her right cheek and eye were already beginning to swell. He wiped the blood off her top lip with his finger and looked at Jim with a dangerous glare. "I already told you I didn't want her hurt!" he exclaimed, keeping his voice low. He pointed his finger at Jim and shook it warningly. "Don't touch her again!"

Jim sat down and grabbed a piece of rope to tie her hands together with. "Well, Pick, she isn't screaming through town, is she? But she might be if you don't get this thing moving!"

Pick glared at him, still angry. "Her father's not paying for a beat-up daughter!"

"And I'm not babysitting a child. She just learned it doesn't pay to scream around me."

8

Saul and Abby Wolf's wedding reception was at the Branson Community Hall on Main Street. It had been a wonderful wedding and an evening of good food, friends, dancing, and laughter. Matt had introduced his sister Annie to Felisha, and then Regina Bannister and Felisha introduced Annie to Truet. Matt had been a bit surprised to see Truet and Annie dancing a few times and sitting together, but he held Felisha in his arms for most the night, quite content to be dancing himself. It felt good to hold her and see her pretty smile and the light shining in her eyes as she looked at him.

When the evening was ending, Lee Bannister's coach and driver parked in front of the community hall to wait for the newlyweds to take them to stay at the Monarch Hotel a few blocks away. It wouldn't be a long ride, but it would be a nice one, just the same. And for once, they would be arriving in style and staying in the most luxurious room for a two-night honeymoon. It was a wedding gift from Lee and Regina. All the guests lined up on opposite sides of the exterior door of the community hall to make a path to the coach. Saul and Abby made their way down an aisle of friends to the open door of the waiting coach, holding hands and excited to begin their life together. Their excitement was nearly childlike and glowed in their smiles as they climbed into the coach and waved at their guests as they drove away.

Matt wasn't blind to the street being nearly empty and three teenagers running down it in a hurry to get somewhere. They were talking to each other in excited voices as they ran. Matt overheard something about a fire.

He yelled, "What's going on?"

The three boys turned toward him without stopping. "The dance hall's on fire!" They turned back to keep running.

"What?" Matt shouted in alarm.

"The dance hall's burning down!"

Matt felt a cold chill of fear fill him. He looked at Felisha with concern. "I have to go!"

She nodded in understanding. "Be careful."

He nodded. "Truet, let's run down there and see if we can help."

Annie spoke quickly. "Give me your house key, and Felisha and I will wait for you there. I'm staying at your place tonight."

Matt tossed her his house key. "See you soon. Tru..." he said, and they began to run down the street toward the dance hall, with a group of men following them.

Annie looked at Felisha. "A fire is one way to ruin a night."

Felisha nodded. "Yes, it is."

Annie sighed. "Regina, as the owner of the Monarch Hotel, you need to go into the men's lounge and get us a bottle or two of wine. We might as well get Felisha used to us, and I can't think of a better way than a girls' night out at Matt's place. It's not our house, so we don't need to clean up. What do you think?"

Regina laughed lightly. "I think you just want to see Truet. But I don't have any children tonight, so I'll drink to that!" she said with a smile. "We can drink three or four bottles at his place, and he can't say anything. I'm his landlord!"

SMOKE WAS COMING out of the building when Matt and his group arrived at the dance hall. The crowd was thick, and the fire brigade was inside, busting into the walls and pouring water in to make sure there was no fire reached the inside of the exterior walls. The fire had damaged the kitchen heavily, as well as part of the main floor of the dance hall near the kitchen. The kitchen was covered with dirt and mud mixed with multiple bags of flour and smelled of burnt wood and soot. The ceilings on the first floor and going upstairs were blackened by the smoke. Matt stepped inside and was looking around when he was approached by Dave, Bella's husband. Dave looked greatly relieved to have been able to save the building despite the damage that had been done and was continuing to be done as the fire brigade swung their axes to open each section of the walls.

"What happened?" Matt asked, looking at the damage.

Dave took a deep breath while shaking his head slowly in disbelief. "Someone started a fire in our kitchen. They used some sort of oil, which smells like kerosene. We keep a bucket of water in the kitchen and behind the bar for putting out fires, but it just spread it like a bucket of fire. There were probably three or four buckets of water thrown on it before we started calling for dirt. If the dance hall wasn't full of capable men, we would have lost this place tonight."

"What is the fire brigade saying about it?"

"Arson. Someone tried to burn us down, and came close to it. We should've had the kitchen door locked. It looks like we are out of business for a few weeks, anyway."

"No one was hurt?" Matt asked.

Dave shook his head. "No one. And I am grateful for that."

"Any idea who did it?"

Dave shook his head. "Not yet. Someone had to see something, though."

"Well, let me know if you hear something. I'm glad it's still here, and it sounds like everything can be fixed. Do you know where Christine is? Is she outside?"

Dave nodded. "Yeah, I don't know what we're going to do tonight. I might just send all the ladies to the hotel for the night."

Matt shook his head with a frown. "Well, you'll be up and running in no time," Matt said as comfortingly as he could and shook Dave's hand. He walked outside and saw Bella standing with her ladies in a group. All of them had blankets wrapped around them, but they were still beginning to shiver in the cold. He walked over to them and looked for Christine, but didn't see her in the group.

"Bella, I'm really sorry to hear about the fire, but it sounds like everything can be fixed. And no one was hurt. That's a good thing."

Bella looked at him, anger flaring in her eyes. "I want you to find the man who did this and put him away!"

Matt nodded. "I will."

Bella continued irately, "You know the sheriff isn't going to do anything about it. I hope you find the person responsible and beat him worse than you did the sheriff!"

Matt frowned. "I'll do my best to find who's responsible. Where's Christine?"

Bella turned around to look through her ladies. "Where is Christine?"

"She went looking for you, Matt," Angela answered simply.

"For me? At my house?" he asked.

Angela shrugged. "I don't know. We were praying, and she got up and said she had to go see you. She looked upset."

"How long ago?" Matt asked.

"Thirty minutes ago, maybe."

"Did anyone go with her?" Bella asked.

Angela shrugged. "I don't think so."

"Damn it, I told all you girls to stay together. Did she say where she was going?" Bella asked sharply.

Angela raised her eyebrows innocently, and her eyes began to tear up from the tone in Bella's voice. "Just to see Matt." Angela was one of the youngest dancers at nineteen, and small in frame and stature. She had blonde hair, and a fragile, innocent expression on her pretty face.

Matt sighed. He wanted to make sure Christine was doing okay. "Hmm, well, she might've gone to my house. There's not much for me to do here, so I'll go back there and maybe meet her on the way. If I miss her, tell her I came by to see how she was, and I'll talk to her in a couple of days."

Bella nodded. "Thank you, Matt. And if you do meet her, walk her back here, please."

Matt agreed. "I will."

9

Annie Lenning took a drink of her wine and looked awkwardly at Felisha. "So, you're telling me that my brother's romantic? Don't believe it, girl. He's lying like a dead, stiff dog. I've talked to Matt about women before, and he doesn't have a clue how to be romantic or what to do with it if he was!"

Felisha laughed lightly. Her face was red, partly due to a glass of wine, and partly because she didn't know if Annie was being sarcastic or serious. "Um, I'm not sure dead, stiff dogs lie too much. We've always just buried them. But I think Matt is romantic. Maybe not overly like some men, but in a very cute and unique way. He makes me smile."

Annie frowned noticeably in thought. "Lie-Lay. They rhyme, and they sound so much alike, they might as well mean the same thing. A dead dog doesn't move much, so it's lying there." She looked at Regina. "It makes sense to me. You?"

Regina nodded as she twirled her wine glass. She

knew Matt didn't have any, so she had brought some from the Monarch Hotel. "I've been married to Lee long enough to understand Bannister babble. Yes, it makes sense." She laughed lightly at Annie.

Annie nodded. "Good. I suppose I'll have to ask the tough questions. Felisha, are you in love with my brother?"

Felisha smiled, and her face reddened more. She took a drink of her wine. "Ahh...yes, I am."

"Really? I heard you were moving over here. Is that because you want to marry him?" Annie asked.

Felisha took a deep breath. "You *are* asking tough questions."

Annie said frankly, "I don't mess around when I'm serious. Matt's my brother, and I love him. I want to know your intentions toward my brother because I don't want to see him get hurt. He's been hurt enough. So...are you hoping to marry him?"

Felisha answered slowly, "We are seeing how it goes. I've been married, as you may or may not know. I do have my son. I don't want to rush into it, nor does he. We want to make sure it's what we both want before we decide to marry. So, to answer your question, do I want to marry him? Yes, I'm thinking so."

Annie frowned. "No, I don't think you understand. It's a yes or no question. If you had to say yes or no, which would it be?"

Felisha looked at Annie and then laughed. "It would be...well, if he asked me tonight if I would marry him, I would have to say no. But that is why I want to move over here—to make sure it's the right thing. I love your brother, but marriage is hard, and I want to make sure this time that I am marrying a man who's right for me. I want to be sure before I say the words 'I do.'"

Annie smiled and nodded her head. She turned to Regina. "I like her. What about you?"

"Yeah, I do too. It's kind of my doing that put them together in the first place. Felisha had my approval a long time ago."

Annie nodded. "Yeah, I like her. So, do you make good bread? Because every Christmas we have a competition, and I'm the champion. You better be there this Christmas with a loaf of bread."

Felisha agreed. "Okay. Any special kind of bread?"

Annie frowned noticeably. "Just bread. Regina brings these fancy breads, but that disqualifies her, because we just make regular bread. Not sesame seed bread with ivory crusts or whatever that was you brought last time."

"I bought that. It was poppyseed with a vanilla glaze. It's a very good dessert bread. It's not meant to be a slop-up-your-chili bread."

"Are you calling me a pig?"

Regina laughed. "Not even close."

"So, Annie," Felisha said. "I have a question for you. You know I've known Truet for a long time. I was best friends with his wife, Jenny Mae, and he is like a brother to me, you'll understand. My question for you is, how long are you going to court Truet before you tell your brother? He thinks you two just met tonight."

Regina laughed. "Yeah, Annie, how about that?"

Annie made a sour face. "Felisha, why would you dampen the mood by asking a question like that? Geez, girl, I thought we were friends." She laughed, then took a breath and answered seriously, "Um...I'm waiting for Truet to be ready."

"I don't understand why you two just don't tell him. Really, I don't," Felisha said with a gentle shrug.

"I know, but Truet's his friend, his deputy, and his roommate. He's worried Matt will be angry, and that could make Truet's life a bit uncomfortable. It's not like we started off by hiding it intentionally from Matt," Annie said softly. She continued, "Truet was helping our new neighbors build their house, and so was I. Some days we worked all day together, and we had a lot of fun. It's not my fault Matt never came to help. Anyway, I began to like him, and he liked me, so we more less started courting without really knowing it. We decided to keep it hidden from Matt until it was time to tell him. Maybe that time is coming up."

Felisha offered, "I think you should. I don't want to see Matt or Truet hurt, and I sure don't want anything to ruin their friendship. I think both of you should sit down with him and tell him. It seems like the only right thing to do. Are you in love with Tru?"

Annie smiled.

"Well?" Regina asked.

"Let's just say, he did a wonderful job fixing my cabinet door, and I'm liking what I'm seeing..." She paused as the door opened and Matt walked in by himself.

"What are you liking?" he asked as he looked at the three ladies sitting in his living room drinking a bottle of wine.

Annie answered quickly, "Felisha. I'm...liking what I'm seeing in Felisha."

Matt looked at the other two ladies as they tried to hide their smiles. "I thought you would. She's a pretty special lady," Matt said, sitting down beside his intended.

"Where's Truet?" Felisha asked.

Matt shook his head. "I lost him in the crowd down there. The fire is out. It burned the kitchen, mostly."

"What started it?" Regina asked.

"Someone started it with lamp oil or kerosene. It was arson."

"Who?"

"I don't know, but somebody had to see someone go into the kitchen. We'll find out who eventually. Tonight, we just have to let the crowd disperse and let the witnesses come to the surface."

"You don't seem too concerned about it," Annie asked more than stated.

"I think they are blessed to still have a building. It was a close call. The fire brigades busted up the walls to make sure there's no fire smoldering in them." He yawned. "And I'm tired."

Regina spoke. "I for one wish it had burned down. I wish that whole street would burn down and run all those people out of town. You know most of the crime happens over there. And when it happens elsewhere, it still stems from there, usually. All those people are fleas on a dog..." She looked at Annie. "I am speaking Bannister babble, right?"

Annie laughed. "Close! But you need more practice. It takes years to perfect."

"Well, you know what I mean. Good riddance," she said with a shrug.

"That's true to a certain point, Regina," Matt said. "But the dance hall is not a place of immorality, it is just a dance hall where men go to have fun. It's not violent like some of the other places over there. There are no prostitutes there, just dancing, and they have a bar, so there is drinking. I agree Rose Street is a nasty place with all kinds of trouble brewing day or night it seems, but the dance hall is the one place that isn't known for that. Not yet, anyway."

"How many husbands do you think go there a night, Matt? Shouldn't they be at home and not tempted by other women and liquor?"

Matt smiled. "That's kind of a crazy way of looking at it. You're trying to end all the single men's fun and their chance of potentially finding a wife because married men go there. It is not the dance hall's fault when a married man makes the choice to go there. That says more about the man's lack of character than the business. An example of that is, Kyle's two friends Sam and Paul are engaged to two of the ladies there, or darn close to it. And all those guys who used to be at Ugly John's fist-fighting and causing trouble are now dancing and minding the rules. So, I would say it's doing more good than harm."

Annie said quietly, "I'm glad Sam and Paul are settling down. It's about time they did. And maybe you should, too."

Matt yawned tiredly as he took hold of Felisha's hand. "In time. She's moving over here, and I think we'll be moving closer to that when the time's right."

Felisha smiled softly. "Why don't you walk me back to the hotel so you can get back here and get some sleep?"

"You could spend the night with us," Regina said to Felisha. "I know Annie wants to stay here tonight."

Felisha laughed at the nervous face Annie made when Regina mentioned her wanting to spend the night there. "No, my friend Rebecca is watching Dillon, and I need to go get him."

"You're staying here?" Matt asked Annie.

Annie answered, "Yeah, I already told you that. You get the davenport. I'm taking over your room. And how come you didn't tell me you had such a handsome deputy, anyway? When is Truet getting back here? He's a lot more fun to talk to than you." She paused, then said before Matt could respond, "He's not my type of guy, though. I'm looking for a cowboy with horse experience. A handsome one, but a cowboy I don't have to watch over this time. I don't have much interest in a useless deputy marshal."

"Good," Matt said simply. "I knew a heck of a cowboy back in Wyoming named Marvin Aggler who would be a great asset for you. He wasn't too handsome, but he could break any horse you put him on. Do you want me to contact him and see if he wants to come west? He'd be a good hand and a good gun if you need more protection over there. I'd trust him with all I have, including you and the ranch."

"If he'll work for basically nothing until we can get things flowing, sure."

Matt nodded. "I'll ask."

Truet stepped inside and smiled. "Hi…" he said, not expecting everyone.

"We've got company, Truet," Matt said. "And Annie's sleeping in my room, and I'll be out here tonight."

"Oh. Okay. She's not going to shoot me in the middle of the night for snoring, is she?"

Annie smiled. "If you snore, I will. I have no tolerance for snoring goats!"

Truet shook his head with a slight laugh. "Do you always compare people to animals?"

Annie nodded. "Pretty much. It's what I know."

10

Christine's hands were tied behind her back as she sat on a horse being led by Jim Hexum through a dark forest that flowed downhill for quite a way. She didn't have a coat and was nearly frozen by the time they had gone at least two miles. It had been a rough ride as she sat straddling the saddle in her ballgown. Aside from her hands being tied uncomfortably and pulling on the muscles in her shoulders, there was a dirty rag of some sort shoved into her mouth with a piece of rope tied tightly around her face to hold it in place.

At the bottom of the hill, they came to a decent-sized pool of water that reflected the moon's light. She could hear a waterfall downriver and running water upriver. The running water would have been a soothing sound to listen to if she wasn't being taken by Bloody Jim Hexum deeper into the forest. He led her horse up the river into a deep, narrow gorge that suddenly surrounded her with towering walls of sheer rock. Jim led her horse farther up the gorge for another mile, she guessed, and then he crossed the river, and they walked through and into another narrow gorge that fed into the one with the river. The gorge they went into was dry, and overgrown with various types of vegetation.

Jim Hexum finally stopped his horse and dismounted. "Welcome home, Catherine," he said as he tied his horse to a small pine tree.

Christine looked around and saw nothing except the dark walls rising above her and tall brush.

Pick Lawson picked up a lantern they had left on the trail and turned the oil up to give them some light. He carried it quickly through the brush toward the gorge wall and disappeared into a mineshaft. "Tie my horse up, would you, Jim? I'll make a fire."

Jim groaned in a tired complaint as he did so. He then tied Christine's horse over to the same tree. He grabbed Christine roughly, pulled her off the horse, and set her on her feet. "Come on," he ordered and led her by the arm along a short trail toward a poorly-constructed door made of scraps of wood blocking an old mine. Inside, there was a firepit that Pick was lighting, and enough wood and kindling stacked along the wall to supply the fire for a day or two. It was so cold that Christine's body shook, and her teeth chattered to the point that she wanted to stand in the flames when they finally began to burn. They had closed the door and put a blanket up over it, leaving a small area up top for the smoke to slip out of the mine. Two wood-framed foldable cots with dark stains covering the canvas were set on the rock floor, and both had two wool blankets thrown on them. There were no pillows or other luxuries, just hard rock, two cots, a firepit, a collection of canned goods, and a pan to cook with.

Christine shivered in her dark surroundings, her face swollen and her left eye nearly closed. She could feel the dried blood from her nose covering her lower face, and her head ached like it never had before. Jim Hexum spun her around, untied the rope holding the gag in her mouth, and pulled the rag out of her mouth. She closed her mouth and opened it again to work the soreness out of her jaw. He untied her hands. "There you go. Sit down and shut up," he ordered, giving her a slight shove toward one of the cots.

Jim had hit her so hard that she was afraid of being hit again and possibly deforming her face with broken bones. On the outside, she appeared calm and serene, but inside, she was terrified. She had no idea who these men were or what they wanted from her, but the isolated mine and the makeshift camp brought the worst of her fears to mind. She had narrowly escaped becoming a slave to Sheriff Tim Wright, and it crossed her mind that Tim might have hired these two thugs to kidnap her and bring her here to finish what he had started. She was too cold not to sit on a cot against the wall and pull both blankets up around her tightly to warm herself. Her ballgown was little protection from the cold that penetrated her skin.

She looked at Jim Hexum in the firelight and recognized him from the day she saw him bring the two dead bodies to Matt's office. She had known who he was when he approached her outside the dance hall, but his words about Matt being stabbed reversed any hesitancy, compared to her determination to get to her friend. She'd had a bad feeling about him from the first moment she saw him that day at Matt's office, and she remembered Matt had called him a predator and a legal killer. Christine knew that much about him, and the fact that he had hit her as hard as he had told her all she wanted to know about him. He cared nothing of human life and was a man to be wary of. He was evil. The other man who drove the wagon had not said a word to her, but she recognized him from the dance hall. She didn't know his name but had danced with him a time or two in the past. Now she was their prisoner.

What she did know was she wasn't alone, despite the fear that tried to drive her into a faithless, desperate panic. She had to take deep breaths and remember that God promised to never leave her, and she had prayed earnestly that the Lord would protect her. She had been praying for the whole hour or longer they had been on horseback since leaving the wagon, which they had hidden in the woods beside the road.

Pick got the fire going well with the help of a can of kerosene and looked at Christine. "Are you hungry?"

She shook her head as she reached up to touch her swollen eye painfully.

"Let me see your eye," he said and moved the lantern closer to look at her. It was swollen closed, and already turning black and blue area. He glared at Jim and said heatedly, "Look what you did to her! I mean it, Jim; don't you dare hit her again. She's a lady, not some two-hundred-pound tough guy in a saloon!" His loud voice echoed out the mine and into the canyons. "Got it?" he demanded.

Jim stood by the door and looked uncaringly at Christine and then at Pick. "Keep her quiet, then." He opened the door and slipped outside into the cold.

Pick took a handkerchief out of his pocket and dipped it into a bucket of water. "Here, let's get you cleaned up a little bit," he said and dabbed her swollen eye with the wet cloth. "I'm sorry, he wasn't supposed to hurt you."

"It's a little late to apologize," she said with no emotion. She looked at him. "What are you going to do to me?" she asked anxiously, then began to sob because of the fear that consumed her. "I just want to go home." She buried her face in her hands.

Pick raised his eyebrows and waited for her to get control of herself. "I'm afraid the dance hall's probably ashes by now, but the good news is, you're going home in a few days. Now, let me help you get your face cleaned up."

Christine closed her eyes while he wiped the dried blood off her face. She said with authority, "You don't want to hang because of me. If you touch me, Matt will hang you. He's a very good friend of mine, and you know he'll be looking for me. Please, just let me go, and I won't say a word to him about this. Please! Just take me home."

Pick smiled softly. "That's kind of why you're here. Once everyone knows what a lying charlatan he is, and soon he won't have a badge anymore. Trust me, I won't hang because of you. Jim and I are going to be rewarded because of you. Ironic, though, isn't it? The title of the song you sang for Matt a couple of weeks ago was *Heroes*, and the only heroes will be me and Jim while Matt scampers to save what's left of his life." He smiled. "Life is so strange, I swear."

Christine grimaced in confusion as she rested her head against the wall and let her tears fall quietly. She had no idea what Pick was talking about, but she was too frightened to talk and too scared to find out what the two men wanted from her. She pulled the blankets tighter around her and wept quietly while crying out to God within.

Pick finished cleaning her face up and said, "I know you're probably scared, Christine, but we're not going to hurt you. Okay? You're safe. We just wanted to keep you here until your parents arrive."

Christine closed her eyes and shook her head slightly as she said strenuously, "I don't have parents. My grandparents raised me."

Pick chuckled. "Right. They'll be here Tuesday to pick you up and take you back home, and we'll get our twenty thousand dollars."

"Twenty thousand dollars from who? I don't know what you're talking about. If you want money from me, I'll give you what I have, but I don't have twenty thousand dollars. And Bella can't pay that much either, I am sure. Especially if the dance hall burned down."

"We're not getting the money from you. Are you kidding me? No, from your parents."

"I don't have parents!" Christine shouted. It hurt her head to shout.

Pick chuckled. "Nice try, Christine."

"I don't know what you're talking about."

"That's all right," Pick said and turned away from her to put another piece of wood on the fire. "You should get some rest. It's been a long night."

The door opened and Jim stepped inside, carrying two saddles. He glared harshly at Christine. "Shut your mouth, or I'll shut it for you! There will be no yelling, do you understand me?"

Christine's eyes widened in fear, and she nodded quietly.

Jim nodded back. "Good. Now, it's getting damn cold out there," he said, setting the saddles down and closing the blanket-covered door behind him. "It feels good in here; it's warming up nicely. We didn't think this through very well, Pick. Someone's going to have to sleep on the rock, and I'm getting too old for that, so I think I'm heading back to town."

"I thought we were taking turns sleeping so one of us could watch over her? If you're tired, you can sleep first. I'll wake you up in four or five hours."

"No, I'm going to town to see if they put the fire out or not. They're going to know she's missing, and I'm sure the marshal will be busting doors down to find her. If anyone seen her leave with me, I'll be a suspect to her disappearing. I need to make myself visible and run point by deflecting that. If by chance I am arrested, keep her here and deliver her on Tuesday like we planned. I won't tell anyone where you two are."

Pick sounded irritated. "It sounds like you're expecting me to stay out here by myself for three days while you enjoy a warm bed and buttered hotcakes. For splitting twenty thousand even, I'd say you're getting a better end of the deal."

Jim looked harshly at Pick. "No one seen you! You can come and go without suspicion. I was the last person seen with her. Now, we have two choices: we can stay out here and let the marshal come here, or I can go into town and deflect them elsewhere for two days."

"Three days!" Pick said bitterly.

"Three days, then. If there's one thing I know, it's when you take the favorite lady in town, the townsmen don't sit idle. If I am a suspect, they'll all be looking at me for answers, and not out here looking. I can tell them I sent her down the falls, and they'll be searching that river all week. Now, would you prefer that, or sitting in here together waiting for someone to spot that wagon and follow the horse tracks to the creek? From there, it's only a matter of time until we're found. And do you think anyone is going to believe we found the Eckmans' daughter? No, they're not! It only makes sense for me to go back. If I don't, they'll come looking for us."

Pick nodded thoughtfully. "Yeah, that's a good idea, actually. On Tuesday, I can hog-tie and gag her in the back of the wagon and take her to town for the delivery. Imagine the surprise on everyone's faces when they see her alive!" He looked at Christine and added, "You should start your own church when you get back home because you'll have been dead and resurrected twice. That's one more than Jesus." He laughed.

Christine looked at him without any humor on her face. "I have no idea what you guys are talking about. My mom died when I was a baby, and I never knew my father. I was raised by my grandparents. I don't know who the Eckmans are, but if you think I'm their daughter, you're wrong!" She looked at Jim and desperately pleaded, "If you take me back to town with you, I promise I will not tell anyone about this. I'll say I went for a long walk or went and got a hotel room or something. Please," she pleaded, tears running down her pretty face.

Jim spat a long flow of tobacco juice onto the rock floor and looked at her. "No. You're here until Tuesday. And listen up, pretty girl, I've killed plenty of men for two hundred dollars or less a shot. You're worth twenty thousand, so you better think about what I'll do for that! Behave, or I'll hog-tie you right now and leave you laying on the rocks and think nothing of it. Pick's a capable man, but if you try to sneak out, just remember I track people down for a living. If I don't find you, I'll find your corpse somewhere out there. Hypothermia will get you before I do if you're lucky." He looked at Pick. "I better get back and make an appearance in the saloon and hotel."

"I like the throwing-her-in-the-river idea. That'll keep them all looking for her clear to Natoma and back."

Jim smiled slightly. "I kind of like that one myself. Keep your eyes on her, and you might take her boots off so she can't run off too fast." He took a deep breath. "I'll check in here and there. Tuesday night, we'll celebrate."

Pick smiled. "You better believe it!"

11

Matt had slept uncomfortably on the davenport while Annie slept in his room. Annie had gotten up early and left the house, waking Matt up when she left. Matt got up and went to his room to get a bit more sleep. He eventually woke up, dressed in a gray suit, and pulled his long dark hair into a ponytail. He had trimmed his beard, and he looked his best on this Sunday morning. He walked out of his bedroom and saw Annie, who had apparently come back, in the dress she had worn the night before. She was standing in front of the cookstove, making a late breakfast. Truet Davis was in the kitchen, watching her cook.

"Are you not going to church?" Matt asked, realizing that neither one was getting dressed to go.

Truet smiled. "No, I thought I would stay home today and make sure your sister doesn't burn the house down. I don't think I've ever seen anyone ever...and I mean, *ever*, burn the potatoes on purpose," Truet said with a questioning expression. "The potatoes were done a long time ago," he said, nodding at the frying pan of shredded potatoes were burnt and still cooking. In another pan, bacon was frying, and there was a plate on the counter with pieces of cooked bacon on it.

Annie flung a hand backward and hit Truet in the stomach. "You'll like them, or you'll starve. They're not done yet."

"You'll like them," Matt agreed. "Where'd you get the bacon? We didn't have that here."

Annie gave Matt a scowl. "I walked to the only market I could find open while you lazy cows slept in. You had nothing here to cook with except potatoes. And apparently, Truet likes them raw."

Truet laughed quietly.

"Add a little salt, and they're not bad at all raw. Almost as good as an apple," Matt replied.

Truet shook his head. "I'm beginning to wish Felisha had stayed here last night so she could cook. She's a great cook, Annie. Maybe she could give you a few tips."

Annie spun around quickly and hit Truet in the stomach again playfully. "Unless you want to get hurt, you'd better rephrase that right now!"

Truet laughed. "I'll try. Maybe Felisha could give you a cooking lesson."

Annie gave him a playful left punch to the ribs, followed by a right to the solar plex. He bent over slightly, and she grabbed his hair with both hands and pulled his head down as she brought up her right knee, stopping short of his face twice. Then she yanked his head upward and pushed him back against the counter, finishing him off by stepping forward with a crushing elbow to his jaw.

She stopped just short of it. She stepped back and glared at him as she said, "Apologize before I do it again for real!"

Truet was laughing too hard to speak.

"Really?" Annie asked threateningly. "You don't think I will? Matt, you better tell your friend to apologize before I put him out of commission for a week."

"You better apologize, Truet. I don't need people saying my best deputy got beat up by a girl."

"I'm...sorry." He kept laughing. He pointed at the potatoes that were smoking on the stove top.

Annie turned around and went quickly to the stove. "You almost made me burn the potatoes!" she accused. "And the bacon, too!"

Truet laughed so hard he doubled over, holding his stomach.

Matt smiled. "Didn't you listen to Aunt Mary? Horseplay in the kitchen only leads to burnt food and burnt hands, or something like that. I never listened."

Annie gave Matt a serious scowl. "Horseplay in the kitchen leads to ass burns and ruined dinners! But you don't cook, so this isn't really a kitchen, now is it?"

Matt shook his head. "Not usually."

Truet regained his composure and asked Matt, "Are you taking Felisha to church?"

"Yeah, and I need to get going, actually. When are you going back to Willow Falls?" he asked Annie.

"Later today. Lee's taking me back around one or so."

He walked over to give his sister a hug. "I probably won't be back by then. I love you, and will see you soon."

"Love you too," Annie said. "And the next time you

invite me to spend the night at your place, clean up your room some."

Matt smiled. "The next time I invite you, I will. Any idea when I'll be inviting you again?"

"You never know, so keep it clean just in case."

A knock on the front door got his attention. Expecting it to be Felisha, he opened it and was surprised to see two of Christine's friends, Helen Monroe and Edith Williams. They appeared to be very cold and looked worried.

Helen spoke through chattering teeth. "Is Christine here?"

Matt's confusion was evident. "No."

Edith said, "She's missing."

"What do you mean, she's missing?" Matt asked with more concern in his voice than anyone was expecting.

"She's missing. She never came home last night."

Matt's eyes narrowed. "Where'd she go?"

Helen looked at Matt strangely. "To see you."

"Me? I didn't see her last night."

Annie said from behind Matt, "Invite them in. They're freezing, Matt."

"Oh! Yeah, come in and tell me what you're talking about. This is my deputy, Truet Davis, and my sister, Annie. This is Helen and Edith, Christine's friends. Have a seat, ladies."

Truet shook their hands, as did Annie. "I'm not a friend of his or anything, just his deputy," Truet said sarcastically.

Matt explained. "Truet is my friend, roommate, and then deputy. So again, where is Christine?"

Annie disappeared and came back with two blankets.

"Thank you," Helen said.

Edith spoke. "Christine is missing, and no one knows where she went. Angela, one of our dancers, said Christine told her she was going to see you and left last night while the fire was burning. We don't know where she is and I'm scared, because this isn't like her."

Matt stared at Edith without saying a word. His face was like stone, and his eyes were slowly turning hard. "Is there anywhere else she would go? Anywhere at all?"

Helen shook her head. "No, there's nowhere else she would willingly go except to see you. And you haven't seen her?"

"No. I was at a wedding reception, and then here. I never saw her."

Truet knelt beside the burning fireplace to add another piece of wood to the flames. "Would she hurt herself if she came by here and saw Matt with Felisha?" he asked.

Edith shook her head. "No! She knew Felisha was in town to see Matt."

Matt asked, "Why was she coming to see me?"

Helen shrugged. "We don't know. The dance hall was on fire, and we were all upset. Maybe she just wanted to cry on your shoulder. I don't know, maybe she just wanted to hear you say everything would be okay."

"She left before I got to the dance hall," Matt said thoughtfully.

Helen nodded. "She didn't tell anyone where she was going. She just said what she did to Angela and disappeared while the fire was still burning."

Matt grunted thoughtfully. "I'll need you to go tell

Bella I will be there soon to speak to all the girls, especially Angela. There's a few places I want to check out first, and then I'll be there." He looked at Truet. "I need your help."

"You got it, boss."

When the two ladies had warmed up and turned down a breakfast of burnt potatoes and bacon and eggs, they left to go back to the dance hall. After Matt closed the door behind them, he looked at Truet. "This is technically out of our jurisdiction, but we're going to overstep our boundaries and bust some heads open if necessary. And I'm starting with Sheriff Wright."

"I'll start asking around down on Rose Street. If she was taken, someone had to see something."

Matt sat down heavily on his davenport.

Annie frowned and sat down beside him. "I thought she was just a friend."

"She is."

She asked gently, "Are you sure there isn't more to this friendship than you know? Because by the sounds of it, there might be." There wasn't any accusation or any bitterness to her statement, but the concern of a caring sister.

Matt smiled and stood up. He looked back down at Annie. "We're just friends." He went into his room and came out with his gun belt wrapped around his waist and his old buffalo-skin coat on. "I'll meet up with you later. Annie, I love you, sis, but I have to go."

Annie looked at Truet after Matt left. "I don't think this a good time to tell him about us."

Truet shook his head. "Probably not right now. I've

seen that look in his eyes before, and...he can be scarier than you."

Annie laughed. "Make me mad and see what happens. Matt's a whipped puppy compared to me."

Truet smiled. "I doubt that."

12

Matt walked seven blocks to 4th Street and knock loudly on the front door of Sheriff Tim Wright's house. He knocked again and waited for the door to open. There was no friendship between the two lawmen since over a month before when Matt had beaten the sheriff and two of his friends with a rifle butt for trying to blackmail Christine and Bella for a bit more than financial gain.

The door opened, and Tim Wright looked at Matt with a nervous expression on his face. "Matt?" he asked, surprised to see him at his door.

"Where's Christine?" Matt asked with a dangerous tone to his voice.

Tim frowned in confusion. "I don't know. Why?"

Matt watched the sheriff's expression closely and saw no obvious sign of him lying. "She's missing."

"Missing? What do you mean, missing?"

"I mean she's gone, and no one knows where she is. Do you?" Matt asked pointedly.

Tim shook his head with a grimace. "No! I hope

you're not thinking I have anything to do with her being missing. I don't!"

Matt took a breath and sighed as he glanced around the street. He looked at Tim and said, "I'd appreciate your help in trying to find her."

"Sure, but how do you know she's not in a warm hotel room somewhere? It was pretty cold last night. She might've gone and got a hotel room somewhere to get out of the cold."

Matt nodded. "That's a possibility, but I doubt it. You could help me by checking the hotels around Rose Street. I'll go to the Monarch Hotel and see if she's there."

"Yeah, that's not a problem. I'll ask around and see what I can find out, and get my men out looking as well." For Tim, it was an opportunity to make the front page of the local paper and add to his reputation as one of Branson's finest sheriffs in the history of the city. He wanted to go down as such, and build a legacy that would be equal to the fame Matt had gained as a deputy marshal.

Matt spoke evenly but had a certain hardness to his eyes that Tim had seen before. "If you do find out who might have her, tell them to bring her back today. It's the only warning I am giving them. Tell them if she's hurt in any way, I won't be abiding by any rules when I find them. And I *will* find them."

"Sure," Tim said hesitantly. If he discovered who took her, he'd arrest them himself and cut Matt out of any glory completely.

"Thank you," Matt said and walked away without saying another word. He headed over to Main Street and turned left to walk two more blocks to the Monarch

Hotel. He went inside and questioned the desk clerk about seeing Christine, but got no results there. He went upstairs to the first floor and knocked on a door.

A moment later, Felisha's eight-year-old son Dillon opened the door. "Matt! Mom says you're late and we missed church. I don't mind, though, because I like seeing the people and wagons go by from up so high. I wanted to spit on them, but Mom got mad. It's like rain is all, right?"

Matt smiled slightly. "I don't know about that, Dillon. It's a little different, I think."

"Nuh-huh! It's not."

"Dillon James, it's not acceptable to spit on anyone ever," Felisha said as she neared Matt. "The boy wanted to open a window and spit on people as they walked by. I don't know where he gets these ideas from."

"Probably from my cousin William."

"We met him when we checked in," Felisha told him.

Matt nodded. "Exactly. He lives here in the hotel and works as security." Matt said to Dillon, "Hey, Dillon, do you know William? The guy with long blond hair and two silver guns?"

"Yeah! He's my friend. He gave me a candy yesterday. Two of them! He said it was lots of fun to spit on people from the window."

Matt looked at Felisha and smiled. "I told you. William likes getting kids in trouble. It entertains him. I am sorry for being late, and even more sorry to have to tell you I must go to work. We have a missing girl, and I think someone took her. I'm not sure yet, but it's very possible."

"Oh, no! Anything I can do to help?" she asked.

"Pray."

"Definitely. Do you know who she is?"

Matt nodded.

"Oh, Matthew, I'm sorry. Well, go find her, and don't worry about us. We'll look for William to step outside and spit on him," she said with a chuckle.

"Really, Mama?" Dillon asked with excitement.

She laughed. "No, Dillon, not really." She gave Matt an empathetic smile. "Go find this girl, and I'll go get on my knees and pray she comes home safely. What's her name?"

Matt looked at her and paused. "Christine."

"I'll pray for Christine, and you go find her. And may the Lord bless your hunting. In fact, let's pray right now." She took hold of his hand, and they prayed for Christine's safe return. Felisha kept hold of his hand. "Do you think I'll see you tonight?"

Matt paused before answering, "I don't know, because I don't know what the day's going to bring. But I will try to come by. You should get out of the hotel and go see Regina or explore the town. Just stay off Rose Street. That's not a good place for you and Dillon to be."

Felisha smiled sadly. "This sure puts a damper on our weekend, doesn't it?"

Matt nodded. "It does. But Lord willing, we will find her today. I went by the city sheriff's, and he's going to help with his men too. I have Truet knocking on doors too, so we might just find her soon."

"But you don't think so, do you? I can see the worry on your face."

Matt hesitated. "No."

"You found Truet, you'll find her too. I have faith that Jesus will help you find her." She hugged Matt and enjoyed his arms holding her. She kissed him. "Go find her so we can spend some time together. Okay?"

He smiled sadly. "I'll do my best. I'll see you later."

Matt left Felisha and went downstairs and found William's room, which was the nearest one to the front desk. He knocked, and William Fasana opened the door, looking like he'd had a rough night of drinking and gambling the night before. He had been woken up by Matt's knocking and was in his long johns. His room smelled of stale liquor and the mess of dinner plates and glasses lying around.

"Matt, what in the hell do you want so early?" he asked as he walked back to his bed and sat on the edge of it.

Matt closed the door behind him and went over to a small davenport along one wall. He sat down.

"What do you want, Matt?" William asked again as he dropped his head into his hands.

"Rough night?" Matt asked.

William gave him a dirty look. "Don't ever play poker with a man named Sebastian. We played all night and drank way too much. Oh, and I lost way too much money to him. You might know him; his name's Sebastian Worthington."

Matt shook his head. "He doesn't sound familiar, no."

"Well, he was asking questions about you. Don't know anything about him, really. A well-dressed man with a pocket full of money, and too damn good at poker to be a businessman. Anyway, why are you here?" he asked, then grabbed a glass of water off his nightstand and drank it.

"What kinds of questions?" Matt asked curiously.

"Oh, basic stuff. Probably the oddest question he asked was if you had a fiancée or was courting someone special. I told him yeah, Felisha's upstairs for a few days. He asked about her. It was just kind of odd talk for a poker game, is all."

"Sounds like. I imagine since you just woke up, you haven't heard any rumors about Christine being missing?"

"Christine who?"

"Christine Knapp. My friend from the dance hall. She disappeared while the dance hall was burning last night, and no one knows where she is. I was hoping you might have heard something in your circle." Matt knew all too well that William knew Sheriff Tim Wright, Josh Slater, and Travis McKnight very well since they all three came to the Monarch Lounge almost nightly. Matt's first inclination was that those three men might have had something to do with Christine's disappearance. If William had heard even the slightest rumor of plans being made, Matt would know where to go.

"No, I didn't know. Let me get dressed and I'll help you look for her, though. You got all the glory for saving Elizabeth last Christmas, so it's my turn. Besides, if I rescue her, I'll be her knight in shining armor instead of you. And I would love to rub that in the face of Travis and Tim," he said with a smile.

Matt smiled. "I'll tell you what, you ask around. I'm going to go get my deputy Phillip and have him sit in the office to relay any messages back and forth. We'll all meet at my office at three and see what we found."

William yawned. "Hey, thanks for coming to get me. A little bit of excitement is exactly what I need today. And don't worry, I have a nose for finding beautiful women!"

13

The damage to the dance hall was significant but repairable. The answer as to who set it was still unknown, and there was a fear of someone returning to set it on fire again. Accusations of who started the fire ran rapidly from Bella accusing Sheriff Tim Wright to some religious extremist who would risk murdering someone in a fire to end what they called immorality. An obsessive gentleman angry that his obsession danced with another man, to a neighboring saloon owner being run out of business. The anxiety of not knowing who had caused the fire or why it had been set was heavy on the minds of Dave and Bella. Fear of a fire being set while everyone was sleeping was the worst scenario Matt heard about while talking to the owners of the dance hall. Of course, the disappearance of Christine was their greatest concern, and they were distraught about her.

Dave sat in his cushioned chair and shook his head, overwhelmed. "I don't even know where to begin. We got a building with significant damage to fix before we can open again, and the only thing I can think about is, where's Christine? And why did she go looking for you? It just makes no sense! She's a smart and careful young lady, who would never just disappear!"

Bella added through her tears as she sat on her davenport in their home behind the bar. "Someone took her. It's the only way she would leave us." She looked at Matt. "You better go find her before it's too late!"

"I am doing my best. I need to talk to Angela. She's the one who saw her leave."

"I'll get her," Bella said and left the davenport in her robe to go get her dancer.

"Dave, someone had to have seen something, and it will come out. My concern right now is finding Christine. In the process of finding her, we'll find the person who set the fire," Matt said, hoping to bring some comfort to Dave.

"What *process* is there in finding Christine?" Dave unexpectedly shouted. He was angry and anxious, and it came out on Matt for his nonchalant attitude toward the repairs that were going to cost a small fortune.

Matt smirked at Dave unconsciously. Dave's tone had struck a nerve, and Matt fought the anger rising within him. His irritation came out in his tone. "I think we're all a bit shook up today, and we'll let it go with that. But there is no *process*, Dave, except patience and asking questions to try to find out more than we know."

"I heard you found a kidnapped woman last Christmas up in the mountains, so you should be able to find Christine without any problems. Right? You are Matt

Bannister, the almighty marshal, right? So, what are you waiting for?"

Matt's eyes hardened. "There is no trail in the snow I can follow this time, and there are no notes telling me who has her! Christine disappeared in a crowd of people too spellbound watching the fire to notice..." He paused in mid-sentence, then closed his eyes and sighed. "I don't know how I missed it."

"What?" Dave asked.

"I don't think Ugly John or anyone else you mentioned started the fire. I think it was a diversion to get everyone outside and focused on it so they could get Christine separated from the crowd somehow and take her without anyone noticing. I say 'they' because it's too big a plan for one man to carry out alone. I don't think we're looking for one man, but a few. The question now becomes why?"

Dave covered his face with his hands. "Oh, Lord. Do you really need to ask that?"

"I do. Because right now, I am lost. I don't know where to look for her. I have people out there asking questions and spreading the word around for anyone who saw anything at all to come forward. I have Sheriff Wright checking the hotels, and my guys are asking around too. That's the only thing I know to do right now. I can't do much without a starting point, and the only starting point I have is right here."

"So, they have her out there somewhere, doing God knows what to her, and the best you can do is stand here and twiddle your thumbs?" Dave asked bitterly.

Matt's eyes flickered with anger. "Do you think you

can do better, Dave? You can start helping by getting your ass out of that chair and start talking to people who might have seen something instead of whining about your burnt floor. Your floor can be fixed! I'm doing what I can, and I assure you I'll find who took her, and they'll wish they never did. Until then, get off your ass and help!"

Dave blinked heavily as moisture filled his eyes. He was a short, stocky man with broad shoulders, short curly brown hair, and a thick mustache on his upper lip. "We love her like a daughter, Matt. We could never have children of our own for whatever reason. These girls are our family. I apologize for being an ass. I have too much on my plate, but she is the most important." He fought his tears. "I have to focus on the repairs because I can't bear to think of what's happening to her." He grimaced against his tears and then pulled himself together. "Forgive me."

"I promise I'll find her," Matt said softly as the door opened.

Bella walked into the apartment and saw her husband sitting in his chair with wet red eyes. He looked up at Bella with an expression of hopelessness and grief.

"What?" Bella asked in alarm.

Dave waved toward her chair not far from his. Bella sat down and told Angela to sit beside Matt on the davenport.

"What's going on?" Bella asked nervously.

"Matt thinks whoever took Christine started the fire as a diversion to take her. He says it was probably more than one man. Like a gang."

"Oh, my Lord! Is that true?" she asked Matt.

Matt nodded. "I think so. I can't prove it yet, but that's what I'm thinking."

Bella's face contorted into a grimace. "The Sperry-Helms Gang? They'll ruin her forever!" She began to cry.

He looked at the very attractive young blonde-haired lady. "You're Angela?"

She nodded nervously, her lips quivering as she fought to keep from sobbing after what she had just heard.

"I need you to tell me what you saw. Anything will help, so tell me what happened."

"Um, we were praying, and she said she had to go see you and got up and left. That's all I saw. She looked worried, but we all were," she said.

Matt felt frustrated by the lack of information she provided. "That's it?"

She nodded.

"That's not very really helpful, Angela. So, there wasn't any explanation why she wanted to see me? Let me ask you, was there anyone near her? Did she leave with anyone? Talk to anyone? Someone had to approach her at some point. Think about it; was there anyone, a man, anyplace near her, or walking away from her?"

Angela frowned as she thought back. "Well, I wasn't really paying attention, but now that you mention it, there was a man who was walking away from her when she got up."

"What did he look like? Do you remember?"

"It was an old man. I know that much."

"How do you know that?" Matt asked.

"Because he had gray hair that touched his shoulders and a long beard, kind of."

Matt's eyes hardened, and his tone grew more intense. "He had long gray hair and a long beard, kind of? What does that mean? Was it a beard or a goatee or a mustache? What was it shaped like? Was he big or small?" His eyes concentrated on her facial expressions and body language.

"I saw his profile, and it was a mustache that went down onto his chin. You know, a lot of men have them like that. It was about this long." She held her finger about three inches below her chin. She pointed at Matt's buffalo-skin coat that hung on a wall hook. "He wore a coat like that one, but it had matted black fur on it."

"Are you sure?" Matt asked dangerously.

"Yup. That's who was walking away from her."

"Was there anyone else walking past or away from her?"

Angela shrugged. "No, most everyone was watching the fire."

"Exactly. Thank you," Matt said and looked at Bella. "He has a black bear coat. Mine's buffalo. I must go. Thank you, Angela, you helped a lot." He stood up.

"You know who took her?" Bella asked.

"I know who she described. Whether he took her or not, we'll find out."

"Who?" Bella asked.

"I can't tell you yet, but I'll let you know." He grabbed his coat off the wall rack by the door.

14

Pick Lawson knelt next to the fire, heating two cans of baked beans poured into a kettle. When it was steaming and ready to eat, he scooped some out onto a tin plate and moved over to the cot Christine was sleeping on. He touched her shoulder lightly. She woke up in alarm and sat up quickly against the wall while pulling the blankets tightly around her. She stared at Pick anxiously.

"I didn't mean to scare you," he explained sincerely. "Here's some breakfast. It isn't much, but it will fill you up for a while." He moved back and sat on the edge of his own cot to watch her. "I know you didn't feel much like talking last night, and maybe you still don't, but my name is Pick Lawson. You don't have to be scared; I'm not going to hurt you."

Christine held the plate of beans and slowly took a bite. She was hungry and the baked beans smelled good, despite coming out of a can. The fire had heated the mineshaft up enough that it was tolerable to sit and eat comfortably. She had not slept for most of the night due to the fear that wouldn't let her go and the cold that wouldn't leave her. She had fallen asleep at some point near daybreak and slept till now. She didn't ask what time it was because she didn't care. The one thing she did need to do was keep up her physical strength, and a meal of beans would help her do that. She had stared at the wooden door throughout the night, thinking she could open it easily and run out while Pick slept. She knew the road was up the hill from the pool they had ridden down the mountain to, but she wasn't sure how far it was from the pool. The steep mountain would be much harder and take a lot longer to climb up on foot, but she feared any noise the horse made or the sound of its iron shoes scraping on a rock would wake up Pick.

If she was to escape, she would have to do it on foot so she could hide easier in case Pick came after her. One important question she had to consider was how far she could go in the freezing cold? They were somewhere in the Blue Mountains, and even though there was no snow on the ground, it was still very cold, even with the sun shining on a clear blue sky. The starry nights were simply brutal. She was not prepared for a midnight walk through the woods in near-freezing temperatures in her lightweight ball dress.

Pick filled his own plate with beans and sat back down on his cot, then faced her. "Not bad, huh? I'm not much of a cook, so canned goods are a staple at my place. I have some canned salmon too, but we'll cook that up tonight for supper. Do you feel like talking today? It's okay if you don't. I'm actually used to being quiet myself."

Christine finished her beans and laid her plate on the

cot. She looked at Pick with a serious expression. "Why did you guys take me?"

"I told you," Pick said with his mouth full of beans. "Your parents are coming to town, and we're turning you back over to them."

Christine grimaced. "Did it ever occur to you that you have the wrong girl? If you think I'm the Eckman girl, you're wrong. The paper said she was dead. Matt found evidence that proved it."

Pick smiled as he swallowed. "Matt's scamming them, and everyone else. He's a fraud, and you're in on it too. I bet you're wondering how I knew it wasn't you and your husband burned in the cabin, huh? The answer is because I know who killed Possum and his wife. You see, Matt may not of thought about it, but two people were killed up there, and those who did it know for a fact that it wasn't you and your husband, Nathan Webster. I know the people who were killed, and they looked nothing like you. You and Matt did a good job of playing it up, though. I'll give you that."

"So, you're saying Matt lied?" she asked skeptically.

"Yes, that's what I'm saying! Like you don't know." He shook his head, laughing quietly. "You are good. Listen, you can play that chord for the next two days if you want to, but the song-and-dance routine won't stop us from turning you over to your parents. Twenty thousand dollars is far too much money to lose."

Christine sat quietly for a moment. "Did you kill those people?"

Pick shook his head. "No. I wasn't there, but a friend of mine was, and he told me about it."

"Then who did it, and why?"

"I can't tell you that. If they heard I said anything to anyone, I'd be the next one killed. And I'll tell you what, I'm lucky to be sitting here as it is! This past summer was a close one," he said with a smile.

Christine watched Pick eat hungrily. He wasn't a handsome man as such. Pick was in his mid-forties and of medium height and build, with short brown hair and clean-shaven, oblong face. A long scar came across his left cheek. His nose was slightly curved from once being broken and his blue eyes appeared dull, yet showed a hint of life while he talked to her. Pick's general appearance was chiseled from a tougher kind of life hardened by the elements he was exposed to. There was no doubt in Christine's mind that Pick was a rough man with a colorful past. His gun belt laid on the ground near his cot. Despite who he might have been, he didn't seem to be a mean man so far, and had sternly spoken up to protect her from being hit again by Jim Hexum. Christine said softly, "It wouldn't hurt to tell me who killed them. Who will I have a chance to tell? If what you're saying is true, Matt's going to be busy trying to explain himself for a while."

"Yeah, he is, but I have too much to lose to risk trusting you. If those guys found out I cut them out of the deal I made with your parents, I'd be a dead man. You see, that's why I brought Jim into the deal—to be the front man and keep my name out of the papers. I dictated the letter sure enough, but if my name was mentioned in the papers, I would be as dead as Possum and his wife are."

"So, this was all your idea?"

Pick nodded. "Sorry. I really am. But I need the money, and you're too good for Branson anyway. You belong back in Sacramento, going to social balls with real gentlemen, not us ruffians around here. Someday you'll thank me," Pick said confidently. "You're too good for this place."

"Did Jim start that fire?" she asked.

He shook his head slowly. "No, I did. Jim's job was to get you away from the crowd and into the wagon. He did, and now you're here. Sorry, Christine, but like I said, someday you'll thank me for getting you out of this place."

"I'll thank you? That's where I make a living! Did the dance hall burn down?" she asked anxiously.

"I don't know. Jim will let us know when he comes back. He'll be here later today, probably. That shouldn't matter to you anymore. You'll have greater opportunities ahead once you go home, Christine. Or should I call you Catherine? Do you have a preference?"

Christine smiled slightly as she shook her head. "You're not going to believe I'm the wrong person no matter what I say, are you?" she asked.

Pick looked at her sternly. "No. Words are cheap, and actions speak louder than words every time. I've been watching you and Matt, so I know I've got the right girl. Matt's not going to like me, but I'll be leaving town as soon as I get my money. He'll never see me again, even if he beats the scandal it's going to cause. Who knows, maybe your pa will be so grateful he will get me a job on the railroad as security or something. I wouldn't mind driving a train."

She looked at him awkwardly. "What makes you think you have the right girl? No, never mind. I suppose I should just wish you luck with that. So, how mad would you be if you turned me over to them and they asked who I am because I'm not their daughter?"

"That's not going to happen, because you are. I do appreciate your efforts to create doubt, and it might work on a lesser man, but I'm not stupid enough to fall for your creativity. Some people fight with their hands, some with weapons, some create plans, and some, like you, try to use words to cause doubt. Doubt becomes second-guessing, and finally the fear of being wrong. It's not going to work with me, so you might as well stop trying. You're here until Tuesday when we take you back to town to meet your parents. If you don't mind me asking, why are you hiding from them anyway?"

Christine sighed. "Okay, I guess I'll play along since you won't believe me," she said with a hint of sarcasm. The worst-case scenario she would be going back in town on Tuesday and being released. Whether Matt lied about the Eckman girl or not, the fact remained, Christine wasn't her. Knowing the motive of her kidnappers relieved some of the worry. She knew she would not be killed or harmed anyway. There had not been any hint of being forced upon, and that was another thing she feared. "Um...before I answer that, I have to use the privy. Do you have a plan for that?" she asked.

Pick yawned. "I do. Take the lantern and go to the

back of the mine. Be careful, because there's a lot of broken glass back there. The boys in the gang get bored hiding up here and like to throw their empty bottles against the wall back there. It's safe, but I wouldn't sit down or take your boots off. I won't see you or anything even if you leave the lantern on, and it should be a lot warmer than going outside."

"And you won't follow?" she asked.

Pick looked at her. "No. You can't go anywhere, so if you wanted to move your cot back there, that's fine too. You're free to move around. I just can't let you go outside."

"I think it would be too cold for me to go outside anyway," she said and took hold of the lantern and walked carefully on the uneven and jagged hard rock floor farther down the mineshaft. She neared the end and almost sprained her ankle on a jagged rock that rose up from the ground. True to Pick's word, shards of broken glass were scattered everywhere. As she squatted to relieve herself, she picked up a piece of glass she could hold firmly in her hand, with a pointed end she could use as a weapon if the need arose.

She ground the edge of the handled part against the rock floor to chip away the sharp edges to make it safer for her to handle, then reached into the pocket sewn into her dress where her dance tickets from the night before were and arranged them to put the piece of glass into her pocket without cutting herself. It was better to have a weapon of some use than none at all. If Pick, despite his promise, tried to force himself upon her, she would have a source of self-defense that would leave him bleeding to death if she sliced him deep enough. If he tried, she would cut him furiously wherever she could, but her first cut would be his throat.

15

Matt Bannister stood in his office staring at a map of Jessup County and then at a map of the city of Branson. He was looking for the most obvious place for Jim Hexum to keep a kidnapped lady. Truet had a man come up to him and tell him he had witnessed a man waiting by a covered wagon across the street from the dance hall. The man had claimed to have gout and couldn't walk, but was standing at the back of his wagon. When Truet asked what the man had looked like, the witness had few details to offer. He had been too preoccupied by the fire to notice.

It at least gave Matt a picture of how they might've gotten her out of there without being noticed, but where to take her? Matt looked at Truet and pointed his finger at the map of the county. "Felisha and I ran into Jim and some other guy here by Slater's Mile. I don't know who the other guy is, but I'll bet they took her out of town somewhere. There are too many people who live in Slater's Mile who would see or hear her yelling to be there, I think. Let's ride out that way and see what we can find. Maybe something will stand out."

"Sure," Truet said simply.

As they were telling Deputy Phillip Forrester where they were going, there was a gunshot out on Main Street. All three men ran outside and heard a commotion from two blocks away. They ran down the boardwalk to see what the commotion was.

In the street in front of the Monarch Hotel, a teenage boy who was dressed poorly and didn't have a coat on, held a revolver pointed at a troublemaker named Ritchie Thorn. He was no stranger to Matt since Ritchie's older brother was Joe Thorn. Joe was the no-good leech who lived with Matt's cousin Billy Jo Fasana. He had fathered her three children but never married her. Joe Thorn was a woman-beater, a drunk, and as faithful to Billy Jo as a flea was to a dead dog. Ritchie was not much different than his brother. Both were troublemakers who thought they owned the world they walked in. Ritchie was in his mid-twenties, a lean, muscular man who labored in the silver mine. Ritchie had short dark hair and a short mustache on his upper lip. He was holding a hand out to the boy and saying, "Put it down, Ollie, before I take it away from you and bust your head open with it!"

The kid was around sixteen or seventeen and had a round, boyish face with unkempt dirty-blond hair. Tears of anger fell down his face as he leveled the gun at Ritchie.

Among a growing crowd were William Fasana, who was standing in front of the hotel, and Sheriff Tim

Wright, who stood off to the side. Neither man held a gun in their hand nor made a move to step between them.

Matt drew his revolver and pointed it at the boy as he walked closer to him. "Put it down," Matt ordered. "Put it down *now*!"

The boy looked at the marshal, surprised to see a gun pointed at him with Matt Bannister holding it. The boy lowered it slightly and spoke through a shaken voice. "He beat my mama, Marshal. He beat her bad!"

Matt looked at Ritchie with no sympathy at all. "Is that right, Ritchie?" he asked pointedly.

Ritchie shrugged his shoulders nonchalantly. "Things got a bit out of control. No big deal, though."

"It is to him. It's his mother you hit!" Matt said sharply and stepped closer to the boy. "Lower the gun. You don't want to ruin your life over this. Why don't you hand it to me?"

The boy lowered the gun. He looked at Matt with a mixture of emotions between rage, heartbreak, and fear. The boy's tears filled his eyes that refused to fall. "She's hurting, and I am sick of him hitting her! I want to kill him, Marshal! And if he comes back to our place, I will! I swear it!"

Ritchie laughed lightly and playfully hit his friend in the belly with his hand.

Matt took the young man's gun. "What's your name?"

"Ollie Hoffman."

"Where do you live, Ollie?"

"The Dogwood Shacks. My mama is crying in pain, Marshal." The Dogwood Shacks were a half-block of small cottages with shared walls in an enclosed half-square shape on Second and Dogwood Streets one block up from Rose. The Dogwood Shacks were owned by John Pederson, the owner of Ugly John's Saloon. They were home to many of the poorest people in Branson and had a nasty reputation.

"How about my deputy Phillip goes home with you to check on her, okay? And if she needs a doctor, he'll get her to one."

Ollie nodded and then glared at Ritchie, who was smiling at him mockingly. "You stay away from my mama!"

"Tell her I'll be by tonight, huh?" Ritchie laughed.

Matt glared at Ritchie harshly. "Get away from here! And if you ever touch his mother again and I hear of it, I will come looking for you and beat you twice as bad!" Matt said coldly. There was no love lost between the Thorn boys and the Bannisters and the Fasana family, especially Matt.

Ritchie smirked at Matt. "It's a funny thing, Marshal. My brother and I were just talking about that. We keep hearing these threats from you, your cousins, and Luther, and yet no one has the balls to do anything. I'm kind of waiting to see if any of you can whip me without your guns. You and William over there are both welcome to try anytime."

Matt's lips grew into a slight smirk. "Let's find out," he said and stepped toward Ritchie.

Felisha's voice stopped him. "Matt...no!"

He saw her standing on the porch near the entrance to the hotel door, holding Dillon close in front of her. They were both watching nervously. He glanced at

Ritchie and wanted to curse because of the frustration he felt at not being able to bust the arrogant fool in the mouth. "You've been warned!" Matt said.

Ritchie laughed as he hit his friend's stomach again. "Told ya! Come on, let's go."

Matt sneered as he watched Ritchie walk away, laughing. He turned to Ollie and asked, "Weren't you one of the boys I caught spitting on Chusi a couple of weeks ago in the alley?"

Ollie looked at Matt, surprised by the question. "Yes, sir."

"Is that how you were taught to treat people?"

"No, sir."

"Then don't ever treat him like that again. Phillip, take Ollie home and check on his mother. Make sure she's okay." Matt looked at Felisha with frustration on his face and then turned to his cousin William. "Why didn't you break that up?" he asked as he walked toward them.

William laughed lightly. "Are you kidding? I was hoping the boy shot him."

"Matt," Felisha asked, "are you okay? Do you have time to eat a late lunch?"

Matt shook his head. "No. We're riding out of town to see what we can find. I have reason to believe the gentlemen we saw on the road yesterday are the ones that took Christine."

"You mean him?" Felisha asked nodding behind Matt.

Matt turned around quickly, and there was Jim Hexum walking across the street toward Matt and the Monarch Hotel. He looked at Matt and smiled. "Boy, you're going to lose respect if you keep letting thugs like him talk you down like that."

"Where's Christine?" Matt asked sharply.

Jim feigned ignorance, stopping short of the board-walk and holding up his hands in surprise. "Whoa, there, Marshal. How would I know? I heard she's missing, though." He paused and pointed at Felisha. "You gotta be torn and half-stuck between your lady there and your bed stock out there somewhere," he said as he stepped up on the boardwalk.

Matt threw an unexpected hard right fist that hit Jim square in the nose, and he fell to his back onto the street, his long, straight nose was broken and bleeding profusely. Jim held his nose with his hands and looked up at Matt, surprised.

Matt pointed at him and said heatedly, "That's for your talking nonsense! Now, where is she? I know you took her!"

Jim Hexum grinned as the blood dripped down his face. He stood up slowly, plugged one nostril, blew out a line of blood onto the ground, and then blew out the other nostril. "You can't prove nothing. I was in my hotel room all night, and I promise no one saw me light a fire. You got nothing but suspicions, and that ain't enough. Nice hit, though. You got me good, but that's nothing compared to what's going to happen to you. If I was you, I'd be looking in the river for Christine. Maybe someone threw her over the falls when they were done with her." He grinned. "You got nothing! Now, if you'll excuse me, I have to go meet someone inside. Have a good day," he said and stepped toward the porch again.

Matt reached his left arm out and put his palm on Jim's chest to block his way. "I have a witness saying she saw you walk away with Christine. That's probable cause to arrest you until we can find her. And your partner was seen at his wagon and entering the kitchen," Matt lied, but he thought it was worth a gamble. "I'm assuming I'll find your partner up beyond where Felisha and I saw you yesterday somewhere. And Christine better be in good health, or I will make damn sure you hang! As for right now, hand over your gun belt, because you're under arrest for the kidnapping of Christine Knapp, arson, and attempted murder!"

"Attempted murder?" Jim asked, surprised by the seriousness of the accusation. "What the hell are you talking about? We never attempted to kill anyone!" he yelled loudly as he grew enraged. Being arrested for such serious charges was not part of the plan. Even if Christine was returned to her parents, the kidnapping, arson, and especially the attempted murder charges would remain, and he could be in jail until a court date. If the jury found his crimes reprehensible enough, he could be sentenced to prison for a long time. He had not foreseen having witnesses notice their every step, and he began to panic. He had no control over the rush of adrenaline that flowed through him and the pounding of his heartbeat as his plan came crashing down.

Matt's face hardened. "Perfect admission, Jim. Now drop your gun belt...slowly." Matt's right hand moved closer to his weapon. Jim's revolver and hunting knife were on it. Knives were just as deadly as guns, or even more so because seldom did a person miss with a knife in their hand. Stabbings were often deadly, but so were slashes across the abdomen or other areas where a man could bleed out before they could get medical help. Matt had seen enough knife wounds in his time that he took no chances when a man had a knife.

Jim sighed heavily and raised his hands as he stepped up on the boardwalk. Matt's left-hand clinched Jim's shirt to guide him. "All right, you got me outgunned. But wait... there's one thing you need to know about Christine."

"What's that?" Matt asked as he reached down to take Jim's revolver out of its holster.

"She hates competition!" he said bitterly, and stepped forward quickly and kicked Dillon in the chest with the bottom of his boot. The force of the kick was absorbed partly by Felisha's forearms as they held Dillon in front of her. The kick sent Dillon and Felisha back into the stone wall of the hotel and then down to the ground.

Jim hit Matt in the face with a short right hook to the jaw and stepped backward off the boardwalk onto the street. He pulled his revolver out of its holster to shoot Matt.

William Fasana had moved his hand nearer to his weapon after seeing Jim's reaction to the news of being arrested. William pulled his reverse-handled revolver with his right hand and fired two quick .45 rounds into Jim's gut an inch apart. Simultaneously, Matt pulled his .45 and placed two quick shots in Jim's chest nearly as fast as William had.

Jim fell to his back, his feet crossing upon impact. The crowd that had gathered to watch Ollie threaten Ritchie was stunned by witnessing a man's death transpire as quickly as it had. There were gasps and words of surprise, but it was Felisha beginning to groan as she rubbed the back of her head and Dillon sobbing in terror that caught Matt's attention. Felisha looked at the blood on her hand.

Matt went to kneel beside her quickly. "Dillon, are you okay?" he asked. "Felisha, let me see the back of your head. You are bleeding."

She looked at him with the most enraged wide eyes he had ever had gaze upon him. "Get away from me! Stay away from us!" She stood up quickly and shoved Matt away with both hands. "Stay away from my son and me!" She grabbed Dillon by the hand and began to walk him into the hotel.

"Let me help you," Matt said, not understanding why she had pushed him away.

Felisha turned around and glared at him with no softness in her eyes. "I never want to see you again! Now leave us alone!" She began to cry as she continued into the hotel at a fast pace. Dillon was still bawling and holding his chest.

"Matt Bannister killed Bloody Jim Hexum!" a man in the crowd yelled and ran toward the newspaper's office.

The marshal turned around as the crowd gathered around the body of Jim Hexum.

William Fasana looked at the crowd around Jim's body and shook his head in disappointment. He stepped near Matt and said, "I saved your life, and you get the credit."

It was true. Matt had been preoccupied, and if William had not been ready, Jim would have gotten the crucial first shot off before Matt did. At such a close range, there was little room for error. "You're right. Thank you."

William nodded. "Any time, cousin."

Matt took a deep breath to calm the storm of emotions that raged within him. It had happened too fast, and the unexpected had left him stunned. His one suspect was dead, which endangered Christine even more. He still had no answers as to where she was or why they had gone through so much trouble to take her. Time was running out, and he could feel the pressure building to get Christine back before she was left in the river or buried in the ground somewhere. The nagging thought kept repeating itself in his head: *Was her body in the river?* Matt had hunted men who had taken innocent, unwilling women to force themselves upon and then disposed of the body. Jim Hexum was a bad man, but he had never been known to harm anyone he didn't have a bounty for. The motive didn't seem right, and Matt couldn't allow himself to believe that Jim Hexum would take her with the intention of harming her. It wasn't his pattern. There had to be a reason, but he could not think it through. Now Jim was dead, and his only hope of finding Christine was being able to identify the other man with him.

He was irritated by Ritchie Thorne and the public mockery he had made of Matt and his family. If it wasn't for Felisha, he would have settled that confrontation right then and there. Felisha and Dillon had been hurt by a man Matt should have taken physical control of and arrested before he had a chance to hurt them. He had failed to keep them safe. Felisha had a head wound, no matter how superficial it might have been, and head wounds bleed a lot. It might have been a large gash; he had no idea because she had refused to let him help her. All he did know was, he allowed it to happen by not taking physical control of Jim Hexum. He had never seen as much fury in Felisha's eyes as when she said she never wanted to see him again. It had cut a path straight through his heart that hurt, and guilt and uncertainty about their future began to fill a strange hollowness that was forming inside him.

Truet stepped to his side and put a hand on his shoulder. "Let her calm down for a few hours. One thing we do know is, we found the right man."

Matt exhaled to calm his emotions. Truet's presence brought his focus back to the problem at hand. "Unfortunately, he can't tell us much. Let's get his body off the street."

William patted Matt on the back. "Well, look at the bright side. Do you know how many wanted men around the country are going to thank us for killing him?" He laughed.

"Matt," Sheriff Tim Wright said, stepping closer with a well-dressed man beside him. "This is Mister Sebastian Worthington from Portland. He is a Pinkerton detective."

Matt looked at the stranger. He was a decent-sized man with a thick chest and round face. He had brown hair cut respectfully short, and a well-trimmed mustache that gave him a professional appearance in his tan suit under his long black wool coat and brown derby hat. The man stepped forward and put out his hand. "Marshal Bannister. Can we go somewhere private to talk for a bit?" he asked.

William Fasana scoffed. "You're a Pinkerton?"

Sebastian nodded to William. "I am." He turned back to Matt. "My room upstairs perhaps would work fine, Marshal."

Matt nodded. "Sure." He looked at Truet. "We will ride out when I'm done speaking to the detective. Get our horses ready and saddled up, please. I'll meet you at the office."

Truet nodded. "I'll have the undertaker come grab Hexum."

Tim Wright spoke quickly. "Don't worry about Jim's body. Me and my men will take care of it." He planned on putting Jim's body in a casket and putting it up in front of sheriff's office for photos to be taken.

Matt nodded quietly. "Thank you."

The detective stepped down and searched Jim's pockets before saying, "Let's go, Marshal. We have a lot to discuss."

16

The room was spacious and quiet, and Matt took a seat in a leather-back padded chair. Sebastian Worthington removed his hat, revealing a balding head in his middle age, and hung it with his coat on a coat rack. "I picked up some brandy from the lounge. Would you like a glass?" he asked Matt.

"No, thank you. So how can I help you, Mister Worthington? I have a missing lady I need to be looking for."

"Call me, Sebastian, or Detective Worthington, if you insist." He poured himself a glass of brandy, carried it to a leather-back davenport, and sat down. On a table in front of the davenport was a pile of papers. He took a deep breath and exhaled. "Do you know why I am here, Matt?"

Matt shook his head. "No."

"I am here to investigate you."

"Me? For what?" he asked.

"Do you know why Jim Hexum was coming to the hotel today?"

Matt frowned and looked at Sebastian quizzically. "No."

"No idea? No guesses?" Sebastian asked almost sarcastically.

"No, I don't. And I don't have time to play guessing games, either. So, if you would be so kind as to tell me why you're investigating me, I would appreciate it." Matt was getting irritated.

Detective Worthington took a drink of his brandy slowly and set the glass down. "Well, Jim Hexum was coming to talk to me. We had an appointment at one o'clock. He didn't make it because you shot him outside the door of the hotel. Which...seems kind of fishy to me. Doesn't it to you?"

Matt didn't answer. He just looked at the detective and waited for him to continue.

"Well, doesn't it?" he asked, watching Matt carefully.

Matt had no idea what the detective was trying to get at, or for what reason he might be subject to an investigation. Matt shook his head. "No. I was arresting him for the kidnapping of Christine Knapp, and he drew his gun. My cousin and I returned fire. It doesn't sound fishy at all. It was unexpected, but not fishy."

"But you didn't return fire, because he never fired his weapon," the detective pointed out.

Matt took a deep, frustrated breath. "You were there. You saw the whole thing, as did many others. Mister Worthington, what is this about?"

He looked at Matt seriously. "Detective Worthington."

"Right. Is this about what happened downstairs? I don't understand where this is going."

"I will get to the point very shortly. This missing girl Jim Hexum apparently kidnapped, is she a friend of yours?"

"She is."

"And would you say you're very good friends with her?"

"I would say we have become good friends, yes."

"Do understand whatever is spoken in here is strictly confidential, meaning it's not leaving this room, so please be honest. I understand you're involved with a lady named…" he looked at a paper on the table, "Felisha Conway, who is staying in the hotel as we speak. Is that right?"

Matt nodded. "Yes."

"And she's the one who got angry with you downstairs, correct?"

"She did."

"Yeah, she did!" Sebastian repeated as a matter of fact. "Are you committed to Felisha? Is your relationship with her strictly monogamous?"

"Yes, it is."

He looked at Matt. "I've been watching her. She seems like a lovely lady."

"She is."

"Great. So why is it you seem to have a unique and let's say questionable relationship with Christine Knapp?"

Matt laughed quietly. "Can you get to your damn point?"

"Answer the question, Marshal Bannister. I assure you the accusations against you are quite serious, and if they are true, you could be facing severe penalties. My witness was killed by you a few minutes ago, and I assure you, to me, it seems suspicious at best. I know you are in a hurry, but please be patient and answer my questions. Here in a minute, you will understand and be able to defend yourself. Now, about Miss Knapp: are you two lovers or in love?"

Matt smiled and shook his head. "Why does everyone keep asking me questions like that about her? No, we are not. We are friends, and that is all. I have never betrayed Felisha, and she is the one I am in love with. Christine is a friend, and that is all." He watched Sebastian writing something on his paper. "Did Felisha hire you to investigate Christine's and my friendship?" Matt asked, perplexed about the line of questioning.

Sebastian laughed. "No. I'm just trying to figure out the relationship you have with Miss Knapp. What happened to her husband? She was married, yes?"

"He was killed in Denver when their wagon train stopped for a few days. He was stabbed in a saloon. That is how she got employed with Bella and the dance hall,"

"Do you know his name?"

"I should, but for the life of me, I can't remember it at the moment."

"Interesting," he said and wrote that down. "Was it Nathan, by chance?"

Matt shook his head. "No, it was more like Daniel or Robert or something."

Sebastian looked at Matt. "Last question. In the line of duty as a United States Marshal, have you ever misled someone or lied about a case?"

Matt shook his head. "No."

"Are you sure about that? You would testify on the Bible under oath that you have never misled or lied about a mystery or case you were working on or solved for monetary gain?"

Matt frowned. "Detective Worthington, I pride myself on being an honest man. I would most definitely stand in a courtroom and swear on the Bible that I have never misled or lied to solve a case, especially for monetary gain. The corruption's elsewhere in town, not in my office."

The detective picked up a typed paper and handed it to Matt. "Jim Hexum sent this letter to Louis and Divinity Eckman, claiming you had lied about the bodies you stated belonged to their daughter Catherine and her husband, Nathan Webster. According to the letter, you planted the evidence that you got from Catherine to fake her death, which would mean she is still alive and somewhere around here. As you can read, Mister Hexum identified Catherine and promised to hold her until her parents' arrival. Which is tomorrow, but the arranged meeting is on Tuesday at noon in front of the newspaper office. The Eckmans requested me to come here and investigate you, and I assure you, if Catherine is brought to the newspaper's office alive by Jim's partner, you will face charges and prison time."

Matt read the transcript of Jim's letter to the Eckmans and laughed. "You can't be serious? They took Christine, thinking she was..." He almost slipped and said Sarah. "Um, what is her name, Catherine?" He laughed.

"As you can see, your friend was not kidnapped

without a cause. They are holding her for a monetary transaction. My guess is she is quite safe and won't be harmed. Jim Hexum was coming to talk to me about you and the evidence he has against you. Shooting him is suspicious for that reason."

Matt laughed. "Well, this the first I have heard of this! I think everyone who was outside will testify that I had no reason to shoot him other than he was pulling his gun to shoot me. This is ridiculous, Detective."

Sebastian Worthington showed no emotion as he continued in a serious tone, "It may seem so. However, the names written in the letter, the named victims, Possum and Ingrid Overguard, do bring up a problem and may lean toward some truth. I did my research, and Richard Overguard was in the state prison and was released back in April. His last known whereabouts were around here. Richard's nickname was 'Possum,' and he was cellmates with Alan Sperry; that is a fact. Do you see where this is going? If that much is true, Marshal, then why would I doubt the rest of Jim's story? Is Christine Knapp really Catherine Eckman?"

Matt laughed. "No, she is not. Just wait until Tuesday and see for yourself."

"Okay. Do you know where Catherine Eckman is?" he asked pointedly.

Matt looked at the detective with a slight smile. "Yeah, I do. She's buried in a cemetery in California somewhere."

"So, you're not hiding her anywhere? Or knowingly misleading me in any way?"

"I've already told you, I'm an honest man. Integrity is

what I stand on, and to my knowledge, the bodies found in that cabin belonged to Catherine Eckman and her husband. How did I come to that conclusion? From the box of pictures and letters I found buried under a pile of rubbish in a corner."

"I talked to the sheriff this morning. He said he found nothing of the sort when he looked through the cabin."

"I know, since he said the same thing to me. But you don't know our sheriff. He's not exactly the kind to get his hands dirty digging through soot and ash. It'll muss his suit. It was buried under quite a buildup of fallen debris. Have you ever dug through a burn barrel and seen a piece of paper that didn't burn? It's the same thing, detective. I have nothing to hide. I did my job, and that's it. Were they killed by someone else? Maybe. I wasn't there, but it could have been a murder-suicide too. And that was my guess."

"What made you think that?" the detective asked with interest.

"It's my experience that living on the run from the law wears people down, and eventually people break down. Maybe they just didn't feel like they could go on living like that, so they ended it. Maybe she was leaving him to go back to her parents, and he shot her. There is no way to know. All I know is she was shot in the chest, and he had a bullet to his head. And it was our sheriff and undertaker who determined that, not me. I just went back up there looking for some something to identify them and found the box buried in debris."

"And the chess set?"

"Correct."

"Did you find a gun?"

"No."

"Either did the sheriff, interestingly enough."

Matt shrugged. "Well, they may have been murdered. I don't know. I haven't heard any rumors or of anyone who knew them. I just found a box, is all."

"And you didn't plant it like Jim accused you of in the letter?"

Matt laughed. "No! I did not plant the evidence to protect Christine. Wait till Tuesday, and you'll see what kind of idiots we have around here. I cannot believe this. Are we done? I need to go tell Bella that Christine is being held prisoner by a couple of fools who have no idea what they are doing." He laughed.

"Detective Worthington, you came all this way for nothing, and worse, so are the Eckmans. You'd think they'd been through enough without this...hoax. There is no other word for it. But in the meantime, I am going to be looking for my friend. I'm sure she's not comfortable wherever she is. Do you have a problem with that, Detective?"

Sebastian raised his eyebrows. "I need to ask you; did you know the Eckmans were coming here?"

"No! I had no idea about any of this crap! But I look forward to hearing what the Eckmans say when they are given Christine." He chuckled.

Sebastian took a deep breath. "I'm afraid it won't be too humorous after all, Marshal Bannister. Yesterday afternoon they were set up and robbed about fifty miles from here on the other side of the Blue Mountains. Louis

Eckman refused to give the money for his daughter's return away and was killed."

"What?" Matt asked, surprised.

"He was killed. One of our detectives riding security was also killed. Another detective and Missus Eckman were not injured. They will be here later tomorrow night, and will meet her daughter on Tuesday as scheduled."

Matt was silent as he absorbed the news. He would have to let Sarah and Nathan know. "I'm...sorry to hear that. Wow, that's a horrible thing. Did they catch the killers?"

"Not yet. But they *will* be caught and tried accordingly."

"It's all for a hoax, Detective Worthington. Their daughter is not here. They are coming for nothing. He was killed for nothing."

Sebastian nodded. "I tend to believe that myself, but I will warn you: if there is any truth at all to these accusations, you will be indicted to the fullest extent of the law."

"I'm not too worried about it, Detective. Do you know who Jim's partner is?" Matt asked.

Sebastian shook his head. "I had hoped to speak to Mister Hexum and find that out myself. No, I don't. But if your story is true, he'll be facing charges himself, so try not to kill him if you find him."

Matt sighed heavily. "Well, at least we know Christine's not floating down the river."

Sebastian chuckled lightly. "She's worth twenty thousand dollars to them alive and well. I doubt they'll hurt her too badly, Marshal."

17

Annie Lenning was wearing in a brown dress with tan ruffles that came down vertically to her waist. Over her dress, she wore a thick black wool coat to keep her warm. Her long dark hair was down and flowed over her coat to below her shoulder blades. She wore a black decorative hat on her head that had black lace and ribbons tied around the band that followed her hair down to her shoulders. A knit red scarf covered her neck, and a pair of warm gloves kept her hands warm as she walked along the street. She seldom made it to Branson, and when she did, it was usually with her children and for a particular purpose. She hardly ever had the chance to wander around and look at the various shops at a leisurely pace and simply enjoy herself. She took advantage of the opportunity and did a little shopping along the way. She had already carried a few items, such as new shoes for her children, back to Matt's house before leaving again. She entered the Monarch Hotel and paused at the reception desk to inquire what room Felisha was in. The

Monarch was a high-class hotel that prided itself on elegance and the best of everything for their guests. The entry was centered in the building, with the Monarch Lounge to the left side of the reception desk and the Monarch Restaurant to the right. The hotel rooms were on the upper three floors. The grand staircase at the end of the corridor led to the upper floors. To the side of the stairs was one room that had been refitted and made into an apartment for Annie's cousin, William Fasana. He had been hired to keep the peace and watch over the hotel after a few lumbermen forced their way into the lounge one night on a drunken binge and caused some trouble and property damage. William got free room and board and a small wage, and could keep any winnings from the gambling tables in the lounge. Being a professional gambler, and with the wealth coming into the hotel, it was an offer he couldn't refuse.

William Fasana had seen Annie walk in from where he was seated in the Monarch Restaurant and stepped quickly out to meet her at the reception desk. "Annie, you missed the show! You should've been here a couple of hours ago," William Fasana said with a smile. "You could've watched your brother and me double up on old Bloody Jim Hexum and put four bullets into him before he could get a shot off. I saved your brother's life," he said proudly.

Annie frowned. "What are you talking about?"

"Well, you should walk down to the sheriff's office and ask Bloody Jim himself. He's just standing around," William said with a smile. Sheriff Tim Wright and his deputies had placed Hexum's body in a casket and had it standing upright against the sheriff office for everyone to see.

Annie frowned. "Stop with the riddles and start talking, William." There was not one ounce of humor for William on her face.

He explained everything that had taken place in front of the hotel and finished with Felisha being knocked down and cutting the back of her head open and then yelling at Matt. He laughed. "Felisha was scarier than Matt and me put together! That woman's got a fiery side, for sure. I suppose that's why I never married, you know? Women are just too unpredictable, and for no reason at all. Not you, though," he added quickly.

"No, you never married because every woman who ever met you wants to kill you," Annie said simply. She continued speaking while William chuckled. "Do you know what room Felisha is in? We're supposed to go buy some things for supper tonight. We're making dinner for Truet and Matt."

"Truet, huh?" he asked, raising his eyebrows up and down teasingly.

"Knock it off, William."

"Oh, he's a nice guy. What's Matt think of you hooking up with Truet, though? I bet he doesn't know yet, does he?"

"No, he doesn't know. We're telling him tonight," Annie said with a slightly nervous smile. "I really can't believe Lee told you that we were courting."

"Lee tells me everything, Annie. You ought to know that by now. What do you think Matt will say?" he asked with an expectant smile.

Annie shrugged. "I really have no idea. We're not children, so he can't say too much."

William laughed. "You sound so unsure about that. So, let me get this straight: you're going to tell him you're courting his best friend the day his fiancé broke it off with him?" He laughed. "I love your timing, Annie! Can I come over for dinner to watch?"

"No!" she said, staring at him without a hint of a smile. "What room is Felisha in?"

ANNIE WALKED up the stairs and knocked on Felisha's hotel room door.

The door opened after a second knock, and Felisha stood in the doorway with an angry expression on her face. "Annie?" she asked, surprised to see her.

"Don't tell me you weren't expecting me. We're supposed to go buy some goods to make dinner for the boys tonight, remember? So, come on, and get your boots on, and let's go."

Felisha smiled sadly. "I'm...not going tonight, Annie. I don't know if you heard what happened, but I'm just not in the mood to see anyone or up to talking about it."

"William told me what happened. How is your head? He said it was bleeding pretty good."

"It hurts, but I'll be all right. Dillon will probably have a bruise on his chest. I was so afraid he had a broken sternum or internal bleeding somewhere that I had the hotel contact the doctor and had him look at Dillon. The doctor said he'll be fine. He gave me three stitches in my head while he was here. William paid the doctor fees for us, which was very kind of him. Matt didn't even stick around long enough to know I needed a doctor." Her hostility showed in her eyes.

"It doesn't sound like you gave him a chance to, according to William," Annie said simply.

"No, I didn't!" Her large brown eyes widened in anger. "My son could have been killed! We were in the middle of a gunfight, and if that man would've pulled the trigger, my son could have been killed! *I* could've been killed, and I'm all Dillon has. We watched Matt kill that man, and you think that's not traumatic for a little boy? It scared the daylights out of me, so what do you think it did to my eight-year-old son? No, I did not want Matt around me, and I still don't! We could've been killed, and we were just standing there! Have you ever seen someone get shot in front of you, Annie? Your brother and William shot him too many times to count, and I was just praying no bullets would hit Dillon or me! It was terrifying, and I never want to experience anything like that again. Maybe I should have never come over here to begin with, but I won't put my son in that position again. Dillon is petrified."

Annie frowned. "I am sorry that happened."

"Have you ever watched someone get shot multiple times and die in front of you?" Felisha asked pointedly.

Annie shook her head. "I haven't. But I grew up around it."

"What do you mean, 'you grew up around it?'"

"Just that. I grew up hearing about gunfights from my uncles, my brothers, and my cousins, and...I remember the day Matt killed the Dobson Gang. I saw their bodies. I grew up around it, Felisha. I knew there would be someone killed when he went after Elizabeth's kidnappers last Christmas, and I wasn't surprised to read about him being in a gunfight when he went after Truet. It comes with the territory of being a US Marshal. Back East, they might sit behind a desk and sign papers, but Matt's not the kind to sit on his duff when there's a murderer on the loose. And he never will be."

Felisha leaned against the doorjamb. "Let me ask you: if you were with Truet and that happened with your son, would you want to be around Truet again?"

Annie shrugged. "Of course. Like I said, I grew up around it. It's a risk you take when you fall in love with a lawman. To answer your question, I'd know to get out of the way. You can see trouble brewing if you watch for it. I would have taken my son inside before it happened and be happy Matt or Truet survived it. What happened to you wasn't Matt's fault, it doesn't sound like to me. He did what he had to do to save his own life. It's not the first time, and it won't be the last.

"Felisha, I asked you last night how serious you were about Matt. I don't want his heart broken, but you need to know he is what he is, and he isn't going to change. He's a lawman, and there will always be people who want him dead. So, my advice is to choose carefully, because he is a wonderful man and he'd treat you like a queen, but he will always be a lawman first. That badge and the responsibility that comes with it is all he knows. He loves you, but you must decide if he's worth loving enough to live with the fears and risks that come with who he is. That badge isn't just a career, it's who he is. And I won't lie to you...the details can be terribly bloody and cruel. Choose carefully, Felisha. I hope you give him a chance, because he had no choice. In fact, his shooting that man may have saved Dillon's life and yours. You think about that for a while."

"It was nice to meet you, Annie," Felisha said shortly. There was moisture in her eyes.

Annie smiled sadly. "Nice to meet you, too. If you get hungry, you know where to find us."

Felisha shook her head. "No, thanks."

Annie nodded and walked away. She had a list of goods in mind that she needed to buy to make dinner. It would be a bit harder to make the meal alone, but she would do it to feed Truet and Matt.

18

Truet knew Matt didn't feel like talking from the expression on his face and his withdrawn body language. He knew Matt well enough to know he would talk when he was ready to, and until then, it was best to give him room to think and time to sort out whatever was on his mind. He could see Matt was troubled, but it was hard to tell if it was having to shoot Jim Hexum or something the detective had said about the shooting or something else. No one other than Matt knew what the detective wanted to talk to him about. What Truet did know was Matt would be concerned and probably confused about why Felisha had lashed out at him at as viciously as she had. It had taken Truet by surprise as well. He had known Felisha for over three years, and he had never seen her act like that before. He had let Matt ride in silence as they headed out of town toward the silver mine's company housing development known as the Slater Mile, but finally, Truet cleared his throat and asked, "Were you able to talk to Felisha?"

Matt shook his head. "I didn't even try."

"I think she was just scared. That whole thing with Jim Hexum was unexpected. Give her some time to calm down, Matt. It'll be all right."

Matt took a deep breath and stopped his horse to speak to Truet in the privacy of the open road. He hesitated before saying, "Do you remember when I told you what I was going to do with the bodies for Sarah and Nathan and you emphatically told me not to?"

Truet looked at Matt with a hint of concern. "Yes. Why?"

Matt smiled. "Jim Hexum wrote a detailed letter to Louis Eckman and named the folks who were killed and accused me of planting the evidence for financial gain. He also stated that I was romantically involved with their daughter. Jim Hexum and whoever his partner is know I planted the evidence. They know Sarah is alive and well somewhere. Unfortunately, they think it's Christine, and took her."

"What?" Truet exclaimed.

"Louis sent the letter to the Pinkertons, and that's why Detective Worthington is here. To investigate me."

Truet raised his voice. "Matt! I told you! You can't cover one crime up with another. You should've found the killers and sent the real dead people's family a notice. You could have written a letter to Sarah's parents at any time to end their bounty on Nathan. Look, I like them too, but you can't risk your life to help them. Not the way you did! I told you that then."

Matt responded calmly, "A letter from me wouldn't end the bounty, it would only let them know where Sarah and Nathan were. Bounty hunters don't care about the law, at least not the ones the Eckmans pay for." He continued, "Louis and Divinity Eckman agreed to pay twenty thousand dollars to get her back. They set up a meeting for Tuesday here in town. Yesterday, they were robbed fifty miles from here, and Louis was killed. His wife will be here tomorrow night to make the trade on Tuesday."

Truet smiled slowly. "That's...insane. You don't know who has Christine, or what proof he has that it wasn't Sarah and Nathan in the cabin?"

Matt shook his head slowly. "In short, no. All I know is what I found in the cabin. If I was wrong, then I was wrong, but it was in the cabin."

Truet scoffed. "You're sticking to your story? If this goes to trial and all the evidence is laid out, with the sheriff's testimony of not finding anything, you're going to lose, because the sheriff's not lying, you are!

"You know as well as I do that once you tell a lie, you have to tell another lie to cover that one, and then another and another just to keep covering your trail of lies. Then someone, probably the prosecutor, will look back and see all the ruts in your story and tear you to shreds. You have someone out there who knows who was killed up there in that cabin, and it sounds like your friend Christine is caught in the middle of it now. Lord willing, she won't go through what Jenny Mae did or be killed in the process of delivering her to the Eckmans!" Truet said heatedly.

"You have put yourself in a puddle of sewer by lying to begin with, and now that puddle is turning into quicksand and you're going to be eating sewer for breakfast, lunch, and dinner if you don't watch every word you say and watch them every step of the way! Matt, your whole reputation is based upon your integrity, and honesty is a big part of that! What's going to happen if it comes out that you lied about this? Can you imagine the humiliation? And what would Felisha say if your lie became the most scandalous scheme since...probably ever around here? And with Louis Eckman being killed over this now, it's becoming national news!"

Matt pressed his lips together and said sincerely, "That's why I need to go tell Sarah and Nathan about her parents and advise them to stay on the ranch. I would go there now, but I'm a bit worried about the detective following me. I don't trust him. I figure if I just stick to my story and they bring the wrong girl, I'll be forgotten about. The humiliation will be on the kidnappers, whoever he or they are. I don't think they can prove a thing as long as Sarah and Nathan stay out of sight." He shrugged. "Everything will be all right."

"I don't like it," Truet said. "Someone out there killed those people, and they know you're lying. I'm not comfortable with not knowing who *they* are."

"I know who killed them. It had to be the Sperry-Helms Gang. The couple murdered were named Richard and Ingrid Overguard. He went by the name 'Possum,' and was a cellmate with a guy named Alan Sperry in prison. My older brothers know Alan Sperry and his brothers, although I don't know them myself. Anyway, Possum was released in April and came here to join up with the gang most likely. The Pinkerton detective told me that much."

"How does he know?"

"The letter the kidnappers wrote to Louis Eckman made a detailed accusation and, researching like a detective should, he discovered the rest. He was pretty thorough."

"I've been hearing a lot about the Sperry-Helms Gang lately. They sound like a bad bunch. Are you sure you want them having that leverage over your head?" Truet asked seriously.

Matt smirked sadly. "They are probably quite excited about it, really. They're getting away with murder. They had ought to appreciate me for it."

"That's not right. Where's the justice for the Overguards? It doesn't seem right their family doesn't know what happened to their loved ones and the murderers are getting away with it."

Matt frowned. "We will try to locate their relatives and notify them. I can always have Uncle Luther make a tombstone or two to stick on a couple of the unknown graves, if necessary."

Truet smiled despite himself. "Missus Overguard is buried in California under a tombstone that says Catherine Eckman. And you're going to put a tombstone for her on an empty grave?"

Matt nodded. "Well, not empty, just unknown. I said if necessary. Anyway, over there is where Felisha and I ran into Jim and his partner. Let's ride into Slater's Mile and ask around. It's very possible they are keeping Christine in a shack out here."

"Has anyone ever told you that you have a twisted sense of justice?" Truet asked.

Matt smiled at the question. "No, they haven't. But it worked with getting you out of Idaho alive."

Truet snorted. "You are the most deceptively honest man I've ever known, Matt."

"Only when it's called for to save someone's life. Let's go."

They left the main road and headed down an access road that went slightly downhill through a thin forest of trees and brush to a wide area that had rows of tiny shacks that were built to give the basics of living and nothing more. It was laid out like a city plat map, with nine small blocks with three roads going vertically and three horizontally. The cabins lined the vertical streets and faced each other across the road. There was very little space between cabins to the sides or to the backs. The small cabins were compacted together to fit as many as they could in the space available.

Privacy and comfort for the company employees was not a concern. Simple housing close to the mine was the objective, and it had been thrown together as fast as they could build it. To accommodate the hundred and fifty cabins, there was a series of three long outhouses with eight stalls in each one on the three vertical streets. Four stalls faced the left side of the road, four stalls faced the right side to serve the homes on that side of the street. The outhouses were separated by a couple of hundred feet and placed near the center of each block.

The company housing community that was supposed to be a benefit for the mine employees may have one time been an attraction, but it had become a slum of discarded trash and filth, leading to a hefty rat population. As they rode into the complex, the stench of an overcrowded and uncared-for community overwhelmed their senses. They watched a homely older woman walk out of one of the privy doors with blackened eyes and a bruised face. She hid her face when she saw Matt and Truet ride by. Another man stood outside his shack urinating beside his porch. The smell of the human waste from the congested privies was noticeable as they rode by the first set.

Up ahead, they saw a man and a woman playing outside with their children in what little grass they had in front of their shack. The woman pointed at Matt and Truet as they neared and her husband turned around. He was a young man in his twenties, with a friendly smile and an affectionate hug for the toddler son he held.

Matt stopped his horse. "Hello. I'm Matt Bannister, and this is my deputy Truet Davis."

The man smiled wider and stepped forward. "Oh, you don't have to introduce yourself, I know who you are. Your deputy, too. It's nice to meet you. I'm Lawrence Barton, and this is my wife, Lucille. And that's our oldest Michael, and this little guy is Ray." He shook Matt's and Truet's hands.

His wife Lucille stepped forward with their five-year-old son Michael. She was a young lady with long curly dark hair and a lean, attractive face. She wasn't what one would expect to be living in such a horrible place. Her husband was a clean-cut, handsome man. They were poor, but their children had shoes and coats on to protect them from the cold. "Hello," she said, with a hint of embarrassment due to her appearance.

"Nice to meet you, folks," Matt said. "We were just riding through and looking around. Have you noticed anything suspicious around here? Maybe some yelling or something that isn't too normal in the past day?"

Lawrence frowned and shook his head. "There's always yelling around here. Every weekend there's fighting and screaming."

"Nothing out of the ordinary that you've noticed?"

Lawrence smiled. "Fat Frank passed out on the privy this morning, and his wife left him there. Other than that, no."

Matt smiled. "Huh. Sounds interesting, but not what I'm looking for."

Lucille asked, "What are you looking for, Marshal? Lawrence works every day, so I might be able to tell you more if I can."

"A lady from the dance hall was taken last night. I have reason to believe she is being held somewhere out here. Maybe right in here somewhere. You'd recognize her if you saw her. She's wearing an elaborate dress, no doubt, and is quite beautiful."

Lawrence and Lucille both shook their heads. "No, I haven't seen her around here, or heard anything out of the ordinary," Lawrence said. "Trust me, the only beautiful lady around here is my wife. I hope you find her, though."

Lucille smiled and looked at her husband affectionately.

A man walked out of a neighboring shack, stumbled

into his yard, and vomited. He bent over and heaved loudly as a yellowish liquid poured out onto the ground. Lucille looked repulsed and she told her children to not watch their neighbor.

Lawrence said, "We're only here until we can afford a place in town. I just started at the mine a few weeks ago. This isn't where we want to raise our kids."

Matt nodded as the vomiting man wiped his mouth with his dirty sleeve, stood upright, and looked at Matt. He saw Matt's badge and walked back inside without saying a word. "I don't blame you. Have you talked to my brother Lee about one of his places?"

Lawrence shook his head. "I don't know who your brother is, Marshal. We just moved here from Utah. I'm afraid we don't know anyone around here."

"Well, I'll ask him for you and get back to you soon enough. You're right, you don't want to raise those boys out here. It's nice to meet you, Lawrence and Lucille. But we have to get going."

"Hey, are you ever in your office? Maybe one of these days we could stop in and chat for a while?" Lawrence asked.

Matt nodded. "Anytime."

"Are you ever looking for another deputy?" Lucille asked. "I hate Lawrence having to go into that mine. It's too dangerous."

"You might not want him to be a deputy marshal either, Missus Barton. Things can get dangerous real fast sometimes," Matt explained.

Truet nodded. "That's true."

"Marshal, that mine is more dangerous." The expression on her face was one of fear for her husband and a desperate plea for work aboveground.

Matt agreed. "Maybe it is. I've never been in the mine. There is always the lumber mill, grist mills, the granite quarry, and a lot of shops and stores. I already have two deputies without experience in law enforcement. If I hire another, he must be an experienced gunman, and you don't look like you are," he said to Lawrence.

Lawrence tightened his lips and shook his head. "That, I'm not. I'm just a laborer."

"Check out the mill or the quarry. Either one is safer than the mine. We're going to go ride around a bit. It was nice to meet you all."

They rode around the community and were glad to leave the filth, rats and cockroaches that had infested the community when they were done. They rode farther past the silver mine than Truet had expected to go, looking for any sign of wagon tracks leading to anywhere suspicious Jim Hexum and his partner could have taken Christine. Truet asked, "We've come a long way, Matt. Speaking of Christine, I don't think Felisha appreciates your friendship with her."

Matt's face grew somber as he said, "I don't think it matters, Truet. She doesn't want to see me anymore."

"Well, we'll find out soon enough."

"What's that mean?"

Truet breathed in deeply before answering. "Annie and Felisha were going to make dinner tonight at our place."

"Huh? I thought Annie was going home today?"

"She changed her mind. Her children are at your

brother Adam's, and she says they won't mind watching them for another day. She was going to wire Willow Falls and let him know."

"Do you think Felisha will be there?"

Truet shrugged. "Do you think Annie will let her miss it?"

"She might try to convince her, but Felisha looked pretty adamant about not seeing me again."

"I guess a better question would be how mad do you think Felisha would be if she did make dinner with Annie and we never showed up? Granted, I didn't tell you about it until now, but I'm getting hungry."

Matt sighed. "I'll be honest with you, Truet: if I knew who was working with Jim, I would have an idea of where Christine might be. But I don't know. She could be anywhere, in a house in Branson or over in Natoma with the Sperry-Helms Gang, for all I know. I thought since I seen them coming back toward town from up here that they may have someplace up here they're keeping her in. Jim Hexum wasn't familiar with this area, so whoever has Christine is the one who knows the area and is behind it all. We've come what, five or six miles, and haven't seen anything worth noting. We may be wasting our time looking up here. We don't even have any useful information to go on since Jim's not saying much."

Matt looked at Truet with a troubled expression and continued, "Truet, I have never given up looking for anyone in my life, but for whatever the reason, I am not thinking clearly. I feel off-kilter and have too much on my mind to focus right. I know Christine is out there somewhere, counting on me to find her, but I don't know where to look! If anything happens to her, I will never forgive myself for not finding her, and maybe that's why I feel the way I do. Maybe...I don't know. I'd look for her all night, but where?" he asked, raising his voice in frustration. "Did they take her to Galt? That's the only place up this road, and that's still miles away. She could be in one of those shacks back there in Slater's Mile, or anywhere in between here and Willow Falls!" He took a breath and added quietly, "I don't know where to look."

Truet spoke softly. "When you don't know what to do, there is only one thing *to* do, and that's pray. Look, you know she'll be in front of the newspaper office on Tuesday. She's worth twenty thousand dollars to someone. I think your detective is right; they're not going to risk losing that much money by harming her. We could search all night long and still not find her. I know you don't want to, but let's go home and see our ladies." He added quickly, "You know, what they made us for *our* dinner, I mean."

Mat took a long, deep breath as his eyes filled with a slight mist. "I've never given up on anyone, Truet, and I sure as hell don't want to give up looking for my friend."

"We're not finding much up here, Matt," Truet said simply. "With all the things going on right now, I suggest we just go home, eat some dinner, enjoy what we can, and be still and know God is working on our behalf like the Bible says He does. I think you'll be able to focus more clearly when you get things situated right with Felisha. That's probably what's got you shaken up. That and Christine missing. I know you care for her. You can't deny that either."

Matt stared straight ahead at the road as it rose higher and made a turn. "If they touch her, I'll kill every one of them," Matt said pointedly.

Truet was taken aback by the words. "When I was standing over Mick Rodman, about to kill him, what was it you said? 'I didn't want to live with the memory of it?' 'I didn't want to be haunted by it,' I believe you said."

Matt smiled sadly. "Truet, the difference is, I already am." He sighed with a hint of defeat. "Let's go home."

They turned around and rode back toward town, not knowing that just ahead around a slight bend, an abandoned covered wagon had been pushed off the road into the trees.

19

Christine Knapp watched with growing anticipation as Pick Lawson yawned and looked to be growing more exhausted as the day dragged on. He had obviously not slept too much the night before, either, and had woken up early. His eyelids were heavy as he laid back on his cot, fighting falling asleep. He sat back up and kicked his legs down to the floor to sit upright. He opened his eyes wide and then yawned again.

She sat on her cot with her back against the rock wall with a blanket across her lap. "You can take a nap, Pick. I'm not going anywhere. I'll wake you up in an hour or two. Maybe I'll even make supper for you," Christine said softly. "I wish you guys would have brought a book to read or something, though." She tried to sound content despite her anxiousness to get away.

Pick looked at her and shook his head slowly. "No, I'm all right. I can't risk you getting away."

"Because of the money you're getting?"

"Yup," he said tiredly. "I have never gotten a break in

my life, Christine. That money will get me away from here, and away from the Sperry-Helms Gang, and started on a new life in San Francisco. I was joking about your father getting me a job with the railroad, but the more I think about it, the more I like the idea if he would. I'd like to go straight and make a living legally. I lost two good friends this past summer running from the law up in the Wallowas, and I don't want to do it anymore. I'm lucky to be alive as it is. Your father's money will change my life."

"Money might help get you started on something, but every dollar you spend is a dollar less. That alone won't change your life. If you really want to change your life, you need to change your heart, and you can't do that without accepting Jesus becoming the Lord of your life. He will change your heart from the inside out."

Pick yawned. "I don't think Jesus wants much to do with me. You can't do what I've done over the years and expect the good Lord to just forget about it, now can you?"

"Actually, yes, you can. Jesus forgives everything you've ever done as soon as you ask him too. We must repent and commit ourselves to him, but forgiveness is exactly why he went to the cross. Jesus wants everything to do with you. He wants you. He can change your life if you let him."

Pick smirked and gave a short chuckle. "I don't see myself becoming one of those bible-thumpers carrying a book to church every Sunday. I don't think a man like me can change into someone like that."

"You'd be surprised what God can do. Matt's a Christian, and he carries his bible to church every Sunday. It certainly hasn't diminished his reputation, has it?" she asked. "And just so you're aware, he's a friend of mine and is looking for me, no doubt. I know he's looking for me by now, even though the lady he is courting is in town," she said confidently.

Pick's lips curved upward just a bit a bit he fought to keep his eyes open. "I don't know who his other lady is, but he sure shines with you."

An expression of sadness flashed across her face. "He's a good man. If you release me and turn yourself in, I will do everything I can to get him to let you go. And you'd still get your money on Tuesday when...my parents come to town." She decided since he wasn't going to believe they weren't her parents, she might as well play along.

"Wish I could believe that. I really do. But I'm afraid I can't risk it." He looked at her empathetically. "Christine, I am sorry, but I need to tie you up. I can't keep my eyes open."

She shook her head. "You don't need to tie me up, Pick. I have nowhere to go."

"Back to town, maybe?" Pick asked sarcastically. "You can't tell me you're enjoying yourself up here." He stood up and stretched with a tired yawn. "I just need to sleep for an hour or two is all."

She argued pointedly, "I don't know where town is, and I'd be a fool to run out into the cold with just a ballgown on, not knowing where I am. You really don't need to tie me up."

"Even a child knows if you follow the creek, it goes to

the river, and the river goes through town. I hate to do it, but I need to tie you up, Christine."

"Pick, honestly, you don't have to. Where I am going to go? I don't know how far from town we are, and it's way too cold to go running through the woods in a ballgown. I'll be right here where it's warm when you wake up. Besides, you're not hurting me, and I'm going back home on Tuesday." She paused to let him speak, but he only looked at her, debating over her words. She added softly, "You've treated me very well, Pick. And I appreciate that, because I know that other guy wouldn't have. The ropes burn my wrists. See?" She held out her arms to reveal the rope burns on her wrists from the night before.

Pick looked at her wrists and frowned. "We'll compromise. I'll take your boots instead."

Christine shook her head. "That won't work either because of the glass back there." She nodded toward the back of the mine.

Pick sat down on the cot. "Fine. I must get some rest. Christine, I apologize about the burns on your wrist and your black eye. I swear to you I won't let Jim touch you again, or tie your hands so tight, either. I'm going to trust you'll be here when I wake up. Please don't leave, because if hypothermia doesn't kill you, Jim might if he catches you outside where I can't protect you. I don't want to see you get hurt."

Christine nodded. "Your friend scares me."

"He's not my friend. Wake me up in a couple of hours, would you? And I'll make up some salmon for us."

"If I'm awake. I may just take a nap too," she said,

lying down on her cot and closing her eyes as she pulled her blankets up over her shoulders.

Half an hour later, Pick was breathing deeply, his eyes moving back and forth under their lids. Knowing he was in a deep sleep, Christine slowly and as quietly as she could stood up from her cot, wrapped her two blankets around her shoulders to cover her, and moved toward the makeshift door. She lifted on one side, moved it just enough to slip out of the mineshaft, and carefully put the door back where it was. She walked through the brush and out into the sunlight stretching down through the sheer cliffs of the gorge. Up above her fifty feet or so, she could see the trees of the forest towering over the walls. Though the gorge she was standing in was dry, she could hear water not too far away. She walked quickly to the mouth of the gorge and gazed in wonder at a jagged cliff overgrown by green moss and other vegetation directly in front of her. It stood much higher than the one the mineshaft was dug into. A shallow river ran through it, a constant flow over the rocks as it followed the cliffs downriver. The place was called Spider Creek Ravine, but it was a series of narrow and deep gorges that splintered off one another in a maze of spectacular beauty and wonder at how they were ever made. The walls of the main gorge were lush with thick green moss and fallen logs that had slipped down the ravine from above. The bottom was rounded river rock, and the water was crystal clear. On a warm sunny day, it would be one of the most beautiful places on Earth to take one's time and explore, but she was in a hurry to get away from Pick before he woke up or Jim Hexum returned. She began following the river through the gorge, which narrowed and widened at inter-mittent places where other gorges branched off like a spider's web of alcoves and narrow passageways barely big enough for a person to fit through, although the next one might be big enough for a train to pass through. Where they went or how far back into the depths of the rock, only God knew. Some drained small flows of water, and others were as dry as the one they had camped in.

Christine was afraid of Pick waking up and coming after her on horseback. She would never be able to outrun Pick's horse, but even more frightening was the possibility of running into Jim Hexum while in the narrow confines of the gorge. She moved quickly along the edge of the river to keep as dry as she could. The afternoon had heated up, but in the heavy shadows of the gorge, it was still as cold as it had been that morning. The coldness was already penetrating her blankets, and her leather boots were soaked from the water.

She passed another arm of the splintered gorge, came around a slight bend, and found herself looking at an open area on her left side where the sheer wall suddenly ceased to exist and a large bank of trees and brush reached down to touch the river. It was a tall forest-covered ridge that seemed to go on forever, but the slope wasn't unmanageable on foot. She could tell by the horse tracks that this was where Jim and Pick had led her down from the road to enter the gorge. A large pool of clear water was before her. At the far end of the pool, the narrow gorge cut through the mountain like they'd never been interrupted and continued downward. Christine had to decide to either go up the steep mountain to the road on top of it or continue to go down through the gorge where the water was. The risk going down the throat of the gorge was getting wet and contracting hypothermia or coming to a large waterfall she couldn't get around. There was a possibility of injury as well, and of not being able to get out of the beautiful yet unknown and unpredictable gorge. She could hear water flowing, and the unmistakable sound of a waterfall from where she stood. Beyond the throat of the gorge, there was no telling what was ahead. On the other hand, if she began climbing up the mountain, her tracks in the dirt would quite possibly be seen, and Pick could find her before she ever reached the top. It would take her too long to climb up and find the road. Pick could wake up in an hour, and be right behind her in no time. Even if she made it to the road, she took the chance of running into Jim Hexum. He had not returned since the night before, and was expected to come back.

Christine walked through the shallow water to get near the bank of the mountain and paused. She looked at the gateway into the gorge and could see no farther than two granite cliffs and the water running between them. She looked back upstream where she had just come from worriedly, and then up the large mountain. She prayed, "Lord, I don't know which way to go." She knew the most reasonable route was to take the mountain to the road, but Pick could not ride his horse into the gorge, she didn't think, not the way the waterfall sounded, anyway. She decided to walk carefully to the entrance of the gorge and look to see if she could get around the waterfall she heard.

The water left the pool with a swift current over solid rock, and when she stepped onto the smooth rock, the current swept her feet out from under her, and she slid on a natural rockslide through the narrow cliffs. She cried out in shock from the cold water and the terror of not knowing what was ahead. She could see the water dropping over an edge, and she had no way of stopping herself since there was nothing for her to grab hold of since the rock was too smooth and slippery to cling to.

She prayed quickly, and her scream echoed through the gorge as she neared the edge. The stream carried her for maybe sixty feet before spitting her over the edge. She dropped about ten feet, and as she fell, her upper body turned downward and she landed face-first in a pool of freezing water about six feet deep. She surfaced in a panic and screamed for help as she tried to swim to the edge hoping for shallow water. The intense cold of the water felt like ice and sent an abrupt shockwave of danger throughout her body. She wanted to curl up in a tight fetal position to fight the cold. Her boots, multi-layered ballgown, and the blankets weighed her down and restricted her swimming motion. The current pushed her past a rock she was reaching out for, but suddenly her head was pulled underwater from the hem of her gown getting caught on an underwater log at the bottom of the pool. She could feel the current gliding past her, and in a panic to break free from the sunken log, she yanked on the dress to rip it free with all the strength she could muster.

On the third pull, her hem ripped free and she was taken by the current backward right into a large stone.

She hit it a jarring blow with her upper back and the back of her head, then spun around the rock and with some desperate steps that slipped on the riverbed, she was able to regain her footing as the river shallowed. She cried out loudly repeatedly as she left the pool below the falls and staggered toward the ravine wall where the water was the least deep. Christine could barely breathe from the unimaginable cold that saturated every bit of her body. She began to wring out what water she could from her dress with her reddened and numb hands. She had lost the wool blankets in the river, and saw one caught on a rock where the water was once more knee-deep just a little way downriver. She ran into the river to grab the blanket, and wrung it out and draped it over the top of her head and shoulders to wrap it tightly around her.

Her body shook uncontrollably, and her breathing was labored. She bent over slightly and crossed her arms over her chest and squeezed her elbows tight to her sides. She stood motionless for a moment while her teeth chattered, and her muscles contracted to force the blood up to her chest. She was freezing, and too cold to move.

Through her chattering teeth and strained voice, she prayed, "Lord, h...h...help me please..." If there was one thing she knew, she couldn't stay where she was, or she would die of hypothermia right where she stood. She was tempted to scale the waterfall if she was able and run back to the mineshaft to the warmth of the fire and a cup of Pick's tart black coffee. If she could have scaled the waterfall, she would have, but there was no way she could do it in her condition. She could stand there and scream for Pick and pray he heard her, but he was a mile away and the roar of the waterfall would most likely drown her voice out. There was no choice but to keep going down the gorge and hope it led to Branson soon. She knew she was in danger of hypothermia, but she wasn't about to lay down and die.

She had no idea how far downriver Branson was, but she would find it, Lord willing. She had to move, and move as fast as she could, despite wanting to curl into a ball and try to warm herself up. Her body temperature was dropping with her layers upon layers of wet clothing. If she had been wearing wool, maybe it would have retained some body heat, but she was wearing cotton undergarments and silk, and neither of those offered any support in a hypothermic situation.

She knew it might be wise to take her wet clothing off, but if she were going to die, she refused to be found naked. The only man that she ever wanted to see her naked was her husband, not someone searching for her or someone who happened to discover her body by accident.

Although her breathing was already labored, she counted to three and forced herself to begin walking along the cliff's edge to stay in the shallow water, or in some areas, out of it completely. To keep her mind focused on something other than the cold that sucked the energy out of her, she began to pray again. "L-lord, I'm... c-c-cold! Please help m-me." She walked as quickly as she could while trying to control the shaking of her body. She focused on talking to the Lord, and the dreams she had for the future. She surrendered all she had in her life to

Him, and tried to remain true to one of her favorite verses in the bible: We walk by faith and not by sight.

However, this time it wasn't just her circumstances that appeared dire, it was her basic survival. She prayed to get back to her friends at the dance hall, and prayed that she still had a home to go to. She had no idea if the dance hall was still standing or was a pile of rubble on the street corner. She prayed God would somehow warm her body, or keep her from freezing to death, at least. She prayed that someday she would marry again, and like Bella had once told her, it would be better than her first marriage. She hoped to have a child again with a man she loved, and raise their child in their own home like a family should.

She had hopes for the future, which gave her a reason to keep walking along the cold, wet, and dark gorge. Christine kept talking to Jesus about her future, since she knew if she focused on the past or the present, her hopes could fall, and she might give up due to the pure exhaustion that was beginning to wear her down. She had pushed herself every step of the way so far and she had no intent of stopping, but her strength was running low, and she had slowed down considerably. She had no idea how far she had walked or how long it had taken her when she walked around a bend and stopped in her tracks.

"No. Lord, no," she said as the sun shone down on her from the open gateway into the gorge. She had come to the end, and it opened into a forest of leaf-bearing trees on both sides of the river. Her escape was only a hundred yards away or so down a straight-as-an-arrow run through the rock cliffs. To her horror, the way out of the gorge was blocked by a log jam that had piled in the narrow walls. It was twenty or thirty yards long, and ten feet or higher above the pool of water backed up behind it. The jam was a jumbled mess of trunks and branches from years of floodwaters raging through the gorge, jamming the logs together wherever and however they seemed to fit. One log was wedged upright between the cliffs. It looked impassable, and the water pooled behind it looked much deeper than any she had waded through so far.

Christine's body was already shaking severely, and she had lost the feeling in her hands and feet. She had no choice but to wade out into the pool of water, although she knew any warmth she had collected from the wool blanket wrapped around her would be lost the moment the cold water penetrated it. Her breath was lost as soon as the water reached above her knees, where she had feeling. She stepped farther into the pool, and it was soon at her waist, and then slowly, the water rose to her chest, and then her neck and chin. She could feel the hem of her dress flowing with the current ahead of her as it was pulled toward the bottom of the log jam.

The log jam seemed massive from the surface of the river, and with every step, the water pulled her toward the logs. It was flowing underneath them, and she noticed the water at the surface was whirling around as it was being sucked down under the logs. Two more steps, and she started to lose her balance on the slippery rocks under her. Only her head was above the water, and her body was being forced toward the logs. She feared with one more step, the water would be over her nose and mouth, and she'd possibly lose her footing and be sucked under the logs. She had no choice but to swim the last ten feet or so and try to climb the log jam. It would be hard to do with the loss of feeling in her hands and feet, but after a short prayer of desperation, she jumped upward and forced herself to swim across the surface toward the logs.

Her dress tangled with her feet and her legs began to sink as she struggled to keep her arms moving. Losing the ability to swim, she slowed down and fought to remain in control of her fear and her body. The worst thing she could do was panic and fail to reason through her situation. She was beginning to sink as the current reached out for her, growing stronger the closer, she got to the jam. She put her eyes on the nearest log and began to dog paddle as best she could. She cried out desperately for the Lord to help her as her head went underwater again, then forced herself up and made a last effort to reach the first log she could.

With all the effort she could muster, she tried to keep her legs parallel to the surface because she feared her gown would get caught on a branch or log under the water again. It was a losing battle, since her legs dropped under the surface and she was soon carried against the logs. She grabbed one log and stepped upward desperately until she could feel something solid under the water, then pushed herself and wrapped her hand around another log and tried to climb up. Her hand slipped off, and she fell back into the water. She wrapped the crook of her arm around a limb at the surface and held on as she looked for a better place to maneuver to get out of the water. With limited use of her hands and feet, climbing a log wall against a flowing current would be much more difficult. Her frustration and fear were getting the better of her.

"Lord Jesus, help me," she said and reached up and pushed up against the log her foot was on. She shoved her hand and wrist between two logs and wedged it by making a fist as an anchor to pull herself up. She then brought her other leg up and tried to find a place to brace it against. Once she found a slight rim of a log, she moved her other hand and wedged it the same way between two logs and pulled with her arms and pushed off with her leg to step up again. Her foot slipped off the slippery rim and she fell back down, but her wedged wrist held, causing her to hang by her wrist. She screamed with the combination of frustration and pain. Blood began to slowly run down from her left wrist to her forearm. She yelled in frustration and scrambled with her feet to find a solid place to get some sort of footing. Lifting her leg higher than before, she wedged her foot into a crevice and pushed.

Now half out of the water, she reached her left hand into another crevice where she could wedge her wrist and make a fist. Using the same technique, she climbed out of the water and up on top of the log jam. Although she was safely out of the water, she now was exposed to the air and physically exhausted. She laid on top of a log for a moment to catch her breath. She no longer had her wool blanket, and the cold air was penetrating her core. Death was imminent if she didn't get warm soon. Laying on a log exposed to the air would never heat her body up, even though the sun was shining.

She forced herself to get on her hands and knees and begin to crawl over the debris. Her left wrist was bleeding, and some skin was pulled back over what looked to be a deep puncture wound. She had a long way to go over uneven and unpredictable logs, limbs, and sticks that had been piled up over years of spring runoffs and flash floods. Her dress snagged on the burrs of ancient branches and the splintered wood of snapped-off trees. Halfway across the log jam, her dress caught on a jagged broken branch and wouldn't break free after a jerk from her hand. She turned parallel on a log, took hold of her dress with both hands, and pulled with all her might to tear the material from the branch. It came loose and her momentum knocked her off balance, and she slipped off the log she was on. She fell four feet down into a hole between the logs, and her left leg slipped farther down between the twisted logs into the water. She cried out in pain since the fall was jarring and the landing hard. She tried to reach up and pull herself up like she had before, but her left leg was wedged tightly in a small triangle-shaped opening between the logs. She tried in desperation to pull her leg free, but it was no use. She was trapped.

Christine knew her life was over, and someday her skeleton would be found among the debris of the log jam. No one would see her unless they climbed up on top of the log jam and looked down into the hole she'd fallen into. She leaned her forehead against a log and began to sob, then her sobbing grew more furious and she began to scream in anger. She wasn't so much afraid of death as angry that her life was ending like this. She tried to pull her leg free, but again, it was useless. She wailed loudly as she sobbed. She was freezing to death, and despite her efforts to survive, she was growing hopeless and unable to help herself.

"Help me!" she screamed, and it echoed up the gorge. She hit the log in front of her hating it and the situation she was in. Her breathing was hard as she sobbed, until it slowly came to an end. Exhausted and coming to terms with her fate, she closed her eyes and leaned against the log in front of her. Her body had stopped shaking, and she was getting too tired to keep fighting. Her leg wasn't going to budge, and her battle was over. She wanted to close her eyes and sleep until the end came.

Of all the good things she had going for herself—the dance hall, singing, finances, and popularity with the customers who paid so much for the last dance of the night—the only thing she regretted in life was not being able to tell Matt she was in love with him. Her life was ending now, and all the hopes she had prayed about while fighting to get out of the gorge were merely dreams of a better life with one of the most amazing men she had ever known. She took a few deep breaths to calm herself and come to terms with her situation.

"Lord, I...d-don't know how, but let M-matt know I love him. And if Felisha w-will...love him the way I w-would, then b-bless their m-marriage. I s-surrender myself to you, Jesus." A tear fell from her eyes.

A few minutes later, she heard a noise, and opened her eyes to listen more carefully. She heard nothing for a moment, and thought it was just a wishful dream, but then what sounded like a stick breaking on the other side of the log jam got her attention.

"Hello?" a man's voice yelled. He was close.

Christine didn't care if it was Matt or Jim Hexum, she spoke as loud as she could. "Help!" Her voice was feeble and slightly slurred. "Help..."

"Where are you?" the man asked. His feet sloshed through the water, then he climbed up onto the log jam.

"I'm...here," she said slowly.

She looked up and saw the same Indian man she had helped Matt walk to his jail. The man was wearing a heavy flannel shirt over a wool sweater, and his long, black hair fell freely.

He looked down at her with a perplexed expression mixed with concern and a touch of surprise. "Why are you here?" he asked while climbing down the hole to her.

"My l-leg's stuck. I...mean, it won't m-move." She found it harder to talk than she had ever known it to be.

Chusi Yellowbear reached down, grabbed her leg, and tried to pull it up with no avail. "This is going to hurt," he said, then took hold of her leg again and pulled, using his legs to power her leg free. Her thigh broke free of the logs and her knee and foot came out easily. He didn't say anything more. He quickly helped her out of the hole, then carried her nimbly across the logs and onto the solid ground on the other side of the log jam. He held her over his shoulder and ran along the river as fast as he could go.

Christine bounced on his shoulder as she watched the back of his feet move quickly across the ground. She did not know where he was taking her, nor did she care. She was far too tired to care. Before too long, he turned away from the river, and in a moment, she was inside a warm teepee with the flap shutting behind her.

Chusi stood her on her feet and turned her around. Using his knife, he cut the buttons off her boots and pulled them off her feet. He straightened, then stepped behind her, slit the back of her dress open, and let it fall heavily to the ground. He cut the her undergarments down to her lower back and stopped. He quickly turned her toward him, held up a heavy wool blanket, and said, "Get your clothes off and cover yourself with this. Hurry!" He went outside the teepee to wait.

Beginning to shake and moving slowly, Christine pushed her undergarments down past her hips and let them fall to the floor at her feet. She wrapped the warm blanket around herself and laid down near the fire.

Chusi peeked in and, seeing she was covered by the blanket, came in with a steaming pot of hot water and a cloth. He set it beside her feet and felt the water with his fingers to make sure it wasn't too hot, then saturated the cloth and wrapped it around her feet.

"Lay down and rest. It's going to hurt, but stay," he said and began rubbing her feet with his hands.

Christine looked at the fire and felt the heat from it immediately. Her feet began to sting. She groaned with the discomfort and grimaced.

Chusi looked at her hands and then moved up to rub her fingers and hands. "It will hurt, but let it," he said.

Christine grimaced, and then shortly began to yell in

pain as her body began to warm up after being nearly frozen.

"Stay put!" Chusi said sharply, then left her momentarily and came back into the teepee with more firewood. He put some on the fire to heat it, then removed the cloth from her feet, dipped it into the warm water, and reapplied it to her feet. He grabbed a heavy blanket made from deer hides and laid it over her. "You warm up, then you eat. I'll make a...soup."

Christine began to cry from the pain in her fingers and toes, hands, feet, and other areas that were the coldest.

An hour later, Christine laid under the deer-hide blanket, beginning to sweat. The pain of warming up was mostly over, but while it lasted, it had been agonizing. Her wrists, leg, and face all still ached, but she was warm and comfortable under the blanket, watching the fire burn. The soft sound of it was soothing. Chusi spoon-fed her hot broth with vegetables and fish of some sort in it. It was a bit bitter, but it helped warm her from the inside out.

"I know you," Chusi said as he fed her another bite. "You are the one who helped me that day."

Christine nodded slowly. "Yes. Thank you for helping me."

Chusi nodded. "Why are you here? What happened to your face? That is not from the logs."

"I was taken and held in an old mine. They're probably looking for me." She laid on her side, motionless, watching the fire.

Chusi frowned. "They probably won't come here, but

if they do, they'll take you again. I must get you to Matt. You're lucky I found you when I did. You'd have lost your leg for sure and your fingers and toes if you were there much longer. You will hurt for a few days, but you'll be good. You'll dance again. I'll get you some clothes to wear." He smiled kindly and fed her another spoonful of the fish soup.

Christine found it hard to stand up, and it hurt to move her hands. Her left knee was bruised, and her thigh was already turning purple. Her feet ached when she stood up, and she winced at the pain. She limped heavily as she took a step covered by the wool blanket.

Chusi held out a set of clothes. "I have no pretty dress, and they're not clean. but they'll cover you."

She stepped painfully forward. "Thank you. I can't walk very well."

Chusi nodded. "Get dressed." He left the teepee to let her get do just that.

The pants he gave her were red and black checkered wool, and the yellow shirt smelled of stale alcohol and body odor. Christine dropped the blanket and put on the pants and shirt without hesitation. Chusi came back into the teepee, opened a leather bag, and pulled out a pair of leather moccasins that had beadwork on them and rabbit fur lining. "Put these on. They were my wife's. Put them on, and we'll go before those men come looking for you."

20

Unlike Lee Bannister and some of the other wealthy men in Branson who had carriage houses on their property to store their buggies and horses in, Matt and Truet had to leave their horses at the livery stable on the north side of town and walk the nine blocks to their house. The biggest question Matt wondered about was whether Felisha would be at his house when he got there. It brought a sense of anxiety, not knowing where he stood with her anymore. Would she be there and apologize, or would she still not want to see him again? He didn't know if it was over with her or not, and it played in his mind like a frightened bat flying back and forth inside a closed barn with nowhere to rest. He hadn't been in a relationship since he was a teenager, and he felt the uneasiness of it tilting on the eroding bank of a flooded river.

"I sure hope Felisha is there because I don't think your sister can cook," Truet said with a slight smile.

"If she is, I wouldn't try anything on my plate. I've

seen kinder eyes than she had on some of the worst killers I've met."

Truet chuckled.

"Did you and Jenny Mae ever argue or have a fight?"

"Sure, we did."

"Did she ever act like Felisha did earlier today?"

Truet chuckled. "No."

"Hmm. I'm wondering if it's over, Truet."

"I don't think you need to worry about that just yet. Like I said, give her some time to calm her nerves down. When it comes to women being angry, you have to learn to give them space and time, and plenty of it." He paused, then continued, "Jenny Mae would get mad at me, and she was pretty verbal about it, but she always had a certain grace about her that made it cute. You know? She'd state her mind and then pout." He laughed sadly. "I sure miss her."

Matt nodded in understanding. "I know it's too soon for you to even think about another relationship, but do know when you're ready to court again, there are some very attractive ladies at the dance hall who would love to get to know you."

Truet frowned uneasily. "No, I think I'll be courting elsewhere, probably. Are you ready to see if Felisha came over or not?" he asked as they came to their house.

Matt shrugged. "Let's go find out."

They walked in and felt the warmth of the cookstove immediately upon entering. It was like a wall of comfort after a long, cold journey. The scent of roasted chicken and fresh bread filled their noses. "Something smells good!" Truet said upon entering. He, like Matt, paused inside the door to take his heavy coat off.

Annie stepped out of the kitchen, wearing a new apron over her dress. "Thank you."

Truet said, "Felisha must be here. It doesn't smell burnt."

"Oh, you're so funny. Ha-ha. Oh!" She doubled over in a fake hysterical laugh. "My side hurts from laughing so much. Ha!" She stood up straight and looked at him seriously. "Maybe humor isn't your God-given gift, Truet, so, don't try it. Did you two hound dogs find the missing woman?" she asked Matt.

Truet chuckled and shook his head at her quick wit.

Matt answered, "No. Nobody seems to know anything, and the only one who did, I had to kill."

"I heard William saved your life. You know, I should charge William fifty dollars for some great advice, and tell him if he paid that Swindall guy at the trading post fifty dollars, he'd write a biography about him. He can't write one about Uncle Charlie or you anymore, but William would love to read one about himself. History would be changed a bit more than likely, like it would be William who killed the Dobson Gang and saved Elizabeth last Christmas. Think he'd pay me for that advice?" she asked.

Matt smiled. "A better question is, would he read it to you himself?"

Annie laughed.

"Felisha's not here?" Truet asked, not seeing her in the kitchen.

Annie looked at him with a fake scowl. "Give it up,

Truet. I told you, you won't get far in a traveling comedy show!"

He laughed.

Annie continued as she looked at Matt, "No, she's not here. She didn't want to come. I think you should go talk to her, Matt. She was traumatized by what she saw today, and if she goes down to the restaurant to eat, you know William probably won't help her by bragging about it. He's not very sensitive about that stuff to begin with. But she did say he paid her doctor bill, so maybe he's softening."

Matt frowned. "Why did she need a doctor? Her head?"

"Yeah, she needed three stitches in it. She was scared Dillon had internal bleeding, so she had the hotel get the doctor. He's fine, and she just needed a few stitches."

"Internal bleeding? He wasn't kicked by a horse," Matt stated.

Annie shrugged. "She's a city girl, she panicked. She was more traumatized by seeing someone get shot. You should talk to her, like I said."

Matt frowned. "I don't think she wants to see me. Wouldn't it be best to give her some space and time to calm down?"

Annie grimaced and shook her head. "No. It would be best if you took the initiative and went to her and showed you cared."

"Hmm. So, you think I should go see her, huh?"

"Isn't that what I just said? Truet, didn't I just say that?"

He nodded quickly. "You did."

"I thought I did. Yes! You should go see her. Truet, wasn't that clear?"

He laughed. "Yes, it was clear."

Matt asked, "What if she doesn't want to see me?"

"Then at least you tried to show her you care. Tell her you'd appreciate having her over for dinner. I made it, so the work's done. She might as well come eat some of the dinner we planned together this morning. If she refuses, then you come back here and have some. Lee and Regina will be here in about half an hour," Annie said simply. "Now, get going, and don't be too late because dinner is in half an hour. And you know the rule: if you're late, you *might* get what's left. I'm not saving nothing."

"Well, I guess I'll go ask her to come over, then."

"Hey! There's an idea," Annie told him sarcastically.

Matt looked at her, shook his head, and walked out the door.

Annie smiled at Truet. "I was counting on Felisha being here when we told Matt about us courting. If he does get a little upset, it would be nice to have an ally to keep him restrained," she said as she gave him a hug.

"He's not going to get violent, Annie. He might get mad, but like Matt always says, 'He'll get over it or he won't.'"

"Yeah, and that's what I'm afraid of."

Truet sighed. "Me, too."

21

Matt took a deep breath and said a silent prayer before knocking on Felisha's hotel room door. A moment passed, and he knocked again.

"Who is it?" her voice asked through the door.

"Matt," he answered with a touch more anxiety than he was used to feeling.

He heard the door unlock, and she held it half-open to look at him. Her facial expression was hard, and she appeared to be angry. "What do you want?" she asked harshly.

"I just wanted to see how you are."

"I'm fine," she said with restrained tension in her voice.

"How's Dillon?"

"He's fine."

Matt nodded uncomfortably. "Hmm. Well, do you think we can talk for a few minutes?"

"I don't have too much to say, Matt."

"Maybe you could invite me in and say what you *do*

have to say, then. I'd prefer not to talk in the hallway if you don't mind."

She opened the door for him to enter. "Don't get too comfortable, because we really don't have too much to talk about."

Matt walked to the davenport and sat down. "Are you going to sit down?" He motioned to the seat beside him.

"No. I'm fine," she said, standing in the middle of the room with her arms crossed. "I was expecting you to stop by before it got too late. That's why Dillon's with Richard and Rebecca. He's not ready to see you and that gun you carry around everywhere you go. It used to be a symbol of goodness to him, now he calls it a loud killing machine." Her tone was cold.

"It's a weapon, not a machine."

She raised her voice. "I know what it is! The point is, he's terrified you're going to kill someone else in front of him, and I can't reassure him you're not going to because just like today, you might. It's just nothing to you, is it? You can kill a man and move on as easily as the man you killed, can't you?"

Matt frowned. "I don't like to, but it happens. I didn't have much of a choice."

"Oh, you never have a choice! Are you going to be able to sleep tonight?"

"It depends if I can sleep in my bed or not. If Annie sleeps on the davenport, I will."

"It's not a time to be funny, Matt! I am serious. Last night I was excited about moving here and starting a life with you, but I think that would be a mistake. I don't want my son growing up around violence. I don't want to live my life worrying if you're going to be killed or hearing that you killed another man. I don't think it's something I can get used to. Annie seems to have grown up around it, and so have you obviously." She took a breath and continued, "I don't want Dillon growing up that way."

Matt sat in silence for a moment.

She sighed heavily and added softly, "See? There's not much to say anymore, except, why did you lie to me?"

Matt looked up at her with a puzzled expression. "I didn't."

"Yes, you did! You said it was 'a girl' taken last night, not your pie-making friend!" Her expression was hard again.

Matt smiled slightly. "Christine is a girl, and I told you Christine was taken. I didn't lie to you."

"You made it sound like a little girl named Christine was missing, not your friend!"

Matt stood up. "Well, it was my friend. If you misunderstood, I apologize, but I told you Christine was missing. And she still is." He walked toward the door. "I'm not going to argue about Christine. I came over to see how you were, not argue. I knew you were upset, and I can understand that. Killing a man is a traumatic and scary thing for anyone, especially when it's unexpected. I am sorry you two were there to see it, but it couldn't be helped. Am I sorry for shooting Jim Hexum? I sure as hell am, because he's the only one who knows where Christine is. He kidnapped her, Felisha. I was arresting him for it, and that's why he went for his gun.

"I am so sorry I didn't grab him before he had a chance to kick Dillon. When a man goes for his gun, there is no time to ask him not to. There is only enough time to kill him. It is never my intention to kill a man, but there are times when it happens. There's no time to debate about it. It is an immediate reaction, and there is no hesitation or questioning about it. When it's over, like today...no, it doesn't feel good. To answer your question, yes, I will sleep, because if I didn't kill him, I'd be dead. Jim Hexum would not have of missed me, and if he had, he could have hit someone else."

"Like Dillon or me!" she spat.

"No, you two were on the ground."

"Because that man kicked my son!" she yelled. "And who's fault was that, Dillon's? No! That man was talking about your other lady and me! Christine doesn't like competition, he said. Remember? Well, when you find Christine, you can tell her she wins! I'm leaving, and I am never coming back. I thought you were the one, Matt," she said and suddenly began to sob into her hands.

Matt stepped forward.

"No, just go," she said and waved him away.

"Felisha," Matt said softly, "I am very sorry things worked out like they did today. Hexum said what he did to aggravate me, just like he did yesterday on our buggy ride. They were setting me up to take the fall for some half-brained idea they had that the Eckman girl is still alive and I'm protecting her. They thought it was Christine, and that's why they took her. Unfortunately, they're wrong, and they're facing arson, kidnapping, and attempted murder charges. That's why he kicked the person nearest to him, which was Dillon. It was his feeble attempt to cause a distraction to kill me, and he hoped to get away. It wasn't smart, but desperate men usually don't make reasonable decisions. I wish I would've done it differently because he should be in jail and not in a box. But it is what it is. It doesn't do me any good to dwell on it. He went for his gun. That's all I need to know to sleep well. I am sorry if that fact bothers you. Maybe we haven't got too much to say, but before I leave here, do know I love you. Do know I am sorry it turned out this way, because the Lord knows I didn't want it to. If you want to go back to Sweethome for good, I'll understand." He paused to take a breath and wipe a bit of moisture from his eyes. "I never wanted us to end. I'll leave you alone. If you don't mind, I would like to say goodbye before you leave." He waited, but she didn't say anything or look at him. "I'll see you at the stage station, then. Despite it all, thank you," he said and walked toward the door.

She turned around as he opened the door. "Thank me for what?" she asked. She wiped the tears from her face.

Matt looked at her softly. "For teaching me that I can love someone after all. You're an amazing lady, Felisha, and I don't want to lose you, but I do understand if you want to go. I'm in a gritty and dangerous business that can be brutal and bloody, but I try to do what's right and make life better for the people around me. I want to make a difference in the world, small though it may be. You made my life shine for a while, and I thank you for that. Take care, my friend."

"Matt..."

He paused.

"I love you too."

He paused with the door open and nodded with a sad smile. "I know."

She spoke suddenly. "Why am I so confused? Part of me wants to run away and not look back, and the other part of me wants to stay with you."

"Are you scared?" he asked softly.

"Of making a mistake, yes."

"Then the best thing to do is pray, then wait and see. Have you eaten anything since this afternoon?" he asked caringly.

She shook her head.

"Then how about you come with me for dinner and spend the evening with Annie, Truet, Lee, Regina, and me?"

"No, I couldn't. I was supposed to help make dinner and would feel awkward."

Matt smiled slightly. "Trust me, they'll all understand. Annie wants you to come over. She was pretty adamant about that."

"I know she does. She and Truet wanted..." She paused in mid-sentence with a slight widening of her eyes and a hint of a smile.

"What?" he asked questionably.

"They wanted...us to make chicken," she said hesitantly. "Maybe I better come over after all," she said with a slight giggle.

"What's funny about that?"

"Give me a few minutes to get ready, okay?"

"Sure, but I can't promise they saved us any."

22

Matt felt the discomfort of not knowing what was going to happen between Felisha and him. He watched her as she sat beside him on the smaller of their two davenports, smiling and acting like there was nothing amiss between them. However, she had refused to hold his hand during the walk to his house, which left Matt slightly confused as to why she took his hand now in front of everyone else. She laughed as she said, "So I had to tell Dillon, 'It doesn't matter what William said, you cannot spit on people out the window.'"

Lee shook his head with a smile. "William…"

Regina spoke through a smirk. "I really don't know why you let him stay at the Monarch Hotel. I don't think he's good for business."

"He hasn't hurt it any, and he has kept it peaceful and quiet since he's been there. We had some trouble with locals wanting to get into the Monarch Lounge and raise a ruckus in the hotel in the middle of the night this past summer, so I hired William to guard the place," he explained to Felisha. "Since then, we've had no issues, and when they come up, William is on top of it. He might be an obnoxious man sometimes, but he's got a great heart to help people, and on the flip side, he isn't afraid of anyone. He just...has a twisted sense of humor." Lee chuckled.

"Twisted is about right," Regina chimed.

Truet spoke to Felisha. "I feel really bad that I haven't got to spend any time with Richard and Rebecca. Are they getting out of the hotel at all since being here?"

Felisha nodded. "They've walked around town and gone into a few stores. They are enjoying the hotel and the area around here. You've been busy helping Matt, and they understand that."

Annie asked, "He's a reverend, right?"

"Yes," Felisha answered. "And a very good one."

Annie continued, "Our reverend is looking to retire pretty soon. He's looking for a suitable replacement to take over the Willow Falls church. Trust me, Reverend Ash won't let just anyone step into his shoes. If your friend wants to move over here, tell him to talk to Reverend Ash in Willow Falls."

"I'll mention it," Felisha said half-heartedly.

Regina asked Felisha, "When are you moving over? I have the cutest little cottage in mind for you and Dillon. I'm even going to have it painted, and new wallpaper put into it. I may even have to hire someone to make some flower beds for the front and plant some tulips or something bright and cheery for spring."

Felisha's face reddened, and she smiled uncomfortably. "I haven't set a date. There's still so much to do. Like

I told Matt, I'll move over here and find employment bookkeeping or something, but I'm not selling my board-inghouse until I'm married. I don't want to give up every-thing I own and discover we aren't...compatible after all."

"That's not going to happen," Regina said pointedly.

"No," Felisha said with a smile, "probably not. I need to get used to a few things, though, like him being a marshal and not a banker. My late husband would run from a confrontation, not start one. I will tell you I was quite shocked today when Matt and William shot that man. I did not handle it well, and almost didn't come over tonight because of it."

Lee said candidly, "A weak lawman is either a corrupt or a dead lawman. There is no room for weakness. That's why we wanted Matt here to begin with. Some people wish he wasn't here now, and our sheriff is one of them. We need law and order to be a functioning society where people like you and Dillon or my family can walk these streets safely. Without it, there is no society, just corrup-tion and victims. My whole point is this: though it can turn violent, most of the time Matt's sitting in his office doing paperwork or out collecting taxes or serving warrants. Most of the time, he looks bored to death. His reputation alone keeps the peace, for the most part. Today was a shock, really, and probably to no one more than him. Am I right?" he asked Matt.

Matt nodded slowly. He had been quiet for most of the evening. "I wasn't expecting it. You just don't know what people will do to avoid jail."

"I was standing right there, and it couldn't be helped," Truet said. "Matt had no choice, Felisha. None at all."

Felisha's face reddened again. "I know that now, but at the time it was horrifying, and I have a boy to raise. It scared me, okay? I'm...seeing it differently now, but at the time..."

Annie asked, "Were you thinking about leaving my brother? I know he's uglier than an old goat, but you have to have a better reason than that!" She continued seriously, "Come on, it's the world we live in." She laughed. "If there wasn't men like Matt and Truet, we wouldn't be safe in our own homes. I would be because I keep a loaded pistol in my kitchen and my bedroom, but you wouldn't be. Jim Hexum will never kick another little boy again, and I doubt that even touches the worst he's done. His death makes the streets that much safer."

"I understand what you're saying, but you didn't see him die, Annie," Felisha explained.

"If I was there, I would have pulled out my derringer and shot the man faster than William and Matt did. Hurting a child is something I won't stand for."

Felisha frowned curiously. "You carry a gun?"

Annie scoffed. "Of course! The holster's strapped to my calf. I know it's not ladylike, but either am I."

"She is no lady," Truet said with a slight smirk.

Annie pointed a finger at him. "If I was you, Goat, I'd shut up."

Truet laughed. "Goat?"

Annie squinted her eyes while making a mock-serious expression. "Yeah, goats think they're comedians, too."

He laughed.

Regina spoke to Felisha. "I hope you and Matt find out you're made for each other. I think you are."

Felisha smiled softly. "I think so. I love this guy," she said and wrapped her arm around his neck and pulled him closer to kiss his mouth. She laughed as she looked at Annie. "Is that unladylike enough?"

"When you make my brother's face turn as red as that, yeah, I think you're getting it." She laughed at Matt's flushed cheeks.

Matt smiled awkwardly as she took his hand again.

Felisha continued, "To answer your earlier question, Regina, I think Dillon and I will move over here after Christmas. I'll need time to organize my belongings and go through a lot of things. I need to find someone to run my boardinghouse who I can trust to not rob me and who will treat the customers as well as I do. I also want them to care for the place so its value stays above what we spent building it. There's a lot to do to make the move over, but I'm thinking soon after Christmas, we can move here and begin our lives together." She nudged Matt's shoulder. "Huh?"

Matt nodded as he looked at her. A sense of relief was coming through him. "Yeah, that would be fine."

"That would be *fine*?" Annie asked with a scowl. "You finally meet a woman who thinks you're not as boring as a stump, and all you can say is, 'Yeah, that would be fine?'"

Felisha laughed delightfully. "Annie, I love you!"

Matt looked at Felisha. "Don't make her feel too at home. She'll come over all the time."

"Well, I do!" Felisha exclaimed. "Don't you, Truet?" she asked with a twinkle in her eye.

Lee smirked, and Regina's eyes widened in surprise. Annie raised her eyebrows and looked at Truet expectantly. Truet's face reddened as he realized everyone was looking at him. "Um..." He had not been expecting to be on the spot. He and Annie had planned on telling Matt they were courting, but this wasn't the way he had seen it. He was feeling the pressure building to say something, but beginning to panic internally now that Matt was staring at him with an expressionless face that could either soften or harden, depending on how he took the news.

He knew Matt had a lot on his mind, troubled by his own relationship with Felisha, Christine missing, and the news of the Pinkertons investigating him. Maybe it just wasn't a good time to tell him he was courting his sister and had been for a few weeks now. Truet knew Annie was waiting, and he hoped Annie wouldn't reach over and grab his hand while he debated on what words to say. If he decided to wait, would Annie understand, or would she call him a possum for playing dead instead of confessing like a man? "Okay, Matt..."

There was a knock on the door and Matt stood up, looking at Truet. "Hold on," he said and stepped toward the door, but paused in the middle of the room to look back at Felisha with a slight smirk. He was going to speak but decided against it.

The knock became a bang. Alarmed, Matt went to the door.

23

Chusi Yellowbear had walked Christine the two miles down a forest trail along the creek to where it entered the Modoc River and then along the Modoc to the bridge that crossed Premro Island into town. He led her across town as quickly as he could to Franklyn Street. He thought he had known which house Matt lived in, but of the two houses he went to, neither was Matt's. The homeowners were as different as night and day. The first homeowner opened the door, saw Chusi, and closed the door, telling him go beg somewhere else. They did not care about the freezing woman he was holding up.

The second home showed more concern and offered to invite them in, but Chusi wanted to get Christine to Matt as fast as he could. The people pointed at a brick house a few lots down and across the street and told him that was where Matt lived. Chusi held Christine up with his right arm around her side, quickly walked her to Matt's front door, and knocked. After a short pause, he banged on the door with urgency. He was cold, but

Christine was shivering, and her breath came through chattering teeth. There were clouds filling the western sky, which meant it would warm up a touch when the clouds blocked the stars, but whether it would bring snow or a cold rain was something a man could gamble on.

"Who is it?" Matt asked through the door.

Chusi could hear other people inside too. "Chusi! Open the door, Matt. She's cold!"

Matt opened the door. His face contorted in concern and then surprise when he saw Chusi holding up a woman with long, dark hair covering her face. She was wearing Chusi's clothes and had a bruised face. It took Matt a second to recognize her. "Oh, my Lord!" he exclaimed, then grabbed Christine and pulled her into the house and into his arms. He moved the hair out of her face with his right hand and looked at her blackened eye.

She moved her eyes up to his and began to sob as she hugged him tightly, crying into his shoulder. Her sobbing was loud and uncontrollable. He just held her quietly since his own eyes had filled with tears of rage.

Truet was quickly beside him. "Chusi, come in and close the door."

Chusi had remained outside, not knowing if he was invited to come inside or not. He stepped into the warm house and closed the door behind him. "She's cold," he said awkwardly.

"I'll get a blanket," Annie said and went to Matt's room.

Matt spoke into Christine's ear. "Shh, you're safe now.

239

I have you, Christine. I got you. Are you okay? Did they hurt you?"

She nodded into his chest. "He hit me. Don't ever let me go, okay?" she said in a high-pitched, shaking voice, and she refused to loosen her grip on him.

Matt's eyes hardened. "I won't." He pulled away from her just enough to turn her face to make eye contact. "I promise no one's going hit you again, but I need to know who did this to you?"

Annie returned with a blanket and wrapped it around her shoulders. Truet was talking to Chusi and getting all the information from him that he could. Lee was standing in the middle of the room listening in while Regina glanced around, surprised to see Chusi in the house and the girl dressed so poorly holding Matt. Felisha sat alone on the smaller davenport, watching Matt hold Christine.

"Come sit down," Annie said, leading Christine away from her embrace of Matt toward the davenport. "Someone get this lady some coffee," she ordered bluntly.

Felisha got up and walked into the kitchen to do so. She had no friendly feelings for Christine, but she could empathize with a scared, beaten, and freezing human being.

Matt looked at Chusi sternly. "Where'd you find her?"

Truet answered, "She came into his camp."

"No," Chusi said.

"No?"

"No. I took her to my camp. I found her. She was stuck in a log jam at the mouth of Spider Creek Ravine. She would have died," Chusi said to Matt and Truet. "Her leg was stuck between logs. She was down in it."

"How'd you find her?" Truet asked.

"I heard her yelling."

Matt turned away from Chusi, stepped to the davenport, and knelt in front of the girl. He grabbed her hands in his. "Christine, I need to know who took you. I know Jim Hexum was one, but who else? Do you know their names?"

"Here's some coffee." Felisha held a cup of warm liquid out for her to take. Annie took the cup for Christine.

"Check her feet. She was in the cold for a long time," Chusi said.

Matt moved his hands down her feet and removed the moccasins. Her feet were red but didn't appear to have any sign of frostbite. He rubbed them to warm them up.

Felisha stood behind Matt. "Shouldn't we get her back home?"

Matt shook his head. "No, she's staying here until I catch the other men who took her."

"All night?" Felisha asked, stunned by his reply.

"For tonight."

"Oh," she said awkwardly.

Matt turned back to Christine. "Christine, I need to know who else is involved."

Christine took a sip of the coffee and looked at Matt. "Pick..."

Felisha spoke. "Well, I suppose I better be leaving."

"No, you can stay here," Regina said quickly. "You

have no reason to leave. Even if the men leave, we can still talk."

"No, I don't think that would be a good idea. So, if you all will excuse me, I'll grab my coat and see you all later." She stepped over to the coat rack and put hers on.

Matt stood up and looked at Felisha. "You don't have to leave."

"I *want* to leave! Trust me, it's for the best," she said, her large, fiery eyes glaring at him.

Matt was annoyed by her tone. He knew her well enough to know that she was angry about Christine staying there for the night, but her anger had been covered by a thin layer of paint for the benefit of their friends. He knew she had been sensitive about Christine since her arrival, and now she was leaving with the same attitude toward him she'd had before they came to the house. "Felisha, you don't have to go. You're more than welcome to stay here even if Truet and I must leave. But I need to find out who else is involved and go arrest them."

For a second, Felisha's eyes showed their anger. "I'm not stopping you. Will I see you tomorrow?"

Matt closed his eyes for a moment. He could feel the pressure coming from multiple directions like an avalanche of situations, and people pulling him in a dozen different ways. Christine needed him to reassure her she was safe, and he needed to know if she was okay. He needed to set their friendship aside and focus on learning what he could about the men who took her. He had questions to ask and information he needed to get to find those responsible before they disappeared. It was important that he ride to Willow Falls in the morning and back to notify Sarah and Nathan about her parents. It was his future on the line if his deception about Sarah was brought to light. He could not take a chance of her mother seeing her, or he would be behind the prison walls himself. There was already an investigation pending the outcome of what he would learn from Christine. And despite it all, Felisha had no clue about any of it, and he couldn't tell her because she only saw her side of the mirror. He understood her disappointment about not being able to spend time with him, but his priorities overruled pleasure. The petty jealousy and nonsense only frustrated him to the point where he wanted her to leave. He had too much going on in his life right now to take the time to console her. He wanted to raise his voice and vent the building frustrations that were beginning to consume him, but he knew better and refused to give in to the emotional yearnings within him. He took a deep breath and answered softly, "I don't know."

Felisha's eyes glazed with tears as she scoffed. "Well, this has been a great weekend, Matt! I came to see you, and you've been so preoccupied with her that I can't even talk to you," she said, pointing at Christine.

"I know, but there's not much I can do about that."

"No, there's nothing you *could* do about it, is there?" she asked bitterly. "I think it stinks that it had to happen on this weekend, and I think it's a pile of crap that all I've heard about since I've come here is you and her! And now she's here. Imagine that?"

Matt answered sharply, "Of course, she's here. I'm the marshal, and now I'm going to get back to doing my job so I can catch the people who did this to her. I'm sorry, Felisha. I really am."

She shrugged. "It doesn't matter. Maybe I'll see you before I leave."

"I will try to see you when I get back if it's not too late."

She shook her head with a sad twist to her lips. "Why do I feel like I'm second place in your life? You're not even going to walk me back to the hotel, are you?"

Matt shook his head. "I can't. I need to talk to Christine to find out what I can about who took her and see if I can find them before they try to disappear. Time is a big factor tonight."

A tear fell from Felisha's eye. "Okay," she said quickly. "I'll see you...sometime."

"Felisha, I am sorry."

"Go find those men," she said and opened the door.

"Felisha, wait," Regina said. "Let us get James to bring the buggy for you."

"No, I'll walk. The streets are quite safe around here, I'm sure!" She directed that at Matt.

"Very safe," Matt responded irritably to her bitter sarcasm.

Annie said to her brother from the couch beside Christine, "Knock it off, Matt."

Christine tried to stand up. "Maybe I should go home. I need to go there anyway."

"No, you're staying put," Matt said sharply, looking back at her.

Felisha's large brown eyes widened a bit as she shook

her head. "I irritate you," she stated, grimacing at him. "Maybe I should make you an apple pie too!"

Matt took a deep breath from frustration. He had to talk to Christine, and the sooner he found out what he needed to know, the better he would feel about locating those involved. He sighed heavily with a roll of his eyes. "That would be nice," he said, shaking his head in annoyance.

She glared at him harshly. "Go to hell!" she yelled, then walked outside and slammed the door behind her.

Regina looked at Matt irritably. "You're just going stand there and let her go?"

"No. I'm not." He looked at Chusi and said, "Chusi, will you do me a favor and follow her to the hotel to make sure she gets there safely? Tell William in private to stop whatever he is doing and come see me, then come on back here, and we'll get you fed and warmed up. Tell no one about bringing Christine here. No one, are we clear?"

Chusi nodded and went outside without a word spoken.

Regina gasped. "That's it?"

"That's it."

Regina spoke heatedly. "You're having that vagrant walk her home?"

"She'll be fine."

"No, it's not fine!" Regina exclaimed angrily. "You're so damn rude!" She walked quickly outside to talk to Felisha.

He put his attention back on Christine as she said, "I'm sorry to cause trouble, Matt. I'm okay with Chusi walking me home."

Matt's irritated frown lifted. "I know you would be, but I need to know who took you. They are probably looking for you, and time's running out to find them. Do you know the names of who took you?"

She nodded.

"Who are they?"

"That man Jim from your office that one day, and Pick is the other one."

"Pick? Do you have a last name?"

"No, but he has a scar on his cheek."

Lee spoke. "A scar right here?" he asked and ran his finger down his left cheek.

Christine nodded.

Lee spoke. "I know him. He rents one of my cottages. His last name's Lawson, Pick Lawson. Rumor has it he's affiliated with the Sperry-Helms Gang, but he pays his rent on time." He shrugged.

"Do you have a key to his place?" Matt asked.

Lee nodded. "At my office."

"I need the key. Can you go get it for me?"

"Sure. Do you want me to go with you?"

Matt shook his head. "Nope. This is between him and me." He looked at Christine. "I need you to stay here tonight. You can sleep in my room and get some rest, okay? This is my sister Annie, and you know Truet. They'll both be here to watch over you. I'm going to go wait for Pick."

Christine grabbed Matt's hand urgently. "Pick was nice to me. Don't hurt him if you don't have to. It was the other man who hit me. Jim scares me, but Pick wouldn't let him hurt me."

Matt answered simply, "Jim's dead."

She stared at Matt blankly.

"How'd you escape? Did Pick let you go?"

"He was sleeping when I left."

Matt stood up. "Truet, stay here and don't let her leave. For twenty thousand dollars, Pick took her right out of the dance hall, so he might come here with his guns blazing. You watch over my sister and my friend. I'll be back when Pick is in jail, if I can get him there." He walked into his room and came out wearing his gun belt and his buffalo coat and hat. "Ready?" he asked Lee. "Let's go get the key to Pick's castle."

Truet asked, "Are you sure you don't want me to go with you? He might have the Sperry-Helms Gang with him."

Matt shook his head. "Your job is to protect Christine and Annie. Do not let her leave. I'll be back later. If William comes by, tell him to meet me at Pick's place. What number is it, Lee?"

"Twenty-five."

Regina came inside and shut the door behind her. She glared at Matt angrily. "You had no right to treat her like that! She came all this way to see you, and this is how you're going to treat her? I expected more from you, Matt. She wishes she never came here now. My goodness, she was ready to give her life to you, and you can't take a moment for her?"

Matt laughed lightly to fight his irritation. "No, I can't! If she wants to leave, so be it. I really don't care right now. Christine is my priority, not Felisha."

Regina grimaced as she pointed at Christine. "That

whore already ruined Annie's marriage, and now she's ruining yours! Can't you see that?"

Matt pointed at the door. He was angry, and it came through in his tone as he shouted, "Lee, get your wife out of my sight! Truet, go with Lee and get the damn key for Pick's place, then get back here!"

Christine began to sob into her hands.

"Regina, let's go," Lee said softly.

Regina stared at Matt in disbelief. "I never thought I'd say this, but Felisha's too good for you anyway. Maybe you and that home-contaminate-like-strychnine can make a go of it, but she's just spinning a web, like black widows do! You should throw her to the street rats and go after Felisha before you lose her for good!"

"Get out! Regina, my word! Just get out!" Matt yelled.

"It's my house!" she yelled. "I don't want her in here! Get her out of my house. I don't have to rent it to you if you don't!"

Lee put Regina's coat over her shoulders. "That's enough," he said gently. "Come on, let's go home."

"You saw how he treated Felisha, Lee!"

"That's between them, not us, dear."

"She's my friend," she was saying as Lee guided her out of the house.

Truet followed. "I'll be right back."

After they had all left, Matt looked at Annie, who was snickering and trying not to laugh.

"What?" he asked.

"Nothing," she said and began laughing. "I'm sorry," she said through her chuckles. They were loud and hard, and she bent over knees, laughing uncontrollably.

"Excuse...me." She got up, walked outside, and began laughing loudly again.

Matt sighed and looked down at Christine, who looked at him with very troubled wet eyes.

"I'm sorry," she said softly as a tear slid down her cheek.

He knelt and took her hands. "You have nothing to be sorry for, Christine. It's not you anyway, it's... This whole weekend's been nothing but trouble. Now that we're alone, I must ask you...did they force themselves upon you or harm you in any way?"

She shook her head. "Pick was a perfect gentleman. Jim was the one who hit me hard until he knocked me out. He made some awful threats and scared me, but Pick wouldn't let him hurt me again even if he tried."

Matt nodded sadly. "Thank the Lord for that. Let's get you something to eat and get you situated for the night, okay?" He paused and then added softly, "I need you to stay here tonight, and tomorrow for me as well. I can't explain why just yet, but I'm asking you to trust me. Blind trust, if you will. I can't tell anyone you've been found safe yet for reasons I can't go into. I know it makes no sense, but trust me, okay? Will you stay here and just make yourself at home? I'll let Bella know you're safe when I get the chance and get some nicer clothes for you. I need to keep this very quiet until Tuesday if I can. Will you trust me?"

Christine looked at Matt with her soft eyes. "Always."

"You'll be all right."

"I know. Matt, why is your sister laughing? Is she laughing at me?"

"I don't know. We'll ask her when she comes in."

Annie came back inside after a moment with an amused smile on her face and wiped the tears from her eyes from laughing so hard.

"Annie, what's so funny?"

She held up a finger to pause as she got control of herself. "I've never seen Regina get so mad." She giggled. "A..." She laughed. "A 'home contaminant like strychnine.' I think Regina has finally found her own style of Bannister babble, but her specialty is poisons." She laughed again.

"I don't think it's funny," Matt said.

"You wouldn't because you're the one she's mad at." Annie snorted. "But when she gets over it, you will."

"It's a little late for introductions, but Annie, this is Christine Knapp. Christine, this is my sister Annie. Kyle's wife."

Christine turned her head to look at Annie in the eyes. "I didn't have anything to do with your husband. I was there that night, but it's nothing like what your sister-in-law thinks. I honestly had nothing to do with him or... his death." Tears slipped out of Christine's eyes. "I just want you to know that."

Annie smiled. "I already know that. Kyle's friends Sam and Paul told me what happened. You've been through enough today to worry about that. Are you hungry? We have some food left over for you and Chusi when he comes back. Let me get some for you, okay?"

Christine nodded. "I'd like that."

24

Felisha walked quickly toward Main Street and looked back for the third time to see the old Indian named Chusi following her from about a half block behind. She turned around and yelled, "Stop following me! Go back to wherever you came from and leave me alone!"

He stopped where he was. "Too cold to argue. Please go," was all he said and waited for her to start walking again. He followed. Matt had asked him for a favor, and he intended to see it through. He would follow the woman and speak to William. Maybe William would buy him a drink, maybe not. What he didn't have was money, but what he did have was a deep appreciation for Matt and his family. Many, if not most, people in Branson treated him like a blot on society and either ignored him completely or like those teen boys had done, humiliated him in public. Some people refused to look at him as he asked for a nickel, some acted like they'd catch a disease from him, some wanted him run out of town like a filthy rat. There were others, though, who treated him kindly, though still hesitant to be seen talking to him. Matt and his family treated him with respect despite his lowly circumstances, simply because he was a human being. It was a debt he could never repay, to be treated like a man of value despite his shortcomings and appearance.

Chusi was a Shoshone, and on a cold January morning in 1863 his tribe was camped for the winter along Bear River in southeastern Idaho. On the morning of the 29th, they could see the steam rising from two hundred soldiers coming toward them in the freezing weather. A small group of men had caused some trouble among the white settlers, but despite their foolish actions, hopes were high that a treaty could be signed that morning with the white soldiers. The Shoshone were warned of rumors of the soldiers' intentions and a few had left, and others were warned by dreams and left, but most were confident a treaty could be signed, and any bloodshed would be avoided. Most believed their peaceful winter camp filled with families and laughter would be unharmed. They stayed where they could play games and enjoy the time of a tribal reunion since many bands of Shoshone had gathered for the winter camp. As the soldiers got closer, some warriors took defensive positions as a precaution just in case the rumors were true. While the mothers hoped it would be a peaceful meeting, they nervously gathered their children near them, knowing there was no promise of a peaceful meeting. While one beautiful Indian baby reached for his mother's nose with a smile, the soldiers attacked without warning and without cause. There was no chance for talking peace or to surrender. Once the first gunshot was fired, the screaming began, and neither the guns nor the screaming stopped until there was no one left to scream. The soldiers' intention was to slaughter every man, woman, and child with Shoshone blood. Chusi and the other warriors fought with everything they had to save the lives of the tribe, including the lives of their own wives, sons, and daughters. If ever there was a motivation to fight, it ran strong through the Shoshone warriors' blood that day. Every weapon in their arsenal was used, but what guns they did have were soon out of ammunition. Their bows, spears, and knives were no match for the guns of two hundred soldiers. Every Shoshone man was killed on sight, and the women and their children were shown no mercy and murdered like they were lice. If there was ever a godless moment, it was being an Indian on that morning when a pair of soldiers gunned down a young mother carrying her beautiful baby boy. Chusi watched the soldiers shoot his little sister in the back as she ran and then stand over his infant nephew and shoot the six-month-old baby like a threatening wolf. Chusi saw his beloved wife trying to save their three children as she led them toward the river to escape in its icy water, but they too were gunned down like rodents before his very eyes. The sound of constant gunfire was everywhere, along with the screams of pain, cries of fear, and yells of fierce anger that died down one by one.

Chusi had fought brutally and killed a few soldiers, but when he saw his family being killed along with hundreds of others, he knew he could stand his ground and die or abandon the massacre to help those who did survive. Chusi ran to the river and dove in as a soldier shot at him. He faked being hit, rolled in the water like a dying beaver, and resurfaced face down as the current took him downstream. Thought to be dead, the other soldiers let him drift down the river. Chusi was found by two other survivors, who warmed his body up.

Now, twenty years later, it was called the Massacre of Bear River. It was hardly ever spoken about, even though over four hundred Shoshone men, women, and children had been murdered. Chusi certainly never talked about it. Guilt for failing to save his people and his own family, layered upon the guilt of surviving when hundreds did not, haunted him day and night. Broken from the loss of family, not just his own, but his whole tribe that he had grown up with, that was mostly left on the frozen ground that day. Whiskey, or firewater as people often mocked, had become a lifestyle. It eased the burden he carried and dimmed the pain he lived with.

He had been on a reservation, but it was difficult to see the broken faces of a once-free people being herded like cattle and taking scraps of bread and beef stew and being told to be thankful. To see the misery in the faces that once knew joy reminded him of his own failure to protect his children, his wife, and the hundreds who were shot down in cold blood. He wanted venison, he wanted trout, and he wanted to pick berries and hear nature, not the sad talk of what used to be. In Branson, he could live alone in the forest and catch fish to sell. Trap for furs, hunt, and live self-sufficiently, close to the way it used to be before Bear River. He was alone, though, and he felt alone. No one cared about him, except the Fasana and Bannister families, who were of mixed blood themselves.

They were not Shoshone, they were Nez Perce, but they treated him like a brother and not a street bum. If Matt wanted him to follow this woman, then he would follow this woman and protect her if necessary. Matt and his family were his friends, even the ones he had never met. His loyalty was committed to their family, whether they knew him or not.

Felisha turned around again and yelled, "Go away!"

Chusi stopped. "Too cold to argue. Go ahead," he repeated loudly on the quiet street. It was dark out, and being a Sunday night, there was no one else on the side street except for the two of them. They were only a block away from Main Street and the Monarch Hotel. His job was almost completed; all he had to do was make sure she got inside safely and then find William to relay a private message.

Felisha huffed. "I'm here, okay? You can leave now! You're not escorting me to my room, so don't even try it. I'll have Willian throw you out!"

Chusi shrugged. "I'm going to see William, Miss. Not you."

Felisha turned around and began walking quickly again. She was visibly upset and wanted to get to her room. She stepped out to cross Main Street in front of three men who were walking up the middle of the road. They appeared to be under the influence of the bottle of whiskey they were drinking. She stopped as they jogged twenty feet or so to meet her in the middle of the road.

"Hey, lady, how much money have you got?" one man asked as he put his arm around her shoulder in a romantic embrace.

She pushed him away. "Get away from me!" she exclaimed and stepped forward to leave them.

"Whoa down there, Jezebel. There's only two kinds of women who walk in front of this hotel alone at night. One answers to 'how much?' And the other to 'how much have you got?'" His friends circled around her, blocking any route of escape. "In other words, give us your money!"

Felisha looked at their faces and recognized the man speaking as the same one Matt had almost gotten into a fight with earlier that day. The same man the boy had aimed a gun at for beating up his mother. The memory of it filled her with a sudden sense of fear since she knew the man was willing to hurt a woman like she was nothing at all. He wasn't a decent man, nor were his two friends, she guessed. She said nervously, "I am courting Matt Bannister. I am returning to the hotel from having dinner with him. Now if you'll excuse me." She hoped Matt's name would clear a path through them like the parting of the Red Sea.

"Whoa!" Richie Thorn said mockingly. "Well, why isn't Matt walking you home then? Oh, it didn't go so well, huh?" It was easy to see that she had been crying by her red and glossy eyes. "Tell him thank you for sending you out alone for me. Now, how about you open your money purse up and give us what you got? In return, I'll let you cross our street unharmed." She had been carrying her floral cloth purse in her hand instead of in her coat pocket.

"Why are you doing this? I just told you Matt and I are courting," she said nervously. She was tempted to make a run for the door of the hotel, but there was no way past the other two men.

Richie shook his head. "Don't lie to me, ma'am. He's courting the dancer, Christine. And we all know that because we all want to be him!" He chuckled at the agreement of his two friends. The man's face hardened. "Last chance. Give us your money or...I'll beat it out of you. Either way, I'm taking your money." He reached over, grabbed the cloth purse, and yanked it out of her hand.

Panic seized her and Felisha blurted in a shaken voice, "Give me my purse! It's all I have." She began to sob.

"Ohh, don't cry," Bruce Ellison, one of the two men blocking her way to the hotel, teased. "Money's easy to get. Just do what we're doing and get some more." He laughed.

Richie chuckled as he opened the purse to take the money.

"Please, give me my money. It's all I have..." she repeated through her fearful tears.

"And it's all we need," he said in reply.

Chusi came running across the street behind Felisha and jumped up and drove his knee into the chest of Bruce Ellison, knocking him to the street with a hard hit to the back of his head. Chusi landed on his feet and turned around to look at the other man who blocked her path to the door, whose name was Bobby Alper. Chusi faked a right fist to the man's face, and when he raised his hands to block the strike, Chusi stepped forward and slammed his right foot into Bobby's groin as hard as he could. Bobby fell to his knees and then face-forward to the street while holding his groin.

"Chusi?" Richie asked, dumbfounded to see him attack his friends.

"Give her the purse, Ritchie!" Chusi said with more authority than Ritchie had ever heard him speak with before.

Ritchie chuckled. "Or what? What do you think you're doing? You don't want to throw fists with me, old man. I'll leave you bleeding on the ground." He sent out an unexpected quick jab, but Chusi pulled his head back just enough for it to miss.

Chusi glanced at Felisha. "Go inside now."

Felisha didn't hesitate. She held her dress up and jogged into the hotel.

"All right," Ritchie said, as he tucked the purse into his coat pocket and put up both of his hands to fight. "I think you had too much firewater tonight, but let's see what you got, old man."

Chusi smirked as he circled at a safe distance. "Years of experience and wisdom," he answered.

"You're a vagrant, so how wise can you be?" Ritchie asked as he leaped forward and swung a wide right toward Chusi's face. Chusi ducked and stepped under the blow toward Ritchie, and ended up behind him when the wild throw came to its end. Ritchie turned to face him quickly.

Chusi noticed Bruce Ellison standing up slowly while holding the back of his head. The Indian circled Ritchie with his hands open to block whatever he might try to do. His eyes darted to Bruce so as to know where he was to avoid turning his back on him. He kept his feet moving back and forth in a semi-circle to keep Ritchie moving and not allow him to take a good stance to make a solid strike.

"Come on and fight, if you're going to!" Ritchie yelled angrily.

"You're too slow for a young man."

"The hell I am!" Angered, Ritchie leapt forward to grab Chusi, but again, Chusi spun to one side and Ritchie was left grabbing air. "Damn it, Chusi! I'm not fighting you. Come on, guys, let's go!" Richie turned his back on Chusi to look at his friends.

Bobby was still on his knees, trying to catch his breath, and Bruce, who was now rubbing his chest, nodded agreeably with Ritchie.

Chusi gave Ritchie's lower back a solid kick that pushed him forward. Ritchie had to make a few steps to stay on his feet. He turned around and reached for Chusi, but couldn't connect. He was faster than Ritchie expected. "All right," Ritchie said. "No more games. If you don't walk away, I'm going to hurt you! Now's your chance, Chusi."

Chusi smirked for the first time like he was enjoying himself. "Horses generally don't play with fire, Ritchie."

"Huh?"

"You're big, bulky, and slow. I'm a Shoshone warrior. If we were in battle, you'd already be dead."

"Oh, yeah?"

Chusi nodded. "Yes."

Ritchie ran forward quickly to grab Chusi, but the wiry old man sidestepped to his left without thinking about Bruce being behind him. Bruce stepped forward and shoved Chusi toward Ritchie, who swung a right fist just as Chusi came into range. The blow caught Chusi on the cheekbone and he dropped to the ground. He began to spring back to his feet when Richie's boot connected with his face with great force. Chusi was knocked to his back and began to roll to his hands and knees. His head was clouded by the two blows, but he was determined to get back up on his feet. Another kick caught him in the ribs and knocked him back down. Bruce stomped on Chusi's chest.

"How's that feel?" Bruce yelled. "Hurts, doesn't it?"

"Not so fast now, are you?" Ritchie asked and kicked him again.

William Fasana came out of the hotel quickly and pulled out one of his .45 stainless steel revolvers as he walked toward the two men kicking Chusi. Without saying a word, he slammed his revolver across the side of Bruce's head. Bruce fell to the ground beside, Chusi holding his ear while crying out and making a painful grimace.

Ritchie stepped back, shocked to see William standing there glaring at him. "He started it, William! He kicked Bruce and Bobby first," he explained.

"Get up, Chusi," William said, his eyes never leaving Ritchie. "Where's Felisha's purse?"

"Well, I don't know her name, but here." He pulled Felisha's purse out of his coat pocket and held it out to William. "We were just horsing around with her for fun when Chusi attacked us. I was going to give it back."

"Sure, you were. Chusi, take the purse and check it for her money." William waited for Chusi to take the purse.

"We were. I don't rob ladies, you know that," Ritchie said nervously.

"No, you just beat them. I heard what you said to Matt today. So, you think we Fasana and Bannister boys are afraid of you and your brother Joe, huh? Well, I'm not afraid, nor are any of my cousins. I can assure you of that."

"I don't want to fight you, William..."

"Of course not. But let's make this interesting. I'm a gambler, right? So, let's gamble a bit. I was hired to be security at the hotel because I'm supposed to be tough enough to do the job. When someone like you is out here on the street calling me a coward and it goes unchallenged, it makes me look like one. I can't have that."

"I didn't call you a coward."

William continued, "Sure, you did! So, right now is your chance to show everyone I work with, our guests and everyone else around here, that you'd be a better man for the job than me. It's a piece-of-cake job with free room and board. You can gamble all night, or drink with the pretty women at your will. You'd love it! The job is great, and it sure beats going down that hole you go into every day at the mine for a few dollars. And it would get you out of that pigsty of Slater's Mile and into luxury. It's an opportunity of a lifetime for you, Ritchie. All you have to do is beat me in a fist fight, and it's yours. I'll make sure Lee hires you if you can whip me. I'm a man of my word. Go for it whenever you're ready," he said and holstered his revolver and unbuckled his gun belt. "Hold this, Chusi."

Ritchie narrowed his eyes, and without hesitating, he threw a hard right fist and connected with William's cheek as he handed his gun belt away. It was a stunning blow that knocked him off-balance, and he stumbled a few steps to remain on his feet. Ritchie followed and threw another hard-right fist to his face. William fell to the ground.

Ritchie paused and looked down at him with a victorious grin. "I didn't want to fight you, William. But without your guns, you're nothing. Clean out your room tonight, because I'm about to move in."

William nodded with a bloody grin from the ground and spat out a mouthful of blood. "Good to hear, but it ain't over yet."

Ritchie stepped forward and kicked him in the ribs once, and then again. Cringing at the boot to his ribs, William scrambled away just far enough to get to his feet. As he was expecting, Ritchie had followed him quickly and threw another hard-right fist toward his head. William raised his left arm in a circular motion and caught Ritchie's right arm in an over-hook. He pulled Ritchie's extended arm in tight to his body to lock it there. Immediately William turned into him and brought his knee up and drove it into Ritchie's abdomen, knocking the wind out of him. William then kneed his abdomen, bending Ritchie over as far as his locked arm would allow him to go. William released the over-hooked arm, grabbed Ritchie by the hair with both hands, and pulled his head down while bringing his knee up in hard blow to the face. He held Ritchie's head in place and drove his knee into his face repeatedly until Ritchie's knees collapsed onto the ground. William let go of his hair, and his head hit the street, barely conscious. Blood flowed heavily from a broken nose, a severely split lip, and a small gash above his eye. His face was swelling and looked like it had been kicked by a horse.

William looked at Ritchie's two friends and spat out some more blood. "Either of you want my job? Now's your chance."

Bruce shook his head. "No."

Bobby just shook his head as he finally stood up.

William nodded and knelt to lift Ritchie's head by the hair. He looked at the bloody face. "Well, I suspect you'll be swinging that pick tomorrow in the depths of the mine after all. I guess it goes to show you greed can get you hurt, huh?" he asked with a bloody grin. "Maybe you shouldn't gamble so much, Richie. Especially when your mouth's bigger than your fight!" He let Ritchie's face fall back to the ground and stood up.

Chusi brought him his gun belt, and William took it and wrapped it around his waist. "Matt sent me to get you. He wants to see you right now."

"Now?" William asked.

"Now."

William frowned. "Do you know why?"

Chusi nodded as he gazed at William. "Say nothing to no one, just go. His words, not mine."

William looked at him for a moment, and then glanced at the door of the hotel, where a crowd of customers from the Monarch Lounge, the desk clerk, and

Felisha all stood watching. "Does Felisha know why he wants me?"

Chusi shook his head. "Say nothing to no one, just go," Chusi emphasized.

William frowned. "Okay, I get it. Give me the purse, and I'll go."

"Say nothing to her," Chusi said.

William walked over to Felisha while his customers greeted him with words of adoration for the night's entertainment. "Your purse, my dear lady. I don't think they'll be harassing you again."

"Thank you," she said without any emotion, then turned away from him and walked into the hotel.

William joined Chusi on the street with a slight smile. "Why do I get the feeling Matt pissed her off again?"

25

Pick Lawson took a deep breath as he opened his eyes to a dark cave and slowly pulled himself out of the depths of sleep. The fire had burnt out except a few red coals, and the coldness from outside was overtaking the mineshaft. He turned his head toward the other cot, expecting to see Christine sleeping, but she wasn't there. "Christine, I'm awake, just so you know," he said, thinking she was in the back of the mineshaft using the privy. When there was no response, it dawned on him that there was no lantern light reflecting on the walls either. "Christine!" he sat up and hollered. "Christine!" he yelled louder.

He began to curse and stood up. He reached for his gun belt and wrapped it around his waist in a hurry, then grabbed his coat and put it on. He stepped out of the mine and yelled, "Christine!" There was no sound except his voice echoing. He saw that the two horses were still tied to a small tree. He saddled his and rode down the main gorge until he came to the pool where he could ride up the ridge. He could hear the waterfall where the gorge continued down a narrow shaft between the cliffs.

It had become all too clear that Christine had taken advantage of his mercy not to tie her up and made a run for it. He had no idea how long he had slept, but it was dark out, so it was far longer than he had wanted to. The ridge alone would take some time for her to climb up, so, there was a chance he could find her along the road, but if not, he needed to get to Jim Hexum and let him know he had lost their ticket for a better tomorrow. They needed to find her before Matt could relocate her and she disappeared into thin air again. The Eckmans would be seeing their daughter in thirty-six hours or so, with twenty thousand dollars just waiting for them. However, it was slipping away faster than a greased pig if he couldn't find her on the way to town. Pick kicked his horse and began to climb the ridge. If he could follow her trail, it would make finding her a lot easier, but it was too dark to see a thing. He rode up the ridge and onto the main road and began riding toward Branson at a steady pace.

Two miles outside Branson, he ran into three mine employees walking back to Slater's Mile. One of them held a rag over his face as they walked. Pick was in a hurry, but he stopped his horse with amusement that he couldn't pass up. "Ritchie, what happened to you? It looks like you ran right into a wall." He knew the three men from the saloons around town. He had no respect for either of the Thorn brothers or the group of friends they hung around with.

Ritchie spoke from under his bloody rag. "If you

know what's good for you, you'll shut up and move on, Pick." His voice was oddly different from the swollen nasal passages.

Pick chuckled. "Talk's about all you got. Looks like someone else thought so too."

Bobby spoke. "It's kind of late for you to be out here so far, isn't it?"

Pick nodded. "I've been looking for that missing girl from the dance hall. I figure there'd be a reward, and I could use the extra money. Any news in town about her tonight?"

Bobby shook his head. "None. Someone's got her. We'll probably never see her again. Which is too bad. She was the prettiest of all the dance hall girls."

"Hmm. You might be right. I found nothing, but she must be somewhere. So, who busted you up, Ritchie? Ugly John finally get tired of your guff?"

Ritchie glared at him over the rag but said nothing.

"William Fasana," Bobby answered.

Pick chuckled. "You had ought to know to leave him alone. Anyway, I need to go," he said and rode forward, leaving the three men behind.

He entered the quiet and empty streets of Branson and rode to Rose Street, curious if Bella's Dance Hall had burned down or not. He was relieved to see it still stood with very little visible damage to the exterior except for some smoke damage to the paint. Lanterns burned in the upstairs windows behind the curtains, and the downstairs windows were lit up faintly as well. The place was closed, but the dance hall was always closed on Sunday night. A sense of relief came over him, knowing it still stood and was livable. His intention in starting the fire was to get Christine out of the building where she could be taken, not particularly wanting to burn the whole place down. It had worked out well for him, and seemed to work well for the dance hall too. He rode past it quickly in case Christine was inside and looked out and saw him. The first thing he needed to do was let Jim know Christine had escaped, so he stopped at the hotel Hexum was staying in. He was a bit sour that Jim had not come back to the mine to check in on them. He tied his horse to the hitching rail and went inside.

"Can I help you?" the desk clerk asked. He was a middle-aged man with severe balding on top and brown hair on the sides. He sounded bored and looked to be suffering from a lack of sleep.

"I'm here to see Jim Hexum. Do you know if he's in his room?"

The man frowned. "Jim Hexum is dead. You'll find him standing outside the sheriff's office if you want to see him, though."

"What?" Pick asked with horror. His concern was noticeable.

"Uh-huh. Matt Bannister shot him dead today outside the Monarch Hotel."

"Matt Bannister?" Pick's breath was sucked out of his body as a wall of fear filled him. "Why?" he heard himself asking.

The man behind the counter shrugged. "Rumor has it Jim took Christine Knapp from the dance hall when it burned. She's still missing, but Matt shot Jim dead for it. Someone said Jim told Matt he killed her and tossed her body in the river. Matt shot him four times in front of everyone for it, too."

Pick put up a hand. "And the girl, she's still missing?"

"To my knowledge. Some folks are searching the river, but no one's found her yet that I'm aware of."

Pick turned around to leave but turned back when he reached the door. "Is Matt searching the river?"

The man shrugged. "I have no idea. All I know is what I hear. He was apparently close to that girl, and killed the man that took her."

Pick nodded and walked outside. "Good Lord," he said, taking his hat off and rubbing his hands through his hair. He could see Bella's Dance Hall up the street a few blocks and considered bursting through the door at gunpoint and demanding Christine come with him with the same hostility that Jim must have felt when he hit her in the wagon. Pick was growing angry, and his fear was turning desperate as he tried to find a way for self-preservation. For the first time since being on Windsor Ridge a few months before, he would have to think through his unexpected change in circumstances. The one thing that he'd had going for him was Matt didn't know who he was. It was most probable that Christine had gone straight to Matt upon reaching town and would tell him she had been held at the mine. She would tell Matt her kidnapper's name was Pick, but to his best recollection, he couldn't remember telling her his last name. Upon investigation around town, it was almost certain that someone would identify him, and even tell Matt where he lived. Over the past two weeks of planning, many people down on Rose Street had seen him with Jim

Hexum. Even Matt had seen them together just the day before.

Pick climbed onto his horse, rode over to Main Street, and stopped in front of Sheriff Tim Wright's office. Two lanterns, one on each side of the pine casket, lit up the body of Bloody Jim Hexum. The man who'd had a hard and dangerous reputation as the most feared bounty hunter in the West was now still, harmless and dead, propped upright in a box. Blood stains on his shirt indicated the four gunshots that had done him in. A large plaque was nailed to the office wall beside the coffin.

It read:

Here lies Bloody Jim Hexum,

Killed by US Marshal Matt Bannister for stealing a woman.

It was obvious that it was placed there for photos to be taken and for the public to view his body. Why he was placed in front of the sheriff's office and not the marshal's? Pick didn't know.

"It's hard to believe Bloody Jim's deader than a doornail, isn't it?" a deputy of Tim Wright's asked as he walked from behind the office around to the front. His name was Mark Theisen, and he was the youngest of the Branson deputies. He was a handsome twenty-five-year-old with a friendly countenance.

"Yeah," Pick said as easily as he could. He knew he had been seen with Jim a lot recently and felt the urge to run. "Taking a woman, though? He deserves it. Any news of her yet?" he asked as naturally as he could.

"Nope. The sheriff has been searching the river but they haven't found her yet."

"And the marshal?"

Mark shrugged. "I haven't seen him much. I have no idea. The talk is he's taking it kind of hard. I'll tell ya, I wouldn't want to be involved in this. If there is anyone else, we'll have two or three more coffins filling our porch when he finds them."

"I'd be running if I was them," Pick said. "Well, have a good night."

Pick turned his horse and began riding toward his home. There was no secondary plan of a deceptive noose to hang from that could keep him out of trouble this time. On Windsor Ridge, he had killed the only witness who could place him at the bank robbery in Loveland. He had then gone to Morton Sperry with a story of being deceived by his friends to rob the bank and frame Morton. He changed the story a bit, and Morton was appreciative enough he helped Pick get a falsified receipt from the tannery for his paint horse, which could have been used to identify him as a bank robber and the murderer of Brent Boyle. He had a receipt that proved he wasn't with his friends when they robbed the Loveland Bank. It had been a terrifying adventure, and he had been lucky to think of ways to get away with it free and clear. His plans had worked, but this time, there was nothing anyone could do for him. He was totally alone and had two choices, but neither one involved the twenty thousand dollars that would have been his if he had just tied Christine up! He was angry, but above and beyond the anger, it was the fear of Matt Bannister finding him that consumed him. Matt might shoot him just as quickly as he had shot Jim, without giving him a chance to surrender. It sure didn't sound like he had given Jim a chance. Pick had no choice but to cut his losses and leave town immediately to save his life. It was only a matter of time until he was identified and ended propped up beside Jim Hexum. The sooner he left town, the better off he would be, because Matt would be looking for him by morning.

He rode quickly to his cottage and tied his horse to a small hitching post. He had a very short time to grab what he could carry in his saddlebags and leave town. Portland seemed like a big enough city to get lost in, and employment could be found somewhere. He could change his name and start over as a law-abiding citizen, for the most part. He unlocked his door and entered his dark home. On the counter to the left of the door was a lantern with a lit wick turned down low. He reached for the knob and turned up the light, and froze when he heard the mechanical click of a revolver's hammer being pulled back behind him. He was afraid to turn around.

"Don't even try it or you'll be as dead as your partner." Matt Bannister's voice sent a chill of foreboding through him.

Pick raised his hands slowly and closed his eyes, expecting to be shot. He knew he was only a moment from death's door. Pick was fast with his gun, but not nearly fast enough to beat a man with his gun already drawn. He slowly turned around and saw Matt sitting comfortably at Pick's own dinner table. It was a small round table with two chairs, one of which Matt reclined in with his boots on the table. Matt looked like a man waiting to kill another, and now his chance had come.

Pick was too scared to speak, and waited to be shot in his own small one-bedroom cottage.

Matt spoke with no emotion on his cold face." Remove your gun belt slowly and throw it over here by me." He nodded to the floor beside him. "And then sit down."

Pick did as he was instructed. He tossed his gun belt to the floor gently and pulled out a chair to sit. Matt moved his feet from the table to the floor.

"Tell me," Matt began, "how did you know Possum Overguard and his wife?"

Pick was taken completely off-guard by the question. "Um..."

Matt spoke coarsely. "Don't 'um' me, answer the question!" His eyes were hardening fast.

"The Sperry-Helms Gang," Pick answered in a shaky voice.

"Are you a member?" The fierceness in Matt's eyes made it perfectly clear why so many people feared the man.

Pick nodded.

"That's how you knew it wasn't the Eckmans' daughter in the fire?" he asked.

Pick nodded.

"What makes you think Christine is their daughter?"

Pick smirked and said in a nervous voice. "I knew you were lying, for one, and when I saw you two together, it only made sense."

"How so?"

"Everyone knows her husband died, and she is different than all the other girls. More elegant and classy, like a socialite. I knew the night she sang that song for you that she would have no other reason to thank you like that. Think about it; her parents thought she was dead. That meant she could now move around freely and marry you," Pick said as he looked at Matt. "You went wrong asking them for the money."

"You think so?" Matt asked, curious as to why Pick would say that.

He nodded. "Listen, I know I'm in a lot of trouble here, but she's a very nice lady. I hope you can make her as happy as she deserves to be. She is amazing."

"She is," Matt agreed, looking at Pick oddly. For being a member of the Sperry-Helms Gang that was known for brutality and intimidation, Pick seemed to be a sincere, caring man at the moment. "Whose idea was it to burn the dance hall and kidnap her?"

"Jim's. I just went along with him," he said, looking in Matt's eyes, and then looked away.

Matt hesitated for a moment to watch Pick's body language. He knew Pick was lying, but he wanted to get a visual of what to look for when he lied. Other than the lack of eye contact, a slight twitch to the right side of his lips was the only indication that showed. Pick was an accomplished liar. "Jim didn't know her from King David, nor did he know the Overguards. Don't lie to me again! Did you know her father, Louis Eckman, was killed yesterday? You probably weren't aware of that, huh?"

Pick's eyes widened and he stared at Matt. "No. How?"

"Their coach was robbed yesterday about fifty miles from here. He wanted his daughter back so much he fought the robbers to keep the money. He was shot and killed." He paused before adding, "You would've had better luck setting this up and then robbing them on the road yourself. Missus Eckman will be here tomorrow night, they say. You're supposed to meet her on Tuesday, right? In front of the Branson Gazette building to make sure it makes the news. Am I right?"

Pick nodded, amazed that Matt knew so many details. "Christine told you that?"

"She filled in some blanks, but I'm a good investigator."

Pick shook his head with frustration. "I'd be that much richer if I had just tied her up like I was going to."

"I would've tracked you down and killed you."

Pick looked at him with a surprised expression. "You're not supposed to be like the Sperrys and the Helms boys. Christine said you were a fair man. What's going to happen now that you've caught me?"

"You're facing quite a few years in prison."

Pick frowned and sighed slowly.

"Unless you're interested in making a deal?" Matt said quietly so no one could hear.

Pick looked at him curiously. "What kind of a deal?"

Matt laid his revolver down on the table. "You have me in a tough place, Pick, and I don't like to be blackmailed."

"I never blackmailed you!" Pick exclaimed quickly.

Matt continued, "No, you tried to expose me for being a fraud. First, you need to know Christine to my knowledge is not the Eckmans' daughter. She probably told you that herself. How do you know the Overguards weren't friends with Nathan Webster and Catherine Eckman? No one knows what happened to those two. When I found that chess set and that metal box of letters, I assumed it was the bodies of Nathan and Catherine.

Apparently, I was wrong, and now I have Pinkerton detectives investigating me and assuming I have hidden Catherine. You have caused me a lot of trouble, and I don't appreciate it," he said sharply. "Because of your mistaken identity, Louis Eckman is dead. Now Divinity Eckman is a fresh widow, and coming here with expectations of getting her daughter. If you had her daughter, she'd give you the money, but you don't. So, here's what I'm going to do for you and what you're going to do for me. You will keep your Tuesday appointment with Missus Eckman and try to swap Christine for the money. She will refuse to do so, and you'll probably be arrested by Sheriff Tim Wright. That much we know will happen. Now you and I are going to get our story straight, so you can walk away from this without prison time, and I get my honorable name back in the eyes of the Pinkertons and this community I serve. Not many people know right now, but on Tuesday, everyone will know about your accusations. And that's what I don't want to happen. Understood? Can you agree with that?"

Pick's disappointment showed. "Christine's really not their daughter?"

"If she was, do you think I'd say you're going to *try* to exchange her for the money? If she is, great. You solved one of the great mysteries the Pinkertons can't solve. You can keep the money, and all is well, except for the arson, attempted murder, and kidnapping charges. But to my knowledge, she is not."

"Attempted murder? I didn't try to kill anyone!" he exclaimed emphatically.

"When you intentionally start a kerosene fire in a building full of people, it becomes attempted murder. You're lucky no one was injured too bad or killed while fighting it. There is a way around that, though, so let's get our story straight so we can both walk away from this."

"I'll tell them whatever you want to get out of here free and clear, and I'll never come back." Pick was very sincere.

Matt nodded. "Good. Now, to be sure that you're not going to talk to anyone about our agreement and keep you out of sight until Tuesday, I am going to keep you in my jail. Don't worry, no charges will be filed, and it's just a temporary holding cell. I will treat you right, and get you whatever you need. But for what you're getting, mainly another chance at life, I'd say that's a fair deal. If you resist, I will charge you with arson, kidnapping, attempted murder, and anything else I can think of to hold you. Right now, unless you have an argument, let's get you to the jail."

Pick frowned. "I don't have much of a choice, do I?"

Matt shook his head. "Not unless you want to try for your gun. But why do that when Christine is back safely, she said you treated her well, and all I want is my reputation intact? The choice is yours, though."

"I was excited to get that money," Pick said disappointedly. "Well, Christine did say you were a fair man. I guess I should believe her."

"I try to be fair."

"So, you keep your career and good name, and I hopefully get out of jail."

"No, I promise I will get you out of jail."

Pick looked at Matt with a slight, sad smile. "I wish she was interested in me because she is a very special lady. When this is all done and over with, you should ask her to marry you, Matt."

Matt frowned and changed the subject. "I already have a lady I am courting."

"You wouldn't know it, watching you and her together. That's what caught my attention, the way you two shine when you're together."

Matt's brows drew together in a questioning expression. He kept his thoughts to himself as he said, "Let's get you to the jail."

Pick sighed. "For the first time in my life, I don't mind going to jail. It's going to be the last time, though. If nothing else, I learned I want to marry someone like Christine and just live life without the fear of getting caught. Maybe working in the mine wouldn't be so bad if you had someone like her to come home to every day."

26

Felisha Conway wiped her eyes as she sat in a comfortable wing chair in the Graces' hotel room. The Graces' children and Dillon were sleeping in one of the bedrooms while Felisha sat with Rebecca and Richard Grace.

"He never mentioned Christine to me in any of his letters, and right now she's in his bed, and is Matt coming here to see me? No. He's out looking for whoever took her. I know it's not her fault and I shouldn't be angry at her for it, but I am. I came here to spend time with Matt, and I haven't spent hardly any time with him since I got here. Tomorrow he is busy doing something, he didn't say what. But he'll be gone most of the day, and then he doesn't know if he'll have time for me or not. Like I told him, I feel like I'm in second place. Second place to his job, and to Christine, tonight anyway." She sighed. "I wish I never came here. I feel like a burden to him."

Rebecca was the first to respond. "The only burden is his own unfaithfulness! You deserve better, Felisha.

He may be a decent man, but he's not cut out to be a father to Dillon or a husband to you. We should have known that from the start, with his violent past. It sounds like his whole family is a passel of heathens and violent men. You don't want Dillon growing up like that."

"No, I don't," she said softly.

"And," Rebecca continued, "you don't want to live your life wondering if he's faithful or downtown dancing with your nemesis."

"Nemesis?" Richard asked. "Rebecca, I think maybe you're being a bit too harsh."

"Harsh? Are you kidding me? Matt has been ignoring her, putting her second to that girl, and acting like she doesn't matter for this whole weekend. He didn't even walk her home tonight, and she was robbed! God knows what could have happened if that Indian hadn't followed her. And why was he following her? Matt has been treated Felisha like dung all weekend. Why would she want to stay around here or even see him again if by chance he has the audacity to show up here at all? Richard, he was making dinner plans with that dancer when he knew Felisha was coming to see him! That should tell you all you need to know."

Richard addressed Felisha. "I don't know what kind of relationship they have, but I watched Matt and you dancing last night at Saul's reception, and there is no doubt he loves you. It was plain to see. And then that fire broke out, and he's been busy since then. His friend was kidnapped and wasn't found until tonight. I am glad of that since we had been praying for her to be found,

Rebecca. I think he's just been busy trying to find her and the men who took her."

Rebecca answered sharply, "Maybe so, but you'd expect him to show more affection toward Felisha, wouldn't you? And not want to share his home with another woman. I think Felisha has a reason to be upset."

"I don't doubt that she has a reason to be upset, but at the same time, I think it has to do with being busy with priorities and not intentional neglect. Matt's a good man, he's just got a lot going on."

Rebecca shook her head heatedly. "No. Maybe it has more to do with him pretending to be a gentleman in Sweethome to impress her. And now that she's here in his hometown and he has a new lady to impress, his true colors are showing."

Richard chuckled. "Felisha, what do you honestly think? With all that's been going on around here, what do you think? You know him better than we do."

Felisha shrugged sadly. "I think I am angry right now, and hurt. He's never treated me like this before. But like Rebecca was saying, I've only seen him in Sweethome and communicated in letters." She sighed heavily. "I don't want my son growing up around the violence, and I can't stand the idea of another husband putting me second to his career."

"And you think Matt will do that?" Richard asked softly.

She smirked sadly. "He already has. I always said I'd never marry a lawman anyway. It was stupid of me to fall for him."

"Matt's busy, I understand," Rebecca said to Richard.

"But if he loved Felisha, then why is she here crying because of the way she has been treated? You'd never made me feel second to anyone or anything except Jesus."

"No, I wouldn't. But I don't have the burden of someone else's life depending on me either. I can't imagine the pressure he is under, so maybe we should give him more grace than we are. You know Truet as well as anyone, Felisha. Why don't you talk to him tomorrow and see what he says?"

Felisha nodded. "Maybe that's a good idea. I haven't had a chance to talk to him much."

"I think that would be a good idea. He'll tell you if you have anything to be concerned about or not. He isn't going to lie to you. It's my opinion that Truet would not stand for Matt not being true to you. He will be able to tell you if Matt is too busy to see you or just saying so. And I think that's what you're really struggling with."

Felisha sighed. "Maybe."

Rebecca continued, "You'll have to forgive me, but seeing that dancer with Matt when we arrived was enough for me. I know women, and she has her sights on him. Women are deceptive, and she knew you were coming this weekend. It wouldn't surprise me if she set this all up to keep you away from him, so she got all his attention."

Felisha smiled. "No, she didn't plan it. Who knows what happened to her, but she came back with a horrible black eye and a bruised-up face. She wasn't faking it."

Richard stared at his wife in disbelief. "Maybe you should be writing books, Rebecca. That's quite a vivid imagination you have."

Rebecca shrugged. "It wouldn't surprise me, is all."

"I'll try to talk to Truet tomorrow," Felisha said.

"Truet is an honorable man," Rebecca offered. "You should marry him, Felisha. I've always thought so since Jenny Mae died. You should leave Matt behind and wait for Truet to be ready to move on with his life."

Felisha frowned as she looked at Rebecca. "Truet has moved on from Jenny Mae already."

"What?" Rebecca asked, leaning forward. "With who?"

Felisha smirked sadly. "Matt's sister, Annie."

"They just met!" Richard remarked with surprise. "They were just introduced last night."

Felisha shook her head. "No, they've been seeing each other for a while now. Matt doesn't know. They were going to tell him tonight, but it was interrupted by Christine."

Rebecca laughed. "Serves him right."

Felisha frowned. "You just don't like him, do you?"

"I did until I seen him with that girl."

"Well, I love him, but this weekend has been horrible. And if he's just ignoring me, then he'll break my heart."

27

Christine had changed out of the clothes Chusi had given her and put on a pair of white one-piece long johns she found in Matt's dresser drawer. They were a bit too big for her, but they were clean and smelled a whole lot better than Chusi's did. She laid in Matt's bed with the lantern down low so she could sleep. She had come into Matt's room soon after he had left to get away from the uncomfortableness of being alone with Truet and Annie. She didn't know either of them and could tell they were both uncomfortable with her as well. It was only expected though; they'd had a nice dinner going when it was interrupted by her and Chusi. Her presence had caused a scene, with both Felisha and Regina leaving soon after. If she had ever felt the discomfort of not being welcome, it was tonight. She wanted to hide, and Matt's room was the only place she could go to be alone.

She was exhausted but couldn't sleep. She turned her face into Matt's pillow and smelled his scent on the linens. She closed her eyes and smiled as she breathed it in. The familiar scent of him was one she breathed in deeply every time she was close to him, whether it was while dancing slowly like they did or a hug like when she had entered his home tonight. She really didn't care about Felisha watching her with those piercing eyes. She had needed to be held, and that was all she'd cared about at that moment. Matt's presence in her life had become one of security and safety since the first time she had danced with him. His arms around her could calm the fiercest storm raging within her. If he was with her, she knew no one could harm her. His scent on the pillow brought the warmth of security to her heart.

Annie's loud laugh was one factor why she couldn't sleep, but the joy in her laughter brought a grin to Christine's own lips. She listened to Truet and Annie horse-playing around the family room like two flirtatious, unruly kids left alone for the first time. Christine had no idea what they were doing, but it sounded like they were running around and jumping over the furniture. Suddenly there was a hard fall that shook the floor, followed by Annie saying, "You jackass!" It was then silent and still. Alarmed that Annie might be hurt or curious if Truet was strangling her, Christine got out of bed and wrapped a blanket around her before walking out of the room. She stopped suddenly when she saw Truet and Annie lying on the rug, embraced in a kiss. Annie gently broke the kiss and opened her eyes to look at Christine, who was staring at them.

"Excuse me," Christine said awkwardly. "I thought... someone might've gotten hurt."

Annie laughed.

Truet smiled with a chuckle. "No."

"Um, this is kind of embarrassing, but do you and Matt have a chamber pot?" she asked quickly to change the subject.

Truet smiled his handsome smile. "No, we don't use those. But we do have a privy out back that's quite a bit nicer than most. Just go out the back door, and you'll see it."

"Okay, thanks." She walked out the back door into the yard and shivered in the cold. She used the privy and came back in the house, keeping her face downward and feeling very awkward as she passed through the family room.

"Nice long johns, sis," Annie teased with a chuckle. She was sitting on the smaller davenport by herself. Truet was standing in the middle of the room, looking like he wanted to say something.

Christine's face reddened. "It's all I could find to wear. Matt won't let me go back to the dance hall tonight."

Annie shrugged. "I wear them too sometimes. They're a bit warmer than a camisole and bloomers on a cold night. There's no shame in that."

"I suppose not. Well, goodnight," she said and stepped toward the bedroom. She was stopped by Truet.

"Christine, before you go." He hesitated for a moment to bite his bottom lip in an awkward pause. "Um, what you saw is a...well, Matt doesn't know. And we'd like to keep it that way if you don't mind."

Annie said pointedly, "That means don't tell Matt what you seen us doing or about us in general."

"We're courting, but not telling Matt yet," Truet explained, with a hint of shame in his voice.

Christine bit her bottom lip while raising her eyebrows in question. "I won't say anything, but you do know if he walked in while you two were on the floor, he'd figure it out. You might want to lock the door."

Truet looked at the front door and groaned. "Yeah, I probably should."

"Well, goodnight," Christine said, then went into the bedroom and laid down in the bed. She covered up and closed her eyes.

AN HOUR LATER, she was woken up by Matt talking to Truet and Annie in the family room. He was talking softly so as to not wake her so she couldn't hear what he was saying. She wanted to get up and go see him, but she remained where she was, hoping he would come in to see her. She didn't have to wait too long since he opened the door gently and peeked in to see if she was awake. He didn't say anything to wake her, he just looked in on her and then began to close the door.

"Did you find Pick?" she asked quietly.

"Did I wake you?" he asked, holding the door half closed.

"No, I was awake. Did you find him?" She turned the lantern up to see him. She moved over to the center of the bed and patted the edge of the bed to invite him to sit down.

He sat down and nodded. "I did. He's resting comfortably in my jail. I wanted to talk to you and thought about waking you up if you were sleeping. I need to leave town in the morning and will be gone most of the day. I need you to stay here with Annie tomorrow. I don't want anyone knowing you've been found yet."

She sat up and crossed her legs on the bed with concern. "Why not? What is going on, Matt?"

Matt ran his hand over his hair anxiously. "I am being investigated by a Pinkerton detective, Christine. Jim and Pick caused a bit of a mess by thinking you were the late Catherine Eckman. Yesterday, Louis Eckman was killed in a robbery attempt. It was a set up by the driver who knew the Eckmans were rich and unfamiliar with the territory. They didn't know about the twenty thousand dollars in the safe Pick and Jim demanded. On Tuesday, Missus Eckman will be here, expecting to collect her daughter from Pick. I don't want to see a big crowd there when Missus Eckman realizes she got her hopes up and lost her husband for nothing. Pick knows he isn't getting any money, but he agreed to escort you to Missus Eckman on Tuesday. So, if you will, stay here with Annie and just hold out for one more day. Please."

"Why not just tell her the truth when she gets here? That way, she doesn't have to go through that second devastation. Why are you having Pick take me to her? There's no reason for that. Are you in trouble, Matt?"

He glanced at the opposite wall and then back at her. "I won't be if you let Pick and me take you there on Tuesday. I don't want to get into too many details, but the reason I want to keep the meeting is that everything I was accused of and suspected of by the Pinkertons will be forgotten about when they realize the accusations were all based on a mistake. A fraud, if you will. I promise I'll have you home and in your best dress by Tuesday afternoon. Right now, the less people know that you're safe, the better off we are. Do you think you could tolerate staying here that long?"

Her lips curved slowly upward into a small smile. "Sure," she said softly. She added," But since you mentioned my attire, I have nothing to wear except your long johns. I won't put Chusi's clothes back on. He saved my life and I owe him a lot, but his clothes stink!"

Matt chuckled. "I'll send Annie to the store in the morning to buy you a dress and something to wear at night."

"That would be nice. So, where are you going tomorrow?" she asked.

Matt hesitated. "I have to go let my brother know Annie's going to be staying here for a few more days. He's watching her children. It's the least I could do so he doesn't worry and come looking for her," he explained.

"I can't go with you?"

"Not this time."

"Are you taking Felisha?"

Matt shook his head. "No. I have to go alone."

"Matt, are you okay?" she asked sincerely.

He nodded tiredly. "I will be."

"Have you spoken to Felisha?" Christine asked softly.

Matt shook his head slowly. "No. And I am too tired to go talk to her tonight. What I really want is you to get out of my bed so I can get some sleep," he said playfully as he leaned back and braced his right arm on the other side of her.

"Really?" she asked.

He chuckled. "No, I'm sleeping on the davenport. My sister will be joining you in here, though."

Christine hooked his right arm with her left and pulled it toward her while the crook of her right arm went across his chin and pulled him backward, then she rolled onto her stomach to pull him onto the bed. She realized by the ache in her arm that she had hit Matt's chin harder than she had intended to. Listening to Annie and Truet horse-playing in the family room had sparked the impulsive playfulness. "Sorry!" She laughed. "I didn't mean to hit you so hard. Is your mouth okay?"

He laid still for a moment, looking at her hovering close over him. "Yeah, I'll be okay. Nice move, though." He yawned.

"I really didn't mean to hurt you." She looked sorry.

"Sure..." Matt rubbed his chin, pretending it ached.

She laid back on the pillow facing Matt with a humored smile. "Thank you, Matt, for being my friend," she said sincerely.

He turned to his side to face her. "Why do you say that?"

"It just feels good knowing I can talk to you and be silly sometimes, and no matter how I look, you're still willing to care for me."

He smiled tiredly. "It's my pleasure. Get some sleep."

"I'm not tired now. Are you sure you don't want to stay here and talk a little longer with me? I'm not going to see you tomorrow."

"You will tomorrow afternoon," he said, his eyes

growing heavy. "I'll be back around..." He had fallen asleep on top of the covers beside her.

She frowned. "You can't sleep in here, Matt. It's not appropriate." She watched him sleep, then got out of bed and walked to the bedroom door. "Annie, could you come here?" she asked.

Annie stepped into the room and looked at Christine, who stood in the loose long johns behind the door, out of view of Truet. Annie chuckled. "You really need to get your own size to wear."

"Matt's sleeping," Christine said with concern. "Should I sleep on the davenport?"

Annie looked at Matt and laughed at the situation Christine had found herself in. "Well, one of us have to sleep in here, and I'd end up shooting him if he snores. So I guess it's you, Chickadee."

"We're not married, or even courting. Don't you think that would be a bit scandalous?"

"Maybe," Annie said with a shrug. "But the good news is, we haven't had a good scandal in the family for a long time."

"Couldn't we share Truet's bed or something?"

Annie raised her eyebrows. "Have you ever seen Truet's bed? It's a cot. I don't think we'll be sharing a cot. Besides, he's on top of the covers, so he isn't going to bother you."

Christine rolled her eyes. "Won't Felisha disapprove? I don't want to cause any more trouble."

Annie chuckled. "I don't think Felisha's going to be coming back tonight. You'll be fine. Just go to bed."

"I haven't slept in the same bed with a man since my

husband. I don't plan to until I am married again. Would you mind if I slept on the davenport?"

Annie frowned. "Do you want my brother to die tonight?"

Christine chuckled from the sincerity that Annie asked with. "No."

"Then I'll take the davenport. Look if anyone asks, just say you were saving his life. And that's not a lie. Nobody's going to know anyway. I'm not going to tell Felisha, and if I tell Regina, it will only be to get her fired up again." She laughed. "Trust me, it'll be fine, and you haven't got much of a choice. We could wake him up and make him go to the davenport, but to be honest, he needs to sleep."

"I know. That's why I didn't want to wake him."

"Honestly, Chickadee, you both need sleep. There's nothing inappropriate going on, right? Then go to sleep with a clear conscious and forget about it. He's not interested in you right now, he's already asleep. And in the morning, we'll get you some real clothes."

Christine's brows came together quizzically. "Matt already talked to you about getting me some new clothes?"

Annie nodded. "Yeah, he did. You can keep the door open if that will make you feel better but get some sleep. We have a lot to talk about tomorrow."

28

Matt opened his eyes, slowly trying to pull himself out of a heavy night's sleep. He stared at the ceiling for a moment and looked over to see Christine sleeping close beside him. A sudden sense of alarm shot through him to see her sleeping in the same bed as him. He was tempted to jump out of bed and separate himself from her, but her head rested on his right arm with his blanket snug around her neck, and she was sleeping soundly. He didn't remember falling asleep but did recall waking up in the middle of the night feeling cold and getting under the covers. He stared at her beautiful, angelic face that slept so peacefully on his arm that he hated to move. Occasionally in a man's life, there was a moment he wished he could save forever. He would give almost anything to have a photographer take a picture of her sleeping just as she was. Her swollen eye and bruised face couldn't take away from how beautiful she appeared while she slept. Her dark hair was ruffled, and a strand of it hung over her face. He reached over and moved the hair out of her face with his left hand. He couldn't help the slight warm smile that formed on his lips as he watched her sleeping. He carefully pulled his arm out from under her head and backed his way out of the bed slowly so he wouldn't wake her. He made sure she was covered and left the room, closing the door behind him quietly.

Annie opened her eyes as he crossed the family room toward the kitchen. "You better pay me five dollars, or I'll tell Felisha you slept with Christine," she said tiredly.

Matt stopped and looked at her seriously. "Why didn't you wake me up and send me to the davenport? If Felisha had come by, there would have been no way to explain it."

"Sure, there would." She yawned. "You both needed some sleep." She closed her eyes and snuggled her face deeper into the pillow she was using. "So do I."

"I'll start a fire for you."

"Uh-huh. Be quiet," Annie said quietly as she tried to go back to sleep.

Matt went into the kitchen and started a fire in the cook stove. When he had finished, he put on his boots and then his gun belt. He was just putting on his buffalo-hide coat when there was a loud knock on the door.

"Geez!" Annie exclaimed and waved toward the door irritably.

"Who is it?" Matt asked in a soft voice.

"It's me! Come on, it's cold out here. Open the door!" William Fasana said loudly.

Matt opened the door, and William stepped inside. "You asked me to let you know when Divinity Eckman arrived. Well, she got here about two in the morning.

Maybe she was tired, or maybe she was mad and needed a bath to cool down, but she was the rudest woman I've ever met. Leave your gun at home when you meet her because you might be tempted to shoot her! Who's that?" he asked, nodding toward the davenport. "Your sweet petunia?"

"Annie."

"Ohhh…" he said quietly, widening his eyes.

"You're sparky this morning, William. I didn't know you were such a morning person," Matt said.

"I haven't been to bed yet," he explained as he stepped toward the back of the davenport quietly. He grabbed the end of the davenport where Annie's head rested and pushed it forward with a hard shove, and then pulled it back with a hard jerk. Annie nearly fell off the davenport but caught herself with one arm on the floor.

"William, damn you!" she exclaimed quietly. "Leave me alone."

He laughed and flicked the top of her head quite hard with his index finger.

She tried to slap him, but he had stepped back, laughing. He looked at Matt and spoke seriously. "By the way Matt, your woman was robbed last night by our pal Ritchie Thorn and his two monkeys, Bruce and Bobby. Luckily, Chusi interfered until Felisha came and got me. They were beating Chusi up pretty good when I got there."

"What do you mean, she was robbed?" Matt asked with a glare in his eyes.

William shrugged. "They took her money. What's

robbing mean to you? Wake up, Matt! They took her money."

"Ritchie did?"

"You're beginning to sound like Adam. Yes, how many times do you need to be told?" he laughed.

"Did she get her money back? I'll go drag his ass out of that mine right now if not!"

"Oh, don't worry. He gave her money back. And I doubt he or his friends will be saying we're afraid of him or his brother anymore, either."

"Did you shoot him?" Matt asked.

"No, but I did work him over a bit. The last I saw of him, his two monkeys were helping him walk down the street. I felt so bad I gave them one of the hotel's towels to cover his face with. I'm not sure he even has a nose anymore, as bad it was broken. But it was fun. Say, do you want me to ride out with you today?"

Matt shook his head. "No, I need some time alone. So...was Felisha upset? Is she okay?"

"Hard to tell. She just took her money and went upstairs."

"You didn't check on her?"

"No. Well, I did go up to check on her, but she was visiting with her friends, the Graces. I could hear her talking through their door. I get the feeling those folks don't like me too much."

Annie quipped from the davenport, "'Moo,' Willy says. Even a dumb bovine could figure that out."

William looked over at her and smiled and then looked back at Matt. "Anyway, I don't know if she's upset or not. I do know her friend gave me a dirty look when I invited her husband into the Monarch Lounge. I don't think she liked the idea of it being a men's lounge only. She wears the britches, I'm betting. Am I right?"

"He's a reverend, William."

He laughed loudly. "Oh, that explains it!"

Matt's bedroom door opened, and Christine stood in the doorway, wrapped in a blanket. She saw William and closed the door quickly.

William looked at Matt and smiled while raising his eyebrows up and down. "You naughty dog! Now *that* would upset Felisha!" He pointed at his bedroom door.

Matt raised his hands and shook his head. "It's not what you're thinking. Nothing like that at all, so get your mind out of the gutter."

Annie giggled.

Truet opened his bedroom door and walked out, tucking his shirt into his pants. "Morning, William," he said louder than he usually did. He was a bit irritated about being woken up earlier than he wanted to be.

"Truet! Have you met Annie?" he asked with a knowing grin.

Truet nodded tiredly. "I have."

"Did you know Matt has a girl in his room? And unless my eyes are deceiving me, it's not his sweet petunia from Idaho. I say, that's a little risqué."

"Get out of here," Matt said with a smile. "You know me well enough to know nothing inappropriate happened."

"Yeah, that's what they said about Elizabeth, too. But there's a little Bannister boy walking around named Gabriel who still doesn't know what he is."

Matt's eyes turned harsh. "We laid that to rest, William. And you know that."

"Yeah, but it doesn't make it right, Matt," he said sincerely. "Someday he's going to find out, you know."

Matt shrugged sadly. "I'll deal with that when the time comes. Until then, I have to leave, and so do you."

"Okay, I'll leave. But I need a drink of water first." He walked to the kitchen, found a glass, and grabbed the pump handle plumbed into the kitchen. He filled the glass and walked back into the family room. "I'm sorry if I offended you, Matt. I just saw your boy last week when I went to Willow Falls, and I thought he needs to know I'm not just a weird stranger. I'm a weird relative!" He laughed.

Matt nodded. "It's fine. Thanks for letting me know Missus Eckman is in town. Any word from the Pinkerton?"

"He's nosing around a bit, but no big deal. Hey, Annie," he said with sincerity.

She sighed tiredly. "What?"

"Wake up!" he yelled and tossed the glass of water on her face.

Annie screamed when the water landed on her. She got out of the blanket she was wrapped in and ran toward him quickly. William was expecting her to do so, so he sprinted out the door and took off running down the street, laughing as he went. "I'm going to hit you so hard, William!" she yelled out the door.

His laughter could be heard in the distance.

Christine stepped out of the bedroom wearing a

blanket around the long johns. "Is your family always like this?" she asked Matt.

Annie turned from closing the door. Water dripped from her face and hair onto her dress. "Pretty much!" There was no smile on her face. "Before I leave here, I am going to get a sack of horse manure from the livery stable, get a key to his room from Lee, and fill his pillow slip with manure."

"Good morning," Matt said to Christine.

"Good morning. Are you leaving already?"

"The earlier I get there, the quicker I'll be back. Annie will buy you some new clothes today, and I should be back this afternoon sometime."

"Matt, can I talk to you in private?" she asked.

"Of course." He followed her back into his bedroom and closed the door behind him.

She stood at the foot of the bed, nervously looking at him. "I just want you to know that I have never slept with any man other than my husband. I have never wanted to spend the night with any man until I was married. I tried to sleep on the davenport last night, but your sister wouldn't let me. I just want you to know that, so you didn't think I was...I don't know, inappropriate or something. I apologize if it ruined your respect for me."

Matt smirked. "I'm sorry I fell asleep on the bed. It was my fault. Did you sleep well?"

"Like a rock."

He nodded. "Then all is well."

29

Felisha had walked to the marshal's office knowing Matt wouldn't be there, but she hoped Truet would be. She had been very close friends with Truet and his deceased wife, Jenny Mae. If there was anyone who would be honest with her, it was Truet. She didn't think Matt would lie to her, and she hated to believe he would, but the thought nagged at her just the same. If Matt was interested in Christine, then it was better for Felisha to know it now rather than change her and Dillon's lives, just to end up alone after all. She wanted to talk to Truet and get his perspective on Matt and her relationship with him.

She stepped into the marshal's office and was struck by the beauty of it. The walls were mahogany, with a short barrier separating the entrance from the office. A big blond-haired young man stood up with a pleased smile.

"Felisha! Oh, my goodness. How are you?" he asked. Nate Robertson had spent nearly a week at Felisha's boardinghouse to keep watch over her while Matt was searching for Truet.

Felisha smiled. "I am well. So, this is where you call home? I didn't realize how nice this place was. It's a very nice office. How are you, Nate?"

"I'm good. Yeah, this place cost a lot, and I don't think those that paid for it are happy with Matt anymore." He chuckled and continued, "Some of the business owners in town built this place just for Matt to be here, but they're all crooked, and you know Matt. He doesn't budge from what's right. He busted up some of the more well-to-do recently, and since then, he's not too popular."

"What do you mean by 'busted them up?'" she asked with interest.

"I mean he broke the sheriff's nose, gave the sawmill manager a new scar on his head, and made the silver king's heir wet himself." He smirked. "Since then, he's not been in their good graces."

"Why did he do that?"

Nate shook his head. "There's only a few people who know that, and I'm not one of them. I do know it had something to do with Christine, but I don't know what."

"Will Truet know?"

"Yeah, he would. But whatever went on is tight-lipped. There's a lot of secrets going on lately, and Phillip and I aren't included. I don't even know where Matt went today or why Truet is staying home. There's even a …" He paused. Matt had come by his house early that morning and told him Pick Lawson was in the jail. No one was supposed to know he was there for any reason. If anyone asked, Pick was in jail for being drunk and disorderly and for first-degree assault on a federal marshal. It was a secret put directly into Nate's hands without any more details than not to mention him being there to anyone.

"There's a what?" she asked.

"Oh, nothing. Anyway, yeah, there's a lot going on, apparently."

Felisha frowned. "Let me ask you, Nate. What do you know about Christine?"

He sighed. "I know she was with Matt's sister Annie's husband when he died. That was a bit of a scandal for a minute. The sheriff tried to arrest her for murder, but there wasn't enough evidence. It was an accident. Our sheriff is always looking for something big to happen to get his moment of fame. Matt's famous, you know, and I think Sheriff Wright is desperate to compete with that fame. He hasn't gotten it yet, but that doesn't mean he isn't trying." He chuckled.

She frowned. "How did Matt get tied up with her?"

Nate shook his head. "I don't think he is tied up with her. You're his lady, you know."

"I know. Well, I came by to talk to Truet, so I'll go to their house and visit with him. Nice to see you, Nate."

"The pleasure's mine. Have a great visit, Felisha."

She walked across town to the brick house on Franklyn Street and knocked on the door.

The door opened, and Truet looked surprised to see her. "Hi..."

"Hi, Truet. I was wondering if I could talk to you."

"Sure. Come on in."

She entered and hung her coat up on the rack as Truet asked if she wanted some coffee. She declined and sat down on the davenport across from Truet, who sat in the smaller one, facing her.

"So, how are you?" he asked.

"Not so good, Tru. I came to talk to you and get your opinion on a few things."

"Okay."

"I guess first, I really need to know what Christine is to Matt. Everywhere I go, it seems someone says they are courting. I was robbed last night, and when I told them I was courting Matt, they didn't believe me because they said he was with Christine. Why does everyone seem to know her? I don't even know how many people have said that to me, and I need to know if it's true or not. I don't know if I can believe Matt anymore," she said softly.

"You were robbed? Are you okay?"

She held up a hand to stop his questions. "William got my money back and then proceeded to beat that man nearly to death, I think. He was very brutal. Which is part of the reason I am here. But first, tell me about Christine."

Truet shrugged. "Matt's been honest with you. She's just a friend of his. He has never mentioned any kind of interest in her to me, and he tells me just about everything. He is only interested in you. You don't have anything to worry about, Felisha," he said reassuringly.

She frowned. "Actually, I do. Tru, do I really want to raise my son in such a violent environment? You were there yesterday. Do you think that's a safe environment to raise a child in?"

"Well, that depends upon how much you love Matt and how willing you are to be with him. Violence is going to happen no matter where you live or who you marry.

The world is full of violent people with criminal intentions everywhere you go. We saw it right there in Sweethome, Felisha. We saw our share of evil every weekend, but unless it affects us personally, we often look right past it. We had a lawman who was bought and there was no justice, and without justice, there is no law. Here it's kind of the same thing. The city sheriff is bought and enforces the laws that benefit him. Luckily, Matt goes by the book of law, and there's not much disrespect when he says something. As lawmen, we don't have a choice. Whether you believe in it or not, violence is a necessary evil that keeps the peace sometimes. No one wants to resort to violence, but occasionally we are not given the choice. No, you don't want Dillon growing up to be a violent man, but it's not going to help him to grow up not knowing there's evil in the world, either. Evil often carries a gun, and the only way to fight it is with another gun. Hexum found out the hard way, as unfortunate as that is."

"Matt didn't seem too bothered by it."

"He was. Keep in mind, Hexum was the only link to Christine. We didn't know if she was dead or alive."

She grimaced and flung her arms out in a wide, all-encompassing fashion. "Because of Christine! See how everything revolves around her? Tru, I really wanted to spend a great weekend with Matt and leave here excited about moving over here to begin a new chapter of my life. A good and better chapter for Dillon and me. But all I've found so far is isolation and a troubled spirit. I'm generally not too bothered by jealousy or stepping aside for a man to do his work, but I feel like I'm second-best to her. I feel like a little ignored doll waiting for some child to play with it. I'm not enjoying this weekend. Aside from Saul and Abby's wedding, I wish I never came here."

Truet sighed thoughtfully. "This has been a strange weekend, for sure. It's never like this. Most weekends are quiet. It's too bad this one isn't."

"Does Matt want me to go home?"

Truet chuckled. "No! He wishes he could spend time with you, but there's a lot going on."

"Why was Christine accused of murder when Annie's husband died?"

Truet frowned. "She had nothing to do with that. I can't go into the details, but I will tell you the sheriff was making those accusations up to make an arrest and it caused a bit of a fake scandal. It was all based on lies."

"Where'd Matt go today?" she asked.

The bedroom door opened, and Christine stepped out of Matt's room wearing Matt's long johns with a blanket wrapped her. Her hair was disheveled, and her eyes revealed she had just woken up. She stepped into the living room and saw Felisha sitting on the davenport staring at her with a combination of surprise and horror. "Oh, I thought you were Annie," Christine said.

"No," Felisha said slowly as she looked at Christine. A sudden burst of anger flickered through her eyes. Her voice became fierce. "Why are you sleeping in Matt's bed? And why are you in his clothes?"

Christine was taken off guard by Felisha's hostility. "I had nothing else to wear," she answered innocently.

"Why are you in Matt's bed? Where did you sleep last night?" Felisha demanded. She stood up, waiting for an answer. She breathed deeply and looked mad enough to assault Christine at any moment.

Christine hesitated before answering, "I assure you, nothing happened..."

"Where did you sleep?" Felisha shouted.

Truet was taken back by Felisha's display of anger.

Christine looked back toward the bedroom. "In there..."

"Who in the hell do you think you are? Matt is my fiancé, and you're wearing his clothes and sleeping in his bed! I know what you're doing, and it isn't going to work! Where did Matt sleep last night?" she demanded.

Truet answered quickly, "He slept on the davenport."

Felisha saw the surprised expression cross Christine's face. She knew by the look and nervousness in Christine's face that Truet was lying, and she looked at him harshly. "Are you lying to me, Tru? Of all the people I thought I could trust, it was you. Are you lying to me? Tell me the truth! It's the least you can do!" Her angry eyes filled with tears that seemed to be puddling over the brims.

He looked down with sorrow for lying to her.

"You lied to me, Truet? I never thought you would! Is there anyone around here who could just tell me the damn truth!" she yelled.

Christine spoke softly. "Nothing happened. He was so exhausted he fell asleep on the bed as soon as he laid down..."

Felisha rolled her head back emotionally and glared at Christine sharply. She shouted, "He's my fiancé! What are you even doing here? This is his place, and I'm his lady!

What in the hell do you think you're doing sharing a bed with my man? You should be ashamed of yourself! You have no right to be so close to him. And you!" She glared painfully at Truet. "I can't believe you'd lie to me to protect her! Where is your integrity, Truet? I thought we were friends?"

"We are. I'm sorry, Felisha. I shouldn't have lied to you. I was trying to avoid this…"

"Did he sleep with her?" Her tears refused to fall.

Christine spoke. "It's not what you think…"

"Shut up!" Felisha screamed, pointing a finger at Christine. "I don't want to hear any more from you. You have no right to steal Matt away from me! But you win, okay? I quit, and you can have him! I won't compete against you. You obviously know what he wants more than I do. But I will never forgive you! I should gouge your eyes out for what you've done to me!" Her breathing was hard, and her expression revealed her pain. "I never should've come here!" She turned around and grabbed her coat from the rack.

"Felisha…" Truet said.

"Don't talk to me. Truet! I've never been more disappointed in my life. Jenny Mae would be so hurt knowing you could sink to their level!" She nodded toward Christine.

Truet could feel his stomach sink to depths he didn't know were possible. "I'm sorry."

She shook her head. "I don't care. I won't see you again. And you," she said Christine. "I hope he hurts you the way he has me. You make me sick to my stomach! You all do!"

Christine shook her head defensively. "I didn't do anything!"

A tear fell down Felisha's cheek silently, and her voice broke as she began to sob. "You ruined my *us*. Tell Matt I don't want to see him again. Or you," she said to Truet. She stepped outside and slammed the door closed behind her.

Truet sat down, stunned by her words.

Christine stood behind him awkwardly. "I didn't do anything," she said softly mostly to herself.

"I shouldn't have lied to her," Truet said, guilt-ridden.

"I probably need to go. I've caused Matt enough trouble," Christine said softly.

Truet turned and looked at her. "No, I can't let you leave, Christine. Matt wants you to stay here, so please, let's not argue about it."

30

Matt rode across the Big Z Ranch without seeing anyone and then entered the land that belonged to his brother Adam. Adam's ranch had been called simply the Bannister Ranch, but Annie and Adam had recently combined the two ranches, doubling the size of the Big Z. Adam was in the process of taking over the management of the cattle while Annie prepared to focus her attention on horses.

There were a lot of changes coming to the ranch, some Matt wasn't fond of, such as constructing a bunkhouse for full-time employees and more barns on the southern rim of the ranch. It meant more people coming and going, and the risk of Sarah and Nathan's secret life being discovered. Matt had taken a huge risk by putting his name, career, and freedom on the line to give them an opportunity to live a decent life, but at what cost if it was discovered? He had not accepted any financial gain, but he had deceived an entire community and the nation since the news of Catherine's body being discovered had ended up becoming national news.

The death of Louis Eckman was big news, and it was making its way across the states. No one had asked why he was in the rural parts of east-central Oregon to begin with, but eventually the question would be posed. Matt only hoped the meeting with Divinity Eckman on Tuesday was not overrun by crowds of onlookers and reporters. His heart went out to Divinity since he knew she must be devastated by the loss of her husband, yet excited to see her daughter again. Unfortunately, she would be heartbroken beyond her means to discover it had all been a mistake. Her travels over rough terrain, the loss of her husband, and the realization she had lost her daughter too would be a horrible moment for her. It was not one Matt would have ever wanted to intentionally inflict upon her. He had intended on not interfering and letting the chips fall where they may, but a large part of him wanted to spare her the humiliation of a public heartbreak. It was in his power to do so, and he was torn between protecting his own future or preventing Divinity's humiliation.

He had seen Adam and Nathan riding back from the western corner of the property, but he figured they'd follow him to Nathan's house. He rode up to the house and dismounted to tie his horse to a hitching rail.

Sarah saw him through a window and opened the door with a welcoming smile. "Matt, what a surprise. Are you here for lunch? Nathan should be here any time," Sarah said with a welcoming smile.

"Yeah, Adam and him are riding up now. If you have some extra, I would appreciate it."

"Of course. So, what brings you all the way out here? Please tell me it's not an official visit, but a friendly one. Have a seat at the table. I'll bring you some hot stew."

"Thank you," he said, removing his coat and hat. "A little bit of both, I'm afraid, but I'll wait for Nathan to get here to tell you." He sat down as she set a bowl of stew in front of him.

She sat across the table and smiled. "We have some new news too, and I can't wait for Nathan to get here to tell you."

"Well, let's hear it!" he said as he tasted a spoonful of hot beef stew. It was perfect after a long, cold ride.

"We're having a baby! I'm pregnant," she announced with great excitement.

Matt smiled. "That is great news. Congratulations!"

She smiled with such pride, happiness, and joy that she glowed. "We just found out Saturday when the doctor came to town. I suspected, of course, but now it's confirmed."

"Congratulations. Does Annie know?"

She shook her head. "Nope. I can't wait to tell her and Aunt Mary. I'm waiting for Annie to get home. Did you bring her?"

Matt shook his head. "No. She'll be here Wednesday, probably."

"Oh. I thought she was just staying until Sunday."

Matt took another bite of the stew and nodded. "She was. I asked her to stay for a few days."

"Any reason why? You just miss her, huh?" She laughed.

"Partly. No, there's some things that came up, and I needed her there for a few days."

She lost her smile and looked at Matt sincerely. "Is something wrong? Is that why you're here?"

"I wanted to wait for Nathan to get here, but the fact is, it mostly involves you."

"What does?" she asked, growing concerned.

The front door opened and Nathan walked in, taking off his coat. "Matt, what brings you out here? Did something happen to Annie? Adam's getting pretty concerned."

Adam stepped inside behind Nathan. "Where's Annie? We've had her kids for four days now."

Matt couldn't help but smile. "Are they trouble?"

"No, but I'd like to know where she is. I don't want her thinking she can disappear for days on end when we're watching her kids." Adam sounded grumpy.

"She's helping me for a few days. I came to tell you that," he said to Adam. He looked at Nathan. "I also need to tell you and Sarah what's happened, and it's going to take a while. So, have a seat, and let's talk for a bit."

WHEN HE HAD FINISHED INFORMING them what had taken place in Branson with Christine being kidnapped, the killing of Jim Hexum, being investigated by the Pinkertons, more less arresting Pick, and her parents coming to town to pay a reward, he informed her that her father was killed in a robbery and that her mother had arrived in

Branson early that morning. He finished by saying, "And so now, I can go to your mother and tell her in private or let her find out tomorrow that Christine isn't you in front of the Branson Gazette newspaper office. It's hard to say how many curiosity seekers and reporters will be there if the story breaks loose. I am leaving that up to you. You tell me what you want me to do."

Sarah had shed no tears for her father, but had grown quiet and looked to be emotionless as she sat there staring at the table. Nathan sat beside her and held her hand comfortingly. "I wouldn't do her any favors, Matt," Nathan said simply.

Adam frowned. "Jim Hexum was a tough man who's been around for years. It's kind of sad to hear he died. He's like the last of the legendary old-time bounty hunters."

Nathan looked at Adam, perplexed. "He was looking for me!"

"Yeah, I know. But it's still kind of sad to see the end of the great ones."

Nathan looked at Matt, rolled his eyes, and shook his head. "So, my dear mother-in-law is in Branson, huh? I can't say she liked me much." His long brown hair hung over his shoulders, and his beard had grown a bit longer since moving to Adam's property. He was a stocky young man with broad shoulders and easy-going eyes.

Matt answered him. "She is. I haven't had the pleasure of speaking to her, but she's not alone. She has some Pinkerton with her."

Sarah moved her eyes to Matt. "That would be Carnell Tallon, my parents' personal assassin. Well, he sees things get done. He has a group of men who do most of his dirty work. Watch out for him, Matt. He may not look like much, but he is dangerous."

Matt nodded. "If you want, I can end it tonight by taking Pick and Christine to her hotel room. It would save her that heartache while mourning your father."

She shook her head. "My mother isn't mourning. She's probably waiting to get back to Sacramento so she can be the centerpiece of a massive funeral for him and make the social pages. Trust me, she's going to suck up the attention of being a traumatized widow for as long as she can. She'll marry again soon enough. She didn't care about my father, nor did he care about her. It was all for show. It was always about the show."

"That's unfortunate," Matt said softly.

She nodded. "Now that we're having a baby, there is one thing I will never do, and that's put finances above our child. I will never let my child go to bed not knowing how much I love them. I will never care more about my appearance than I do about my child. I will never say let's go to church to make a good impression and then go cheat on my husband." She looked at Matt. "My mother has always wanted to be in the papers, so let her go there and find out Christine's not me. I have nothing to say to her. Let her think I'm dead, because when it comes to my parents, I am."

Matt shrugged. "Okay."

"Do you know if Jane came with her? I'd love to see Jane. I'd love for her to move here. Any chance you could arrange that?" she asked.

"I was told it was it was your mother and another

man, a Pinkerton who arrived. I'm assuming no one else came with them. Who is Jane?"

"The maid. If anyone influenced me, it was her."

"It would be kind of odd if I asked your mother about her maid."

Sarah smiled slightly. "I suppose it would. You know what is sad? My child won't have any grandparents. Nathan's parents have passed on, and mine? Well, my baby is better off never knowing who they are. We don't have any family."

Adam said softly, "Sure, you do. We all might be a little rough around the edges, but you two fit right in."

"Thank you, Adam," she told him.

They talked for over an hour at the table, then Matt said, "Well, thank you for the stew, but I need to be getting back. Felisha has been here all weekend, and I haven't gotten to see her much. It's not going so well, either. She was robbed last night by Joe Thorn's little brother and his friends when she walked to the hotel. I haven't seen her yet today."

"Oh, Matt!" Sarah said loudly. It was her first true expression of emotion since hearing about her parents coming to town. She continued, "You can't do that to her. Was she hurt? I didn't have to know my mother was here or that my father died. You should've spent today with her. That poor girl has been sitting around waiting for you all weekend. When is she going home?"

Matt took a deep breath. "Tomorrow at the same time your mother's meeting Pick and Christine. No, she wasn't hurt. William got her money back and put a beating on Ritchie."

Nathan chuckled. "Boy, you sure know how to enter-
tain your guests. I am curious, how is she liking
Christine?"

"Not well at all."

Adam looked at Matt sincerely. "You know, Matt, I'm
not the most romantic man around, but did I hear right?
You let her walk across town alone at night? In Branson?"

Matt nodded. "I was busy trying to talk to Christine."

"You need to go apologize," Sarah said pointedly.

"Wait," Nathan said with an amused smile. "So, you
have Annie staying at your place with Christine? How
does Felisha like that?"

Matt frowned. "Not too well. I never expected her to
be jealous, but she seems to be."

"Of course, she is!" Sarah exclaimed. "Go take her out
for a nice dinner somewhere and apologize to her."

"I'd kind of like to follow along and watch this dinner
myself," Nathan said.

Adam chuckled. "Me, too. Mind if we come along? It
might help to have two experienced married men across
the room, holding signs up for you to read. You know, like
sign number one will say, 'Take hold of her hand.' Sign
number two, 'Look into her eyes.' Sign number three,
'Say I'm sorry.' You know, step by step instructions. That's
what big brothers are for."

Nathan chuckled. "Unless we get the signs mixed up
and one says just for our own entertainment, 'Wow,
Christine looks great!'"

Adam laughed.

Sarah slapped his arm. "That's not funny, Nathan!"

"Oh, I'm sorry, Matt." He laughed. "But dang, you're

dumb when it comes to women! You don't keep the woman Felisha's jealous of in your house for two nights without her! I wish I could be a fly on the wall when you see her tonight."

Adam grimaced and added seriously, "You may not walk normal for a week or two when she's done with you. Do you want me to run point and clear the way for you? I could tell her you would spend time with her if it wasn't for that much better-looking woman staying in your home." He broke into laughter, as did Nathan.

Matt smiled. "You guys are awful."

"Is she better-looking?" Nathan asked Adam.

"Than a woodchuck? Probably not. Oh, I'm just kidding, Matt." He and Nathan both laughed.

Sarah touched Matt's arm. "Ignore them. You go spend some time with Felisha."

Matt pointed at the two of them with a smile. "This is like a bad friendship. You two are going to run every employee off this ranch with your joking around." He stood up and gave Sarah a hug. "Congratulations to both of you!"

31

Carnell Tallon pointed at Saul Wolf as he walked into the Monarch Restaurant with his new bride Abby for dinner. Saul was dressed in a black pair of pants and a black long-sleeve shirt. He looked massive and powerful next to his slim and fragile-looking wife. She was wearing a pink dress and had her red hair up in a bun, exposing her neck. "That's him. Saul Wolf, known for a time as the Unbeatable Goliath in the prize-fighting ring. He fought a bout against Jacques Christy in July and beat him to death. He looks like he could hurt someone if he hit them. With the death of Tom, he might be exactly what I'm looking for." Carnell's friend Tom Picard had been carrying the shotgun on the coach when he was shot and killed in the robbery.

Sebastian Worthington added as he took a bite of his salmon dinner, "He's Matt Bannister's friend. He works for Matt's uncle at the granite quarry. It shouldn't be too hard to recruit him."

The two men were eating dinner with Divinity

Eckman at a private table set apart from the others in the restaurant. She was dressed in an expensive gown that stated perfectly that she was quite well to do. She looked at Saul and Abby with interest. "He's not a handsome man at all, is he?" she asked simply.

"Handsome or not, the man can damage anyone he hits. It would be quite handy for protecting you and for keeping the longshoremen in line when they get rowdy. We could even get him back into the fighting game and win some more spending money when you go to Europe this summer. He would have multiple purposes," Carnell said to Divinity.

"Invite him over, and let's see if he is someone I could tolerate around the house," she said.

Carnell left the table and approached Saul and Abby. A moment later, Saul and Abby sat down at the table. "Saul and Abby, this is my associate Sebastian Worthington, and this lady is Missus Divinity Eckman. Again, my name is Carnell Tallon. I am employed by Missus Eckman, and Sebastian works for me. We understand you two were just married, and wanted to say congratulations and share a meal with you. Our treat, so order anything you'd like. Nothing is off limits at this table."

Saul looked uncomfortable as he thanked them. Abby smiled at the introductions.

Carnell spoke. "Before we go any further, I don't know if you've heard, but my employer and Missus Eckman's husband, Louis, was fatally injured in a robbery on our way here. So before either of you bring it up, I will let you know it has been a devastating time, but we got her out here tonight to eat with us. It isn't something she wants to discuss, so let's just please refrain from bringing it up. She is still quite emotional."

Abby looked at her compassionately. "I won't mention it again, but my sincere condolences to you and your family. That's horrible."

Divinity gave a slight forced tight-lipped smile and nodded once.

"Saul, I understand you're a fighter?" Sebastian asked.

"I was. I don't fight anymore, though."

"What are you doing now?"

He answered with a touch of uncomfortableness, "I work in a granite quarry."

"Hard work," Sebastian stated. "Do they pay you as much as you made fighting?"

He scoffed. "I didn't make nothing fighting. My manager kept all the winnings, mostly, so yeah, it pays more." He laughed.

Carnell spoke. "And now you have a wife to care for. Soon you'll have children and a family to support. Can you do so working in the granite quarry?"

He tilted his head awkwardly. "Others have, so I suppose so, yes."

Divinity spoke for the first time. "Would you just get by, or prosper? The American dream is to prosper, Mister..." She looked at Carnell.

"Wolf," he answered for her.

"Mister Wolf, would you struggle to feed your family, or would you be able to enjoy life?"

"I imagine we'd get along all right. I already enjoy life, ma'am."

"Missus Eckman, please," Divinity said simply. "How

can you enjoy life when you're stuck in a..." She looked at Carnell.

"Quarry."

"Yes, one of those."

Saul shrugged nonchalantly. "I like the men I work with, and it keeps me strong. I like to sweat, and a day's labor feels good when I can afford to buy a flower or two for my wife. What more do I really need to enjoy life? Compared to what I came from, I'd say I have it made."

Carnell asked, "What are you going to do when your body gets too old for all that hard labor? You need to think about that too."

"I'm afraid that's about all I know."

"You know how to fight," Sebastian said.

Saul frowned as he looked at Sebastian and then at Carnell. "I'm not interested if you're looking for me to start fighting again."

"Not again, no," Carnell said. "But I thought you'd like to think over a job offer. I have an opening for a security position to watch over Missus Eckman. I think it may be providence that we ran into you. I don't believe anyone would go near Missus Eckman if you were watching out for her. It would pay very well, and you'd be living in a palace compared to what you have now, I am sure. Does that sound like something you'd be interested in so far?"

"I don't know...um."

"Are you moving to town?" Abby asked quickly.

Carnell chuckled. "No. The position would require you to move to Sacramento, California, but a change of environment can be very exciting. Plus, you'd get to see some of the more beautiful places and people in the world. This summer Missus Eckman is traveling to Europe for a two-month trip to Portugal, England, and many other places. All expenses paid, and your wage would be sizable, like I mentioned. And all you'd have to do is watch over Missus Eckman and her daughter, Catherine."

Abby frowned. "Catherine Eckman? Why does that sound so familiar?"

Carnell answered, "That is probably due to your marshal stating she was killed in a fire. New evidence has come to light that proves he lied, and she will be back with her mother tomorrow."

"Matt lied?" Saul asked.

Sebastian nodded. "It appears so."

Saul shook his head. "No, he wouldn't do that. Especially about something so awful. He's a Christian man. He wouldn't do that."

Divinity said with a touch of hostility in her tone, "My husband was a Christian too, Mister...Wolf. That didn't stop him from lying and cheating on me. I assume your marshal is cut from about the same type of material. A man is only a man, whether he's a Christian or not."

"I'm afraid some men are cut from a different cloth than what you're apparently used to. Matt wouldn't lie to you. And when he does get married one of these days, I can personally guarantee you he won't cheat on his wife. Integrity, ma'am. Some men have it, and others don't even know what it means. Matt is one man who has it."

"Fine, Matt didn't lie. We'll find out tomorrow either way," Carnell said, sounding annoyed. "Back to the job offer." He leaned forward to look at Abby. "Wouldn't it be nice to have money in the bank and a nice home? To wear beautiful gowns and see your husband getting the respect he deserves? Come back to Sacramento with us, and you'll suddenly be first-class citizens in the greatest city on Earth."

Abby shook her head. "I'm sorry, Mister..."

"Tallon," he answered.

"Mister Tallon. I can tell you right now, thank you for the offer, but we must refuse."

"Don't you want to think about it?"

She shook her head. "No. I will never leave my parents, and they live here. So, unless Saul wants to divorce me two days after our wedding, he isn't going anywhere either."

Saul agreed. "Yeah, sorry, gentlemen. It sounds great and all, but I can't take the job."

Divinity frowned. "You haven't heard how much it pays yet. How can you make a decision without knowing the financial benefits?"

Abby answered quickly, "I won't leave my parents. It's as simple as that."

"You won't leave your mother and father?" Divinity asked, perplexed. "You're giving up a life of pleasure because of them?"

"Yes. I will never leave them until the Lord takes them home. I love my parents, Missus Eckman. There's no amount of money you could offer Saul that would change my mind on that. My mother's my best friend. Money comes and goes, but it sure doesn't buy happiness. We'll be happiest right here with our family and friends."

"I think you're making a mistake," Divinity said. Her

words sounded cold, but within her, the envy of Abby's relationship with her mother was tearing her heart in two. She wasn't sure where she had gone wrong with Catherine, but she wished she could do it all over again and somehow build a relationship with her only daughter like Abby had with her mother. She longed to have that kind of relationship with anyone. For the first time in a very long time, the boldness of her loneliness struck her harder than a fist from Saul ever could. She longed to have Catherine back and promised herself she would work on earning that kind of love and respect from her own daughter.

"I don't think so," Abby replied.

"Well, it was nice to meet you two, but I must retire to my room for the night. I am meeting my daughter tomorrow after a very long time." She paused to look at Abby sincerely. "I hope to have a relationship like yours someday. Good night. Carnell, give them a wedding gift before you leave," she said and walked away. Unknown to them, her eyes clouded with foreign tears that broke loose as she climbed the stairs to reach her room.

Carnell looked at them both. "What do I have to do to get you to reconsider joining up with us?"

Saul answered simply, "Move to Branson."

"That's not going to happen."

Saul shrugged. "Like I said, I am perfectly happy right where I am. Just out of curiosity, since I turned your job offer down, are you still buying our dinner, or should we go back to our table? I don't want to be rude, but we don't have time to order the poached salmon or any expensive meals. We were just going to grab some chili really quick and go home. My honeymoon's over, and I have to go to work tomorrow."

Carnell frowned. "Well, how about we call that your wedding gift? Your two bowls of fifty-cent chili are on Missus Eckman and me. I'm sure we can afford a dollar."

"Thank you," Saul said. "But I usually get two bowls for me, so three bowls altogether, if you don't mind."

32

Matt knocked on Felisha's hotel room door and waited for it to open. He knocked again.

"Go away!" she called through the door.

"It's me," he answered, taken off-guard.

"Go away!"

He frowned. "Felisha, are you okay?"

"I don't want to talk to you. I'm going home tomorrow, and I'm not coming back! It's over, Matt!"

A wave of emotion rolled through him like a small sink with a large drain that had been pulled open. "What?" he asked, surprised. He was trying to think of anything that might've given her a reason to be mad.

"You heard me, it's over. You can leave now!" she hollered through the door.

Matt hesitated. "I could, but I'd rather talk to you."

"No! Go talk to Christine! She's waiting for you to come home and sleep with her again, I am sure! Just get away from me." Her anger was clear.

Matt sighed, and a quick flash of anger ran through

him like lightning. No one was supposed to tell her about sleeping in the same bed as Christine. He leaned his forearm on the door and rested his head on it for a moment. If there was anything he could understand, it was why she was angry. He said in a soft voice, "Felisha, I fell asleep. I didn't plan on sleeping in the bed...on the bed!" he added quickly. "I wasn't under the covers, just so you know. I can understand why you're mad, but nothing is going on. I don't know how to make you believe me, but..." He paused, then continued, "I am so sorry for not walking you back here last night. I am sorry things worked out the way they have. I wanted to do so much more than I've had a chance to. I'm sorry you're mad. It seems like it's becoming a daily thing."

The door jerked open and Felisha stepped out of the room, her large brown eyes burning with anger. She pushed Matt away from her door and yelled, "I'm not mad, I'm hurt! You hurt me! You betrayed me! You lied, and you tore my heart out and stomped on it! You treated me like crap next to your friend! Oh, your special friend! She's wearing your long johns and sleeping in your bed. How do you think that makes me feel? She knows you better than I do! Maybe she's the one you should be with, not me! This is goodbye, so leave!"

A hotel room door down the hall opened, and Rebecca Grace stepped out of her room. "Better get going, Matt," she said. "Felisha isn't interested in you anymore."

Richard Grace said as he pulled her gently back inside, "Close the door, Rebecca. It's none of your concern. It's between them, not you and them."

"She's my friend, and he's cheating on her. I want to

make sure she isn't going back..." Her voice faded as Richard led her inside and closed the door.

Matt looked back at Felisha with a perplexed expression and shook his head. "I never cheated on you. Are you not going to let me explain?"

"No! You don't understand the difference between being mad and being hurt! What could you explain that isn't going to make me mad, according to you? Hurt! I am hurt! It's a painful experience, not an emotional one!"

"I'm sorry for hurting you. It wasn't intentional."

"Oh, Lord. Nothing is ever intentional with you! This whole weekend has been unintentional when it comes to you. But yet, it is intentional, isn't it? Your special friend is probably in your bed right now, just waiting for you to come home and fall asleep. I am done! It is finished, and I don't want to see or talk *to* you again. And don't try to use that 'Thank you for teaching me that I can love someone again' line either. I fell for it once, but I never will again! Let me ask you something. If we were all caught in a raging flood and you had a hold of Christine's and my hand but could only save one of us, whose hand would you let go of, hers or mine?"

Matt frowned. "We're not in a flood plain."

"Just answer the damn question!" she shouted.

"I wouldn't let go of either of your hands. I'd try to make sure you were both safe, and rather it was me who drowned."

Her face contorted with disgust. "Good luck with her! I hope you enjoy your damn apple pie!" she yelled, then stepped into her room and slammed the door behind her.

"Oh, come on, Felisha! Can we just talk? I already told

you I fell asleep. Haven't you ever been so exhausted that you fell asleep and woke up the next day not remembering falling asleep? It's not that uncommon. I know I haven't spent much time with you, but I have a job to do, and time was of the essence. I couldn't take the time to be with you. Certainly, you can understand that. You wouldn't want me visiting with you over coffee if it was Dillon taken, would you? It's the same thing. My profession does not allow for a set timeline. I could have been gone for a week or more, but luckily, it worked out differently. We can fight and end what we have, or we can have a conversation without the door between us and the *neighbors*," he emphasized loudly, "listening in. Felisha, talk to me. I don't want what we have to end."

The door opened again, and Felisha stood in the doorway looking at him with a certain coldness to her eyes. "Matt," she said calmly in a soft voice. "I am going to make this short and sweet because I just don't have it in me anymore to keep trying to fool myself. Yesterday I watched that man die, shot four times by you and your cousin. You both meant to kill him—"

"Of course. You don't shoot someone in the leg when they're holding a gun."

"Shh! Let me finish! Now he's dead and propped up on the boardwalk like a trophy with your name on him. Congratulations! Last night I had to walk home alone because of you, and I was robbed by three men. Thank you for sending that Indian man to follow me. I watched your cousin beat that robber near to death with one of the most brutal and ruthless expressions on his face that I have ever seen. I imagine if you had fought that man earlier that day when I stopped you, you would have had that same expression, or one very close to it. I have been here since Friday, and rumors do get around about you. Not only about Christine and you, but about the violence too. You are a tough man. You are a good man, but you're not the man for me."

"Felisha, can we go inside and talk about this?"

She shook her head, and her eyes watered. "No. I don't want my son growing up in a home where violence is just another day's work. Annie told me she grew up hearing stories about killing and gunfights from people in your family. I don't want Dillon or me to become so hardened to death and violence that it just becomes expected. I don't want him thinking it's normal, because it's not! You come from a violent family, and I don't want Dillon around it. *I* don't want to be around it. I am taking Dillon home, and that's where we will be living. I am breaking our courtship off, and will not be corresponding with you through the mail anymore. And if you come to Sweethome for any reason, stay in the hotel, please. We are no longer a couple. That's all I have to say, and there is nothing you can say that will change my mind. I have decided, and feel good about the decision. It's final. You can leave now."

Matt looked at the ceiling and took a deep breath. "So, being in love with you isn't enough, huh?"

"Just because you love someone doesn't mean it's right to be with them. You're not right for me, and I'm not right for you." She sighed. "And maybe that's all we need to know to go our own ways. I never thought about it that way until just now, but I think it's best to just say good-night and part ways."

Matt frowned and bit his bottom lip emotionally. "Goodbye, Felisha," he said sadly.

"Goodbye," she said, fighting the tears that clouded her eyes. She closed the door and locked it with him standing there. Matt stood at her door for a moment, not knowing what else to say. The months of excitement, love, and joy he had known with Felisha were suddenly gone. Emptiness began to form in the pit of his stomach as he realized what they had shared was over. He longed for some magic words that would heal the pain he had caused her and wipe away the reservations she had about being with him, but there was absolutely nothing coming to mind except that it was over. She had said her peace, and though he hated to, it was sometimes better to walk away. He was walking down the hall toward the stairway when Richard Grace opened his door and stepped out. "I am really sorry, Matt."

Matt looked at him blankly. "Listening in, huh?"

Richard's eyes opened wider as he shook his head defensively. "It's not like that. No..."

"Well, you might've heard me say I didn't want this."

"I know, my friend," he said as Matt walked toward the staircase. "Hey, Matt, I know it hurts right now, but remember God has you right here in the palm of his hands." He put his hands together as if he were carrying water in them. "It'll be okay."

Matt nodded and turned the corner to go downstairs. He stopped when he saw his cousin William standing midway up the stairs, listening to the conversation. He expected William to laugh or say something sarcastic. "Not today, William," he said as he passed him going downstairs.

William frowned. "Asparagus doesn't make a good pie. It's just not sweet enough."

Matt turned around irritably and glared at his cousin. "What? What are you talking about?"

William shrugged with a sincere expression on his face and then smiled slightly. "I like apple pie too, Matt," he said simply with a wink and continued upstairs, then turned the corner and went up to the third floor of the hotel.

Matt shook his head, walked out onto the street, and looked up at the lit window of Felisha's room. The curtain was closed, and she didn't look out the window to watch him walk away. It was over.

Matt didn't feel like going home and confronting whoever had told her about sleeping with Christine just yet. He wanted to be alone for a while and just sit and think. He walked to his office, unlocked the front door, and stepped inside. He could sit in his office for as long as he liked. but he decided to check in on Pick Lawson before he did. He went to the back of the office and opened the heavy steel door that led to the jail cells. He only had one person in the jail, and Pick stood up when Matt entered.

"You didn't tell me it was going to be so isolated and quiet in here! I'm telling you, Matt, I could use some company. Your deputies aren't much fun to talk to, and I've been left alone. I don't mind being alone so much, but being trapped in here without a window is harsh!"

Pick said irritably. "I never should've agreed to this. Had I known this place was like solitary confinement in prison, I never would have agreed to it!"

Matt sat down in a chair provided for visitors in front of the cell. "It's only for one more night, Pick."

"Yeah, I know, and it's driving me crazy! I have nothing to do except read the Bible, and it's putting me to sleep!"

"You don't believe in it?" Matt asked.

"I believe in God, but I don't want to read about him."

"No?" Matt asked. "Someday you're going to face the God you say you believe in, but you're not going to know him. If you don't know him, what's going to be your excuse? 'Sorry God, I just didn't think you were important enough to get to know.'" Matt paused before continuing, "Unfortunately, everyone wants to go to heaven, but you don't get there by believing in a god, you get there by believing in Jesus and what he did for you on the cross. The secret to happiness, peace like you wouldn't understand, and knowing who God is and why Jesus and the cross are so important are all in that book. That book has the answers to why we exist and why there's so much evil in the world. Why good people suffer, and how faithful God is to those who belong to him. You should read it. It might change your life, and give you a purpose and new understanding of what's important. For me, nothing is more important than knowing Jesus Christ. Do you want to know why? It's in the Bible. Read it."

"Why? Tomorrow, I'm getting out of here, and soon I'll be starting a new life somewhere else. I'll be happy to get away from here. I'm really looking forward to getting out of this dungeon you have here, though."

"I bet. This place might seem like a dungeon because it's designed that way. I wanted it to be a place no one wanted to come back to once they left. It's punishment for breaking the law." He paused and continued, "I don't want to preach to you, Pick, but I will tell you the consequences for not getting to know Jesus Christ are eternal, and quite a bit worse than this place. The only thing separating heaven from hell is the message in that Bible. It is up to you to believe it or not. It is up to you to seek the Lord or not. And ultimately, where you spend eternity is totally up to you. God loves you. He's more than willing to save you and wants to accept you into his family, but you must make that decision. You've had all this time to read the Bible, and you have no interest. Just remember when you stand before Jesus, he lived and died a painful death for you to be able to join him in heaven. It couldn't be easier to avoid hell, but you have to want to know him. You have to be interested in getting to know him. The Bible's a good way of doing that."

"Okay, I'll give it a try. Why not? So, what do you think about tomorrow? Is Missus Eckman here yet?"

"Yes, she is. And I imagine she's excited to see her daughter," he said slowly. "Remember, the sheriff will probably arrest you since he'll have an audience, but don't worry about him. I can have those charges dropped if you give Sheriff Wright the story we agreed upon. Hexum started the fire, it was all his idea, and you let Christine escape. She will back you up on that."

Pick chuckled. "I'm not changing my story, not on my life."

"And you were never here."

"Nope. I've never even met you before."

"Good. There is one other thing we need to clear up. As you might know, I do things a bit differently. Like for example, when a bank robber kills another bank robber, I think they did society a favor. Just between you and me, were you the fourth bank robber in Loveland this past summer?"

"Why would you ask me that?" The question was completely unexpected and had caught him off-guard.

Matt shrugged tiredly. "You fit the description offered by my brother Adam and my uncle Luther. Rumor has it you had a black and white paint horse until that week-end. My brother owns that paint now, by the way. Considering you're affiliated with the Sperry-Helms Gang, my guess is you were the fourth rider, am I correct? All I have to do is bring that paint to the livery stable and have old Pete identify it. He said he'd know it by the markings if he seen it."

"I suppose it wouldn't do me any good to lie, now would it?" Pick asked, realizing he was finally caught for killing Brent Boyle.

"No."

"Are you reneging on our deal?"

Matt shook his head slowly. "We still have a deal. However, if you change your story tomorrow in the slightest, I will charge you with bank robbery and murder. You won't leave my jail except for court and finally prison or the gallows."

"I told you I wouldn't change a word!" Pick exclaimed.

"Good. Then you have nothing to worry about. Out of curiosity, why did you try to set up Morton Sperry and the others you named in the bank? Were you trying to take over the gang if they were arrested?"

Pick took a deep breath. "No. Allan Sperry is getting out of prison in the spring, so it wouldn't do any good to try to do that. Allan is apparently more dangerous than Morton."

"Then why claim to be them when you robbed the bank?"

Pick sat down on his bed and leaned against the stone wall separating each cell. "To frame them and end the gang. Marshal, you can't just leave the Sperry-Helms Gang alone. Possum was talking too much, and Mort and Jessie murdered him and his wife as an example to the rest of us. Deuce, Karl, and I were all wanting out as safely as we could get out. Framing them was the whole idea of that bank robbery. The money wasn't the object, Marshal. Framing them was. Everything went wrong, though."

"And Brent, the young man you shot, was in the gang too?"

Pick shook his head slowly. "He wanted in the gang, but Deuce refused to introduce him to the gang because Brent would have gotten himself killed by his mouth alone."

"Brent got himself killed anyway, didn't he?"

Pick nodded slowly.

"Why'd you shoot him? My brother saw it and said it was quick and unexpected."

"Your brother's a hell of a shot. We were in a gully with just our heads above ground, and he killed Deuce too easily. I was running before I was killed next. Brent was injured and would have slowed me down or identified me if I left him behind. Like I said, everything went wrong."

"Do you think the Sperry-Helms Gang will try to blackmail me, knowing it wasn't the Eckmans' daughter killed in that cabin?" Matt asked.

Pick shook his head. "No. As long as you leave them alone about that, they'll leave you alone. Besides, the way we wrote up that confession, they can't say one way or the other."

"How come you didn't invite them to join you in this scheme with Christine?"

Pick scoffed. "Because they'd hurt her and probably kill her if they didn't get the money. Besides, I needed Jim Hexum because of his name. It was more credible that way."

"Who in the gang do I need to look out for in the future?"

"Aside from Morton and his brothers, the Helms brothers, the Crowe brothers, and be wary of my old partner Cass Travers, too. He's right up there with them when it comes to being mean-spirited and deadly. Do not trust anyone with the name Sperry or Helms. They're all bad news."

"What about you? How do you compare to them with your gun?"

Pick smirked sadly. "I've had my share of gunplay, but I'm not that proud of it."

Matt looked at him closely. "No one of worth is. Well, I am going to go do some work in my office for a couple of hours. Do you want some coffee?"

"I'd love some. Can I sit out there with you?"

Matt shook his head. "No. I want to be alone for a while."

"We could trade places! I can personally guarantee you won't see or hear anyone in here!"

Matt smiled slightly. "That's the way I designed it. My jail is not meant to be pleasurable in any way, shape, or form."

"Well, let me commend you. It's not!"

33

It was getting late when Matt opened the door to his house and stepped inside. Annie was sitting on one end of the davenport, while Truet sat on the other end. Christine sat alone on the shorter one and laughed lightly as Matt stepped through the door.

"Where have you been?" Annie asked. "We were about to send out a search party for you. It shouldn't take this long to go to my house and back. What did Adam say? Is he mad?"

Matt took his coat and gun belt off and hung them up by the door. "No, he's not mad, just curious where you are."

"Are my children doing okay?" she asked.

"They're fine."

"What do you think?" Christine asked, standing up to show off her new clothes. Annie had bought her a long brown skirt and a light-blue button-up blouse.

"You look very nice," he said without his usual enthusiasm.

"It's nice to wear something other than a ballgown and dresses. It's been forever since I wore a shirt like this. I love it!"

Matt smiled. "You look great."

Annie asked, "What's wrong with you? You don't look very happy tonight. Is something wrong?"

He looked at her and took a deep breath. "Who told Felisha I slept with Christine last night?"

"Uh-oh," Annie said, looking at Truet and then Christine. "I wasn't here when she came by."

Truet frowned. "I'm afraid it was me, Matt," he said, leaning forward and putting his elbows on his knees. "Felisha came over, and she was very upset to see Christine come out of your room."

"I thought she was Annie," Christine added apologetically.

Truet continued, "I told her you slept on the davenport, but she knew I was lying." He looked at Matt with a troubled expression. "I ended up telling her the truth because I felt like garbage, lying to her the way I did."

Christine, still standing, leaned against the armrest of the smaller davenport and crossed her arms. "I told her nothing happened. I told her you had fallen asleep, but she got mad and only got madder the more I tried to explain. You must have talked to her already, though, if you're asking. How'd that go?" she asked with sincerity.

Matt looked at her. "I didn't really get to say much. She won't be coming back, though. We are through."

Truet spoke first. "I was afraid of that happening."

Annie followed with a sympathetic frown. "Sorry to hear that, big brother."

"There's not much I can do about it." He looked at Christine. "Apparently, she wasn't mad, she was hurt. She emphasized that very clearly a few times." His eyes went back to Truet and Annie. "We are no longer courting, and she doesn't want to see me again. I suppose we should break that news to Regina before she remodels one of her cottages."

"She was pretty excited about Felisha moving over," Annie agreed.

"Yeah, she'll be heartbroken," Matt said quietly with a roll of his eyes.

"What did Felisha say?" Annie asked.

He looked at her solemnly. "When she was yelling or talking normally? When she was yelling, it was that she was hurt, not mad. When speaking normally, I come from a violent family, and she doesn't want Dillon growing up to be like you, Annie."

"Like me?" Annie asked, perplexed.

"Yeah. You're so accustomed to hearing about violence that it doesn't bother you. You didn't lose any sleep after hearing I shot Jim Hexum. That's not normal, apparently."

Annie widened her eyes. "Oh... Well, how many people died in New York City today? Felisha should be crying all week long if that's the case. What do I care if Jim Hexum was killed? I didn't know him. I'm just glad you killed him before he killed you or William. She's not normal!"

"I'm too violent for her, and that's one of the reasons she wanted to end it. She doesn't want Dillon growing up to be violent."

Annie laughed. "I am sorry. I really am, but that's ridiculous." She looked at Matt curiously. "You're not going to run away again because you're heartbroken, are you? I mean, you haven't had your heart broken since Elizabeth. We were all kind of talking about that before you got here."

Matt smiled, amused, and shook his head. "No, I'm not going to run away."

"Good. Because I'd just track you down and kick your butt all the way back here. Heartbreak is just a temporary inconvenience that gets in the way of the priorities of everyday life if you let it."

He sat down on the far end of the smaller davenport. "I remember when Elizabeth married Tom; I was devastated at the time. Uncle Charlie and I were cutting wood, and he knew my heart was broken. His words of wisdom went something like this: 'Get used to it, because it won't be the last time your heart will be broken.' I was pretty incensed at the time, but I'm thinking he might've known I wouldn't be very good at relationships in the future." Matt smiled. "I'll be fine. I don't need to run away this time, Annie."

Truet offered, "I don't think it has anything to do with being bad at relationships. You two got along fine. I think it was just the busyness and being preoccupied with finding Christine and everything else happening as it did. Felisha had said she felt second to everything else going on, including Christine, and in fact, she *was* second to Christine. But in your defense, that's the way it's going to be in any relationship you have if you're still a lawman. That goes for me as well."

Matt nodded in agreement. "It's been bad timing all the way around, and it is what it is. She's going back tomorrow, and I will probably never see her again until you get married," Matt said to Truet. "Don't hurry it. Otherwise, she might begin screaming at me during your 'I dos.'" He smirked. "I still don't understand why she's so mad."

Annie chimed in with a chuckle, "She's hurt, Matt. I thought she emphasized that a few times, but you still don't get it?"

"Apparently not."

Christine sat down beside Matt and asked quietly, "Do you want to go for a walk?"

"I don't want anyone to see you before tomorrow."

Her eyes widened as she said dramatically, "I don't want anyone to see me with my face looking like this, either. Trust me, I'm going to be bundled up so much anyone who sees me will think I have leprosy."

He chuckled. "Yeah, let's go."

OUTSIDE, they decided to walk within the residential district and stay away from the main streets. There was no one else out this late at on a Monday night, especially with the temperature as low as it was. As they crossed the street, Christine asked with her usual sincerity, "Matt, how are you, honestly?"

"I am okay. I was taken off-guard by Felisha's hostility, and there was no talking to her about it. She asked the darndest question about whose hand I'd let go of if I was holding both of your hands in a flood and could only save one of you, and that seemed to be the final straw. She slammed the door in my face."

Christine frowned. "What did you say?"

"I told her I wouldn't let go of either of your hands, and I'd make sure you were both safe before I let the water take me away."

She chuckled. "Matt, you were supposed to tell her you'd let mine go and hold hers with both hands and never let her go. I appreciate you not letting my hand go, but that wasn't the answer she was looking for."

"I was just being honest. She is a wonderful lady, and I was looking forward to her moving over here."

"You weren't ready to marry her, were you?"

"No. It would have taken some time to be sure we could get along well. Also, to see if I was ready to be a father to her son. There was a lot to think about, and we both agreed to take it slow to be sure before we decided to make a family together. I'm thinking it wouldn't have worked out so well if one measly weekend could break us up like this."

She stopped at the corner and turned to face him. "Matt, I am sorry for any part I had in her ending her relationship with you. I know I had some to do with it, and I am sorry."

"Christine," he said softly, "you have nothing to be sorry for. You really had nothing to do with it. You were my concern and my priority, and then my responsibility. I'm just thankful that you're here, because quite frankly, I was getting a bit scared I wouldn't find you. Truet's right; Felisha *was* second to you, and I won't apologize for that because finding you was all I cared about." He began walking again.

"Do you ever think we're getting too close, Matt?" she asked with a sad tone in her voice.

"I don't think having a friend to talk to is ever a bad thing. Do you?"

"No, but if it's going to interfere with your relationship with Felisha, then who's to say it won't interfere with the next lady in your life?"

"You wouldn't have interfered if you hadn't been taken against your will. Christine, you are an amazing and beautiful lady who I think the world of, but Felisha was my lady. She would have been my priority if you had not been taken. There were obviously some cracks in the foundation of our relationship for it to be broken up so easily. I don't know if I failed to reassure her that I loved her enough to trust me or if her reactions were unjustified jealousy. I'm not sure of either one, but either way, it's over now. I was talking to Pick tonight, and he said I should ask you to marry me when this is all over. I told him I was courting someone else, and his response surprised me. He said he couldn't tell when we were together because we shined."

"He told me the same thing. I've had a few people ask if we were courting," she interrupted.

"I know, the rumors are getting around. You asked if we were getting too close and the answer's no, but if our friendship is getting in the way of other things, then maybe we need to back off a bit." He stopped walking to turn to look at her. "I am not going to jump into another relationship because my heart is broken. I'm not that kind of guy. I don't know if you do or not, but as your friend, I need to tell you that if you were hoping we were going to get together here real soon, the answer is no. I think you're wonderful, but if it ever happens, I want the foundation of our relationship to be as strong as cured concrete, and not one that just looks cured on the outside for people to see like it was with Felisha. I thought her and I had built a strong foundation, but apparently not. If you and I were to ever start courting, I want the foundation to be made of concrete and steel. I wouldn't want it to end when the tough times came. Do you understand?"

She smiled sadly. "I understand completely. I don't want to rush into anything too quickly either, Matt. Let's take our time, and if our friendship grows into more, then great. But if not, at least we can still be friends, right?"

"Of course."

"Okay, then. So, what's going to happen tomorrow?" she asked as they began walking again.

"Are you nervous?" Matt asked.

"No, but it seems like you're not telling me everything. You've told me a lot about what's going on, but it feels like you're hiding something important, and I'm feeling a bit in the dark. Can you enlighten me on what's missing?"

Matt grimaced. "How about I just promise you will understand when the time comes?"

She raised her eyebrows in question. "That much of a secret, huh? Matt, I really wish you would trust me enough to let me into your private world like trusted friends do."

"Christine, it's better that you don't know anything

aside from what you already know. Again, all I can say is, no matter what happens tomorrow, just trust me. Okay?"

She looked at him quizzically and stopped walking. "You know where she is, don't you? You're hiding her from her parents, aren't you?"

Matt looked at her without any sign of emotion. "Christine, I believe I've told you before that when someone breaks confidentiality or betrays me, my walls go up and they never come back down. Do you really want to know the answer to that, or leave it be?"

She looked into his eyes. "You can trust me."

"Then yes, I know where she is."

"She doesn't like her parents?"

"They put a twenty-thousand-dollar bounty on her husband's life just for her eloping with him. Would *you* like them?"

Christine grimaced. "No. That's horrible."

"Those are the kind of people we are dealing with. They have their own private Pinkertons. Ex-Pinkertons, I learned today, who still carry their badges. They are hired killers, and they are investigating me. If Pick brings you to them tomorrow, then everyone will know it was a mistake, and the real Catherine was murdered and burned in that cabin. At least, that's my hope."

34

The Branson Gazette newspaper office was set back about twenty yards in an alcove on Main Street. It was the only business that wasn't lined up with the rest of the buildings on either side of the street. The owner of the Branson Gazette, Louis Sorenson, could not purchase two lots side by side, so he had bought two lots horizontally aligned. City ordinances stated both lots had to be built upon after purchasing, so he built his office and printing shop on the center line of both lots. He believed he would need to expand in the future, and this gave him the means to expand in both directions, and add a second floor if it was ever necessary. It was a sore spot with some of the city officials and other business owners on Main Street that Louis only paid taxes on one place of business for two lots of prime business real estate.

People were crowding along the edges of the alcove in front of the newspaper office to get a look at what was turning out to be a public attraction. Everyone had heard about the death of Louis Eckman and came to see the poor widow get her missing daughter back alive and well after nearly four years. No one knew she had eloped with her fiancé. The story had been spread years ago that she had been taken. Today, Catherine Eckman would be returned to her mother, and it was big news in Branson. Matt didn't know where the misinformation had come from or how the word had spread so fast, but when Matt turned the corner to enter the alcove, he was surprised to see so many people waiting for the arrival of Catherine Eckman. There was a simple black coach with black velvet shades pulled down over the windows parked in front of the office, waiting. Matt had no doubt the Eckmans had bought the coach to make long journeys out of town with all the comforts of home, yet the exterior looked as plain as any other to deter the interest of the criminal element that often waited along the roads outside the city limits. Divinity Eckman sat within the coach with the door open a few inches so she could talk to the group of men standing around it. Matt smirked when he saw the Branson Sheriff, Tim Wright, standing tall and important as he spoke with the Pinkerton detective, Sebastian Worthington and a smaller man with a thin frame and short brown hair under a brown derby. The man wore wire-rim spectacles and had a slight light brown mustache a shade or two off from his hair. From the description Sarah Pierce had given him, Matt concluded the fragile-looking man was Carnell Tallon, the brains behind all the Eckman blood money.

"It's Matt! They're going to arrest him when Catherine gets here!" Matt heard a lady say a bit too loudly to her husband as he walked by.

"Shh, Matt's right there," he heard another man say to his two friends.

Matt ignored the gossip and had to hide his smile when he saw one of Tim's deputies nonchalantly say something with a nod toward Matt, then look away. The other men watched him nearing with resentful expressions.

"Gentlemen," Matt said in a friendly greeting.

Tim Wright looked at him with a pleased smile on his crooked lips. "Hello, Matt. Hey, this is the first time you haven't been able to find your man, isn't it?" he asked pointedly.

Matt nodded. "Yeah, it is. I suppose we're all here for the same reason, to see if it's Christine or Catherine someone brings in, huh? If they show up at all, that is," he said, scanning the faces of the lawmen around him. His eyes stopped on Carnell Tallon, who looked at him with a cold glare.

Carnell said in a threatening tone, "For your sake, they better show up, huh?"

Matt's eyebrows rose in reaction to the unexpected statement, which had taken him a bit off-guard. He was immediately irritated by the tone of Carnell's voice and the look in his eyes as he waited for Matt's reaction. The smaller man wanted to make sure everyone knew he was in control and Matt was the weaker of the two. A slight upward curve appeared on Matt's lips as he looked at the other lawmen and then back at Carnell. "Ironically, I was just thinking that very same thing. I was thinking I sure hope they show up with Christine for my sake because some guy is going to do...what, exactly?"

he said with a shrug. "That's exactly what I was thinking on my way over here," he finished with a chuckle. He had not met Carnell previously, but Matt didn't like him already.

Carnell raised his eyebrows. "You would be surprised by what I could do, Marshal."

Matt's eyes widened. "Look, I don't know who you are or why you're here. What I will tell you is I've been hunting the worst of mankind for many years. Men like you, who like to talk real tough, are a dime a dozen. Cheap as eggs."

Sebastian said quickly, "Matt, you're talking to Carnell Tallon, a Pinkerton detective and the Eckmans' personal security manager. If you don't mind me saying so, you might not want to aggravate him. Because if Catherine is brought in today, Carnell may be your only friend or your worst nightmare. He has a lot to say about any consequences you may face. That is who you are talking to right now."

"More so than the law?" he asked Sebastian. He didn't wait for an answer and looked at Carnell. "Personal security manager, huh? I am sorry to hear about what happened to Mister Eckman. In truth, I'm a bit surprised a man with your knowledge and experience didn't reconsider hiring local drivers to carry such important people through lawless territory. The driver never should have known what he was hauling or who until you got there. It's not uncommon for local drivers to arrange for his pals to rob the coach, especially if the passengers are rich. You're lucky they didn't find your twenty-thousand-dollars, or you'd all be dead. That's a fortune for boys who make less than two dollars a day if they're working at all in that part of the country.

"There's people up in those hills who will stab you for a dollar, and you'd never see the Missus in there again." He nodded toward the coach. "I have no idea why you folks came across the wild country when you could've come up the Columbia River in a lot more comfort in a sternwheeler most of the way. Let me give you a bit of advice: put on some working men's clothes on your way back, because wearing suits in these backwoods invites trouble. I hope you all get home safely if you're headed back the same way."

"That sounds like a threat, Marshal."

"Common sense shouldn't be a threat to you. If it is, you're in the wrong line of work."

Carnell was annoyed. "If Catherine is delivered today, I will personally escort you to jail. If we get that far," Carnell added quietly.

Matt laughed. "That almost sounded like a threat, if I was easily threatened. Which I'm not."

There was no doubt the two men didn't like each other, and the tension was rising. Tim Wright stepped forward and said to Matt, "Christine might be their daughter, Matt. We don't know."

"That surprises me, coming from you, Tim. But if she is, no one will be more surprised than me. And no one should be more concerned than you, considering what you tried to do to her, huh?"

"Carnell?" Divinity's voice was heard from inside the coach. He turned his attention to her. She continued,

"Have him move away from my carriage. I don't want him near me."

Carnell turned to Matt. "Would you please step away from the coach? Your presence is not welcome here."

"I'm beginning to feel most unwelcome," Matt said, not caring how sarcastic it sounded. He had no respect for Carnell or the widow behind the covered windows of the coach.

"You are," Carnell said bluntly.

Matt smiled. "When she says 'hop,' do you jump like a good monkey? Never mind. I'll be right over there when you're ready to start looking for me." He pointed toward the brick wall of the neighboring business. It was then that he saw Dave and Bella standing along the wall with the crowd, looking at him. He glanced back at Carnell. "I don't want you to lose me."

"Trust me, you're in my sights," Carnell said coldly as Matt walked away.

Matt walked over to Bella. "Let me guess, a rumor told you Christine was being brought in today?"

Bella looked at him with a disappointed expression. "I should have heard it from you. You were supposed to keep us updated, but we heard nothing."

"I was busy looking for her."

Bella spoke with great anxiety. "I hope they didn't hurt her. Some girls never recover after being taken. I've seen it before, Matt. Many of them end up committing suicide."

Matt's eyes focused on a tall man at the corner of the building wearing a bull-hide coat. It was his brother Adam, just standing there quietly. "I'm confident she'll be fine," he said to Bella. "Excuse me," he said and worked his way through the crowd of people to Adam.

"What in the world are you doing here?" Matt asked.

"Oh, I came to see the show."

"Yeah, me too. None of those guys over there like me much today, and I don't think Missus Eckman does either," Matt offered.

Adam moved a bit closer to him. "By the way, you don't know Nathan and Sarah."

Matt frowned and spoke quietly so as to not be overheard by those around him. "Don't tell me they're here."

Adam nodded slowly as he stared at the black coach and the men around it. "Somewhere. But you're not supposed to know them."

"Okay, but I really am not liking the sound of this. Why are they here?" Anxiety went through him like an ocean wave. If Sarah wanted to get back in her mother's good graces and told her what Matt had done, it was reasonable that Carnell could arrest him. It would turn into a gunfight before that happened, though. He could tell by the coldness in Carnell's eyes that he wouldn't live through the night if he allowed Carnell to arrest him. The whole idea of it made Matt's heart beat faster. He'd had a plan, and it was being thwarted by the one person who literally had his future in the palm of her hands. If Sarah was as devious as she made her mother out to be, then he had a reason to feel the fear that was overtaking him. He looked around to spot her and Nathan, but he couldn't see them in the crowd. "Where are they?" he asked Adam.

Adam shrugged nonchalantly. "I don't know. You just remember that you don't know them. That means you don't know who they are, understand?" Adam asked firmly.

Matt frowned. "They're not going to shoot me in the back, are they?" he asked quietly.

Adam scoffed lightly. "Nathan isn't wearing a gun today. He thought you might be mad at him for teasing you about your lady yesterday. How'd it go last night, anyway?"

"Let's just say I'm single again."

"Rory's single. You should marry her anyway."

Matt ignored the statement and nodded toward Main Street where Pick was leading Christine's horse toward them. "The show's about to start."

Adam's eyes narrowed as they rode closer. "I know him. That's the man I saw up on the hill. The one who shot at Uncle Luther and killed his friend. He tried to shoot me!" he said loud enough to be overheard by those around him. A few people looked back at Adam as they listened.

"Adam, don't complicate things!" Matt hissed under his breath.

"Huh? I'm telling you who he is. That's the man from up on Windsor Ridge! I have his horse. You know he was the fourth bank robber that day."

"Adam, shut up!" Matt said, glaring at his brother.

Adam grimaced at his brother's expression. "What?"

"You're going to scare him away. I know who he is."

"Well, you should have said so," he said as the crowd gasped and spoke about the coming riders.

"Here she comes!"

"I didn't know it was her."

"Oh, my...her?"

All those things were being said by the crowd nearest to Main Street. The rest turned to see the missing daughter of Louis and Divinity Eckman in expectation.

Carnell Tallon pulled the coach door open and held out his hand to help Divinity step out. She was wearing a long red pleated dress with a long mink coat to keep her warm. A large decorative hat with a variety of colorful feathers mixed with a few flowers was set carefully upon her well-done hair, which was up under the hat. She was quite an attractive lady, and the men in the crowd eyed her in wonder, while many women looked at her with envy. She had it all—wealth, fame, and beauty. She was every young lady's dream come true. She stood between Carnell and Sebastian, waiting to get the first look at her daughter. Divinity wiped a tear from her eyes with an embroidered handkerchief.

Pick wore his gun belt, but Truet'd had instructions to make sure Pick's revolver was empty. Not knowing what to expect, Matt stepped away from Adam and walked back to where Dave and Bella were standing, closer to the coach. He casually pulled the leather thong from his revolver's hammer as he walked. He stopped beside Bella. "Here they come."

She looked at him awkwardly as she noticed his thumb remove the thong, but her attention went toward the street when Pick led Christine's horse into the alcove. "Oh, my Lord!" Bella gasped and began to cry when she saw Christine's beaten face.

Pick led Christine's horse to where Carnell waited with Divinity.

"Here she is," he said. "Got my money?"

Carnell's face hardened. "What are you trying to pull? Where's Catherine?"

Pick pointed at Christine. "Right here!"

Divinity's face contorted into a perplexed grimace. "Where's my daughter?" her anguished voice asked. "You said you had my daughter? Where's Catherine?" she yelled. "You said you had my daughter!"

Christine looked at Pick with tear-filled eyes. "I told you I wasn't her." She slid out of the saddle and looked at Divinity. "I am so sorry you were put through this. I told them I wasn't your daughter."

Divinity glanced at her with a hate-filled sneer and then looked at Pick. "Where's my daughter?" she yelled.

Christine ran to Matt and wrapped her arms around him as she began to weep. He held her close with his eyes on Carnell.

Carnell shouted harshly, "You brought us out here for nothing! Louis Eckman was killed protecting this money for nothing! You stupid son of a bitch! You deserve to die!" He pulled his revolver out of his shoulder holster and aimed it at Pick.

Matt drew his revolver and stepped away from Christine. "Put it down!" he yelled. His attention went back to Christine. "Go over there." He pointed toward Bella with his left hand. "Put it down, Carnell! He's not your prisoner, he's Tim's. Tim, arrest your man!"

Carnell looked at Matt with fury on his face. "How dare you aim a weapon at me? I am a Pinkerton detective on a kidnapping case!"

"This is Tim's jurisdiction, not yours. Your case is over,

and has been over for a long time as far as I'm concerned. Now lower that gun before I pull the trigger!"

Pick volunteered nervously, "My gun's empty."

Matt yelled, "Tim, grow a spine and arrest him!" Tim had not moved.

Carnell lowered his gun. "Go ahead, Sheriff." He looked at Pick. "I know where to find you. You'll be interrogated by me soon enough." He put his gun away and looked at Matt. "Happy?"

Matt nodded once as he lowered the hammer and put his revolver back in its holster.

Tim and his deputies surrounded Pick with their weapons aimed at him as Tim pulled the man down off his horse and took his gun. With a crowd that big watching him, Tim made a show of making the arrest and spoke much louder than he usually did.

Divinity turned toward Matt and took a few steps toward him. "Do you know where my daughter is?"

Matt sighed. "To my knowledge, you buried her."

"So I lost my husband for nothing?"

Matt nodded. "I'm afraid so."

Her expression became one of fury. "I want that man hanged! I want him charged with my husband's murder, and I want to be reimbursed for my travels! I want his body burned beyond recognition and tossed in a ditch where it belongs!" she yelled bitterly.

"Well, you're probably not going to get that," Matt told her simply.

She glared at Matt wickedly. "I *will* get that! I'll have it done myself, no matter what it costs me!"

Matt shook his head. "Some things can't be bought,

Missus, especially if you want to be reimbursed." He heard his brother Adam chuckling through the silence of the crowd.

"Go to hell! All of you can go to hell," she yelled, turning toward the crowd. She froze when she saw her daughter and Nathan standing in the open, staring at her. "Catherine?"

Sarah Pierce stood in a plain light green dress with a brown coat and a black yarn scarf wrapped around her neck. She wore a rabbit fur hat made by Adam's wife Hazel to cover her ears against the cold and had her long dark-blonde hair in a ponytail. She said harshly, "What are you doing here, Mother? I told you I never wanted to see you or Father again when I left." She turned to the crowd and yelled, "I'm Catherine Eckman, and I was never missing, I ran away to marry my husband. This woman," she pointed at her mother, "and my father put out a twenty-thousand-dollar reward for the first hired killer, like that man," she pointed at Carnell, "to kill my husband and take me back home like a slave. Why? Because my husband wasn't good enough for them! None of you are good enough for them either. When those hired killers couldn't find us, they put out a ten-thou- sand-dollar reward for anyone who killed my husband. I love my husband, and I gave up my family of my own free adult will to be with him!" She looked at her mother. "I'm pregnant with his child. Are you still going to have Nathan murdered? He's right here, Carnell, so why don't you do it now?" She turned back to the crowd. "That's my parents. They'd rather have my husband killed just so I could be forced to marry someone they thought would benefit them! We've been hiding, but I'm not hiding anymore! Mother, you can leave!"

"Catherine, you look like a peasant dressed like that. Come home with me, and let's get you cleaned up," she said, walking to her daughter to give her a hug.

"A peasant? Do you understand English? I'm not going anywhere with you! Stay away from me," she yelled as her mother came closer. "I don't want you to touch me!"

"What is wrong with you?" Divinity asked sharply. "Has he brainwashed you? Are you afraid to leave him? He can't hurt you now. Carnell is here, sweetie. Nobody can hurt you now. Come now, let's get you cleaned up and into some decent clothes. You don't have to worry about that piece of rubbish anymore, and I know a great surgeon who can get rid of that cancer in your belly for us. Everything will be fine."

"Cancer? It's a baby, you sick, selfish witch! I love my husband, and we're having a baby. It's not a cancer or a blob of fat. It's a baby! That's one thing, though; it's always about you. How I dress, how I eat, who I marry, and whose child I am carrying! I am not going to abort my baby, nor am I going to leave my husband, and you are crazy to even think so. I am happy, and want nothing to do with you! The only danger I am in is from you and him!" She pointed at Carnell. "I don't want anything from you!"

"Then why are you here?" Divinity asked bitterly. "Certainly, you need money! Did you come to collect the twenty thousand because that street rat can't provide for you? Was this all a ruse to get your inheritance? All you had to do was come home, Catherine. You can still have the best life has to offer. I know, come to Europe with me and see every-thing there is to see. I know you always wanted to go to England when you were little. Of course, traveling would be easier and less trouble if we erased your mistake." She nodded at Sarah's belly, which wasn't showing yet.

Sarah shook her head with disgust. "I'm not a little girl anymore, and it was Scotland, not England. And no, I don't need money. The only reason I am here is that I heard someone kidnapped me! The nonsense has gone on long enough. I'm not dead, and I wasn't kidnapped! I don't know who that man is or why he thought that woman was me, but enough! I don't want any of your money or an inheritance. I never want to see you again, either. My child will never know who you are, so you don't have to worry about any little street rats knocking on your door begging for table scraps. And if anything happens to my husband, I will make sure everyone in your city knows exactly how selfish, narcissistic, and wicked you really are! You know, it's a shame. Most girls want to be like their mother, but I don't even want to know you. I have nothing left to say except goodbye."

Carnell asked sharply, "Who were the Overguards?"

Sarah shook her head, a bit perplexed by the ques-tion. "My friends. They were murdered by someone, but I don't know who. Why?"

"I'm curious how Matt Bannister found your things in their place?"

"I read about that nonsense too. Those were things I

left behind because there wasn't room for them in the saddlebags when we left their place."

"How well do you know Matt Bannister?" Carnell asked quickly.

Sarah scoffed with disgust. "I know his name and who he is, but I've never met him! Is there anything else, Carnell?"

He shook his head. "Come join us for lunch and let's talk."

"Why would a lamb dine with the wolf pack? No, thanks," she said and turned around to walk away.

Divinity shouted with an emotional sob, "Your father is dead! Doesn't that matter to you?"

Sarah turned around and shook her head. "No. And it doesn't matter that much to you either, I am sure."

"Don't you dare talk to me like that! I am your mother!"

"I don't care."

Carnell stepped forward. "Catherine, wait a minute. We came all this way because your parents love you. Your father died protecting the money to get you back. That must mean something."

"Yeah, it means he had some kind of agenda." She turned around to leave again.

Carnell said sharply, "Catherine! You are wrong. Your parents love you and were coming to save you. Now, we came all this way, I can't just let you walk away without talking to us without him there." He pointed at Nathan and stepped forward to grab her.

Nathan glared at Carnell fiercely. "Come any closer, and I'll bust your face up for you!"

He stopped. "I have a warrant for you, dead or alive! If I was you, I'd shut up and do as you're advised," he said in a threatening tone, with murderous intentions burning in his eyes. "You've been on my list for a long time. I'd stay out of this if I was you."

Nathan shook his head slightly. "If you think I'm going to stay out of this, you're crazier than that woman! This is my wife! She's not going anywhere with you or her. It's not a crime to marry a woman without her parents' permission, so take your warrant and shove it where the sun don't shine. Good luck trying to make it stick in a court of law!" He looked at Sarah. "Are you ready to go home?"

She nodded, and they put their arms around each other and began to walk away.

Divinity yelled, "You're not leaving me again! Catherine, you're not leaving me. I won't let you!" She looked at Carnell. "Shoot him, damn it! Don't you dare let him take her away from me again! Shoot him now!"

Nathan spun around, placing his body in front of Sarah.

Carnell spoke. "Catherine, you're coming with us one way or another! I suggest you get into the coach with your mother right now. Do not force me!" He pulled his revolver out of his shoulder holster and started to raise it toward Nathan.

Matt pulled his revolver and aimed it at Carnell's head. He yelled, "Lower the gun, Carnell! He's no threat to you."

"Stay out of this, Marshal! This doesn't concern you."

Divinity screamed at Carnell, "Shoot him!"

"Put it down right now or I'll blow your head off, Carnell!" Matt ordered loudly. "One...two..."

Carnell looked at Matt with an enraged snarl on his lips. With a growl from deep within, he turned his body quickly to Matt, swinging his revolver toward him as fast as he could.

Matt pulled the trigger of his Colt .45, and the right side of Carnell's forehead exploded in a spray of blood, bone, and brain matter as he fell to the ground at Divinity's feet. She began to scream in horror at seeing her friend and caretaker lying dead on the ground.

Sarah looked at her mother and then turned her back and walked away with Nathan. Divinity looked up and wailed just in time to see her daughter turn the corner, leaving her all alone.

Matt stepped forward and spoke to Sebastian Worthington while he tried to console Divinity. "I suggest you take her back to the hotel and leave town in the morning. If that reward for Nathan is not rescinded immediately, I will have the Missus here arrested and tell the world about it."

Divinity glared at Matt through her tears. She screamed bitterly, "You murdered him!"

"No, ma'am," Matt said simply. "You did! He'd still be alive if it wasn't for you." He turned around and looked at the crowd of bystanders, who were displaying a wide range of emotions between shock and horror. Three ladies and one young man were vomiting from the head wound they had witnessed. Most were walking away quickly, while others stared in awe. Pick had been having shackles put on his wrists when the shooting happened, and since then, neither of the deputies had finished securing his wrists. They just stared at Matt, trying to digest what they'd seen. Matt's eyes fell on Christine as she was being led away by Bella and Dave. Christine's eyes didn't leave Matt's as she turned the corner and disappeared.

As Sebastian coerced Divinity into the coach and closed the door, Matt looked at the dispersing crowd and saw Adam Bannister standing like a granite pillar against the brick wall. Adam gave him a single nod of approval.

35

Christine Knapp was greeted at the dance hall with tears and a great deal of excitement by the other ladies. She had a lot to tell them, and all were relieved that despite her black eye and bruised cheek, she had been well cared for. She did not tell them she had been at Matt's or any of the things Matt had shared with her. She blamed the fire in the dance hall on Jim Hexum and praised Pick for keeping her safe from him. The damage to the dance hall was extensive in the kitchen, but the floor and walls could be repaired, and the rest of the smoke damage as well. There was nothing that couldn't be replaced, and the love she felt upon returning home assured her that she was the greatest concern of everyone there. After a warm bath and washing her hair, she put on a clean dress and left the dance hall unattended to walk over to Matt's house, but he wasn't there. Annie had gone back home with her brother Adam, and Truet didn't know where Matt was. He offered to walk her back to the dance hall because it was getting dark, but she declined. She went to the marshal's office, but Matt wasn't there, either. She was walking back to the dance hall feeling quite disappointed when she saw him sitting on a bench under the wide covered porch of the stagecoach station. She went over, climbed up the two steps to the wide platform, and smiled empathetically as they made eye contact. She sat down beside him and remained silent to let Matt say something if he wanted to.

He said sadly, "I had hoped to get here early enough to see Felisha and Dillon before they left. I would've liked to have said goodbye properly. I hate that it ended on bad terms with her. Felisha's right, though; I would not be a good father to Dillon." He held up his right hand and turned it palm up. "This hand has killed more men than most of the worst outlaws you've heard about. It's beaten countless men, and can be brutal, I suppose. I never thought of myself as a violent man, but if you knew about all this hand's done over the years, the fact is, I am. I am a very violent man, Christine. She was right. If there was any one thing I could have said to her before she left, it would be, 'You're right.' That's all. I'm glad she left before she heard about what happened today."

"Would you have stopped her from going if you could?" she asked gently.

Matt shook his head slowly. "No. She needs to go back home and raise her son to be a proper boy with a good education. Lord willing, the boy will never pick up a gun, or ever need to."

"Maybe that's where you come in," she told him softly. "You make the world safer for all the rest of us. That hand that's seen so much violence didn't do it in vain. You're not a violent man, Matt. You have a violent profession that calls for violence at times. You're a very gentle and loving man. Don't get your trade and your character confused. You're a wonderful man with a violent trade. There's nothing wrong with that."

"I've shot two men in what three days. I don't take much pride in that."

"And that's what makes you perfect for the job. You're only violent when you need to be. Some people call that being a man. I think of King David, who was sensitive enough to write the psalms and play the harp beautifully. He was a man with a good heart filled with compassion, love, and sensitivity, and he always wanted to do the right thing. He was a man of gentleness and great honor, yet he had the courage to face a giant with nothing more than a sling, a small stone, and knowing God was with him. He had such amazing faith in God, and such a righteous heart that God called him a man after His own heart. But he was also a man of war, and could be extremely violent. There's a lot to be said for strength under control, and that's the way you are. You are capable of so much damage, but you're not a threat to anyone until they cross the line of the law. That does not make you a violent man. It's just too bad Felisha couldn't see that. I think you'll make a wonderful father and husband."

"I've had so much on my mind this weekend that I didn't have a chance to think too much about Felisha and how she felt. After everything was over today, I had time to sit down and relax, and that's when losing her hit me. I wandered down here, and have been sitting here thinking."

"Have you eaten anything today?" she asked.

"No."

"Let's go get some supper at the Monarch Restaurant. And if you'll let me, I'll pay. It's the least I can do."

"Oh, no! I'll pay."

"I won't argue, but one of these days, I will repay you for what you've done for me. And can we talk about what's going to happen to Pick?"

Matt took a deep breath. "Well, I kind of ran into an issue with Pick."

"Like what kind of issue?"

Matt hesitated. "Like one that's not going to make him very happy. Let me just say that the Eckmans were an exception to my normal rules of conduct because of Sarah and Nathan. I put myself on the line to protect them. Truet warned me not to contact the Eckmans and say I found their daughter, but I never expected someone like Pick to come along and do what he did."

He looked at Christine and continued pointedly, "I just discovered he was the fourth bank robber in the Loveland bank robbery, and he killed a young man named Brent Boyle. My brother witnessed that killing. I'm the only one who knows that, aside from my brother. Everyone else thinks the fourth rider is still hanging in a tree somewhere up in the Wallowas. Rumor has it the bank's gold and money are buried underneath wherever his noose is hanging. It's not, because Adam returned it to the bank. But people talk, and a hundred years from now, it'll probably be a legend. The hanging man's lost gold or something. Anyway, I'm going to arrest him for murder after freeing him from the local charges tomorrow. I made a deal with him before I knew that, and I can't look the other way. Pick belongs in prison or hanging from gallows for his crimes."

She closed her eyes and sighed. "I was really hoping he would be able to change his life like he told me he wanted to. He was so sincere when he told me that all he wanted was to get away from here and start over again the honest way. It's almost too bad you couldn't give him the chance to do that. You know, if Pick changed his life and becomes an honest and respectable citizen, he would owe it all to you and the grace you gave him. Kind of like the grace God gives us to make changes in our lives when we don't deserve it. You'd be giving him an undeserved chance at a new life."

"And if he doesn't, and ends up going back to the Sperry-Helms Gang and hurts someone else? I could let him walk away and pretend like I don't know anything. I've always said when a criminal kills another criminal, it only helps the innocent citizens, but I'd always know he got away with murder."

She sighed. "I guess the bigger question is, would you be able to live with yourself if he did hurt someone else?"

Matt shook his head slowly. "No, I wouldn't. I like to think I'm keeping the people around here safe from men like him. I don't think I can afford to have him roaming free and promise every one of the folks around here that he's harmless. You do know none of this would have happened if I hadn't tried to deceive the Eckmans in the first place, don't you? You never would have been kidnapped, so Jim Hexum would still be alive, and Mister Eckman would still be alive, along with Carnell. You never would have gotten a black eye, the dance hall never would have caught fire, Pick would still be doing whatever he does, and Felisha would still be my lady and moving over here. I think I made a mess out of everything."

He looked at Christine sadly. "I made a mistake and brought you and Pick into it as well. I asked you both to give false statements to keep my friends safe, not knowing Sarah would come out of hiding and make her story public. I could leave everything well enough alone right now and it would turn out fine, but I couldn't live with myself if Pick went back to the Sperry-Helms Gang and killed someone else. I like to be known as a man of my word, but I've done enough wrong with this whole Eckman situation. My one little lie meant for good has caused so much harm to so many lives, and that little lie could have cost your life too. That's the weight I am carrying today."

Christine frowned compassionately. "Matt, all I care about is how you will see yourself in the mirror from this day forward. You're too good a man to not walk that narrow line of integrity. Maybe you're forgetting that your friend, Sarah and her husband are now free. Your plan may have been a bad decision to begin with and had some unforeseen consequences, but your goal was a success. Sarah and Nathan are free to live their lives as they please now. As for the others who lost their lives, they all made the choices that got them killed. That badge on your chest hasn't been corrupted yet, so wash your hands of that weight you feel and go look in the mirror for a while. I think you're one of the finest men I have ever known. There's far more to you than that badge, and the people around here are lucky it's worn by you. Carry it with honor, my friend."

"Thank you. I appreciate you saying that."

"Of course. Shall we go get something to eat before the restaurant closes?"

"I suppose we better if we're going to eat at all, huh?"

36

Sheriff Tim Wright was woken up by the loud knocking on his door. He reached over and turned up the lantern beside his bed. He looked at his timepiece and wondered who was banging on his door near midnight, then got out of bed and went to his door and opened it. He backed up immediately as Morton Sperry and Jesse Helms invited themselves in. Jesse closed the door behind them.

Morton spoke with no nonsense in his voice. "I heard Pick's in your jail. Give me the keys." He held out his hand out, waiting. He wasn't a tall man, but he was broad-shouldered and stocky. He had neck-length brown hair and a goatee. His fierce green eyes were cold and dangerous in his hard face.

Jesse Helms was a bit taller and just as broad and stocky. He leaned against the doorjamb with his left hand near his holstered gun.

Tim shook his head. "I can't just give you the keys! What am I going to tell Matt?"

Morton glared at him. "Tell him he escaped. Keys."

"Escaped? How's he going to escape? I must protect myself here, Morton. If you want to get Pick out, you know Matt's going to come after him. You don't want him with you when Matt finds him."

"That's not your problem. I want my man out of your jail. I can go get him, or you can come release him, but he's coming with us. If you don't think so, just say so," Morton challenged.

Tim hesitated for a moment, then, with a frustrated sigh, he walked over to a desk in his family room and grabbed a ring of skeleton keys. He tossed them to Morton. "Close the door behind you when you leave, and put the keys in my desk, please! I'll tell Matt in the morning that he escaped somehow."

Morton smirked as he put the keys in his pocket. "Good. Nice working with you, Tim. Have a good night," he said and left.

Jesse snorted in through his nose, sucked the mucus into his mouth, and spat the mouthful out onto Tim's floor. "Have a good night, Tim," he said and stepped outside, closing the door behind him.

Tim sat down on a chair and took a deep breath.

PICK WAS nervous as he rode between Morton and Jesse out of town to the north toward the granite quarry. Morton and Jesse were in good spirits, it seemed, and were curious about what kind of mess Pick had gotten himself into this time. He explained as well as he could without mentioning his deal with Matt. Pick acted grateful to be free from jail, and played along as well as he could to satisfy the curious minds of Morton and Jesse. He told them the same story he had told Sheriff Wright and was confident that they believed him. He was curious why they were traveling north when the Sperry home was west in Natoma. It didn't take long before he saw the glare of a small fire at the granite quarry. The rest of the gang was standing around the fire, talking and drinking. nearby homes. The noise of the donkey engines, dynamite exploding, and the daily work in the quarry and finishing buildings was enough to keep most people from moving too close to the quarry. Pick stopped his horse and thought about running for his life when he saw a noose tied to the end of a small hand-cranked derrick with a twenty-five-foot boom. The boom was a thick, movable piece of oak connected to a base that pivoted to lift the heavy blocks of granite out of the quarry hole and swing them onto a wagon to take them to one of the buildings for cutting and shaping. There were two larger derricks with steel cables and towering structures that helped keep the derricks stationary as they brought up large pieces of granite. Both larger derricks were connected to donkey engines for stronger pulling power. At the moment, though, the one that had Pick's attention was the smaller derrick with the noose.

"What's this?" Pick asked nervously. Morton had thrown Pick's gun belt to him when they woke him up, but his gun was empty. Truet had emptied the cylinder of its bullets earlier that day.

"Relax," Jesse said, noticing the fear in Pick's expression. "We're not going to hang you."

Morton smiled in amusement. "No. On the contrary, do you remember when you told me about rigging up that fake noose to get away from that man on Windsor Ridge? With the marshal in town, I thought it might be a good idea for you to show us how to rig that up. It might have given any of us the advantage if Bloody Jim Hexum had come after one of us. Are you up to it?"

"Oh, sure," Pick said with a relieved smile. "It sure worked when I used it."

"I know. That's why I would like for you to show us before you leave town. This is your farewell party, Pick. The marshal is going to be looking for you in the morning, so you need to leave us. Get out while the getting's good. I recommend you head north to Canada where he can't follow you. And while he's chasing you, we're going to rob that stagecoach that has your money on it." Morton laughed. "You're out of luck on that one, Pick, but I'll give you some money before you leave," he said as they rode up to the fire.

"Fellas, Pick came up with a brilliant strategy to escape the law, and it's a way to fake a suicidal hanging. Pay attention, because it might just save your life if we get separated on the run and outnumbered," Morton said to the group of men at the fire near the derrick.

Pick's old friend Cass Travers put out his hand to welcome Pick back. "Good to see you in one piece, old friend. How'd you come up with this gimmick, anyhow? I've fiddled with some ropes and couldn't figure anything out that worked. Here's some thinner rope than what they use here," he said, handing Pick about ten feet of braided rope.

Pick chuckled as he took a drink from the bottle handed to him by young Jack Sperry. "I had no choice. Time was short, and I just did it. Let me untie this noose and show you." It became clear that his friends had cut the much thicker rope used by the granite quarry off along the boom and tied a thinner triple braided rope to the end for him to use.

The men watched, joked, and drank as Pick explained each step of his design. He measured about four feet of rope off the ten-foot length Cass had handed him and cut it off with his knife, then tied it to the rope coming down from the boom. After tying a bowline knot about three feet from the end of the main rope, he verified that his shorter rope wouldn't slip. He made a loop with the remainder of his short piece and tied another bowline knot just below the first knot. He pulled the loop he had made over his head and shoulders so it wrapped around his chest and under his arms. Satisfied that it fit well, he took the last three feet of the thin rope and wrapped it around the main rope, covering the two bowline knots with a noose. Pick pulled the noose over his head so it tightened around his neck.

He said, "There you have it, boys. If you act don't move, they'll think you're dead and either leave you hanging or throw you over a horse. Either way, just play dead until you can escape."

"And..." Morton said, stepping over to Pick, "this is a

good idea, and one we should all be aware of in case it's a last option. So, carry rope." He walked behind Pick and looked at the two lines going down toward his armpits. "Let me look at this for a minute. So, will this really support your weight?"

"Oh, yeah. The only bad thing about doing this is it burns your skin."

"And what happens if one of these two ropes breaks?" Morton asked curiously.

"Then you'd strangle to death, so check your knots before trusting them. And if you don't know how to tie..."

Morton pulled his knife, cut one of the ropes that supported Pick's weight, and shoved Pick over the edge of the quarry. Pick scrambled to reach the edge with his feet while trying to pull his body weight up enough to loosen the noose around his throat. He gasped for air and made eye contact with Morton, reaching his hand out for Morton to save him.

Morton grabbed his hand and pulled him part way up, just enough for Pick's toes to reach the edge of the landing. "I'm tired of your one-man shows, Pick. I can't trust you, bud," Morton said loudly. "Everyone, say goodbye to Pick."

Pick tried to speak, but the noose was too tight around his throat. He tried to shake his head, but the noose allowed little movement. His desperation showed in his eyes.

"Goodbye, Pick," Morton said, and let go of his hand and then pushed the boom out over the quarry, far above the dark hole below him.

"Bye, Pick."

"Catch ya later, old pal."

It didn't take too long for Pick to go limp and hang lifeless over the quarry in the firelight. Morton looked at Jesse. "You have that note?"

Jesse nodded.

"Bring him in. We've got a little note for the Marshal."

37

It was four in the morning when the first employee of the granite quarry showed up for work. The workday didn't start until seven, except for a few Chinese employees who worked in the cutting and shaping building. They often started early and worked late, depending on their workload, of their own accord. It was one of them named Ah See who had seen the man hanging and ran to notify Robert Fasana. Robert was the son of Joel Fasana, who, along with his brother Luther, had spent their lives to make the quarry what it was today. Robert had worked in the quarry his whole life as well and had learned each job of the trade. Now that Joel had retired and Luther was nearing retirement, Robert managed the family business. It was Robert who came to Matt's house just after five in the morning and woke him up to tell him there was a dead man hanging from their equipment. Matt and Truet rode out to the quarry and found a small crowd of men awkwardly staring at the body dangling over their quarry pit as the sun rose in the eastern sky.

"Matt, we got a problem," his Uncle Luther said. He had just arrived himself. "Someone cut our rope and tied a man on the end of our boom instead. Think you can get him off there?"

Matt dismounted from his horse. "Pretty sure of it. Did anyone see anything?"

"No. It happened overnight."

Matt looked closer at the man's clothes and hair. He sighed irritably. "That's Pick Lawson. He's supposed to be in jail. Swing him over here!" Matt shouted as some of the employees began turning the boom to bring the body to the edge of the hole. They set him on the ground, and Matt turned him over to his back. A note was nailed to his chest. It was written in Chinese, and couldn't be read by Matt. He pulled the paper off the nail and held it in his hands.

"What's it say?" Truet asked tiredly.

Matt shrugged. "Uncle Luther, do you have anyone who can read Chinese and speak English?"

Luther nodded. "Find Ah See. Ah See!" he yelled.

"He speaks English?" Matt asked.

"Better than most. He can translate for you. Ah See, come here!" He looked at Matt. "Here he comes."

A short Chinese man in his thirties wearing denim jeans and a blue V-neck shirt came quickly toward them. He had long black hair in a ponytail, and his face was clear of hair. He smiled at Matt. "Yes?"

"What's this say?" Matt asked, handing the paper to Ah See.

The man frowned, then looked puzzled. He ran his

finger down the three lines of odd-looking marks. "See no evil, hear no evil, speak no evil."

"Really?" Matt asked.

Ah See nodded once.

"What's that mean?" Luther asked.

"I have a pretty good idea. Thank you," Matt said to Ah See.

Truet pointed at the extinguished fire from the night before. "They were here for a while, it looks like. Any idea how he got out of jail?"

Matt shook his head. "No, but I'm going to find out. Truet, will you take Pick's body to Uncle Solomon and tell him to charge the city of Branson, namely the sheriff's office, for this one? I'll go have a little talk with Tim and let him know he's paying for the funeral."

Matt rode to the sheriff's office, found the front door unlocked, and stepped inside. He looked around and saw that the cell door was open, with a set of keys still in the lock. The sheriff's office opened at eight in the morning, and it was still a bit early for Tim and his boys to come walking in. In the meantime, Matt made a fire in the woodstove and sat down behind the sheriff's desk. He read the statement given by Pick and the one given by Christine; both had said exactly what they were supposed to say. He found what the sheriff had written up for his official report. There was nothing written in it that Matt hadn't expected, and very little written about him, aside from the killing of Jim Hexum and Carnell Tallon. Both killings had been self-defense, with many witnesses. He closed the sheriff's report and waited.

The door opened, and Tim Wright stepped inside

and paused when he saw Matt sitting in his chair. "Matt! What are you doing here?" he asked as he closed the door behind him. He looked toward the jail cell and asked quickly, "Where's Pick? What did you do with Pick?"

Matt stood up and walked toward the cell slowly. "That's a good question, Tim. Where was he when you went home last night?"

"Here! Where is he?" Tim asked in a demanding tone.

Matt turned around and looked at him, exhaustion showing on his face. "Dead. He was found this morning hanging from one of the quarry's derricks."

"Suicide?" Tim asked.

Matt shook his head. "No. Someone hung him. Probably the same people who took him out of here. What do you know about that?" he asked pointedly.

"Me? Nothing! I'm wondering why he isn't in my jail." If Matt hadn't known Tim was lying, he might have believed him.

"Nothing's broken in here. Nothing's disorganized. It's almost like they had keys, Tim. I didn't hear you unlock the door, either. Where are your keys?"

"I didn't need them. I saw the smoke from the stovepipe."

"Where are your keys?" Matt asked again.

Tim sat down at his desk casually, opened his desk drawer, and frowned when he saw they were not there. He looked at Matt like a child caught in a lie. "I must've forgotten them at home."

Matt reached into his pocket, pulled the keys out, and threw them at him. Tim ducked to dodge the keys flying at him. They hit the wall behind him with a loud bang and bounced to the floor.

Matt shouted fiercely, "They were left in the cell door! Now, who'd you give your keys to?" he demanded.

"No one! I must've left them in the cell door by accident."

"And Pick just walked out of here and went and hung himself?" Matt asked harshly. "Is that really going to be your story? Don't you get sick of lying? Don't you get sick of being pushed around by the leaders of this town and the filth of the streets? I know it was the Sperry-Helms Gang that hung Pick! They left a note, Tim. Now, how in the hell did they get your keys?" he demanded. He did not know for a fact that the Sperry-Helms Gang were to blame, but it was the most reasonable guess, and worth the gamble to corner Tim.

The sheriff sighed and said softly, "They came to my house and demanded them. I had no choice, Matt. They would've killed me if I didn't hand them over. I didn't know they were going to kill him, I swear! I had no choice. You wouldn't either if they came to your house in the middle of the night. You would've done the same thing if Morton and Jesse were standing in your house. You might kill one of them, but not both! What difference does it make anyway, huh? Pick was one of them. Let them take care of their own. It's just one less outlaw we have to worry about, right?"

Matt sat down in a chair near the cells and said calmly, "That's just it, Tim. They wouldn't come to my house. I'm not intimidated by heathens, and they know that."

Tim frowned. "Matt, I'll admit I've done some things I shouldn't have in my time as sheriff, but when it comes to those guys, there's too many of them, and they're all the same. I'm not crossing them."

"What's that mean?" Matt asked as his eyes narrowed.

"That means, my official story is going to be I accidentally left my keys in the lock when I went home. Pick made the decision to escape and hung himself. 'Yes, Mayor, it is my fault, and it won't happen again. Sorry, city council members, I messed up.'" He paused and looked at Matt before continuing, "That's my official story. What I won't do is have those guys coming to my house looking to get revenge for betraying them. Firebombs, Matt. That's one of their weapons of choice. I'll not be burned alive or my house burned down because they wanted to hang one of their own men. What's it matter to me? That's not my battle and it's none of my business! I suggest you leave them alone too. Throw that note they wrote in the fire right now and forget about it. It's not worth it to get on their bad side."

"Are you going to let them take over your town, Tim? You represent the law for all the citizens here. You're responsible for protecting them and their way of life. It's your duty as the elected sheriff of this city."

Tim chuckled. "Matt, I respect you and what you stand for, but it's not as simple as you make it sound. There are people around here you just don't argue with, and if they want something, you do it. But when it comes to the Sperry-Helms Gang, I'll give you some advice: let them do whatever it is they're going to do. You're not going to stop them without a whole lot of bloodshed on both sides, and even if you win, you're going to lose because the next one in line is going to ambush you. You're right, they're heathens, and it's just best to let them be heathens elsewhere, because they don't cause any trouble in my town. What they do outside of town is none of my concern. That's your problem. But again, I highly suggest you just let them be. They're not your usual drunken toughs. These are killers, brutal ones who hide it well."

"Tim, I can't go after them for killing Pick without your official statement saying it was them that took him out of here. I can't arrest them without your help."

The sheriff laughed. "Like I said, I accidentally left my keys in the cell when I went home. Mister Pick Lawson chose to leave the jail and committed suicide, to my knowledge. Because if there is a note, I haven't seen it!"

Matt glared at him for a moment. He pulled the note out of his pocket and handed it to him. "Suicides don't normally hammer a nail into their own chest to leave a note."

"Better yet, some Chinese men hung him! Do you know what it says?"

"I do."

"Of course, you do," he said with a hint of sarcasm. "What's it say?"

"See no evil, hear no evil, speak no evil."

Tim smirked with a slight nod. "It sounds like good advice, Matt. It's a warning, you know. Listen, for both of our sakes, let's just say Pick crossed some Chinese and they hung him. There is a gang of Chinese that I understand is controlling Chinatown with an iron fist. Apparently, they are quite dangerous to their own kind if they don't pay their fees or whatever. I really don't care either way. But this works out perfectly for us. Pick crossed that gang of Chinese and got what he deserved."

Matt stood up, frustrated. "It's pointless talking to you!"

"No. I'm doing you a favor, Matt! Leave them be for your own good. They will kill you, or your family if they can't get to you. You have no idea what they will do to get to you! They are evil men, every one of them, including Pick. Let it go before you get hurt or someone you love does! Nothing is off limits with them. Nothing!"

"My hands are tied without your honest statement."

"I left my keys in the cell door by accident."

"You are a simple coward!"

Tim chuckled bitterly. "Better a coward with a healthy and long life than a courageous fool long since buried! You're going to get yourself or someone else killed, Matt."

"A coward might live longer, maybe. But he'll have a hard time looking at himself in the mirror eventually. We all die sooner or later, and I'm going to Heaven either way when the time comes. In the meantime, tell your buddies I'm not intimidated by anyone. And if they ever go near my family, I will leave my badge at home, and there will be no mercy or prisoners when I'm done. I've done it before, but I'm better at it now! Because of you, they're getting away with killing Pick today, but eventually, they will face me. And I won't back down," he said, glaring at Tim with hard eyes. "You make me sick, Tim," he said as he walked out of the sheriff's office and let the door close behind him.

Outside, Matt felt the first drops and breathed in the fresh scent of the morning rain. He was angry and took a deep breath of the fresh air to calm down as Truet rode his horse to meet him.

"I got Pick's arrangements all taken care of, courtesy of the sheriff. Are you all right, Matt? You look angry this morning."

Matt looked at him, indignation clear in his eyes. "Truet, when the next election comes around, I want you to run for city sheriff." He turned back toward the sheriff's office and said loudly, "Maybe when we have someone with a spine as sheriff, we can clean this city up!" He looked back at Truet. "Until then, we are waiting for some heathens to make a mistake."

"Do you want to tell me what's going on?" Truet asked.

"Yeah, but later. I think I need to go for a long ride."

"Not going to Sweethome to see Felisha, are you?"

Matt smirked despite his frustration. "No. I think I might take a few days off and go up to the cabin on Lake Jessup and read a book or two. No, I have too much to do. But I think I *will* take today off and go for a ride. Maybe I'll stop by the dance hall and see if Christine wants to go for a buggy ride. Or maybe I'll just ride out to the Big Z and see what Annie's doing. Adam told me he hired a couple of new cowboys, and Annie's been sneaking around to meet up with one of them a lot. It seems like she has two or three men who want to court her out there. Anyway, you got the office while I'm gone."

Truet frowned noticeably. "Hey, Matt, do you think I could ride out there with you? It would be kind of neat to see her again. You know, she's a pretty amazing lady, and if it's all right with you, I wouldn't mind getting to know her better myself."

Matt shook his head with a disgusted expression. "She can't cook worth beans, and trust me, you don't want to know her. So no, you stay here, and maybe think about meeting Angela or one of the other ladies at the dance hall. I have to go meet this new guy and see what he's like. Adam likes him a lot. Adam and Uncle Charlie both think there's some embers burning in that fire between them already."

Truet's eyes hardened just a bit. "She never mentioned hiring anyone new."

"She didn't. Adam hired him. He's a cowboy, just the kind of man she needs around there. And he treats her kids well. Adam said he treats them better than Kyle did, and that's awesome if you ask me. I wanted to go meet him and welcome him onto the Big Z. Aunt Mary really likes him too, apparently, so it may not be too long until we get to watch Uncle Charlie walk her down the aisle if what I hear is true."

"You're lying!" Truet accused.

"No. Why would I lie about that?"

"There's not another guy! She would have told me," Truet said quickly. He closed his eyes, knowing he just said too much.

"Oh? Why's that?" Matt asked, staring at Truet with a serious expression.

Truet took a deep breath. "Well, because she and I are kind of courting."

Matt's eyes hardened, and anger twisted his lips into a

snarl. "That's my sister, Truet! Don't even joke about that."

"Um, I'm not kidding."

Matt raised his voice. "You just met her! So, what the...what the... What do you mean, you're courting her? No, don't even go there! You're not serious, are you?" he asked, glaring at Truet.

Truet frowned and shook his head slightly. "No."

"Good!" Matt said and quickly rode away with a grin on his lips. Matt had been a marshal for a long time and had made a career of reading people for his own survival. It didn't take a Pinkerton detective to figure out that Annie was hooked on Truet and Truet was falling for her like a stone pushed off a cliff. They were trying to sneak a growing relationship behind his back, and failing poorly at hiding it. In truth, he couldn't think of a better man for his sister to start courting than Truet. Someday, when he and Annie had the courage, they would tell him they were courting. Until then, Matt would continue to put the fear of his wrath into them. He enjoyed making Annie and Truet sweat a little bit. It was entertaining, and rather amusing to watch. But then again, that's what big brothers and best friends were for...causing problems.

ACKNOWLEDGMENTS

For my family.

This story and the others I've written never would have been without your support, interest and encouragement. To my wife, Cathy, thank you for all the drives down the coastline talking about this story. It amazes me how I can get so frustrated in a tangled web of details and you can make those same complicated details sound so simple. To my son, Keith, your devoted interest, care and feedback are absolutely invaluable. I want to thank you for that! I want to thank my daughters and son-in-law's as well for always being supportive and believing in me. I love you all.

I want to thank Mike Bray, Lauren Bridges and the rest of the staff at CKN Christian Publishing for their hard work to make this book possible. You're the best at what you do, and I have so much respect and appreciation for all of you. Thank you.

ABOUT THE AUTHOR

Ken Pratt and his wife, Cathy, have been married for 22 years and are blessed with five children and six grand-children. They live on the Oregon Coast where they are raising the youngest of their children. Ken Pratt grew up in the small farming community of Dayton, Oregon.

Ken worked to make a living, but his passion has always been writing. Having a busy family, the only "free" time he had to write was late at night getting no more than five hours of sleep a night. He has penned several novels that are being published along with several children stories as well.